Silver

by

Scott Cairns

ISBN-13: 978-1479132287
ISBN-10: 1479132284

Author Website: www.scott-cairns.com

PROLOGUE

A Beginning

Upon few things in life you can rely. That you were born is certain and that you will die, irrefutable. What happens in between is a matter of opinion. This story is no different from life. What is certain is that Avery Silver was born and that Avery Silver died. What happened in between is merely opinion.

The birth was straightforward; the first one anyway. It was 1849 and Mrs. Mary Silver had been in a painful labour for over 27 hours when finally a very overdue and plump baby was delivered to the Silver household. As was customary of the time, her husband, Mr. Toby Silver, was not present at the birth, preferring to remain in the company of his associates many streets away. He had been warned of the distress that a birth causes the mother and he felt sure that Mary would prefer him not to hear her in such a state. So it was that, Mary Silver was attended by a reputable doctor beforehand and by a skilled and expensive midwife, Alice Simms, during the labour. Alice was pleased the Silver's had taken her on for this particular birth as many women were now choosing to accept the help of surgical intervention and, given the long labour, she felt sure that the doctors would have taken a knife to Mrs. Silver in the interim. In Alice Simms's experience, babies that were late were bound to take longer to come into the world. Such babies were larger and, she believed, lazier. However, the length of the labour had worried even Mrs. Simms, as none of the assembled maids, herself or Mrs. Silver had slept in over a day and the last few hours had been wretched for all concerned. There had been a lot of noise but little production. The head had been visible for an age and a large and healthy one it had looked; the hair was thick and dark with blood. After a full three hours of painful exertion, the child's head had finally emerged and from there the shoulders followed in a rush of slippery limbs. The room in which Mary Silver's confinement had been broken was silent for the first time in many hours as the attending midwives held their breath. After a few moments, the infant drew its first breath and, as if there had been a link between those waiting and the arrival of the child, there was a collective sigh of relief; a recycling of life-giving air. Avery Silver had been born; one way or another.

A Middle

In the years that followed, many thousands of infants were born to expectant and adoring families. Some would live to lead lives of privilege or service, whilst others would succumb to the diseases of the period or the poverty of their situation. Some births would prove a cause of celebration, whilst others were greeted with the horror of circumstance that having a child out of wedlock, however this had happened, could bring. That Imogen was the progeny of one such

2

coupling had not been her fault but it was her destiny. In a similar rush of limbs, she had been received by a waiting midwife, and then passed to the mother. Though the mother clutched her tenderly, there was an instant air of distance between them.

"Please take her from me. I can't bear to see her and then to lose her." The mother whispered, hoarse from labour, to the waiting woman.

The woman nodded knowingly and stepped forward to lift the child from the warmth of the mother's chest. As if she was aware of the situation, the child let out a mewl of protest. A last-minute bid to state her case.

"Are you quite sure you want to do this?" The midwife already knew the answer and had begun to turn away before the mother nodded weakly. The child needed feeding and if the mother would not feed it then she wanted to deliver her to the foundling hospital as soon as possible.

"You should give her a name." she offered, as she wrapped the child tightly in her cloak, preparing to brave the February chill. The mother turned her head away and the midwife suspected she had begun to cry. "You should give her a name in case you change your mind."

She was met with silence and, though her sympathy lay with the young woman, the midwife's own maternal instinct was to feed the baby swaddled in her arms. She understood the circumstance into which this particular child had been born and, though not her place to say, she half suspected the mother would regret giving the child away. The silence turned into minutes but was broken with the hungry rooting of the

3

nameless baby girl. The midwife sighed and, pulling her hood up, she stooped to pick up her bag and leave.

"Imogen." came the mother's voice. "Her name is Imogen."

The midwife turned and caught the damp gaze of the exhausted young woman who lay on the labour bed.

"Imogen." she said and then she was gone.

An End

It is many years later in another bedroom where the next certainty in life is played out. It is gloomy around the edges; the furniture around the walls shies away from the amber glow of the bedside table preferring instead the anonymity of the dark.

A glow emanates from an oil lamp, whose wick is turned up high, casting a sphere of yellow light around the bed and up the wall behind. Your attention is drawn to the bed and its occupant. An ornate brass bedstead is dressed with stark white sheets; the crisp linen is ruffled by the body of an unruffled, silver-haired gentleman reading a book. Silver by nature and by name; let me introduce you to Avery Silver.

Avery is propped against the bedstead with an array of pillows, his head bent in study. You would be forgiven for thinking him far beyond his sixty years. The angle of his head and the light has cast an unflattering shadow, emphasising the lines across his face. His shoulders are slumped in rest and he looks as frail as a cobweb. It is past midnight on the third day of the New

Year, 1911 and Avery is wakeful. Since his wife died some years ago, he finds night time the hardest. The step over which most of us tumble into sleep, Avery seems only to falter at. On the threshold of dormancy, he imagines she is still lain beside him and he starts awake in his bed; his hand smoothes across the sheets beside him to find only nothing. The years have turned this ritual into a habit and he finds himself quite unable to sleep before the small hours. Tonight is no different. Avery is supporting a weighty leather book, his reading glasses perched on the end of his nose. The book is well thumbed, the pages soft beneath his fingertips as he tentatively holds a page aloft, ready to turn. His lips move silently as he scans the words.

'I don't agree to that - it may make them dangers. We know too much about people in these days; we hear too much. Our ears, our minds, our mouths, are stuffed with personalities. Don't mind anything any one tells you about anyone else. Judge everyone and everything for yourself.'

Avery's focus changes as he stops reading. His concentration shifts from the written page as he considers these words in his head. As he does so, he glances up to look at the gloomy room. His eyes sparkle as the light catches them. His thoughts are far away and he sees only the dark outline of the curtains. His countenance clouds and the expression upon his face shifts to one of deep consideration.

'Don't mind anything anyone tells you about anyone else. Judge everyone and everything for yourself.'

It is but one ordinary word placed after another but in the ordinary can be found the extraordinary. In this ordinary room, something very normal will take place. This sleepy eyed gentleman with his long nose, down which he now peers at the fuzzy words on the page, is going to die. He is going to die before he even finishes the sentence he is trying to read. Now, before your pulse starts racing, I am afraid there is nothing spectacular to witness here. If you are excited by the dramatic entrance of a dark haired assailant then this is the wrong sort of story for you. There will be no death at the hands of a deranged madman.

Avery Silver will depart this world in the most common of ways: His skin will flush hot, and then cold, and he will draw a sharp breath. He will look around into the gloom of the room for some assistance, knowing there to be none. He will cry out a little as a crushing pain over his chest threatens to squeeze the air from his lungs. His body, were you to touch it, would be clammy and cool. The thin skin across his aging bones will be pale and you will suspect he is dead already. His shoulder will hunch to his ear as he draws up his hand to clutch at his heart. His book will fall to the floor beside his bed, the pages curling under the weight of the binding. He will blink once and look around to where his wife used to lay, his eyes wide with fear, and he will slump towards the empty bed, his hands smoothing the sheets before him.

All manner of deaths are recorded in black and white and this one shall not be any different, for in the end they all stop breathing, their hearts stop beating and their chests fall with one final sigh.

Chapter One - Imogen, 1911

After spending Christmas with my husband's family we returned home to Hampstead in the New Year. As we swept in through the front door with our bags and our hails of a Happy New Year to the house and its occupants, we were greeted by a cheerless mob. Our butler, Stokes, was standing in the hall and appeared very sombre indeed. From beyond the corridor, I could make out the faces of our maid, and the housekeeper, peering from the basement stairs. I was most perturbed that they should be so grim-faced amidst our jolly mood. My heart sank as I considered the cause of their sullen one. I wondered if our neighbour, poor old Mrs. Crossfield, had taken a turn for the worse. Oblivious to the ominous faces around them, the boys were dancing around their father, still singing a carol, holding hands and encircling his legs.

"Nanny Hewitt," I beckoned to the tall drab woman following us in. "will you take Thomas and Sebastian to the nursery."

She hadn't waited for me to finish but had stepped forward and ushered the boys up the stairs without a further word. They reluctantly followed the lead of their imposing nanny and cast doleful glances through the banisters as they went. Thomas, older than Sebastian by a year, had noticed the solemn faces of the staff and was pressing Mrs. Hewitt in hushed tones for the news.

"Hush, boy." she admonished and swept them out of view, her shushing skirts the only noise in the whole house save for the grandfather clock, which now ticked ominously.

"What is it, Stokes?" John enquired of our po-faced butler.

My husband continued to shrug off his great coat, Maud rushing forward to assist. I watched as Stokes looked from my husband back to me. I noticed with a feeling of dread that he didn't catch my eye. John handed over his scarf and gloves before rounding back on Stokes, waiting.

"Come on man, out with it." he coaxed after a brief pause.

"Sir, Madam," he ventured, and then, stepping aside, he gestured to the parlour. John's impeccable manners forced him to wait for me to enter the room, but he was hot on my heels and impatient for the news as Stokes closed the door behind us.

"It is Mrs. Bancroft's father," he began.

I knew he was dead without John having to ask. The tone was all too familiar of my mother's death and my heart slowed down. I watched John's face fall and he looked over at me. My ears filled up and the steady voice of Stokes became like the sound of a distant hum. John had taken a few steps towards me but something Stokes said made him stop dead.

"...police constable.....happened suddenly..."

A few of Stokes' words reached inside my shock. I must have sat down and John, still shaking his head angrily at Stokes, was at my side in a moment. He knelt with my hand in his, mouthing words at me and patting my arm. I watched as he said something to Stokes; the butler's expression changed and his head hung low as he mumbled a response.

"..appears to be a problem....the police are suggesting.....Mr. Silver's body."

John turned sharply and then his face clouded with unmistakable anger.

"Can't it wait," he shouted again. The noise burst through the fog in my head and I was, all at once, back in the room. "Where is he?" John hissed, struggling to keep his temper.

Glancing quickly at me, he clutched my hand almost protectively and then turned to dismiss Stokes.

"Imogen? Are you all right?" He stood again, one hand against his brow as he considered me. The other hand, I noticed, was shaking. "I shall ring for Maud to take you upstairs."

I shook my head and tried to stop him as he strode across the room and pressed the bell at the fireside.

"..must be some mistake..." he muttered. "I'll speak to the police constable and get to the bottom of this nonsense and then go to Avery's house myself and..."

John was upset about something I had missed and I needed to know what it was.

"What did Stokes say, John?"

"...there'll be hell to answer for with his superiors. Just see if there isn't. This must be able to wait."

At that moment, the door opened and Maud stepped into the room. She dipped into a brief curtsey and John indicated to me, saying, "Mrs. Bancroft has had rather a shock and she would like to go to her room."

Maud's face was pale and she approached me warily.

"I'm sorry for your loss Mrs. Bancroft. Shall we get you upstairs?"

John was trying to gently coax me out of the chair as the door opened again and Stokes indicated to him that someone was waiting in the hall. He nodded and strode across the room throwing last instructions to Maud

"See that Mrs. Bancroft is not disturbed, Maud, I don't want her being upset."

Having just been advised of my father's death, I failed to see what else could upset me and I was starting to feel an impatience rise within me. I felt as though I was being treated like an invalid.

"John,' I shouted. 'What did Stokes say?"

I stood up to deliver this and I shook with the effort of making myself heard over Maud's twittering, and John and Stokes' hushed parlay at the door. All three of them stopped what they were doing and looked at me aghast. John's mouth opened and closed and opened again before he decided he could not repeat what Stokes had said. I turned to Stokes, who seemed also to have been struck dumb. He could not look at me and instead looked to his employer for his leave. Amidst the silence and the gawping, a third face appeared at the door behind John and Stokes. He was a tall, slender man in a black woollen suit, his face gaunt and lined with tiredness. I took him for an age similar to my father but as he brushed past Stokes and my husband and spoke, I recognised in him a wealth, not of years but of weariness.

"Mrs. Bancroft," he enquired, and I nodded. "I am Inspector Charles Hurst, Madam. I think we should perhaps sit down. May I?" he added indicating the seat in front of my own. He stepped forward and stood before the armchair in front of mine. As I sat down, he looked back to John, who regained himself and dismissed the staff before joining me with the Inspector.

"This may come as a great shock to you, Mrs. Bancroft. You may wish to stay seated."

~o~

As the carriage pulled up at my father's house, I noticed first the crowd of people standing outside the railings. They numbered more than twenty and they peered curiously into the cab, wondering who else had come to join the rumpus. At first, I did not recognise any of the faces staring at me. Most were men, clutching notepads and pressing each other to get the best vantage of those freshly arrived upon the scene. They took in John more than myself, perhaps mistaking him for a senior inspector or perhaps another doctor come to examine my father's corpse. As the carriage drew to a stop, I surveyed the sea of faces and recognised one of them towards the back of the crowd. A neighbour of my parents for some years, the usually jolly Mrs. Phelps was pale with the cold. She looked half frozen from the bitter fog but, as her eyes lit upon mine, her face at once was alive. Caught up in the excitement of this hubbub, she began directing the reporters as soon as she recognised me. At once, the noise about us began to rise.

"Mrs. Bancroft!"

"Over here! Did you know your father's secret?"

The men at the front of the group began pushing to get to the door. The bridled horse danced nervously with the cluster of people at his flank.

"Get back," called the driver. "Get back, I say!" A large man, he brandished his furled whip menacingly, the horse rearing a little at his tone.

"Whoa. Easy."

Inside the cab I clutched John's arm; the solemn and quiet of our contemplation on the journey had been broken and now we were to face the reality of this horrible situation. It was at once both surreal and horribly real. The ugly commotion outside my father's house was most scandalous. This area was respectable and unaccustomed to such scenes. Those neighbours that were not joined in the throng of people outside the cab were peering from behind curtains, the staff standing behind railings or pressed at the attic windows. There were people in the crowd who did not belong in the area. Two young women dressed in shabby evening wear, with thin shawls around their shoulders that barely concealed the raw blue of their skin, stood gawping from the corner of the street. We had passed small huddles of people leaning on one another, passing hushed laughter behind their hands, all the while pointing in the direction of my father's house. All the people who did not belong and all those who did, had been drawn by the same heady scent of scandal, and had followed their noses to my father's house. My respectable, quiet father would have been appalled at the scenes but it was he himself that lay at the very heart of the circus. John leaned across me and climbed down from the cab only to be pressed by half a dozen men.

"Did you know he was keeping something from you?"

"Is it true?"

"Gentlemen, please. My wife is grieving. We have nothing to comment." John reached back inside to take my hand and led me from the carriage through the throng and to the front door. The crowd fell silent as I stepped down from the cab and parted to let us through; a moment's peace at seeing my grief, perhaps to preserve some decorum. Those few yards seemed an eternity to walk; all eyes were watching and I leaned on John for support, fearing I would collapse under the weight of their gaze. At the top of the steps, my father's elderly butler, Heston was waiting. As we reached the door there was a shout from a way off and I turned. The two women from the corner had walked across the square and had called out.

"Come on, Immy." John gently guided me towards the door when the shout came again. This time I made it out quite clearly.

" 'er dad has no cock but 'er mother did!" Her companion hooted and the two of them fell about cackling to each other. As the crowd around us watched this exchange, the noise began to rise again. The ludicrous suggestion by a bawdy house tart had stirred the men of the press from their modesty and we were jostled the remaining few steps to the door.

Ushering us into the house quickly, Heston called out to the mob.

"You should be ashamed of yourselves," he shouted and there was a hush. Pens poised, they waited, collectively holding their breath at the tantalising show of emotion. Perhaps something was to be divulged. "All of you," he added in a quieter tone, scanning the faces at the front of his master's house. Composing himself, he turned back inside the house and his anger was barely concealed as he shut the door with a shaking hand. He turned to face John and myself and apologised.

"I am so sorry for your loss, Mrs. Bancroft. I didn't mean to lose my temper."

It had hardly been an outburst, but for the gentle and softly spoken butler, that was indeed the most irate one could expect to see him. His normally well-ordered life was in disarray and he coloured at his impropriety.

I was cheered a little to see a familiar face and for that face not to conceal any contempt, and I placed a hand on his arm. It remained there but for a few seconds; the white gloved hand of a lady upon this servant's sombre black uniform was uncomfortably out of place, and immediately reminded me of the strangeness of what had brought me to the house. Heston straightened immediately and with a military air resumed his role of transferring us into my father's study, where a police constable and suited man were waiting. The man was my father's age, once tall but now seeming not to fit his clothes as perhaps he once did. He had in his hand a book from my father's bookcase and was leaning towards the window the better to read the inscription. I recognised the binding instantly; a collection of classic verse from Milton and Wordsworth. I knew the books well. They had been a gift of my mother's to my father on their Silver wedding anniversary. A collection of romantic poetry, I had cherished that particular volume when John and I were courting. Cryptic as always, the inscription was one of my mother's.

'What God has torn apart, let man lovingly make whole.'

Before I could enquire of this man what business he had rifling through my father's belongings, he had put the book down on the desk and stepped forwards to introduce himself.

"Inspector Greene," he proffered his hand first to John and then he addressed me directly.

"You have my condolences, Mrs. Bancroft. I take it you have been briefed by my colleague?"

I nodded and beckoned to Heston who brought me a chair. The Inspector waited until I was seated and then leaned back against the desk, behind which my poor father would never again sit. I was taken by this melancholy thought and a tear began to slip down my cheek. It was apparent that this disturbed the Inspector's sense of dignity and he watched me solemnly for a moment before offering his handkerchief. He turned to face John and directed a summary of the proceedings to him in hushed tones.

"I must apologise again, Mr. Bancroft, but these circumstances are most unusual. As you know, the deceased has been identified by a doctor and one of the staff here but in the circumstances, we would prefer a more formal identification by family. I take it you will be undertaking this duty?" I heard John agree and then I heard my own voice.

"No. He is my father and I will make the identification."

Both men looked at me disapprovingly but John was the first to air his feelings on the matter.

"Now look here Imogen, you're upset and grieving. Naturally you want to see your father, but under the circumstances I think it's best if I tend to these matters," his moustache bristled with importance and, having spoken succinctly but forcefully, he clearly thought that should be an end to the matter.

"No, John," I said gently. "I must see him. I must make them see what a mistake they have made. There must be no doubt."

And I did believe sitting in my father's study, surrounded by the comforting familiarity of his things, that perhaps it was just a silly mistake. That I would be called to my father's bedroom and be able to deny that the person they had found there was my father. Since leaving Hampstead Heath, I had willed into existence some love affair between my father and some woman who had now come to be found dead in his bed, and for some curious reason they believed it to be my father. The more I thought of this woman the more I could believe in the fact that my father, perhaps ashamed by her death, was safe and well. I imagined he had gone to his club and he was at that moment nursing a whiskey and a cigar, bemoaning his situation with some chums. My spirits lifted and I found I was not dreading walking into my father's bedroom but I was eager to do so, for the sooner I ascended the stairs and showed them the truth of the matter, the sooner I could put an end to all the nonsense. I would send Heston to fetch my father from his club after I undertook the task. With a renewed sense of vigour, I rose from my chair and proceeded directly out of the room. Heston opened the door swiftly and I was away up the stairs, John and the Inspector at my heels.

16

"Imogen. Really, I must insist."

I was in such a rush to get to the first floor that I tripped near the top and had to steady myself against the banister. Heston's face stared up at me, his expression one of great pity and sadness. Wildly, I took the next few stairs two at a time and came to stand outside my parents' bedroom. I was at the door, my hand upon the great brass knob, and the sense to knock took me by such surprise that I was compelled to do so. As I raised my hand to knock, I caught sight of John and Inspector Greene alighting the landing beside me. Seeing this action as foolish, I brought my fist instead to my forehead and opened the door. The last time I was in this room was when my mother was alive. On my wedding day, after I was dressed, Mother had invited me to sit at her dressing table as she had put the finishing touches to my hair. As I sat looking at myself in the mirror, my mother behind me, I had begun to weep. Mother was shocked and a little taken aback. I hadn't been sad but moved and nervous about the future. My life at home in my parents' loving care was now at an end and, although I had been looking forward to my adulthood, I was all at once nervous of what lay in store.

"How did you feel on your wedding day?" I had asked my mother. There was a long pause; her hand hovered above my forehead before she continued with her task, carefully combing my auburn hair.

"Mother?" I prompted, but still she was silent. I watched her reflection in the mirror as words formed on, and then disappeared from, her lips, all the while her hands seemingly busy at my hair but not touching me at all. In the silence, I could hear the clock on the great mantel ticking, dutifully marking the passage of this time. After what seemed an age, she had finally found the words she had struggled for.

"I was sad I think. Don't look like that. I was sad for us both that not one of our family could share our future together. As you know, our parents were dead and," she paused. "your father and I.....we......"

Not one to ever be lost or struggling for words, I had frowned at her as I watched her in the mirror. She had blushed and her eyes had flickered as though she were embarrassed. She caught my eye and smiled.

"And happy too. Excited and nervous and a little scared."

"Why scared?" I felt a little relieved to hear her say this and I waited anxiously to hear her reply. Far from having to consider this, she placed her hands on my shoulders and addressed my reflection head on.

"Just like you and John, mine and your father's stars have been aligned since the first day we met and it was destiny that we should end our days together; it is the same destiny that will see you and John very happily joined together." She smiled at me, her eyes misting a little with tears, and hugged me to her. I felt myself well up, all at once feeling the little girl, safe in her mother's arms. The door opened behind us and I heard my father's voice.

"What's all this?" his tone was hearty, mixed with a hint of concern. I drew myself away from my mother and composed myself, ready to face my father's close inspection.

"I'll see you downstairs," my mother whispered to me, planting a kiss on my head, her own face now streaked by tears. As she turned to leave the room, she placed a gentle hand on my father's shoulder. He closed his eyes, leant his head to one side and kissed it. It was a moment's tender affection, genuine and heartfelt, but it was that one gesture that alleviated my fears and my anxious feelings, I knew in that instant that I wanted to marry John. I wanted to stand in twenty or thirty years' time and share exactly a moment such as that with my own husband. As the door closed behind my mother, my father held out his hands for mine and I stood before him.

"I don't need to ask you this as it's been written on your face these past months, but tradition insists I do." Here, he had fixed me with his most concerned face and gripped my hands more tightly. "Now, do you love John and want to marry him today?"

I matched his serious question with my own solemn face and replied with a most heartfelt and vigorous nod. Smiling broadly, I added, "Without any question, Father."

"I haven't the words enough to tell you how proud I am of you, Immy. Your mother and I both are. You look..." he had stepped back and surveyed me, "...beautiful."

He had paused and I felt on the verge of sadness again, but now resolved to the excitement, I wanted to stave off any tears. I had stepped forward and stretched a little to place a kiss on his cheek. I stepped back and smiled at him.

"I love you, Father."

He had smiled then too; a dazzling beam of satisfaction that radiated his pleasure at my words and his affection for me. I had basked in the warmth of it and felt happy. I remembered the feeling even then as I stood upon the threshold of his death. The room was not as I remembered it from that occasion; the curtains were drawn and my mother was long gone. The fire had not been lit that day and the walls exuded a chill air penetrating from outside. The bed too was smaller than I remembered it and the body lain within it seemed too big for the room. I avoided looking at it. I was stood upon the threshold, at the very edge of lies about to step into truth.

"Imogen?" John's voice was gentle and the questioning tone enquired only if I was sure of what I was about to do. His hand was upon my shoulder and I leant my cheek against it, my eyes closed. At once, I was both grateful for him being behind me but I also needed to do this alone, and after a moment, I kissed his hand and stepped forward into the room. The gaslights cast my shadow across the bed and the sheet that had been pulled up over the body was beyond the reach of the gloomy light. My father, usually a forward thinking and modern man, refused to be connected to an electricity supply and so, with a surprisingly steady hand, I took up a lamp from the dresser and lit my father's bedside oil lamp. The light jumped up the glass chimney and I turned down the wick to settle the flame. I glanced towards John who was still standing in the door frame, his jaw set in defiance at the lie we were about to prove false.

I tried to smile at him but my mouth and lips were too dry and they would not form into any cheery expression; instead, I looked grimly down at the white sheet and lay a hand upon its cover. I held my breath and turned back the sheet enough to see the face beneath it. The flesh was drained and ashen, giving the skin a blue glow, as if Jack Frost himself lay upon my father's bed. There was no doubting though that the face was my father's and a great choking sob rose from deep within me. The sheet fell from my hand and covered the face again. John stepped forward and was beside me in three great strides but I was like stone. Whilst a great surge of sorrow shook me, I was not yet done; for now, there was no escaping the terrible lies that had been spoken, excepting human error, a farcical mistake, unkind lies. John tried to steer me from the bed and one foot followed under the weight of his guiding hands, but I shook him off.

"Imogen, really, you don't need to do this."

"On the contrary, John, I absolutely must do this," I retorted.

My tone was glacial, a shield of distance for the grim task ahead. With renewed courage, I gripped the corner of the sheet and gently pulled it back revealing his nightshirt, unbuttoned and pulled back across his shoulders. Familiar and strong, they were diminished little in death from those that had carried me as a tiny child fast down the stairs of this very house, taking my breath away and making me squeal with delight. I inched the sheet towards his chest, feeling vindicated by the contours of the linen.

As I raised the sheet, his chest appeared flat beneath his nightshirt and I felt somewhat calmer, as I leant forward to pull aside his nightshirt. As I did so, a fresh band of crêpe bandages were revealed and my first thought was what injury had caused him to be dressed so. The shock to my heart was for his manner of death; perhaps he had not died peacefully but been murdered in his bed and dressed by his killer. Without

21

thinking, I pulled at the loosened bandages to see his wound, ready to call out to the dunderhead of an Inspector who, instead of searching for my father's killer, was spreading lies about him.

As the bandages came away from my father's chest, it took me a while to focus on what I was seeing. Flat and small, bound under the crêpe bandages, were two lumps on my father's chest. I drew in breath sharply and peered hard. More than answer any questions, the ambiguity of their slight feminine form only made their positive identification more difficult. Whatever error had been made, it could not be corrected by this evidence. I closed my eyes and threw the sheet to the end of the bed.

My father's nightshirt was covering his groin, but his legs had been drawn wide apart at the hips and his knees were bent. He resembled a frog pinned for dissection and the comparison with my own close inspection made me feel suddenly intrusive. Aware at last of my husband stood behind me, the fact that strangers had picked over my father so, had arranged his body thus and had inspected him like a specimen, made me feel sick. Struggling with the urge to run from the room and the desire to know the truth, I lifted my father's nightshirt and both wished to see and not to see his manhood. The light only made it harder to make out, but what wasn't there could not be forced into being by better light. There was nothing there. In the thick, dark triangle of my father's pubic hair there was not one small protruding piece of flesh that could be mistaken for anything else. I stared at the place where my father's member should have been and I felt my skin drain of all its colour. My eyes prickled with the effort of not blinking, but closing my eyes to do so might break the spell and I didn't know if I could stand to face the revelation yet.

"My God! It's true!" John's voice was loud behind me and I jumped, my eyes darting around, looking for any truth I could fix on to keep me standing; I did not dare trust the walls in case they weren't solid or the light, in case it burnt my eyes. My ears were ringing with John's words. It was true. It was true. I felt light-headed and sick, and I staggered past John, pushing aside his entreating arms. I crashed into the door, struggling to remain upright, and ran to my old bedroom down the corridor. My heart was pounding in my throat and my stomach was knotted in my shoes. I felt upside down as I threw open the door, slammed it and locked it behind me. The door shook with John's knocking and he tried the handle, calling all the while to me.

"Imogen. Let me in. Imogen."

And so he went on; all the while I shut out the sounds of the truth and, instead, turned my head back to the lies. In the gloom of my childhood room, I could see my mother's face in the mirror on my wedding day, the look in her eyes as she had chewed on the words of how she had felt on the morn of her own wedding. I knew now why she had been so evasive. The lie of it and the truth of it had been that there had been no wedding. The truth of it was that my father was a woman.

Chapter Two- Avery, 1869

Through the crack in the heavy linen curtains, a shard of light edged itself across a fine rug. Like a dusty finger, it pointed accusingly at the bed and its sleeping occupant. The first fronds of pale grey morning stretched themselves, as if from a weary sleep and tried to penetrate Avery's dreams beneath the crisp linen sheets. His head rested heavily on the plump pillows. His thick, sleep-ruffled hair, a dark contrast to the white of the linen, was the same colour as the mahogany furniture which loomed from the edges of the room. Avery was in the middle of a dream. His eyes, shielded by sleep-weary lids, flickered, seeing yet not seeing his hidden fantasy.

It is summer in his dream and the sun is brighter than the gloom of his bedroom. There is a lake which, at first glance, appears deserted. Stirring the stillness of the velvet greens of the surrounding parkland and the cornflower blue sky, there is a couple picnicking. They are shielded from view by the dancing yellow-green skirts of a willow tree. From the path, anyone watching could make out a young lady attired in a plain white dress, lounging against some cushions scattered about the picnic blanket; her hat has been cast aside, and some curls from her hair have come loose and now frame her pale face with auburn. She is Kate Ward and, in truth, she is a young servant girl in the Silvers' house; far from enjoying a picnic on a day like this, she should be working up a sweat cleaning silver or changing bed linen. The young man leaning over her is

Avery Silver. He is Avery Silver as he appears to himself.

Avery is smartly dressed, from his polished shoes to his immaculate shirt, his expensive jacket and trousers to the luxury oil taming his thick mahogany locks. A cooling breeze picks up off of the lake, beside which they lay, and carries the scent of the picnic and the sound of their hushed laughter and mumbling. Avery has exaggerated his own body shape; his shoulders aren't usually that broad, he isn't normally quite so tall. Avery's back obscures the view of Kate and you would have to be almost upon them before her state of undress is revealed. Avery is leaning across her, one hand tugging down an arm of her summer dress to reveal her firm pale breast. Her nipple, despite the warmth of the summer's day, is pert and erect and it is this nipple that Avery now takes in his mouth. Kate's head lolls backwards and she bites her lower lip, allowing the small sigh of pleasure rising in her throat to escape her.

In the bedroom in which the sleeping Avery lay dreaming, the sounds of morning began to fill the air as, one by one, the birds in the square outside shook themselves awake. Avery's leg moved beneath the sheets and created a ripple of white light in the beam of dawn, like a river cresting over a rock. The sound of broken glass punctuates the silence in the room and Avery's head reared up briefly. His eyes, heavy with sleep, look about, confused as he noted only the intrusion of the dawn. His thick chestnut sleep-tussled hair was thrown up in surprise and he promptly collapsed back into the pillows. The curtains seemed to draw open of their own volition as the morning outside them stained the shaft of light from grey to blue, then from blue to violet, pregnant with the impending sun, to the warming yellow and the promise of a glorious summer's day. Avery shifted again. His dream was becoming more distant, more polluted by the stirring noises from the house below. A distant door closed; the creak of the floorboard above him; the far-off mumble of voices. Avery groaned and pulled a pillow over his head. 3, Cornwall Gardens was coming alive and he wanted nothing to do with it.

Soon the chorus of birdsong outside began to play second fiddle to the industrious sounds of the city. The distant clatter was of horse's hooves as the Omnibus collected and deposited its early commuters. The faint masculine cries were that of early morning tradesmen passing up the Cromwell Road. Some way off, the hazy shriek of a seagull can be heard as it wheels across land, the Thames beneath disappearing from view as barges clogged the snaking black highway.

Avery began to protest beneath the sheets. His dream had been coming to its conclusion; the same impotent ending as was common of all his dreams. Kate would be breathless with longing and her chest rising and falling with a great weight of passion; her collarbone glistening in the heat of the summer sun, reflecting across the surface of the lake. Avery too would be alert with arousal, blood surging to his head and he would hear only his own breathing, long and deeply drawn through his open mouth. His eyes flickered in his head as he tried to stay inside his dream.

He is inhaling Kate's words as she whispers to him, urges him on. He is drawing himself up above her and gazing down at his lover, and sees his own desire mirrored in her eyes. He traces his fingers down between her breasts, across her stomach and embraces her thighs and hips. He is arrested by Kate's sharp intake of breath and he watches as she bites her lip and her eyes flicker backwards with a moment's indecision; Kate's own hands grip tighter around Avery's neck and she presses herself upwards into his embrace, nudging her hip into his groin. Avery pushes his hand up under her petticoat, his knuckles raking the inside of her thighs. Her breath is hot about his ears as she whispers to him. The same phrase Avery has heard in his dreams every night for the last two months. 'Be gentle, Avery.'

A pulse in his head throbbed and all at once he is filled with both an insatiable hunger and an impotent rage. Before either of these emotions can be explored, the image of the lake vanished like a grey mist and he woke with a start in his bed. His breathing, as in his dream, was heavy and he struggled to bring himself back to the waking reality. The sounds from the window were more insistent now and Avery glanced at the mantel clock. It was before eight and presently the real Kate would be arriving to rouse him. Avery groaned and rubbed his eyes, wiping the sleep away and trying to banish the fast fading images of Kate from his mind. He wished he could wipe away his feeling of shame and guilt so easily.

There was a gentle tapping at the door, barely discernible to Avery, who was anticipating such an intrusion. He ignored it, yet the door opened without his command, as he knew it would, and the soft rustling of Kate's skirts entered the room before her. A young, slight figure, she made her way around the room. As he watched her through his sleep veiled eyes, he could discern a hint of amusement as she picked up the first of Avery's clothes from the floor. She set down a porcelain bowl and jug on the dresser and collected the chamber pot beneath the bed, before padding her way back out of the room. As the door opened, allowing cooler air to briefly permeate the dusty room, Avery could smell the familiar scent of her on the brief breeze and then she was gone.

Avery had been holding his breath and he allowed himself a long sigh before rolling back under the sheets, thankful for a few more minutes before Kate would return. His dreams were becoming awkward and he was worried she would see something of them still playing across his mind. He closed his eyes again and tried to call to mind how he should see Kate; the obedient and dutiful face swimming before him. He pictured her in her maid's attire; the black dress, the starched white collar and apron, but even as he imagined her, he was drawn by her petite frame and her sweet face. The familiar milk-white skin at her neck, he imagined his own lips pressed against it.

"Oh, give me peace!" he called out, screwing up his eyes and pulling the sheets up over his head. After only a few minutes and before, it seemed, Avery had even closed his eyes, the door opened and closed again.

"Are you awake, Miss Silver?" Kate whispered the words only just audible. Her Yorkshire accent was soft but unmistakable. She walked to the nightstand and on it carefully placed a glass of something milky.

"Miss Alice?" she ventured softly, leaning across the great bed. "Truly, you stretch my sympathy."

Avery finally rolled to face the maid and pulled a face before sitting up. He reached for the glass and, making another face, threw the contents down the back of his throat.

"Yeugh!" he exclaimed, his eyes closed and his mouth wide. "Foul concoction. I don't know why my father insists on such measures. Am I not the very picture of health?"

"Indeed, Miss!" Kate retorted, raising an eyebrow. Kate smiled and took the glass from Avery, her fingers brushing his. An innocent gesture, which sent a shot of nervous pleasure straight to Avery's stomach. He recoiled and looked away before adding, "Thank you, Kate."

His tone was perfunctory and Kate straightened up, a hint of concern on her small face. The gesture did not go unnoticed and Avery added in conciliation, "I expect I shall live." Kate nodded and stepped back from the bed busying herself, instead, at the wardrobe.

"Your father has risen early this morning and has already gone to visit Mrs. Fearncott. He will be gone much of the day. Shall I?" she added, gesturing at the curtains. Avery nodded reluctantly, and watched as Kate drew the heavy curtains. She was immediately thrown into silhouette by the bright sunshine and Avery had to squint to measure up the day outside. The window revealed a promising blue sky peppered with puffy cloud and he found himself cheered by the prospect of such a day.

"I don't know where he finds the strength to be up so early; he is at least three times my age."

He tried to keep his tone level and betray none of the thoughts so vivid in his mind as he watched the young girl potter around, tidying the disarray of the room. There was little about Kate that differed from his dream, so well has he studied her. The face was as alluring as he has imagined it and her slight frame just as appealing. As Avery watched, Kate seemed to become aware of his eyes upon her and eventually she turned to face him, a ready smile on her lips.

"If you want to help, Miss, you only have to ask."

With that she tossed a blouse across to Avery, still sitting in bed. Avery laughed. Kate was singularly the cheekiest maid he had ever known of. Though she was good at her job, he felt sure she would not keep a position very long with her ready wit and easy cheek. He was glad of it for, had she secured a permanent position in Yorkshire, she would never have found herself in London and into his household a few months ago. Without knowing it, that simple gesture had diffused the tension that Avery had felt since he woke and he began to feel more relaxed in her company. Kate busied herself once more and Avery began to think how he would spend the day, unexpectedly without his father's prying eyes. Kate pulled out a dress from the wardrobe and glanced at Avery who shuddered and shook his head.

"No, the grey one I think," he ventured, rising from the bed, his nightshirt falling across his muscled legs. He blushed as he saw Kate watching him.

"I need some new clothes," he said quietly.

At this comment Kate looked surprised. Her mistress's wardrobe was full of dresses, from the drab greys and blacks of mourning to delicate creams and lilacs. Had she herself but a quarter of its contents she would never want for anything more. Most of the prettier dresses were hardly worn but she said nothing. Instead, she hurriedly put the dress back into the wardrobe, extracting instead a pale grey silk outfit. She hung it on the wardrobe and began to straighten out the bodice and brush the skirt with a clothes brush.

"Your father's taken the carriage. Shall I send for a cab?"

"No. I shall walk and perhaps catch the Omnibus. It's a beautiful day and I fancy I would enjoy the exercise. You don't approve, Kate?" he asked, seeing her frown.

"Miss Silver..." Kate didn't need to glance up to know that Avery was frowning at her, his mouth open, ready to argue. She changed tack. "What you do is your own business and I'm all for walking, Miss, but it's your father. He's the one what pays me wages," she grumbled, picking up a book from where it had fallen from the bed. "I don't intend losing this position 'cos your fancy takes you up town. You know 'ow he worries about you."

Aware she had probably spoken out of turn, she faced Avery, chewing her lower lip, waiting. Avery nodded and walked across to the dresser where a plainly decorated ceramic bowl was filled with warm water. He leant over it, scooped up a handful of water and splashed it across his face.

"Well, you mustn't worry so, Kate. We will simply take in the morning at Kensington Gardens and then I have an errand to run."

"What errand, Miss?"

31

Shaking his head, he drew himself up to face his reflection across the dresser top. The mirror showed a handsome young face. The brown eyes, although red and weary looking, were filled with sparkle. Thick brown hair, tousled from his restless sleep, clung about his face where it lay damp. The lips were full and the mouth was upturned slightly into what always seemed a look of amusement. He considered himself for a moment and he was both pleased and angry by what he saw. His eyes flashed over the contours of his chest beneath the nightshirt and he flinched, his jaw set in angry contempt. Over his right shoulder, he saw Kate's face, small with perspective, her eyes narrowed with curiosity as she watched him appraise his reflection in such a way.

"Are you okay, Miss?" she said, frowning.

Without so much as a glance upwards, Avery nodded. 'Yes!' His tone contained a warning undercurrent and Kate seemed less than satisfied with both his assurances and his reluctant smile. Frowning, she stepped forward, her face growing larger in the mirror, and Avery turned his back on their reflections and faced her. For the first time that morning Avery smiled directly at her and leant forwards, taking Kate's hands in his own.

"I can't tell you what I must do today, only that I need your help to do it. You will advise Arthur that we are to take a walk in the park and that we shall be taking lunch somewhere, perhaps Cravens or The Regent. Will you help me?"

Annoyed with herself at the way her stomach lurched at his touch, Kate lowered her eyes to meet Avery's and she set her jaw, resolute to her own voice nagging her to remain firm. She could already imagine the disapproving look with which Arthur would receive this news. As head butler, Arthur fancied himself the head of the household in the absence of Toby Silver.

"Of course, Miss," she heard herself saying and, drinking in the approving nod, she pulled away from him and turned to the wardrobe once more.

Avery sat himself before his mirror and watched Kate as she busied herself once more. As she moved, she talked aloud to him, her pink lips opening and closing at such a rate he felt dizzy by the speed. Her bright blue eyes were moist and the colour of her slender cheekbones seemed pinker against the ivory of her skin. After a few moments, she stopped abruptly and turned to catch him staring at her. A hot flush spread across his cheeks and he grinned sheepishly.

"If you want to admire perfection Miss, you must only commission my portrait and you can look upon it as oft as you like."

Avery spun around to see Kate seated demurely upon the blanket box at the foot of his bed, her knees drawn to one side and her head turned to look over her shoulder; the pose similar to a portrait that hung in the hall. He laughed out loud. She was unlike anyone he had ever been in the company of, either staff or otherwise. She always seemed to say and do whatever was on her mind and it is this, as much as her beauty that charmed him.

"And if THAT is all it takes to turn your foul mood around, I recommend you start work on it as soon as you can," she added, scooping up the few used pieces of crockery and, placing them on her tray, she whisked out of the room. Avery shook his head, smiling to himself, as he tracked the sound of his maid drifting from the corridor humming tunelessly. His face was still set in a smile but Kate had taken his cheer with him and he wasn't ready to let it go. He stood silently for a moment, his breathing the only sound in the seemingly otherwise still house. Kate had disappeared down the back stairs and he felt an impulse to follow her and, abruptly, he hurried out of his room. He stood for a moment at the head of the stairs and listened to ensure she had reached the bottom before he followed. As he reached the foot of the bottom flight, he found the door to the kitchen ajar and he could sense, rather than see, the hustle and bustle of the staff as they went about their morning duties. He listened and watched as he edged closer to the crack in the door, gradually bringing the scene beyond into full focus.

"Hush, girl," admonished the stern voice of Mrs. Druce, the cook. "I won't hear talk like that in my kitchen. If you'll only listen to yourself," she continued out of earshot, grumbling about how service had been in her day. The kitchen was a rush to Avery's head, filled with steam from the adjoining laundry room and from the stove where Mrs. Druce was orchestrating breakfast. Two pans were providing the percussion, lids rattling, one with boiling eggs and one with milk. A kettle was whistling merrily and Mrs. Druce appeared to be whirling, in a dance from the kitchen table to the stove, pulling out a kipper from the oven steamer before lifting the lid of saucepan. The fragile steam pirouetted against Mrs. Druce's white cap before vanishing into the dense fog that gathered above everyone's heads; there, it mingled with the warm, soapy scents and the smell of food. The scullery maid,

Jane, scuttled around and looked to Avery as though she were busy but Mrs. Druce seemed to notice that she was without purpose.

"For heaven's sake, child," she barked. "What on earth are you doing? You're wearing out my tiles!"

Jane stopped abruptly and dropped her hands to her side. Her bottom lip trembled as she weighed up if she should speak out or keep quiet. The moment's indecision was just enough for Mrs. Druce to draw fresh breath and begin berating Jane for all that had gone wrong in the house that morning. Behind the large frame of a pious Mrs. Druce, her symphony of breakfast was reaching its crescendo, a fact that Jane seemed to be trying to signal.

"Mrs. Druce?" Jane offered timidly.

"Hold your tongue, girl. I've not finished."

At that moment the assembled room noticed the arrival of Kate through the back door; the first of the day's locks of hair had come unpinned from beneath her cap and her cheeks were red.

"Mrs. Druce," she nodded her head. "Mary-Ann. Jane," she added, without looking at either. She hurried past them both to drain the jug and busied herself with the dishes that Mrs. Druce has prepared. It was enough to deflect the tongue-lashing from Jane straight to Kate.

"And here's another one come to get under my feet. If you ask me..."

Kate did not let her finish and interjected immediately.

"Your eggs are done, Mrs. Druce, and the milk is going to burn."

Jane, shocked by the polite insolence with which this was delivered, quickly spun around to see Mrs. Druce's reaction. Surely, as if it were her own children and not breakfast about to be ruined, Mrs. Druce, oblivious to the impropriety of Kate's impertinence, set about rescuing the eggs and milk with flustered cries of, "Heavens!" and "Saints, preserve us!" Jane cast a shocked glance at Kate, indicating how narrowly she escaped a berating.

It was no secret that Jane and Mary-Ann were jealous of how Kate had risen to the position of ladies' maid above them and how they thought Kate simple because of her accent. Mary-Ann and Jane had been with the Silvers longer and Avery himself had overheard Mary-Ann bemoaning her ill-fate to have been passed over to be his maid for the likes of Kate. Kate knew these things only too well and avoided eye contact as she loaded breakfast onto the waiting tray.

"I'll take those," Mary-Ann had pushed in front of Kate and was now leaning to take the tray.

"As you wish," Kate replied curtly.

Mary-Ann smiled smugly and walked out of the side door to change her pinafore for a cleaner one. Kate watched after her for a moment, smiling.

"And what are you so pleased with yourself about?"

Mrs. Druce had been watching Kate from the kitchen table, her eyebrows were arched in a permanent look of suspicion which cast shadows over her plump face. Breakfast out of the way, she had ordered Jane to the sink and was now settling herself with a cup of tea and a slice of cold meat before the next preparations must be made.

"I don't know how you can stand to be idle, Katherine. I am sure there are any number of things to keep your hands from the devil."

Kate took the hint and turned again to the sink beside Jane, washing out a jug and standing it on the wooden counter top. She turned to look for a cloth to wipe it and noticed Mrs. Druce's still watching her.

"And how does the young Miss do this morning?"

"Very well I gather, Mrs. Druce. Miss Alice and I shall be going out for the day."

"Where might you be going on such a fine day?"

Kate said nothing and avoided the narrowed gaze of Mrs. Druce as she walked to the sideboard and began untying her apron.

"I take it the master is aware of the young Miss's plans?" Mrs. Druce added, with an unpleasant smile. Avery's own stomach knotted. He knew that his father had not approved any such plans and he wondered what Kate would say,

"It is Miss Alice's wish to take in the air at the park and then to take lunch in Kensington," Kate advised. "I expect we shall return before tea. Have no fear, I shall make Arthur aware of our intentions, Mrs. Druce," she added levelly. The old woman's lips pursed with distaste and she muttered something that Avery could not catch. However, he was unable to miss the tongue which Kate poked at Mrs. Druce as she walked behind her to take down her coat from the back door.

Avery stifled a laugh and quickly retreated from the door as he heard the return of Mary-Ann to take up the breakfast platter. Taking the steps two at a time, he darted back up the stairs to the ground floor and slipped into the dining room. He was a few moments ahead of Mary-Ann and had just gathered his breath when the door swung open to reveal Mary-Ann's sour face. Preferable though Kate's presence may be, Avery was yet to compose himself from that morning's exchange and he was grateful for some time to reflect on his dreams. Mary-Ann set the food down around him, scowling as she raised the coffee pot in anticipation.

"Yes, please, Mary-Ann." Avery watched her pour a careful stream of hot coffee into his cup. Her hands were steady and Avery could not help but think that she would have made a far more prudent choice as ladies' maid than Kate. As he watched Mary-Ann bustle competently about the dining room, he remembered how clumsy Kate had been that morning helping him dress. What a fuss it had been! For his part, he had been nervous around her, guiltily shying away from her touch as if her skin were aflame. As he had stepped into the grey dress, he had felt foolish in his underclothes and he had tried to hurry her along. Kate's inept and heavy handed buttoning and hooking was preferable to her delicate and light touch, which teased his senses. His hurrying her had made her more fingers and thumbs than usual. It had been her hands about his shoulders and neck, roughly tugging at the collar hooks, that called to mind the most vivid memory of that morning's dream, her arms flung about him in a fit of passion not duty, and he had snapped at Kate rather than disgrace himself.

"Thank you, Mary-Ann."

"Yes, Miss," and with a simple bob, Mary-Ann retreated to the hallway whereupon the tall figure of Jamieson stepped forward to take her place.

"Arthur? When do you expect my father home?" Avery enquired of the butler.

"I believe he is expected back for supper, Miss Silver."

"Thank you, Arthur. That will be all."

"Very good, Miss." With a practiced hand, the door closed behind Arthur Jamieson with a delicate click and Avery was left alone to his breakfast, yet found himself without an appetite. Insatiable though his hunger was, there was nothing before him that would satisfy it. In a week's time, Avery would be twenty and life so far, was not unfolding the way he had expected. He pushed his chair away from the table and walked to the fireplace. Above it, an ornate mirror was hung, he stood before it and tried to see anything of himself in the girl staring back at him. Her hair had been pinned up and pulled back, making her neck look long and her ears more prominent. Eschewing any make-up, the girl had a tired and much older look about her than she should; to Avery, the girl did not look very happy and he could sympathise fully with her. Neither of them could bear to spend another minute with the other.

"Damn!" Avery's quiet curse was swallowed by the silence of the room and he bowed his head, his fists balled against the mantelpiece. His eyes burnt with angry tears. His heart and his head were of one accord but his body was not. He was no fool, but since he could remember, he always imagined that at some point in the future, as part of his passing into adulthood, as a rite of passage or puberty, he would become a man. As time had gone on and he had grown older, he had always known that this could never happen. Standing in the family dining room, an uneaten breakfast for two on the table, dressed in a grey silk dress stained with his own tears, Avery realised his own folly. His dreams of Kate were not foolishness; his dreams of himself were. Furious at himself he wiped hard at his eyes with his knuckles and he peered again at the girl in the mirror. Eyes fixed on each other, Avery stared her down. Unblinkingly, he leant in to whisper, "If the wind will not serve, take to the oars."

Chapter Three - Imogen, 1911

I recall vividly that first evening spent under my father's roof after his death. I didn't sleep at all but lay curled under the eiderdown upon my childhood bed. The room was chill from the January air seeping around the ill-fitting frames. With the draft behind them, the heavy curtains seemed to breathe on their own, like great velvet bellows moving in time with my own deep breathing.

My face was dry; I was quite unable to call to mind any grief at my loss. The opposite was true as I could not lay claim on any one emotion for long. Confusion tried to wash over me but its cold fingers were at once met by the scorching edge of fury. I lay stunned like a small bird who had flown, unknowingly, into a dazzling window.

John had stayed at the door for only a few moments. I imagine he was in a state of shock of his own and did not stay to try to talk me from my room. I had heard the muffled sounds of his voice and another man's in the hall below. Heston's? The Inspector's? Then I heard the front door slam and the distant sound of those ghastly men outside rose to greet him and then the house fell silent.

I stayed in the same position all night, my body seemingly frozen both by the cold and the shock of what had come to pass. My mind, however, was feverish. Images of my father loomed out of the black of night.

… Christmas just gone, my father, the attentive grandparent; his hair, once dark, now silvery in the

wintry light from the window. He was listening intently, the hint of a smile playing across his face as Sebastian questioned why the three wise men brought the baby Jesus Gold, Myrrh and Frank Insects…

… Green Park, a picnic is laid out on the velvet grass. My mother seated on one corner of the blanket, a parasol shielding her pale skin from the summer sun. Her eyes were twinkling as she watched her husband with pride. I am smiling too as I follow her gaze. His summer suit is crisp and well fitting; his hair is well oiled and he is making a play of being a waiter as he un-packs the basket across the blanket. He is laughing…

…I am in the nursery with one of my nannies; she is berating me for spilling my milk again. I am crestfallen and on the verge of tears when the door opens and my Father's face appears. He is pulling a sullen face, as long as, I suppose, my own must have been.

'What's this?' he enquires before kneeling down, his arms outstretched. Nanny Owen sighs and rolls her eyes as my indulgent father sweeps me up and dries my eyes…

…I am waiting in the parlour with my mother; John is in my father's study asking for my hand in marriage. They have both suspected for a while and Mother has been stitching the same row on the hem of an old skirt for the past half an hour. The door opens and my father has his hand upon John's shoulder, ushering him in to the room. There is little between them in height and whenever I see them together, I marvel at the similarity in features. John's own darkly oiled hair, the same set of the jaw and the tall, slim build even heir eyes are cast from the same mould: a steely grey, shot with

blue. Only, John has a moustache in the new style and my father's face, as always, is clean-shaven. They are both looking dour and my heart falls into my stomach like a cherry stone. Mother stands, her eyebrows raised.

"It seems we are to have a son at last."

My father's face breaks into an almighty smile and he slaps John on the back. I am the happiest I have ever been…

In all the scenes that play out, I am watching him, him and my mother with an enormous sense of pride. "That is my Father." I seem to be saying, "That man is my Papa and he is my rock."

Tired and confused, I lay upon the bed trying to push out the image of my father's dead body and the more I tried, the more it seemed possible I had imagined the previous night's events.

I could sense the dawn approaching beyond the curtains and I was filled with a longing to return home, to see my children and to get away from that house. I felt quite sure that if I could put some distance between myself and that room then I could pretend, for a while at least, that it was not happening. My limbs were stiff and I shivered as I became sensible to the cold of the room. Padding quietly across the carpet, I unlocked the door and slipped out on to the landing. I was not surprised to see Heston asleep on a chair beside the door. I suppose John may have asked him to keep a vigil but such was his nature, I half expected he would have done so anyway.

Quiet as I had tried to be, he roused instantly and stood to attention. In the gloom of the landing, his expression was hard to make out and I sensed, rather than noticed, his look of great sorrow. For his part, he had served my father above and beyond the call of his duty over the years, often forgoing personal engagements to better meet the needs of my father. In this new age, Heston seemed more comfortable with the old traditions and placed his loyalty to my father above all others. His loss seemed comparable to my own. I forget how long Heston had been my father's man but I cannot remember a time without him. The grey haired man must have been a similar age to my father and I felt a pang of pity for his having slept in a corridor on my account. His eyes met mine for a brief moment before he composed himself; his sleep-crumpled clothes the only clue to the strangeness of the circumstance. I cleared my throat; the noise seemed loud in the silence of the house.

"I have to be home," The words didn't seem right and I felt a need to explain.   "I have to be with my family." The word sounded hollow as the realisation broke over us both that no such thing existed within these walls anymore. I opened my mouth to go on but Heston's voice filled the void.

"Of course, Madam," He stepped aside allowing me to pass before swiftly disappearing down the hall to use the back stairs.

When I descended the staircase several minutes later, somewhat more composed, Heston was waiting for me. He too was looking less disheveled having found the time to pull on a fresh jacket.

"Can I bring you some tea before you go Mrs. Bancroft?"

"No thank you Heston. I just want to get home."

"Very good Madam. I will call for a cab."

I stepped into the parlour and waited, the clock on the mantel had been stopped, its hands frozen at ten past ten. I wondered if the clock had simply not been wound or if it had been stopped to separate the now from then. After several minutes Heston returned.

"There is a cab waiting outside Mrs. Bancroft."

I passed him into the hallway and allowed him to help me back into my coat and took my gloves without meeting his eyes.

"Are the....," I started to say, gesturing towards the front door. "Have they gone?" I managed to finish.

"Yes, Madam. For now at least we are to be left in peace."

"Thank you Heston." Our eyes met and I managed a weak smile. "Look after him."

The stiff butler nodded solemnly, bowing his head before opening the door to the cold January air. As the cabbie ushered me into his waiting carriage, I glanced back towards my father's house, the curtains drawn at the master bedroom window and allowed myself a moment to imagine the respectable man that lay within.

As the cab tumbled along the uneven roads across the fringe of the city, my gaze was jolted with it as I stared from the window. It was early, yet all manner of life was unfolding beyond the dusty pane. A man was out walking two large dogs, one pulling him in haste, the other dawdling to sniff at some delicious scent along a wall. The man looked about to be drawn in two. His eyes were heavily lidded as if caught in moment of deep slumber. It occurred to me as I took him in that if my father could be a woman, then so could he. I frowned, closing my eyes, my head swaying with the tilt of the carriage. I tried to summon an image of my father but try as I might I could not repress the vision of him as last I had seen him. I rubbed my eyes before alighting on the next scene as the cab slowed down at a junction. A girl of about sixteen was stood in the shade of a tree blowing her hands and jigging, to keep her feet from absorbing the ice cold from the flagstones beneath. Her clothes were dull and worn and she blended in very well with the streets behind her. I caught myself leaning forward, taking a grip of the window ledge as the cab began to move and with it my view of the girl. I stared hard. Could there be any doubting that she was female? Had she not wide hips and a narrow waist evident even in her heavy winter clothes? As the distance began to grow, I could no longer discern her features but instead I filled in my father's face across her own plain one. I could not see how it could ever be so. Yet had I not seen it with my own eyes? My eyes could not rest upon anything for long as I looked around the shabby interior of the cab for some answers. Familiar as I was with John's anatomy, could it be that all men were endowed equally? Mine was not a mind accustomed to such thoughts and I felt strange, imagining the naked form of my father, but perhaps there was a more satisfying answer to all of this than at first was thought. I began to fancy that perhaps a medical condition of age could cause such a change. I had not been aware of my shoulders having been drawn up tight but along with this thought, I had relaxed them and at once had grown weary. I imagined then that the matter could instead be a medical peculiarity rather than admit that my father, my own life, my own parents had been a lie.

46

At the moment that it dawned on me, a sudden emptiness washed over me. My mother had known! How could she not? The enormity of this realisation struck me cold across my cheek and I felt as if she herself had slapped me. The familiar sense of struggling to breathe inside a thick fog threatened to choke me. My mother had known and she had not shared it with me. I considered the ramifications of this latest revelation. She must have known everything! For some reason, this felt like an even bigger betrayal and such was the distance of my grief for my loss of her that it felt easier to be angrier at her all of a sudden. How could she have not known?

In my sleep-deprived state of shock, a jumble of images chased themselves across my mind; my mother waving from the bank of the lake as my father rowed me and a friend around the water in a lopsided circle. I must have been about 12 or so and the friend turned out to be a petty girl, Melanie, whom I would later fall out with rather spectacularly about John. I remember I rather sullenly chastised him for his idiocy but secretly, my heart was filled with pride as Melanie giggled at him. Her own father, I remember, was quite the bully and was permanently finding new ways to demean either one of his three daughters. Evidently, he had so wanted a son that he failed quite completely to take any pleasure in his children. Whilst I had often longed for a brother or a sister, I was glad at times not to have to share my father and this was one of those times. The images faded and another replaced it. My father sat at the breakfast table as I entered the dining room, my mother stood behind him as she leaned across to take some of his bread. She giggled as my father caught her wrist and pulled her bodily into the back of his chair. He was beaming broadly as he caught sight of me, and winked. When she saw me, she blushed and hurried to straighten her blouse.

"Your father is a devil, is he not Imogen?"
They were always so affectionate and they were how I had imagined my own life with John to be. That it was not thus was surely my own fault and not John's. The more I knew of his family, the more I knew my own to be unusual with their warmth. As the image faded, I wonder to whom I owed the trait and then it hit me. The thought that had been hovering for the whole journey home, had now settled on my mind. My father was not only a woman but, of course, how could he be related to me? I had lost him entirely. Far from being the only terrible thought, I wondered whether my mother had really been my mother. I groaned aloud and balled my fists up tight to my eyes. I had been set adrift from my family and as the cab finally rumbled to a halt outside my home, I felt certain that stormy weather was still to come.

I had expected to find my home peacefully waking up to the crisp winter's day and was surprised to be met by a hive of activity. As the door opened to my knock, I was taken aback to find the hallway filled with domestic staff. Evidently, John had called them to the front parlour and they had just been dismissed. I was not expecting to see so many familiar faces so soon and their looks were an unsettling mixture of sympathy and pity.

"Good morning Mrs. Bancroft." Maud's voice at my elbow was cool and devoid of any telling emotion as

I handed her my coat and gloves. "Shall I tell Mrs. Harkness to ready the breakfast things?"

"What are you all doing in the parlour, Maud? Where is my husband?"

The young girl had only been in our service for a few months and she looked a little surprised, as if I should be aware of the exchange that had just taken place. She looked behind her towards the retreating backs of the rest of the staff returning to their duties and cast about for words.

"...We...er....."

"Imogen!" John's interruption saved her from any awkwardness and the young girl was palpably relieved not to be having any further conversation with me.

John was at the door to the parlour. He was smartly dressed in a fresh black suit, officially marking a period of mourning, but it was clear from the dark rings around his eyes that he had not slept. He glanced towards Maud trying to make out what she had said.

"That will be all thank you Maud," he said.

"Very good sir." She dipped into a brief curtsey and scuttled down the corridor, unburdened, to join her colleagues.

"What was that all about?" I immediately enquired, noting John's furtive glance after the maid.

"Not here, Imogen. In my study." He walked quickly ahead of me, his heels clipping across the polished tiles with a military air. I followed wearily, suddenly aware of how heavy my limbs felt and how empty my stomach seemed. As he closed the door of the study behind us, he checked again that there were no staff straggling in the hallway before firmly pressing the door into the frame, clicking the lock across the handle to secure us inside. He crossed the carpet and was standing in front of his desk, his arms folded and his face set in a stern countenance.

"You should have told me Imogen."

Anger weighed down upon his brow so that his eyes, fixed on mine, appeared narrower than usual.

"Told you what, John?"

Where a few moments before I had yearned to be safe in my own house, I felt a sudden desire to be alone again. I knew that this conversation had to be had but I was still not prepared to lend words to my own dizzying thoughts.

"John. I am so very weary and I know we need to talk but can we discuss this later?" I didn't look at him as I spoke and I began to turn back to the door, fully expecting any understanding and sympathetic husband to let me go with an "*Of course, of course.*"

"Later?" His tone was shrill and his face thrown into a parody of bemusement. "Absolutely not, Imogen. We will discuss this now."

"John, please." I turned again to the door. He was at my side in three strides, gripping my arm tightly.

"I said, we will discuss this now," he pulled me away from the door and led me to the chair opposite his desk before depositing me roughly in its seat.

"John, you're hurting me."

"How long did you both think to keep this from me?" He leaned over me, his hands resting on the arms of the chair. His face was sallow with lack of sleep but his eyes flickered over my face intently.

"I beg your pardon?" His tone was so strange, his voice so authoritative. It was a side of John I had not seen before. The side of him reserved for his business associates. I was stunned into silence.

"Well," he asked a little more quietly. "I mean, good God, do you expect me to believe that you didn't know?"

There was coldness in his voice and the accusation stung me.

"I didn't know." The words came out so weakly they seemed to founder in the air. It sounded foolish after the strength of John's words. I felt like a small child in front of her father, only mine had never behaved like this. "I didn't know," I repeated. The words dawned on me and I shook my head slowly and my face grew hot with shame.

John had continued to watch me turn pink and seemed agitated but distracted. He drew his hand through his hair and mumbled to himself that he wanted to believe me.

"I need you to be absolutely honest and clear with me, Imogen." He levelled his gaze at me. "Are you telling me you had no inkling? No clue? Absolutely no idea that your *'father'* was masquerading as a man?" A small amount of spittle flew from his lips as he spat out the word 'father'. He wiped his mouth, looking at the door before adding more quietly. "This is a ghastly business. No, it's more than that. It's absolutely monstrous. What on earth was he.....or I suppose I should say, SHE thinking?"

He had thrown his hands in the air, a fresh energy animating him as incredulity took hold of him. He paced in front of the desk, continuing to run his hands through his hair.

51

"Have you any idea of the scandal this is going to cause?" he waited for a response. "Have you any idea what this could do to my reputation? Your children's reputation?"

At the mention of the boys, I looked up at him, his familiar features pulled into a strange look of contempt. There was a wild look of panic about him as the truth of his concerns became clear. Reputation.

"I didn't know, John. I didn't know. I didn't know." I snapped, throwing my hands into the air, my own anger finding fuel in his crass remarks and shallow self-pity. I wanted him to believe me but, more than that, I wanted him to put his arm around me and to say that it would all be right, even if it would not be. I stood up and took a step towards him but the grief, the anger, the tiredness was too much and I stumbled faintly. His instincts took hold and he stepped forwards and caught me to his chest, his arms holding my elbows.

"Imogen," he said simply pushing me at arm's length so he could study my face. A modicum of sentiment returned to his voice as his concern for me momentarily overshadowed his concern for himself. But it was to be a brief lapse in his demeanour.

"Please, take a hold of yourself." His grip tightened as I sensed him cast about for somewhere to put me. Where moments before, all I had longed for was to be held in his arms to seek comfort on his broad chest, now I wanted to be out of his grip. I stepped backwards and sat back down in the chair. A noise sounded heavily on the floorboards above us as someone dropped something in one of the bedrooms. I watched as he straightened his waistcoat, walked around his desk and sat down. After a moments silence, John cleared his throat. He lowered his voice.

"I have spoken with the staff and they have been informed of your..." he paused whilst he considered what word to use. "...father's demise. They were aware that there were some....irregularities.....with the death but I have made it plain that gossip will not be tolerated."

He waited seemingly for some acknowledgement from me and in the absence of one he continued a little haltingly.

"I am meeting with the police commissioner later this morning, to discuss how this thing can best be handled. As you know, the press seem to have got wind of it and those that I haven't managed to pay to keep quiet will have it all over town by lunchtime.' His voice wavered as his anger seemed once again to get the better of him. 'There will be a storm to deal with this afternoon and I would prefer it if you were not around."

His gaze dropped to the desk and I felt my face burn as his intentions grew clearer.

"I shall arrange for the boys to return to Worcester until this matter has died down. I shall deal with this matter."

"But what about my father? The funeral? There are arrangements to be......"

"Your father?" he answered quietly his eyes narrowed questioningly. "Who was your father, Imogen?"

The question took all of my breath from me, the ready answer fresh on my tongue turned stale, as John awaited a response and Oh! Forgive me but I faltered, there in my husband's study, and instead of the pride I

53

had always associated with my father, I felt only shame.

"Imogen, you had no father. That woman has made fools of us all," he spoke softly struggling to convey his anger but trying to keep his volume down. "SHE was not your father and whether you kept her secret or not, it will cost me a small fortune to try and bury it with her."

In delivering this, he had sunk backwards into his chair, his large hand gripping on to the edge of the desk to prevent him slumping entirely. I felt his exhaustion wash through the both of us and I was adrift. I watched him across the desk as I struggled to find words in response but none came. John's gaze fell to his desk upon which this situation had no doubt doubled his workload. I looked beyond him to his mantel where the clock was still, no-one having entered his study this morning to wind it. The silence it afforded in the room was all incongruous with the crowded, angry words that hung in the air around us. I felt defeated and each minute, of silence that it marked, put us beyond the others reach more acutely than any miles could. After several moments had passed awkwardly, John rose from his seat and walked around his desk to stand before me. He held out his hand for my own and he pulled me into an awkward embrace. I felt his familiar arms around me and they afforded me no solace, but I tried to find some comfort in the gesture. The next week would no doubt bring many more battles and we would both need strength to get through them.

Chapter Four - Avery, 1869

Rounding Cornwall Gardens onto the Gloucester Road, the sun at their back, Avery Silver and his maid, Kate Ward, cut a path through the bustle of the busy streets up towards Kensington. Having assured Arthur that he had told his father of his intended outing, Avery's thoughts of home were soon forgotten as the summer's day transformed the neighbouring streets from the bleak familiarity to the sunny prospect of discovery. Avery's step, at first quick to escape the oppressive stare of his home, slowed a little and Kate drew alongside him. Being several inches taller, Avery's stride was longer, and, being more disposed to rush at this opportunity than Kate, he had covered some distance alone. As they fell into step with one another, Avery watched the people they passed by. Gentlemen in suits tipped their hats, ladies on their arms held parasols raised against the sun, tourists headed to the Palace or the South Kensington Museum hurried excitedly past; foreigners, struck by the vastness of the city that he was underwhelmed by. As the numbers of people on the busy thoroughfare increased, Kate was pressed to his side and he wondered how she found the hustle and bustle in comparison to a Yorkshire town.

"Weather such as this would be much improved were it not for the number of people enjoying it. Don't you think?" he asked. Kate rolled her eyes in acknowledgement of the masses around them.

"Believe me, Miss, the great unwashed of London have seen far more of a bar of soap than in Harrogate or Leeds."

Avery smiled, he hardly ever thought about what life Kate had before she had joined the household. She had appeared without references just as Avery had dispatched the last in a long line of useless girls. He knew from experience that she disliked talking about her previous life and he was encouraged by her mentioning her home cities to enquire further.

"Tell me, how do you find London?"

He knew that most of her free time was spent around this area and he himself had noticed that she was no longer inclined to look up at the buildings in the same wonder but rather seemed to hurry on to make the most of her precious liberty. She had one or two friends she had made in service and these she would meet with occasionally, to walk in the parks or share ice cream or tea with. There was little about these meetings that he did not know, so prone was she to gabble constantly whilst she was busying herself in his rooms or around the house. During her first month, she had kept her head down and busied herself at her post being almost wary of Avery. She had seemed a morose girl and he had wondered if in fact she might not be a little slow. He had found her guardedness a challenge and he remembered how stunned he was when she unexpectedly confided in him. Aware that her strange accent made her stand out, one of the local girls had made fun of her and he had found her in his room that evening, folding clothes into his press with a face like thunder.

"Miss Ward? Are you alright?"

She seemed to have been waiting for his arrival and she answered simply and honestly.

"No, Miss Silver. I'm not."

"It looks for all the world that those clothes have slighted you Miss Ward and by all accounts you are giving them what for." She had not smiled. He closed the door behind him and moved to the chaise longue beneath the window. Seating himself awkwardly, he had tipped his head to one side and offered the seat beside him with a well placed hand. It was a gesture that invited intimacy and evidently was all that Kate was waiting for.

"Do you know, sometimes I can barely understand every second word that Mary-Ann utters but I hold my tongue. I don't think her slow, I don't think her stupid and I don't think myself better than her."

Avery had not expected any such outburst and hardly knew how to respond before she continued with her rant as she strode around the room.

"I've put up with it for weeks now and today they tried to get me in hot water. I don't go in for tireless gossip Miss Silver. Never have and never will. I won't get into trouble because they see fit to talk about their betters. I've worked hard here, haven't I? Its not fair if they get me into trouble just because I was born a hundred miles away."

"Kate. Kate," Avery had had to repeat himself to halt the flow. "You're not making any sense. What on earth has happened?"

Kate had drawn herself up on the spot and turned to face him properly. She hesitated, some of her own anger had dissipated in her own little tirade and she may have been content to apologise for the outburst and disappear without a further word, but Avery was intrigued by this other side to the quiet young girl.

"Please. Don't stop. Just tell me what has happened?" he nodded for her to continue, an encouraging smile upon his lips. He tapped the seat beside him again and, with some of the wind taken from her sails, she let out a huge sigh and flopped down beside him. It was the first, but not the last time he would feel his chest lurch at her proximity and, as she leaned back against the window frame, he was envious of the ease she seemed to feel being inside her own body. Her own chest was tight against her uniform and the material stretched around the buttons revealing a shadow where her bosom swelled. Avery felt his mouth prickle and he barely heard the remainder of her story as he imagined what lay beneath the dark cotton dress

Avery had felt his cheeks grow hot as he listened to her story but could not drag his eyes away from her breasts. Evidently, two of the girls in the household had been teasing her relentlessly. She had put up with the mimicking of her accent and the deviling over her seeming slowness when she misunderstood their cockney phrases. That day, she had broken with the pressure and there had been some altercation or other below stairs. One of the girls had begun badgering Kate about her lack of references and had begun conjecturing on the reasons. It seems Mary-Ann had touched a nerve by suggesting the reason Kate had not arrived with any references was because she was running away from something.

"Alice?" Kate's voice startled him and he looked around to note they were now walking across Kensington Gore to the Gardens. Glancing at Kate, he saw her waiting for him to reply.

"I'm sorry," he blushed. "What did you say?"

"I said, London is a curious place, full of curious people but it's home now."

"Tell me, do you miss your family? You never speak of them Kate and you certainly have never been away from Cornwall Gardens long enough to visit."

He noticed immediately the change in her body language and regretted asking the question, curious as he was to know the reason for her obvious discomfort.

"Why do you ask, Miss?"

"I suppose I know very little of your life before Cornwall Gardens and..," he paused. "....I am curious, that's all." He considered her surreptitiously as they maneuvered themselves through the wrought iron gates to enter the park. He did not want Kate to feel uncomfortable, not that day, and he wanted to change the subject.

"I am glad you feel London is home to you."

They ambled along the footpath, bordered by a vibrant display of summer blooms and Avery pulled at the sleeves of his dress. The plump heads of yellow begonias drooped over lazy pink primulas and sullen golden marigolds. The park was alive with riotous colour and seemed alert with the expectation of a long and glorious day. They walked on in silence for a few minutes, taking in the heady scents, before Avery added, 'We have come to be quite close have we not?' There was a pause and his cheeks grew hot. He wondered if she could see any of his dreams upon his face. With few friends he was more than just fond of the intimacy he shared with Kate, they were close in age and he felt less like she was a servant to him and more of a companion. Much as this pleased him, he was cautious to remind himself daily of the proper role that he must play in their relationship.

"Yes, Miss."

Avery glanced at the path ahead, which was busy with ladies sauntering in the pleasant sunshine. After an unforgiving winter and a late spring, the weather was causing much abandon among their neighbours. A few young gents were basking on the grass, hats tipped to shield their eyes, arms behind their heads, catching a little extra sleep; the local brigade of nannies were also out en masse, pushing great black and silver perambulators, each appraising the others' baby carriages before deciding upon whom to bestow their morning's greetings. The Round Pond sparkled in the morning sun reflecting the great blue sky and making it seem that one could step through the very earth itself and fall through the heavens. Avoiding the throng of people in front of them, Avery veered off the main path and headed down past the waterside and up towards the Porchester Terrace Gate. He had thought long and hard about this moment and he decided it was now or never.

"I have a favour to ask of you, Kate," Avery stopped and Kate continued past, turning after a few steps so that they were some distance from each other, when Kate replied, "Yes Miss?"

"I have two things to ask of you and I am afraid you may find both strange. The first is an errand that I wish to run in St Giles," he held up a hand as Kate's face fell, the area around St Giles being of questionable character. "I will explain what I wish to do in a moment and I shall understand if you will not come with me. However, if you do, I need your assurances that the details of where we go must remain with only the two of us."

He kept his eyes on Kate's as she nodded slowly at him, indicating only that she understood. She was hesitant but her curiosity forbade her from denying him.

"Yes, of course, Miss," she answered. "And the second thing, Miss Silver?" she asked neutrally. She seemed nervous of the serious turn that this conversation had taken but her eyes sparkled with delight. Avery's cheek twitched as she addressed him and he hesitated, considering again what he was about to ask of her.

"I would like you to stop calling me Miss or Alice."

Her face lit up in a smile. She seemed relieved that this outlandish request was all that seemed to be vexing her young mistress. However, noticing how solemn Avery's face became she stifled a laugh and instead enquired. "What am I to call you then?"

He waited nervously and the girl looked confused, her eyebrows knitted together expectantly.

"I should like you to call me, Avery." He stated simply. "Or perhaps you would like to call me, Sir," he added. He kept his eyes fixed unblinkingly on her own as he waited for her reaction. His stomach knotted as something like recognition dawned over her face. There was no doubt that she was puzzled and she stepped backwards slightly to look at him.

To anyone who cared to consider it, Avery was a tall and handsome woman who seemed to go to extraordinary lengths to refuse to wear anything which could make him more beautiful. He always chose plain and drab dresses and refused to have either his hair or his face made up, which made him seem much older than his twenty years. Kate had always professed this to be strange and she openly coveted the fine fabrics her mistress refused to take pleasure in. Many supposed that Avery was in want of a mother figure to guide him in the fashionable changes to which a young girl ought to be devoted. Avery watched, almost shyly, as Kate continued to look puzzled by what she was being asked.

"What is the errand in St Giles?" she asked.

"I told you already," he answered cautiously. "Avery needs some new clothes."

Avery's words hung in the air between them as Kate looked at him curiously. As they stood facing each other on the path, a trio of young girls passed them, their arms interlocked, giggling and pointing at a young man asleep down by the pond. A family of ducks was investigating his straw hat and was about to make off with it. The spell of their stare was broken as Avery stepped aside to allow the girls room on the path and he watched until they disappeared beyond earshot. When he looked back at Kate, she was walking away from him towards the gate. With an anxious start, Avery hurried to catch up with her and placed a restraining hand upon her arm.

"Kate?"

She stopped and, looking up at her mistress, smiled nervously.

"If we hurry we can catch the next bus to St Giles, Miss, " she caught herself from finishing and looked up expectantly at Avery. The dread rush of icy cold surging to his heart was replaced, at once, by a warming pleasure and he smiled broadly. Kate

62

returned his excited beam as she finished her sentence. "...Sir."

~o~

As the Omnibus rolled off along Shaftesbury Avenue, Avery Silver and Kate Ward appeared fairly ordinary figures by the light of the splendid, summer sun. There were plenty of ladies and gentlemen ambling along towards Piccadilly Circus and few noticed the two drably dressed women as they strayed down Mercer Street. The narrow road was bustling with people intent on making hay whilst the sun shone. Several ramshackle stalls had been thrown up along the side street. Two barrow boys competed for an audience, shouting cheekily to sell their fruit and vegetables. A man in a moth-eaten suit tried to demonstrate something mechanical out of a battered suitcase. He struggled with his sales patter as some parts fell off his machine. His audience stared at him warily with a mixture of curiosity and pity and some openly laughed. A woman, shabbily dressed in the offcuts of what was once a fine dress, paraded around an upturned crate stacked high with parasols. The contents were neither new nor in very good condition and Avery eyed her suspiciously, wondering how such a down-at-heel woman could have acquired so many parasols. Kate too had spotted the woman and she quickly glanced away as the woman noticed her admiring her wares.

"Jus wot you need ter keep yer fair skin shaded from the sun, Miss. Only 'alf a shilling. Good as new,

63

Miss." The woman tried to press the parasol she was holding into Kate's hand. Kate shook her head and Avery was quick to intervene.

"We have no need of a parasol today, good lady. The sun has been a stranger too long and we intend to make the most of what warmth he offers." He pressed a penny into the woman's hand and strode onwards more purposefully. Kate smiled at the woman and hurried to catch up with her mistress. As they approached the junction with an even narrower street, Kate glanced down it nervously. The sun did not seem to penetrate this passageway and the number of people in fine clothes had diminished. Instead, the buildings cast a shadow upon a duller palette of colour. The drab grey of those who earned their way from harder means was evident and Kate did not look keen that Avery lead her down that particular passage. Not wishing to appear lost, Avery slowed but did not stop, looking all the while for an indication of the street name. As if drawn by an invisible string, a young girl ambled out of the gloom and Avery beckoned to her.

"What street is this?" he asked.

"Fer a penny, Miss, I'll tell ya."

"Tell me first and then we shall see."

"S'erlam Street, Miss," the girl offered, holding out her hand expectantly.

"Earlham Street? Do you know the tailor, Mr. Fry?" he asked.

The girl narrowed her eyes at Avery, wondering what this strange looking lady would want with a workman's tailor. She looked Avery up and down and seemed to weigh up her chances of seeing a penny if she didn't tell her. The girl noticed a boy out of the corner of her eye, eager to snatch the chance of an easy fee if she herself did not take the opportunity.

"Two pennies, Miss, and I'll take you there."

Avery nodded and gestured for the girl to lead on. Avery beckoned to Kate who rolled her eyes as the girl turned on her heel and skipped down the same dirty side street which Kate had been eyeing nervously.

"That's right, you skip off and take the penny and we'll just get our throats cut for our troubles," Kate muttered. Avery laughed out loud and pulled her after him, trying to keep up with the young girl. They followed the girl to a run-down shop set back from the road. Handing the girl two pennies, Avery turned to Kate and put his fingers to his lips, indicating she should stay silent. The door to the shop was open and Avery stepped inside. Despite the gloom of the street, the shop was stuffy and warm. There was only one room that was full to bursting but seemingly had very little to sell. A large cutting table filled most of the space upon which laid a bolt of heavy woollen cloth and over which an elderly man was stooped. He did not glance up as they entered the shop but merely threw a curt greeting at them from his work.

"I'll be with you in a minute, gents."

He continued to chalk upon the cloth as he drew around a paper design for sleeves of some sort, a great oil lamp throwing light upon his task. Avery smiled to Kate but she was unable to force her face into a similar gesture and instead she looked around the room. A tailor's dummy stood beside the small window, blocking out what little of the light had managed to make it up the dark street, and was clothed itself in cobwebs and dust. A couple of crates were stacked against a sidewall, their labels indicating yet more of the same drab cloth. The custom here appeared to be for functional work wear and nothing more besides. The man, still busy at his task, carefully finished off his dusty lines, muttering to himself as he did so. His hair was thinning and a pair of glasses sitting atop his balding pate slipped a little as he leaned ever more forwards across the cloth. Several minutes passed in silence and Kate glanced at Avery again as the man seemed to forget about their presence entirely.

"And, done," he concluded, straightening up and pushing his glasses back to his nose. "How can I help you, gents?" His mouth dropped open and he peered about his small shop searching for someone else. "Pardon me, ladies, I thought you were gentlemen!" he stammered. He wore a slightly confused expression and scratched his head. Evidently, he did not entertain many unaccompanied ladies at his premises and for a moment he acted stunned. "Have you come to collect something?" he ventured.

"I wish to have a suit made," Avery announced, fixing the man with an unblinking stare. "I wish to have quite a few fine suits made."

The tailor looked a little confused and indicated around his shop. "Begging your pardon, Miss, but your husband might prefer to go somewhere a little more..." he smiled, searching for a word that offended neither himself nor Avery "...upmarket."

"I do not have a husband, Mr. Fry, but I shall pay well and I will pay even better for your absolute discretion."

Fry's eyes sparkled at the mention of money but he still looked at Avery warily.

"Discretion about what, Miss? Who are the suits for?"

Avery glanced at Kate and then back towards the open door. Taking his hint, Kate stepped to the entrance, glanced sideways up the street before nodding to Avery that they could speak freely.

"The suits, Mr. Fry, are for myself," Avery stepped forward and fingered the cloth upon the table, all the while keeping his eyes on the tailor. If the man was shocked by the statement, he did not allow his face to convey it and he waited for Avery to come to the point. This was business and, on the matter of money, Fry was most serious.

"I will provide you with money for good material and I will pay you double your usual rate for a good job. To start, I would like a light summer suit in linen, a formal suit for daywear and a dress suit for the theatre. Do you have any questions?"

The old man glanced at Kate to confirm that this strange young woman spoke in earnest and, seeing her solemn face, he began to add up the sum in his head, eager to calculate this rather odd turn of fortune. He licked his lips.

"Of course I'll need a deposit, and then there's the rate for my 'discretion'," He smiled slowly at Avery, his hands braced wide on his table. Avery considered him for a moment and then broke into a smile too.

"'Indeed, Mr. Fry. Shall we say an extra ten percent?"

The old man agreed, rather too hastily for which he would chide himself later, and offered his hand on the bargain. As the young woman took his hand, his eyebrows shot up in surprise. Her grip was firm, the hands dry and large.

"I will need to take some measurements, Miss...?" he fished for a name.

"My maid will take what measurements you need and have them sent to you this evening," Avery replied, laying out some notes on the table. "A deposit, Mr. Fry. You will not be able to contact me but I shall arrange for the package to be collected a week tomorrow."

Fry nodded and snatched up the money, stuffing it into a drawer under the table, glancing nervously at the door.

"How do you know I can be trusted?" the old man ventured.

Avery looked at him in surprise and considered the man before stating, matter of factly. "Because, I shall need a whole winter wardrobe too, Mr. Fry, and for that I shall pay handsomely."

The old tailor's eyes sparkled with glee. He had not expected half such luck that morning when he had crawled out of bed and opened the doors of his miserable little shop. He wrote out a list of the measurements he would need of Avery and handed it to Kate and then shuffled to the other side of his table to escort the strange lady to the door.

"What shall I call you, Miss?" he asked, his voice soft to acknowledge the price which such information could be worth.

Avery put his head to one side and furrowed his brow.

"You shall call me Mr. Silver," he whispered conspiratorially, leaning in to the old man.

Kate spun around and threw Avery a look of concern. This errand was dangerous enough as it was and what had seemed exciting in the bright sunlit park that morning now seemed foolish folly. That Avery was now being indiscrete with his name made her especially nervous. Smiling, the old man leaned forwards to watch them disappear back towards the warmth of Mercer Street.

"For what you're paying me, I'll call you Mother Mary herself," he muttered to himself, shaking his head in bemusement.

Chapter Five - Imogen, 1911

Having won some small ground with John that I would stay in London but that the boys should return to Worcester, I gladly slipped out of his office. As the door closed behind me, I was not surprised to see my eldest son, Sebastian lurking in the hallway. As I caught his eye, I tried a smile but it would not break across my face and instead I merely ushered him silently back up to the nursery. On the way up the stairs, he asked me directly.

"Is Grandpapa dead?"

I continued on to the first floor landing and, noticing he had paused behind me, I looked at him directly. At nine, he was a young man in the making. Where his brother still had his infant curls and sported the odd childish frills about his clothes, Sebastian was becoming aware of his future and it wrought upon him a most serious demeanour. I looked at him carefully, knowing he had most likely already been told the news and wondered what more he wanted me to tell him.

"Yes, Sebastian. He is dead."

He was a few steps below me and the angle of his face thrown up into the light made him appear all at once, much younger than he was. He was fighting his natural childish curiosity to ask more but all too aware that something was wrong. I was weary but in a way I wanted to talk and, at that moment, Sebastian was intent on listening.

"What is it, Sebastian?"

My tone must have been inviting as he stepped up to join me on the landing. As he did so, he looked carefully over the banisters to see into the hallway below. Satisfied that we were alone but with an air of caution, he whispered to me.

"Last night, after Nanny Hewitt had put us to bed, I heard voices from the back stairs. I knew you and Father had gone out urgently so I got out of bed," he looked from each of my eyes, scanning my face for some hint of reprisal. When none came, he continued. "Thomas was already asleep," he assured me. "As I said, the voices were coming from the back stairs. They were hushed but angry and I thought perhaps something was wrong. From the top of the stairs, I could hear Mrs. Harkness and Beth below me. I think Beth was crying but Mrs. Harkness was cross. Very cross."

I opened my mouth to chastise him for eavesdropping but I needed to know what he had heard. Sebastian was waiting for me to reprimand him and he waited nervously, still holding on to whatever information he wanted assurances on. I knew of course that I should be cross with him, for leaving his bed in the night and now for telling tales but my own curiosity was aroused.

"Why was Mrs. Harkness cross, Sebastian?"

My lack of disapproval had broken a dam and the rest of the story spilled out.

"Mrs. Harkness was furious with something Beth had said. She kept saying over and over again that she was a liar and that she would tell the master in the morning. Beth just kept on arguing with her, insisting she had been right and that she didn't care if the master found out because she was not going to work a minute longer for this house. She called Father a liar and she called you a liar and she called Grandmamma a tom and Grandpa a molly.'

I had not been expecting my mother to be brought into this and the shock of it stung me. All at once, I was filled with ice where my heart was and my head swam. I did not fully understand the words he had used and half imagined that he had misheard them. I doubted very much that they were complimentary all the same. Sebastian hesitated, his pale face rosy cheeked with fury. His voice had risen and I looked up and down the stairs. I could hear a door closing below us and I grabbed Sebastian by his hand and led him quickly to the guest bedroom. I glanced down the corridor again before closing the door behind us. The change in scenery had stemmed Sebastian's flow and he looked awkward as he recalled the words Beth had used the night before. I bent down before him so I could look up at him. He wore an expression of concern and I knew he was anxious about this secrecy.

"Sebastian," I started softly. "I don't know what you overheard or you think you overheard last night."

He opened his mouth in silent protest but I held up a hand and closed my eyes. The incline of my head made it impossible for him to argue with me. "I don't need to remind you that you should not be out of your bed and I think this is a perfect example of why one must not eavesdrop. You must be mistaken."

Again, a defiant look was silenced with a disapproving glance. "Be rest assured that I shall deal with this."

His eyes were shining with the onset of tears. No doubt he felt frustrated. He was angry and he was confused and he wanted the clarity which I was unwilling, and unable, to give him. I felt sure that John was right in his decision to send the boys away and, filled with the sense of their imminent departure, I drew up my eldest son in my arms and held him tight.

~o~

I was aware of Nanny Hewitt's eyes upon me as I deposited Sebastian into her care and affirmed my wish that the boys be readied for their return to John's parents. She seemed less than pleased that she too would be removed from the epicenter of whatever scandal was breaking here in Hampstead and she met my gaze with a peculiar obstinacy. As I closed the nursery door behind me, I was overcome with exhaustion and I went directly to my bedroom. The bed had been drawn ready in anticipation and I wondered, with a sudden anger, whether Beth had readied the sheets. The thought that she was in my employ and had uttered those words in my own home filled me with anger and I was fuelled with another surge of energy. I crossed the room to the fireplace and pressed the bell push for the kitchen. As I waited, I poured myself a glass of water from the bedside table and crossed to the window. It was only a few moments later when Maud arrived. Evidently the household were on a state of high alert as she appeared quite breathless.

"Yes Ma'am?"

I had hoped Beth herself would attend and I could have the immediate satisfaction of terminating her employment myself.

"Maud, would you have Beth come and see me please."

"Beth, Ma'am?" The girl looked awkwardly to the floor. Evidently, Sebastian and I were not the only ones aware of last night's altercation.

"Yes. Beth. The short, dumpy one," I added spitefully.

"She's not here Ma'am." The poor girl looked as if she would rather be bobbing adrift in the Channel than reporting to me. "She's gone."

"Where has she gone?"

"Begging your pardon Mrs. Bancroft but I don't rightly know. She took off a few minutes ago. After you came back, she went to see Stokes and then she left Ma'am. Bags an' all."

I watched with a feeling of pity as the young girl in front of me tried desperately to distance herself from the actions of her counterpart. Maud was a good maid but was a dreadful orator and stammered terribly. It gave me no pleasure watching her squirm under interrogation and after a few more minutes of her struggling with her words I dismissed her.

"I would not be disturbed for a few hours, Maud. Make sure Mrs. Harkness is given some assistance with her packing but be sure they don't leave without my seeing them off."

With a little bob, she backed out of the room, grateful for not being questioned further on any of the rumours flying around below stairs. I suppose I must have slept a little as a few hours later, I started heavily with the sound of knocking at my door. I had been in the middle of a strange dream.

"Yes?" I called out. "Come in."

The door opened cautiously and Maud's face appeared around the frame.

"Mrs. Bancroft? The cab is here for the children."

"What? What's the time?" I fumbled with the nightstand and drew up my watch. It was half past two in the afternoon.

"Very well. Help me get ready." Maud closed the door and hurried to the wardrobe, immediately withdrawing the black dress of which I had been so fond when my mother had died. The sight of it made my head swim again and I considered I had not eaten for almost a day. The thought of food made me feel more giddy but I knew I had to eat something otherwise I would pass out. I suffered terribly from nausea and giddiness when I was carrying Thomas and the signs were familiar.

"Have Mrs. Harkness ready some dry toast and serve it in the parlour with tea in half an hour?"

Maud buttoned me up and then retreated from the room, whilst I tidied my hair. The mirror at the dressing table reflected a poor image of me and I was shocked by the toll only a day could take on someone. One's own face should be as familiar to us as the walls in our home but how often do we find ourselves studying our own walls? Yet, as with walls, it is all too obvious when cracks begin to appear. My eyes were red rimmed and bloodshot, dark shadows were beginning to surface beneath them. My skin looked crumpled from the sleep I had had and my complexion was grey. Normally, I was content with my appearance and had every reason to consider myself a reasonable beauty but on this inspection I was revealed as being older than I thought myself to appear, and I was taken rather suddenly with the fact that age comes to us all. The thought did nothing to alleviate my mood and I pinned up my hair in the old fashioned way, succumbing to the grim and familiar sense of grief that had taken up residence within me once again.

As I descended the stairs, Sebastian did not look directly at me and I could sense his annoyance that he was to be treated as a child being sent away. Thomas, however, was quite perturbed.

"Why are we going back to grandfather's house? Will you and Father come too? Are we having another Christmas?"

I was unsure how to answer him as, in truth, I did not wish either of the boys to be sent away. I felt with every fibre of myself that I needed to hold them tight to me. It was for this same reason that they had to go. I could not yet accept what had happened to myself let alone explain it to a child.

"No Thomas. You and Sebastian need to help Father and me by staying in the country until after the funeral."

The word was familiar to him but it was evident that he understood little of the situation. He had the good sense however to refrain from asking any more questions and, instead, watched silently as I embraced Sebastian, who was grateful to receive only a kiss to his forehead, save I embarrassed him in front of the staff. John accompanied them to the station with Nanny Hewitt and he seemed grateful to be leaving the house. As the door closed after their receding voices and the hallway had begun to return to its familiar muffled enclave, I was immediately sensible to the eyes that avoided my own. Maud, stood to one side of the hallway, awaited some indication of my intentions so that she could usefully employ herself to my service.

Although I was sure she did not normally meet my gaze, her eyes appeared to dance around the room in a concerted effort to watch me but not to see me. The hairs on the back of my neck prickled with the paranoia of the thought and I knew I ought to take advantage of the peace and get some more rest. There was a lingering sense of foreboding which I knew would prevent me from settling and so, I was rather grateful when, just moments after the door was closed, the bell sounded. I immediately thought it was John, forgotten something, and I lingered in the hall behind Stokes as he crossed the tiles to draw the door open.

As soon as the door opened, I could see it was not John but a shorter man silhouetted against the crisp blue winter sky. He wore a bowler hat and was stooped with age. It took but a second before I was able to place a name to the face beyond Stokes.

"Geoffrey!" I announced warmly.

My father's solicitor was barely over the threshold when he saw me and his face lit up in a genuine show of affection. His expression, however, was muddled as I crossed the hall to greet him.

"Imogen, I can't tell you how sorry I am to learn of your father's death. I am deeply sorry for your loss." He took up my hand in his own and placed his own paper thin fingers across the back of mine, patting me absently. His eyes searched my face as if he was seeking some comfort from me too.

"Thank you Geoffrey. Thank you for coming. Won't you come through?"

I walked through to the parlour. Stokes passed Geoffrey's hat and coat to Amy and followed us.

"Can I offer you a drink? A sherry perhaps?"

Geoffrey Leech had been the Silver family solicitor for as long as I can remember. He was an elderly man himself and had recently taken retirement yet retained a few of his personal clients. I knew that he and my father were members of the same club in St James and I considered them to also be friends. It occurred to me that perhaps he knew something. Stokes served two glasses of sherry and we sat ourselves opposite one another.

"Ah, thank you Stokes' he accepted his glass. 'Is John home?"

"You've just missed him. He has gone to Kings Cross. We thought it best in the circumstances to send the boys back to the country."

"Of course. As you see fit. I really do need to see both of you. Shall he be long?"

My ears filled with a faraway rushing as my heart beat loudly. Geoffrey had some more news and, by the look on his face, it was not good.

"He should be back within the hour. Of course you can wait but please tell me what it is Geoffrey. I cannot bear it."

He looked up at me, immediately anxious at the distress in my voice. I knew the colour had drained from me and my already gaunt face must have seemed quite pale.

"Oh good Lord, Imogen. I'm so sorry. I shouldn't have said anything. It is nothing unusual in the circumstances. Although in the circumstances all must be considered quite unusual..." He leaned forward quickly setting his glass down before resuming his muddled speech. 'That is to say, of course, I am naturally shocked by the circumstances and.....' The old man looked at me, appealing for some assistance as he struggled to find the words. He was an astute and confident man and I was astonished by this rather guarded display. He glanced towards Stokes and I understood a little of his predicament.

"That will be all thank you Stokes. You may leave us."

The butler gave nothing away in his expression as he inclined his head with a polite 'Madam' and reversed out of the room. Geoffrey had taken out his handkerchief and was now stood mopping his brow and, if I was not mistaken, his eyes.

"Forgive me, Imogen. I cannot begin to tell you how upsetting all of this is but of course...'" He looked at me with another apology fresh on his lips, a slightly embarrassed expression that he should forget my own grief.

"Geoffrey, I can't thank you enough for your kind words but please tell me what you have come to say. I must hear it now. Please."

He nodded and sat down once again, leaning forward slightly so that he could keep his voice low.

"There is to be a coroner's inquiry tomorrow morning. The police have submitted a report to the coroner, who is to perform a post mortem. Your father was not so very old and it is likely that his death was a coronary disease. As you will know, he suffered from palpitations of the chest and he was receiving some treatment from a doctor in Belgravia."

This was news indeed to me. I had not known that my father was anything but in perfect health. I had not known my father to be anything but my father though and how wrong that assumption proved to be. I could only listen as Geoffrey continued.

"In the circumstances, it is not the death itself which they are trying to determine but of course, given the nature of the.....facts of the case.....as they stand......" Once again, Geoffrey's characteristic assuredness faltered as he struggled to find the words, if indeed they existed in his mind. "Imogen, what I am trying to say is that they are trying to prove, for the purposes of the death certificate and for the Will, your father's true biological gender."

He had said it and, once out, the statement seemed to suck all other sounds from the room leaving only that word. There were many questions, not least of which I wanted to know where and when this inquiry was being held. The post mortem? Had that already been carried out? Didn't I or John have to have given our consent to that? I wasn't sure what they would be subjecting him to but the image once more of my father being pinned to a table like the subject of a science experiment swam before me and I felt giddy and sick. I pushed all of the questions to the back of my mind and asked the one thing upon which I could feel solid.

"What do you think?"

Geoffrey levelled his gaze at me and fixed me with his most assured stare.

"Your father was a good and decent man Imogen. Nothing will change that."

The pain behind my eyes that had been raging all day, momentarily burst forth leaving only a numb feeling, and I closed my eyes gripping the bridge of my nose as if that were the only way of holding on to some truth. John would say a few hours later that it was the lack of food and sleep that caused me to slip off my chair in the parlour and crumple to the floor in front of Geoffrey Leech. No doubt, he would also feel that the solicitor should not have told me any of the details about the Coroner's Inquiry and he was partly to blame for my distress. However, I firmly believe that a person's brain is only capable of simple truth and, quite unable to deal with the truth as it was unfolding; I had simply abandoned thinking about it at all.

Chapter Six - Avery, 1869

"Avery?"

The sound of Kate's voice seemed further away than the few feet she was. The familiar dressing screen had been drawn across the middle of the room, whilst Avery had begun imbuing the flat, lifeless clothes that had been smuggled into Cornwall Gardens only a few hours ago, with the life Avery intended for them. Kate's voice seemed tentative as if she were unsure of who else might be lurking behind the screen besides her mistress. Avery finally stole a glance at the mirror he had thus far been avoiding. The effect of the clothes was at once alarming and electrifying. Fry had done a good job with the measurements. The cloth, although not the best, looked fine in the light of the room. Avery stood taller than ever in a jet black evening suit, the tails of the coat accentuated his natural height and the style was very forgiving across his hips which, although slight, now appeared almost invisible. The crisp white shirt collars stood up at his neck and his shoulder length dark hair had been lacquered and swept backwards. As he looked at himself in the mirror, he cocked his head to one side and thought how odd it was that he had not seen it before. His hair had always been untidy but the untidiness was a perfect imitation of the confident young men around Covent Garden. There was roguishness about them and Avery recognized it in himself too. His shoulders, naturally broad for a woman carried the jacket well and the flat line of the shirt that hung smoothly below his neck disguised his breasts, which were bound tightly to his chest. The effect of this created a defined and well-muscled tone. He smiled with relief.

"Avery? Do you need some help?"

"No!" he replied, curtly.

The darkened room absorbed the sound of their voices, leaving an oppressive silence into which Kate issued an audible sigh. Avery adjusted his position so that he could see the profile of Kate in a corner of the mirror as she sat upon the edge of his bed. The lamplight from the walls flickered as the gas waned; although it did this frequently as other lamps were drawn in other rooms, Kate jumped. The shadows from behind the screen seemed to shrink before leaping upwards again, as the light returned to its previous glow. He watched as she leant back on her hands upon his bed, seemingly comfortable to wait a while longer. He wondered what she would think when he stepped from behind the screen. When she had arrived with the clothes that afternoon, she had seemed almost as excited as he had been but he wondered whether he had mistaken his own eagerness with her anxiety. The room was warm and the lamplight soothing and he watched as she bent her head to examine her hands. The skin on the back of them was rough and defied her youth. Although the tips of her fingers had long since stopped puckering from her hard labour, they had instead developed the tell-tale rough calluses of domestic service. He briefly considered the sum he had just spent on clothes she perhaps could not wear outside the walls of the house and wondered if Kate herself would ever be able to afford some kid gloves with which to conceal her hands. He wondered if she would accept them as a gift from him.

"Well?" The sound of his own voice startled him and Kate looked up in surprise. As she did so, she could not stop the involuntary intake of breath that escaped her. Her reaction was simple.

"Oh my God!"

There passed a few awkward moments of silence before Kate could add any more; all the while, Avery watched her earnestly, self-consciously awaiting her approval. The young girl looked quite pale and confused beneath her beaming smile.

"I can't believe how well it fits. I mean I can believe it of course, I see so with my own eyes but...I just thought it wouldn't look so well on you. I mean, your clothes always look well on you Miss, I mean, Sir. I mean you always look fine but these make you look even finer." She looked embarrassed as, in the search for the right words, she found the perfect ones. She blushed.

"Just tell me what you think Kate. Honestly," he added, grinning.

"Turn around," she instructed, her head cocked to one side as she considered him more critically.

Now it was Avery's turn to blush and he revolved slowly, holding his arms out to the sides avoiding her gaze, which had turned more serious.

"Well?" Avery asked again.

Kate narrowed her gaze and searched his face, as if truly understanding for the first time what Avery hoped to achieve from this whimsy. Her voice, when it came, was deliberate as if stating a fact she had only just found to be true.

"You look just like a gentleman."

Her tone troubled him and Avery held her gaze trying to determine how what the young girl was feeling. It was important that she remain in his confidence and above all, that she was not spooked by this queer turn of events. The gas jets hissed again and the light danced across the room. It was enough to break the spell. Kate looked to the door and looked reassured as she noted the bolt drawn tightly across.

"It fits you very well, Miss," she offered again quietly, not looking directly at him.

Avery felt bolder; there was something in the way that she had been looking at him that made him feel taller, a look that had not been there when he had been dressed as a woman. It was as though the clothes, rather than concealing more of him, had revealed another side to him; a hungrier side, a side that was more at home in its own skin.

"Kate?" Avery's voice was husky as he tried to lower the register in which he spoke.

The girl looked up nervously and her face was once more wide with wonder at the sight of a man stood in her mistress' bedroom.

"If you call me Miss one more time, I shall have to report you to your mistress." A broad grin crackled across his lips as he spoke and Kate released a suppressed giggle, throwing a cushion at Avery's head.

"Yes Sir!"

~o~

Toby Silver had left for the evening for a dinner at Mrs. Fearncott's. Avery had taken supper and indicated to Kate that he would probably have an early night as he was suffering from a headache. With the rest of the staff downstairs availing themselves of the break with an unexpected night off, Kate had gone up ahead to make ready his clothes and prepare an escape route. As Avery mounted the stairs hurriedly and reached the door to his own room, he stopped to consider the consequences of what he was about to do. What had seemed yesterday a private and thrilling secret, was now on the cusp of becoming something altogether more dangerous. Avery was unsure what excited him the most, the risk that he was running at discovery or the fact that his secret would no longer be his alone. At the thought of the way Kate had looked at him, his heart seared hot in his chest and he flushed just thinking of it. He wanted to be looked upon by the world as she had done, with recognition and maybe desire. He turned the handle and slipped inside the room.

"It is only me... Kate?" Avery whispered in to the gloom.

The young girl said nothing but held out the crisp shirt as she stood waiting to dress him.

"I think I'd rather dress myself. If you don't mind," he added.

Kate looked a little hurt.

"I thought it would save time if I helped you."

Avery wondered why it mattered to him that he dress himself, after all hadn't Kate been helping him dress for the last three months? Why should it matter? Hadn't she seen every part that he despised? Perhaps it was for this very reason, that for the first time, when he was dressed in these clothes, there was a part of his outer self he no longer despised.

"I will dress myself," he repeated.

Kate lowered her eyes; her jaw set upon many objections over which she now chewed and handed over the shirt. Twenty minutes later, Avery stepped out from the screen and looked again at his reflection in the mirror. The dull glow of the lights cast a shadow around his face highlighting hollows of his cheekbones and the angular set of his jaw. As he admired his reflection, Kate stepped behind him.

"Are you sure you want to do this?" she asked.

"Are you sure **you** want to do this?" Avery replied, turning to face her.

Kate bit her lip and, closing one eye, squinted at Avery through the other, one half of a smile formed on her lips as she tried to contain her nerves. Just as a cat that would pounce on his prey, Avery stepped forward in the split second it took for Kate to nod her head and planted a grateful and excited kiss full on her forehead.

"I shall be back within the hour. I will pass the house once and then wait in the square for your signal, just like we agreed?"

Kate's eyes widened at his bold kiss and she touched a hand to her mouth before nodding her assent. A few moments later, they had descended the main staircase, Kate in the front and Avery scuttling between landings and doorways like a burglar. Had anyone have encountered him, they would no doubt have smashed a lamp over his head believing him to be pursuing her down the stairs. Had the danger of his discovery not been so very real, the absurdity would have made him burst out laughing. As she reached the front door and opened it with a click, the faint ambience of the evening noise of the city burst forth. Avery's heart gave a great lurch of fright as the danger of it all became suddenly obvious. What looked acceptable within these four walls would of course be ridiculous in the plain eyes of the world beyond the front door. Avery froze on the threshold and considered retreat.

"Good evening to you, Sir," Kate offered loudly and all but pushed him out of the door.

~o~

That first evening Avery had been too self-conscious to enjoy the feeling of his new-found freedom. Surrounded by familiar houses and streets, he had been convinced of discovery. Faces seemed to loom from the windows that he passed in abject horror and he had started to act furtively. He had drawn himself away from the light and skirted the shadows, keeping his head low and his shoulders rolled forwards to hide his features. This sort of activity had only drawn more attention to him and a few pedestrians had eyed him longer than most trying to divine his intentions. After only half an hour, he had returned home, where an ashen faced Kate admitted him entry as though he were the devil himself.

"Well," she had probed him when they were safely concealed within his bedroom. "Did nobody recognise you?"

Avery had remained silent, half ashamed by his lack of nerves and the other half disappointed that he felt no different.

"I hope you aren't going to make a habit of this. My nerves won't stand it. You were only gone a minute when I thought I heard your father come back. I reckon

I stopped breathing. I almost ran down the stairs and out the back door never to come back..."

Her voice had trailed off as Avery had whipped around and grabbed at her wrists firmly.

"Kate, promise me you won't leave." He knew that he needed her. It was true, he needed her help to execute that evenings outing but more than that, she was the only one to whom he could acknowledge this secret inside of him. She had been surprised by his earnest appeal and had considered him a few moments before assuring him.

"I promise I won't leave." She had smiled at him and returned to the business of brushing down the jacket that he had removed.

As Avery listened to Kate's busy voice, as she concealed his discarded clothes, he knew that there would certainly be repeats of that evening. His disappointment was already waning and he realised he would need to go further abroad in the city to fully escape his self-consciousness and the prospect of discovery.

When he ambled down Jermyn Street several weeks later, he was well practiced in his casual walk. The set of his face was a rehearsed look of assurance. He knew from hours spent in front of a mirror how he looked from all angles and he was confident of the smiles he bestowed on passers-by. With his father out most evenings courting the widow Fearncott, he was at liberty at least two or three evenings a week to spread his wings and fly free in the broad city. After each outing, he returned to Kate's worried face and, whilst she de-constructed his façade, berating him a little more each time with how long he had been gone,

Avery analysed his performance and made mental notes about changes he should make to his attire, to his mannerisms or his posture. Thus far, he had restricted himself to merely walking the city streets, watching other gentlemen, nodding or tipping his hat to the odd stranger but one night, he had stumbled across a pub in Westminster and been emboldened by the inviting glow to step inside. He had fallen to idle chat with a few young graduates, Bateman and Goodwin. They had got along very well and Avery had agreed to meet them again for a repeat of the entertainment.

"Silver!" The bar was busy: the air was thick with the smell of ale and the sounds of conversations being held at every volume. He looked around for the source of the voice but the noise of the place seemed to fill the air like fog; the words from the private conversations of gents in corners skulked at ankle height whereas the animated chatter of old friends paraded at chest height, peppering the air with friendly tones. "Silver!" the bark of Bateman was cheery and soared above the fug, so when Avery caught it a second time, it invited him to turn and head towards the two men seated by a window.

"We had almost given you up for good," Goodwin stood and clamped his firm hand around Avery's own, pumping his arm in a good natured welcome. Goodwin's eyes twinkled in the gaslight, they were watering from the smoke in the room and they were wide with intoxication. Avery could see a good cluster of glasses before them on the table.

"So much so that we have been unable to locate the drink we ordered for you," Bateman picked up a few glasses as though searching for Avery's.

"So we ordered you another one," Goodwin joined in, pushing the glasses aside and lifting his hat. "But we lost that one too."

"So we ordered another one," Bateman eyed Silver with a mock sheepish grin before clapping him about the shoulders and calling across to the barmaid. "Three more beers over here Sally."

Avery's smile broadened as a woman from the bar delivered another round of flowing mugs of beer and he watched her expression change as she took him in. Appraising his height and his clothes, she evidently judged him worthy of a wink and a smile in return. Avery's heart ballooned with satisfaction. He felt the promise of the evening spark an expectation inside him and he grinned to himself. The barmaid's face was framed by blonde hair, that many years ago may have shone like a moonlit path, but now hung like a lank mane. Her mouth and eyes had a hard pinched look, which made her seem harsher than she probably was, and Avery was not in the least aroused by her presence. Unwittingly however, she had breathed some life and confidence into him and Avery relaxed back in to the settle. Beside him, Bateman was animatedly recanting an earlier dalliance that rendered Goodwin mute with embarrassment.

"...and then she whipped his arse with a fire poker!" Bateman's roar was matched only in strength by the burning of Goodwin's ears. Avery, both astonished and thrilled by the coarseness, smirked into his beer before leaning across to clap Goodwin on the back in a good natured way.

"Never mind Goodwin, maybe next time?"

Goodwin's face softened and he allowed a smile to steal across his lips as he watched Avery. He downed his beer and called to Sally to bring another round. Avery felt his shoulders relax.

"Silver. I am afraid that last time we met, you managed to wriggle out of telling us what it is exactly you are in." Goodwin tried to deflect some of the attention from himself. Avery noted with relief that the man looked less than bright but rather his eyes had begun to take on a slightly crossed glaze.

"In?" Avery questioned.
He noted awkwardly that Bateman's brow furrowed a little before he was able to recover himself.

"In! Oh Goodwin, my dear fellow! I am 'In' to everything!" he roared good humouredly and watched with some pleasure as his two companions slapped the table and threw back their drinks. Avery had not given much thought to his cover story and he was thrown slightly by the question. He knew that his carefully constructed camouflage could easily be dismantled by not answering this carefully. Thus far, he had not thought much about the implications of his 'sojourns' into town but he could only imagine how they would be received by his father. As he watched Goodwin's amused face flush redder still, he was confident that he would not recall much of the detail of this evening's conversation but Bateman was once again on the appeal for information.

"Where did you school? Don't say you are an Oxbridge man?"

Avery knew little of either institution but suddenly caught by a moment's inspiration.

"Je suis tres desolee monsieur! I am afraid I was schooled *en Francais,*" he watched tentatively to see how this was received. Bateman's eyes shot up. Goodwin leapt to his feet.

"A frog! In our midst sirs!" Bateman howled with laughter and cuffed his friend lightly. All the same, the slight touch threw the man off balance and the three men were once more caught up in mutual glee.

"Ah! I knew there was something odd about your accent and that explains it," Bateman erupted. "A pseudo-Frenchman in our midst eh?" Evidently, this epiphany explained any misgivings Bateman had over Silver and a palpable air of generosity swept Avery back into the centre of the evening. That simple phrase continued to grow legs and become a subterfuge on its own account with only the occasional need of Avery's creativity.

"So are you in trade of some sort," Goodwin declared.

"Only the finest!"

"Exporting Art eh? Typical!" Bateman declared. "Anything good in this country and the frogs want it. Well Silver, you can take it from me that some of the finest artists are Englishmen, envied by the French and not the other way around."

And that was as easy as it was, Mr. Avery Silver was suddenly a fine arts exporter and no further questions were asked. His money was as good as theirs and they were not inclined to question him further. As the evening swept onwards, the conversations that merged in the air above them were deteriorating in tone and the suggestive words became more common in the thick air until Bateman was roused by them into action.

"Gentlemen," he swayed slightly in the heady cloud of words. "Shall we try our luck in St Giles? Bucknall Street?"

He winked suggestively at Avery as if the street name should mean something to him. Goodwin groaned loudly but, eager not to appear unknowledgeable, Avery returned Bateman's look with a narrowed gaze, rubbing his hands together gleefully. As they rolled out of the pub on to the streets of Westminster, Avery was glad to see there was a full moon and, as a result, the streets of the City were brightly lit.

The air was still warm from the heat of the day and he was heady with the beer inside him. As he glanced across at his new friends, he thought for the first time that he was filled with a sense of belonging. They all caught a cab from Westminster and, with a knowing smile, the driver deposited the three men in the heart of St Giles.

In a strange part of the City, Avery began to feel a little anxious. The streets were narrower and the moonlight less able to penetrate the huddle of buildings that seemed to close in on them. As the cab drew off and the sound of the hooves and wheels became more distant, he could hear a new language coming from the street. There was a muttering of disapproval from a doorway and the heavy breath of an old man lying across the step. Something smashed some streets away and the sound of a dog barking in response came from closer by. Avery looked to his companions for support and was relieved to see their faces alight with glee instead of fear.

At first, the streets looked no different to the heart of the west end and Piccadilly but in truth they were much darker. The facades of the buildings more grey, the dark windows like teeth knocked from a gaping mouth. There were women milling with baskets selling snacks, exchanging turgid fruit for filthy coins, hastily concealed behind their grey shawls. Much to Avery's surprise, the press of life swarming in the streets seemed to come from all walks of life. Men in toppers walked tall amongst the crowd and women, whom Avery took to be ladies, milled around on the arms of Gentlemen. Yet as Avery watched, he noticed the women's clothes were shabbier than they first seemed. The men upon whose arm they tilted were leering, the gestures between them, obscene. The suggestive smile that Bateman had offered in the cab became clear. After only a few minutes, they were approached by two women.

"By my word, Mr. Smith. If it aint a pleasure to see you tonight."

The taller of the two had pressed her skirts against Bateman and was fingering the collars of his shirt. Evidently, Bateman was a regular here.

"And your good friend Mr. Brown, a pleasure as always Gents. I was telling me friend here about the both of you only earlier, wasn't I Sarah?"

The other girl was smiling at Avery and he tried to avoid her gaze by stepping into Bateman's shadow.

"Miss Connie!" Bateman effused, overplaying a sweep of his hat in greeting. "Your warm welcome has much improved my standing this evening. And a man in want of a standing may be warmed by one such as you." He winked at Avery and pulled the woman closer to him, burying his face into her chest. The woman, Connie, shrieked with an attempt at amusement but Avery caught the tired, repetitive gesture and flinched in embarrassment. The other girl, Sarah, he noticed was hanging back. She was not nearly so eager as her friend and Avery could see immediately she was tired. Despite her best efforts to appear attentive, her eyes drooped and she stifled a yawn from escaping her drawn mouth. Most of her face was in shadow but there was something familiar about the girl.

"We need another one," Goodwin's voice was loud behind Avery and he jumped a little at the proximity of the man. Connie, quick to spot a business opportunity, grabbed his arm suggestively.

"I'm worth waiting for aint I Mr. Smith? I can do your friend for half price if he'll wait," she offered.

Bateman's nose turned up at this suggestion and he was momentarily turned off by the very idea. Her eyes darted around as the possibility of her last customers of the evening dwindled.

"Another man's seconds? Not even Goodwin here would use another man's oil to grease his spoon. Come on Avery. There's a place off the Tottenham Court Road I hear has a good line in dark eyed girls. I saw the way you looked at Sally earlier."

Connie was quick to try to recover the situation.

"Alright! Don't go wasting any shoe leather on my account. If it's blondes you want, why don't you see to this one, Sarah and..." she spun round desperately looking for someone she could call upon. Her eyes lit up, she had seen someone she could use.

"Ellen!"

A fresh faced girl with a spiky nose and wide comfortable hips sauntered over, her black hair slick to her face.

"Alright Ellen? I reckon this could be your lucky night. This 'ere is Mr. Smith, Mr. Brown and..." she raised her eyebrows expectantly at Avery.

"Mr. White," Bateman interjected smoothly.

The new girl was wary at first but soon warmed as Goodwin jangled the coins in his pockets. He was taken with the fresh faced girl and, stepping past his companions, he took her by the shoulders and allowed himself to be led towards a darkened alley. As the intention of the evening's entertainment became clearer and the location promised to be so uncompromising, Avery began to panic.

"I am afraid I will have to pass..." he stammered, trying to clear his mind and regretting that last ale which now dulled his wits. "I don't think..." he flapped his hands for some inspiration.

"Don't worry Mr. White, we'll soon have '*Him*' up!" and with that Connie had taken him by the hand and pulled him after Bateman and Goodwin. Although only a few moments behind, the two men were already pressed into doorways and Avery could no longer discern the flickering shadows as his companions.

"Come on. This way." Connie led him deeper down the alleyway until they drew level with the dark mass that was Bateman and Sarah. The dark was dense and it was only the stark white of flesh that leapt out from the gloom. Avery was shocked to see that the girl already had Batemans cock out and she was knelt down before him taking his flaccid member into her mouth. There was a look of Kate about the girl and the image at once both excited him but made him feel protective of her. Bateman's own hands were large about her head and he pulled her by the neck to take more of his rising need inside her mouth. Before he could take any more of the scene in, Avery was pulled away by the woman holding his hand.

"It's more if you want to watch Sir."

She pulled him further along the alley before stopping alongside a recessed window. She pressed against him and, before he knew it, she had grabbed his crotch and immediately her eyebrows knitted together into questioning disbelief.

"What..?"

Avery pressed his hand across her mouth and dipped his head to her ear.

"Say nothing and I will pay you double."

He leaned back and watched her eyes dawn in recognition and he withdrew his hand from her mouth.

"I've not been fooled by a tom before," she slurred at him. "Well, it's my lucky night ain't it? Double pay and no mess for the bother."

A shout from down the alley made both of them look up in alarm.

"Fine fillies, eh Silver?"

It was Bateman. His voice was hoarse as if he was trying hard not to breathe. The gaslight from the distant street threw down long and strange shadows and Avery could discern one to be that of Bateman thrusting himself against the wall. "Not a patch on the French, eh?"

Avery paused, imagining the girl Bateman was pushing himself into, the resemblance of Kate drawn into his mind, before calling out in response "Easy Bateman!" He turned back to the woman before him, aroused by the turn the night had taken and feeling emboldened by his successful disguise.

"Make this convincing and you can take the rest of the night off."

There was not a moment's hesitation from the woman and Avery's lip curled in satisfaction as the whore pressed him down on to the windowsill so he was sitting. In the gloom of the alley she made a play of fumbling at the front of his trousers. She didn't take her eyes from his as she lifted up her skirt and petticoats and stood astride him. As she lowered herself onto his lap she fumbled around under her skirts as if to guide him into her. In the intimacy of the light she winked at him and then rolled her eyes as he 'entered' and threw her head back, her chin pointing to the darkened skyline. Avery followed her gaze and watched the moonlit grey sky, streaked with sooty swirls of fireside smoke furling in the air above. The dense curls from fireside hearths, their respective occupants oblivious to the whore and her client who stared up at the product of their domestic bliss. Avery's hands, at first loose by his side clutched the woman by the hips and, as she drew herself up, he could feel the muscles in her thigh tense. As she collided with his lap on her downward bounce Avery was all too aware of his missing member but felt his arousal swell just the same. His eyes focused on the bare skin at her chest. Her dress was cut low and her ample breasts were bursting from beneath her thin bodice. As she rode him to a hard canter, he imagined his phantom cock standing erect from his trousers and how it would be wet with the juices of this bawdy tart. He was alert with his own state of arousal and his own hips thrust underneath the woman so that they met with a force. His grip was tight on her and it was his own urgent rhythm which set the pace and he was suddenly aware of her little whimpers as she cried out, feigning his rough sex penetrating her hard. She clutched at his head and leaned into him, whispering in a matter of fact way.

"You'd better spend soon. You aint no guardsman you know."

He was hardly aware of how it happened but before he knew it, the whore had clutched him to her breast and begun to moan, all the while she was shaking and grinding herself into his crotch. He found it hard to breathe as he was filled with the musky scent of her cleavage, all the while his own desire was ardent. He realised she was finishing off her performance and he was left feeling unfulfilled. He groaned loudly.

"Better make it an extra sixpence. You took longer than I thought, Sir," she said loudly.

As she un-straddled him arranging her skirts, Avery too made a play of putting himself away before they both emerged from the alley where Bateman and Goodwin were already waiting. Bateman had a smile on his face but Goodwin was looking a little worse for wear.

"Vomited before he could get his spoon out," Bateman clapped his friend about the shoulder and between him and Avery they supported him back to the main thoroughfare. As they approached the brighter lights, Avery glanced behind them but all three women had been swallowed into the dark. He stood for a moment trying to discern the alley from which they had just emerged but it too had been eaten up by the night. As he caught up with his companions, there was an elegant carriage drawn up beside a well-lit public house. As they approached, a smart jacketed young man hopped down from the seat and stood at attention beside the now open cab door. The man eyed Bateman with suspicion but immediately and, with a well-trained hand, guided the staggering Goodwin into the plush seat.

"Will he be alright?" Silver asked Bateman.

"Who cares!" Bateman declared loudly with a wolfish grin.

Silver stepped forwards and addressed the young man.

"You will take him home?"

"Yes sir."

"You are Goodwin's man?"

The young man's eyes flicked over Silver's face.

"Of course, Sir."

"Good. Well, look after him."

"I always do sir."

The young man closed the door after his master and, acknowledging Bateman very briefly, climbed up beside the driver.

"Good old Heston!" Bateman exclaimed. "Goodwin would be lost without him. Right Silver, shall we try somewhere else for a night cap?"

The carriage rattled off but Silver was perturbed to note the young servant turn in his seat and eye him suspiciously. Luck had been on his side already this evening and the dalliance in the alley had left him rattled.

"Another time Bateman."

Chapter Seven - Imogen, 1911

It was difficult to set eyes for long on any one individual, such was the bustle on the steps of the coroner's court. The building loomed out of the surrounding smog, half of its roof obscured by a dense grey cloud of smoke. In London, there has always been an industry which thrives on death and I was not surprised to see so many people. Anyone would be forgiven for thinking the cacophony had all been stirred up by the death of my father but life continues to go on and all manner of business was conducted there, including many other deaths being investigated. There was a stream of visitors entering the building seeking answers and just as many leaving; either satisfied or not. As we got closer, there was a throng of people assembled at the foot of the steps leading to the grand doors. They ranged on a spectrum of patient to impatient; from those leaning nonchalantly against the railings, to those extracting a pocket watch every couple of minutes and crossly tapping their feet.

In the light of the cold winters day, I saw Geoffrey amongst the faces, looking even older than the day before. His white hair caught the light of the low winter sun and he had an ethereal glow. He shivered in the cold and I was struck by how frail he seemed. I thought of my father and his heart. Why hadn't he told me about that?

"Leech, thank goodness you are here." John extended a hand to the old man.

He tipped his head to me, his face clouded in concern. His distress at my being present at the proceeding was evident. I must have given the impression of being in shock, having not registered Leech's presence; instead, I merely chewed on my bottom lip and looked into the distance. "Might I have a word with you," he indicated to John. When they were at sufficient distance from me, Leech continued.

"I have no wish to repeat what I said to you last night but as you know, I have known Imogen for many years and her nature is impulsive and strong. I am as fond of her as I am my own daughter and I would not wish her to witness the scene inside this court."

Johns face was as dispassionate as it was the previous night when Leech had advised against both him and me attending the enquiry. Leech was waiting expectantly and, seeing John's stubborn jaw, he lost his temper a little.

"So help me John, I am just trying to look after her. You would be well advised to do the same."

He had delivered this a little too loudly and I started from my reverie as if only just aware of his presence. The two of them stepped away from one another. I smiled at Leech gratefully and jerked towards him like a marionette suddenly pulled up by my strings.

"Geoffrey," I walked to greet him warmly. "Have they spoken to you yet?" My voice was tainted with edgy concern as though it may rise in a panic at any moment. I was tense and nervous and Geoffrey looked tenderly at me when he replied. "You know that there is nothing you can do. This is not a criminal court or a civil hearing."

I nodded as he spoke, agreeing again that I knew all of this. He continued to repeat what he told me the previous evening.

"But Geoffrey," I managed to interrupt at last "they have called me to be a witness."

Evidently this was quite a surprise, as he spun around to question John who looked worn and tired. On the other hand, I was not surprised when an official from the coroner's court called early that morning requesting my presence as a witness. John rolled his eyes and shrugged.

"Let's get this over with, shall we?" he indicated for Leech to lead the way up the steps to the Coroner's Office.

Leech sighed, his shoulders sloping to accentuate his age depleted frame yet further. We followed him at an easy pace through the doors, which were too tall by half and across the marbled floor to a normal sized door marked 'Private'. A few heads turned in our direction and acknowledged Leech with a raised hat or a cheery salutation, for his was a familiar face. As we reached the clerk's desk however, he was met with the stony face of bureaucracy.

"Name?"

It was clear that the clerk knew full well who Geoffrey Leech was and I could hazard that he probably knew why he was here.

"Leech. Geoffrey Leech."

"Deceased's name"

Leech licked his lips to lubricate his dry mouth before the words could slip out.

"Silver," he intoned quietly. "Avery Silver."

The clerk did not miss a single beat but merely consulted his lists and replied in a steady voice.

"You will be in room number five Mr. Leech. The body was brought in at ten o'clock. Mr. Schofield has already convened the jurors for the first inspection."

The clerk had not looked up at all but his clear voice had alerted a few curious passersby to our arrival.

"Geoffrey!" An amiable looking man some twenty years Leech's junior strode across the room. As he approached, the younger man proffered his hand and rounded a welcoming arm across Leech's back, guiding him away from the officious desk of the clerk and from John and myself. "What a surprise to see you here? I thought you were enjoying your retirement on some god forsaken estate in Wales! Something tasty tempted you back to the office eh, Geoffrey?" The man narrowed his eyes conspiratorially. I did not recognise the man but it was evident from the charged atmosphere that there was no love to be lost in this conversation and I was not surprised by Leech's cool response.

"It is something of a family matter, Mr. Taylor and I am afraid you have rather caught me at an inopportune moment. Will you excuse me?" he removed himself expertly from the younger man's grip who was left watching the retreating back of Leech, a sneer already formed on his lips.

Leech rejoined us with an apologetic face. I tried to smile but was all too aware of the mask into which my face had formed. John and I followed Leech through a side door and along a wide corridor off which there were several doors, all marked with numbers in great brass Roman numerals. There was a strange smell as we walked down the hallway, it was an

106

unfamiliar smell for such a building. I suppose I had expected the dusty odour of books and paper; of learning and justice instead there was the sour smell of too many bodies in one place, of chlorine and bleach and the metallic smell of blood. The numbers descended from *X* and I found myself considering the scenes playing out behind each of these. The door to room *VII* stood open and as John and Mr. Leech hurried past, I paused for a moment, lingering on the threshold to see inside. The room beyond was large and perfectly square. In the centre of the room, there was a table and to one side, a large desk opposite which there were a collection of twenty or so chairs The room would have been perfectly innocuous were it not for the body which lay upon the table in the centre. Before I could even determine the poor soul's age, the door had closed shut again and I had to walk on quickly to catch up with Leech. Behind each door I passed, I could only think of the room beyond, the table upon which a body lay and the collection of men turning it over to determine how each had come to meet their end. As Geoffrey and my husband drew level with Room *V*, I found my legs unwilling to continue and I had to lean on the wall for support as all about me began to swim.

"Imogen," John hurried to my side and took my weight. His breath was warm on my face as he hissed to Leech. "What are they thinking, calling her to witness such absurdity? Look at her!"

Geoffrey remained motionless; his mouth opened and closed in a comic expression as words tried to form on his dry lips.

"I'm taking you home."

John started to turn me to return the way we had already walked.

"No," I tried to shake him off but his grip was strong. "John. I want to stay."

"I have no doubt you do Imogen but Leech and I will manage."

"Geoffrey," I implored the old man. "I am absolutely fine. I assure you." I managed to extricate my arm from John's grip just as a door further down the corridor opened and a clerk appeared, investigating the commotion. He watched for a moment as John continued to press me into leaving before disappearing back inside his courtroom.

"Mr. Bancroft, if the Coroner has requested Imogen's presence, it really would be most helpful if she remained."

John opened his mouth.

"That is, if she is feeling up to it." Leech finished before John could reply

John was about to retort when the door to room number five opened again and an official looking man stepped out and called us in. Torn between duty and his eagerness to escape the scandal, John lingered for a moment before gesturing me in through the open door before him.

The room was similar to Room *VII* but arranged around the table were a dozen or so men obscuring our view of the table and the body over which they were deliberating. There were two men who were seated beyond the mob at the table, looking nauseous and holding their heads in their hands. They had not noticed our entrance and Leech lingered on the periphery of the scene awaiting his leave from the Coroner. The clerk, having closed the door behind us, ushered us to seats on the far side of the room. He talked as he walked, not to Leech but to himself.

"Rather straight forward if you ask me. Should be quite quick."

"Gentlemen," the raised voice was immediately identifiable with the tall figure of a man who was jacketless before the centre table, the Coroner. "If you would kindly please re-take your seats."

There was a small amount of commotion as the assembled throng redistributed themselves amongst the seats directly opposite the Coroner's desks. One or two of the men lingered a little longer at the table, staring hard at the body that was laid upon it. It was a few moments before I could focus on the form and understand that the body was that of my father's.

"Oh for pity's sake!"

John stood and tried to shield my gaze, as he did so I was sensible only to a great shift inside my heart, a cold numbness.

"Imogen, don't look."

Geoffrey too had stood, he was flustered and evidently he also had not expected my father's body to be on show when we were called. As both men flapped around trying to prevent me from seeing my father's corpse lain before me, I was granted instead a flickering view like the pages of a children's book thumbed at the edges. But instead of stick figures, I watched, unblinkingly, at the two young men who were entranced by the body of my father. Their faces were a paragon of astonishment and concentration. They seemed to be willing themselves to see my father as a man and to believe it but they did not yet trust what they saw. I followed their gaze to the face of my father, still recognisable from the previous day but decomposition and whatever had been undertaken during the post mortem had given his skin a much dingier and waxen complexion. A sheet, no doubt for preserving what modesty and dignity he could still claim, had been drawn down to his legs revealing his naked form.

"What is going on over there?"

The voice of the man stood at the head of the room, whom I assumed to be the Coroner, had noticed the commotion between the clerk and John as they tried to obscure my view of the body on display. I ignored him and continued to stare at my father. Between the curves of my husband's arm, I noticed first the misshapen chest that was at odds with the rest of his body. In the stark electric light, I could see then that his chest could pass as either male or female in form; there were two small breasts flattened and aged lying tight against the chest cavity. Evidently a lifetime of binding these tightly had rendered them paler than any of the surrounding skin tissue and it looked as though he was still wearing those grey bandages across his chest. The more I stared, the more I was inclined to disagree with the clerk and concur that the matter of determining my father's gender was not as simple as it would first appear, and I again allowed myself to hope that this would all be some mistake.

"Can't you cover him...I mean her. God damn it man, just cover it up!"

John crossed in front of me, his voice rising to a shrill pitch, but I could not focus on his words. I could see now why the two gentlemen sitting down were

110

coloured so I saw the fresh post mortem cuts made between my father's legs. An incision had been made at the top of my father's pubic bone and circumferentially across his hips. Another single incision had been made, exposing the shaft of his sex which protruded like a miniature erection. Despite the urge to turn my face away, I found I could not. As the clerk rushed to recover the cloth and to shroud my father, I found I needed to witness this last invasion to prove to myself beyond any doubt of the truth. It is the erect sex which the two men who had lingered were staring at and I could immediately see why. The shape of the organ released from its surrounding skin must have been familiar to them and I blushed harder myself when I recognised it. In form it was a miniature version of a phallus. To them and to me, the cut and dry of this case was no longer straight forward as we each considered the form of the sex between my father's legs and I shuddered.

"Imogen?"

A dark canvas cloth was pulled over my father's corpse and, once removed from sight, the spell of calm seemed to break and I was all at once aware of the commotion about me. Geoffrey's voice was full of concern and he lowered his face level to my own to enquire again.

"Imogen. Do you want John to take you home?"

From somewhere, I steeled myself against the raging desire to run from the room and I blinked back the tears which had been building.

"Thank you but no."

"Imogen, this is hardly suitable," John interrupted.

111

"On the contrary John," I countered levelly "This is entirely suitable."

"Gentlemen, please." Having nodded his gratitude to the clerk, the Coroner directed his attention to the two remaining men stood by the table who glanced up, first at the Coroner and then rather sheepishly at one another, unwilling to acknowledge the thought which had been occurring to them both. The Coroner watched over the top of his spectacles as they returned to their seats. "Thank you." He turned his attention to the gallery where Geoffrey, John and I were seated.

"My apologies." He attempted what seemed to be a placatory smile toward John but which presented itself instead as a grimace. John muttered something inaudible but the Coroner's attention had already been drawn by the files upon his desk. He read some notes from the top file then motioned towards the clerk and whispered something in his ear before continuing.

"Gentlemen, you have had the opportunity to view the body and ask questions relating to what was discovered during the Post Mortem. You will now have the opportunity to question witnesses in order to form your conclusions upon the matters already discussed. May I remind you again that no foul play is suspected in this case and your primary purpose as a jury is to agree on both the cause of death and, in this particular case, the gender of the deceased. Again, this is not a criminal court but rather your decision here will be used in any civil disputes over the last will and testament of the deceased and, most importantly, in ensuring the accuracy of the death records. For the benefit of the clerk, I shall now summarise the findings of the Post Mortem and the initial viewing of the body."

On cue, the clerk placed his spectacles on his face and took up his position with his stenograph. He coughed lightly; a well-practiced mannerism which seemed to indicate his readiness as the ringleader of the circus. The Coroner shifted in his seat and turned his attention directly to the table before him, as if in viewing my father's body he could better recall the facts of the case. As in many vocations, each person has something peculiar to the way they work. With this Coroner it seemed he had a certain word blindness for, as verbose and as verbally effusive as he seemed, he was quite unable to retain facts when he read them written down. He was a tactile man and had found in his line of work that he could better recall a corpse's bruises if he has touched them himself rather than read a report of his own writing with detailed findings.

"The deceased lain before you has been positively identified as having been known by the name, Avery Silver of Hamble Gardens, Parsons Green. The first identification was made by a long serving member of staff who was the same person who made the discovery of death, one George Heston. The second by a locum GP, a Dr. William Stevens and thirdly by his daughter Mrs. Imogen Bancroft. The deceased was discovered in the morning of 4th January 1911 lain in bed by the aforementioned Mr. Heston. The alarm was raised to call for a GP who confirmed, as must have already been evident...," he added raising his eyebrows across to the jury in a conspiratorial fashion. '...that the deceased had been so for some hours."

113

The coroner leaned forwards across his desk on to his elbows and crossed his feet at the ankle underneath his chair. He continued.

"The police report, of which you have been given a copy, does not detect anything unusual in the accounts of any witnesses, nor was anything untoward present at the scene of death. No burglary was made of the premises, no intrusion, and no violence was committed upon the body."

He allowed a brief silence to fill the room, for those listening to absorb his words from the air, before he added, in a yet more superior tone.

"It has, apparently, come as a great shock to all three of the persons aforementioned that the deceased's gender is in question. Put plainly, they believed the deceased to have been a man and that closer inspection reveals this to be in doubt."

There was a shuffling beside me and I glanced to my right to look at Leech. Although he was sitting with his body turned away from that of my father, his head was bowed reverentially and inclined towards the Coroner, I noticed his attention was not on the words being announced but rather his attention was wholly on not looking at the body of his friend. I looked around the rest of the room and took in the faces of the men which made up this court. There was an all pervading feeling of curiosity within the room that seemed to soak up the facts which the Coroner was reeling off and what was left seemed only to be mere fiction.

"...bilateral incision of the abdominal cavity revealed ovaries and fallopian tubes. A further incision to the uterus revealed a small tumour..."

His confident voice was obscured by the fug of confusion around the room and, despite the clarity of his voice and of the medical facts he was regurgitating for them all, the faces of the men before him were clouded with doubt.

"...Hypertrophy of the Labia Majora and Labia Minoris and an enlarged Clitoris."

This last word hung in the air for a few moments as it dawned on everyone that the Coroner had finished. The words meant very little to them all a few hours ago but the image of that little piece of flesh being cut away from its surrounding tissue was fresh in all their minds. The shape of the head and the hood of protective skin gave even the least squeamish among them a shiver of queasiness.

"In my opinion, the case is as clear, not so much by what we have found as by what we have not found." The coroner tilted his head, addressing the balance of his own words. Evidently, he considered it an adequate summary of the case thus far and he removed his spectacles. He used them to indicate across the room towards Geoffrey Leech, who had only half listened to the summary. I noticed as I watched him that he had winced at the intimacy of the details but as yet, had not once looked in the direction of the table and where his client, his friend now lay under that thin shroud.

"This is Mr. Geoffrey Leech. He is a solicitor who, as I understand it." Here he replaced his spectacles and quickly glanced back down to his notes. Evidently having not inspected Leech first hand, he was unable to summarise him. "Ah yes, here we go. Leech has been the family solicitor since 1880. He has dealt with all aspects of the deceased's affairs from property acquisitions, land registry, probate, wills and marriage." He looked at Leech with incredulity, as if he could not understand how such a simple matter of a client's gender had been missed. Leech rose and made his way to the front of the courtroom to a leather chair placed in good view of the jurors.

"Mr. Leech is a witness who has a vested interest in today's outcome. There will be quite some unpicking to do of the deceased's affairs if the result is not found in favour."

This last statement was not said too loudly, evidently being for the benefit of the clerk who was busily taking notes at his side. The officious looking man glanced up at his superior, a quizzical expression on his face.

"Shall I note that last bit, Sir?"

The Coroner rolled his eyes heavenward and clapped his hands on the table before leaning backwards in his chair. The noise was loud and punctuated the end of his monologue. His official role now being to orchestrate and steer the jury before him to the obvious conclusions, he seemed pleased to announce to the room that the witness may be questioned. Having listened intently to the Coroner's diatribe it was clear how he viewed the verdict. However, there appeared to be some considerable thought going on with some members of the jury. I had been watching one of the young men who had been slow to return to his seat after the physical examination and who still wore an expression of utter puzzlement. He had not taken his eyes from the body. As the Coroner raised his voice to invite questions of them for the witness, the young man started in his chair and looked guiltily at his feet.

"Mr. Leech, Sir. How well did you know the deceased?"

A well-dressed young man with a finely clipped pencil thin moustache and well-oiled hair addressed him.

"I have known Avery for just over thirty years. We were introduced by a mutual friend at the St James club in Mayfair. I saw him a few times again, once or twice to play cards with or to have a drink and a chat too. Then he came to see me in the summer of 1880 with a property acquisition. The family home as is. A nice house in Parsons Green, somewhere he and his wife could bring up their daughter."

The man behind the speaker coughed loudly to interrupt Leech straying from the point, and looked a little embarrassed on the old man's account.

"Sir," continued the moustachioed gent. "Are you saying that at no time during your first meetings with the deceased that you found anything out of the ordinary?"

Leech took a moment. He had wanted to respond confidently to any questions and he gave this question much thought. As he cast his mind back, he considered the smooth and ready face of his friend. Had he thought anything unusual about him when first they met? In truth there had been one thing, a small thing at the time that now seemed an obvious oversight and he considered not mentioning this to the assembled room.

"Mr. Leech?" the juror prompted.

"His voice," Leech responded quietly. "Avery was a tall man and his frame was solid. When he first spoke, he had much less of a presence than I had expected. Nothing incongruous or strange just...," he tried to think of the right word. "...surprising," he decided after a moment.

The juror nodded and looked over towards the body. He was trying to imagine the corpse of my father in life, animating this figure with the form of a woman and a softly spoken voice and trying to imagine how, and if, he could be fooled. It was all too obvious by his superior smile that he thought he would not be. Having decided the fate of this verdict in his own mind, he was already considering how he may spend the rest of his day's leisure. His suit was fine and striped like many of John's colleagues. He was a man of the city; his trade probably stocks and shares; paper not people. He belonged to the new century and like many of those of his generation, already considered himself several steps ahead of the likes of Leech, the Coroner and my father. These dusty, grey haired relics belonged to the last century and he would not be fooled by the small footed corpse that kept him from his city bank on a trading day. As he calculated the potential losses from his earnings through this day's duty, the thought made him cross and cast a shadow across his features. The man behind him who coughed, his lips parted wishing to speak, finally interjected into the silence, raising his hand as he did so as he if wished to use the bathroom.

"If I may, Sir?" he addressed the Coroner who gestured towards Leech with a wide sweep of his arm. "Thank you. Yes. Mr. Leech. This may sound unorthodox but could you describe the deceased for us. It is difficult, on the face of the evidence, to imagine how on earth this fellow conducted himself."

"Or herself?" his neighbour piped up. A long faced old man, his arms folded guardedly. He blushed slightly as attention was drawn upon him and he proceeded to shuffle awkwardly in his seat, adjusting his position until he was back in exactly the same pose, closed.

"Of course, or herself," the original speaker agreed.

The hairs on the back of my neck had begun to rise and I was shocked by the impertinence of these young men. In life, my father had run rings around men like them. I was growing frustrated at the manner in which these people referred to him. Leech however, had been prepared for this. As he had travelled by cab this morning from his home in Battersea, he had tried to imagine what he would be asking someone if he was placed in a similar position. He cleared his throat; age was beginning to endow him with troublesome phlegm that settled on his chest, promoting a rather unhealthy rattle.

"Silver was someone upon whose judgment I relied very heavily. He was a sober and astute man who was strong in character but who reserved judgment on people and issues." As he spoke, he levelled his gaze upon each juror individually, most of whom were listening intently but some men's attention had strayed to the clerk, the corpse or their fellow jurors. "Avery was about as solid a friend as a man could choose. He was knowledgeable, loyal and a convivial companion."

"You were friends a long time. Twenty years you say?" the Juror prompted.

"Thereabouts, yes."

119

"And in those twenty years, you were members of the same club, so presumably you spent many evenings together?"

Leech nodded, a little nonplussed.

"Not infrequently."

"And what would you do on those evenings?"

Leech, unsure of where this line of questioning was leading, seemed fairly content to indulge the fellow a little.

"More often than not, we would discuss any pending business matters. I was always interested to talk with Avery as he has....had," he corrected himself. "...he had an uncanny knack for riding his investments very skillfully. He would seem to know weeks, days before a collapse to sell or when to buy just before a big boom. As I said, he was a very knowledgeable chap. We would discuss the day's events. His opinion usually differed from mine and we would sometimes debate an item in the news. More often than not, we would both concede the others point and agree to disagree."

"Did you drink together?"

"Of course,'" Leech scoffed and looked to the Coroner in amusement. The old boy's eyes twinkled in companionable accord at the suggestion that one would spend an evening at one's club without a few glasses of something.

"What did the deceased drink?"

Leech frowned

"What a question."

"This is wasting our time." Another juror called out from the end of the row. He had been waiting for a while on the edge of his seat. It was clear he also had a question.

"What did the deceased drink?"

Leech looked from the juror to the coroner. It was not clear what the man was trying to get at but Leech was sure he would be disappointed. The coroner shrugged at Leech as if to say, 'Answer if you like.'

"Avery was a whiskey drinker and a good one at that."

There was a moment's pause and the patient man at the end of the row took his turn to direct the proceedings.

"Mr. Leech..." the new juror started but evidently the previous juror had not finished

"Sorry. Can I just ask one more question and then I'm done?" his smile was simpering toward the chap at the end of the row, who scowled in return. "So, if the deceased was a big drinker and you spent many evenings at the club together and you were good friends, might it be reasonable to assume that you visited the gents at some point together over the course of twenty years?"

Leech had not been expecting that and his first response was one of professional admiration. He had simply not seen where the young man's line of questioning had been leading. Had this been any other circumstances, he may well have congratulated the young man on his astute mind. However, the more overriding emotion was one of irritation at being asked something he had not given any thought to. He felt slightly disconcerted but then was filled with a momentary boost as he recalled occasion after occasion when he and Avery had been in the gents.

121

Perhaps here was some evidence to suggest Avery was hermaphrodite. He was about to respond positively but to his annoyance he found he could not recollect any occasion when he had seen Avery at the urinals. As each recollection scrolled through his mind, he saw Avery disappearing to a stall, returning from a stall, closing the door. Again, he had not thought anything of it at the time. Plenty of men prefer privacy in the toilet and why would Avery be any different? Leech mumbled his response.

"Yes and he always used the stalls."

There was a murmuring from the jurors as they looked to one another and back again at the original speaker with a renewed admiration. The chap looked immensely pleased with himself but modesty only allowed a small amount of colour to flush his cheeks before he retook his seat apologizing, once more, to the gentleman on the end.

"Mr. Leech. Just a quick question. What can you tell us about the relationship between the deceased and the woman who purported to be his wife, er…Mrs. Silver? I am curious. Do you think she knew the truth or is it feasible to assume she was ignorant of this?"

The mention of my mother was as much a shock for Geoffrey Leech as it had been for me. He looked directly at me, startled as if I were the one who had uttered her name. It was obvious he had not considered her at all. Her death eight years ago had been quite a shock to us all and one from which we had only just seemed to recover. Her death was most untimely and wholly unexpected. She was a petite woman but with the most robust constitution. Along with her hearty nature, I had always assumed she would just live to a ripe old age.

I suppose I had not even given it so much thought as that even, at the time it was impossible to imagine mother without father or he without her. In the end she had died of a large tumour in her stomach. Her last months were terribly hard on us all but father bore the worst of it. Even as an adult they were protecting me as if I were a child and they both made sure that I never endured any of the details of the awful treatments that the doctors tried on her. Geoffrey had seen it too. He was a regular visitor to Hamble Gardens in those last few months, I know father and he shared more than business during that time.

As I stared back at Geoffrey, his tired grey eyes sparkled with tears. He would never speak of any of that in this room. He had seen my father cry on a few occasions but in truth what man would not in such horrendous circumstances. Geoffrey himself had lost his own wife a few years after him and then he too had cried. Avery had been the natural choice of all his friends in whom to confide and to lean on. The question posed by the young man was a touch too far and Leech visibly prickled as the young man, feeling awkward in the silence created by Leech, repeated himself. Leech weighed up how much he was willing to share in the matter of public interest and what was adequate in a legal investigation such as this.

"I don't see that this has any bearing on this inquiry," he settled upon, looking to the Coroner for assistance. The Coroner merely tipped his head on one side, considering the matter before reluctantly addressing the juror.

"I think, whilst we can say it would throw some more light on the life of the deceased, it does not serve this inquiry in determining the cause of death nor the question in hand as to gender."

An argument was ready on the lips of the young man; he was evidently cross that he had not had the opportunity to have his own line of questioning praised as had the previous gentleman. He decided against putting words to his disgruntled thoughts and instead crossed his legs and turned his back on the room a little. It was an insolent and immature gesture that did not go unnoticed by the Coroner who rolled his eyes.

"Does anyone have any more questions of Mr. Leech? That are pertinent to the aims here today," he added. The jurors looked at each other blankly, most seemed to be more intrigued by the details which evidently were not to be investigated.

"Well if that is all, then Mr. Leech you are free to go." The Coroner indicated the free chairs to the back of the room and Leech walked as directed to sit beside me once more. "We will take a five minute break."

Chapter Eight - Avery, 1869

It wasn't the breeze ruffling the hair at the nape of his neck which made him feel empowered, though the recent trim Kate had skillfully administered and the lack of hair clips and ribbons was, of course, refreshing. Nor was it the feeling across his chest as the tight crepe bandages compressed his small breasts though, unsurprisingly, this gave him the confidence to stand taller than he had since he was a child. And, though the shoes he was wearing gave him a new gait, a relaxed amble that made his arms swing loosely beside him, it was not these that endowed him with the secret pride he was carrying. The whole ensemble he wore was made of expertly crafted pieces and yet none of it was responsible for making him feel whole. It was not the gold cuff links or the pocket-chain he had borrowed from his father. It wasn't his trousers, his jacket or his hat. Nor was it his underpants but what was inside them which made him stand tall.

On that first evening, when he had taken the packages which Kate had collected from Fry's and hurried them into his room, he had locked the door and opened each of the boxes and inspected the fine clothes with a deep reverence, as if each item contained an element of magic; as if in wearing them he would become something else. That they would not only serve to shroud the body he had inhabited but that in doing so would reveal something in its place. He had laid the first suit across his bed sheets and he had itched to try it on. He had pulled out a shirt and the draw was too great; having checked the lock was drawn across his door, he pulled the stifling grey dress over his head, tearing a few delicate buttons from their threads. Not comfortable naked, he kept his stays on and drew the white shirt over his back and buttoned it up, the smooth cotton causing his nipples to pucker and protrude. He glanced at the mirror and pressed his hand under the shirt and crushed his chest. The line he created was pleasing and he nodded to himself, he could see a solution and strode across the floor to draw out some crepe bandages from a side drawer. He dropped the shirt to the floor and made haste binding his breasts tightly, his chin dropped on his chest as he watched them disappear with a satisfied grin. He eagerly picked up the shirt and drew it back on. He buttoned it completely before turning to face the mirror once more. The flat line was remarkable and he wished immediately that the change could be unalterable. He had smoothed his hand down the front of the shirt and his reflection glowed with approval. Then, as he had unwrapped the paper from a third but smaller package and, having folded back the tissue, he had discovered underwear. Rather than revere them, he had instantly thrown them down. They had surprised him. All of the other garments, he was outwardly familiar and they also served to conceal what he already had; yet these were both unfamiliar and were designed to display what he should have had. The light within Avery's stomach had been briefly tempered and he had crushed up the underwear, his fist balled around the fabric. He had been angry and had used the material to stifle his own suffocated sobs, his teeth clenched. As his anger diminished and self-pity began to glow within him, so too did an idea. At first it was a crude and ill-formed thought but his ambitious mind excelled himself and he found himself smiling over his tears. Of course the idea had its flaws; Avery had never seen a male appendage before. There were sculptures of course but one was not allowed to linger long enough to inspect them for design. Paintings, art and imagination were all he could rely upon and for the moment it was enough to form an image in his head. From what little he knew of anatomy he could be sure that it had to be soft but hard enough to stand erect and he would need some way to attach it to himself so that it would not slip out of his underpants and slide down his trouser leg. His mind had raced as he reached yet another dead end. How on earth could he fashion something which would fit the bill? Where on earth would he be able to do it and from what could he make it?

It had given Avery several days of heartache and he had begun to sink into a depression so deep that it threatened to overtake him all together. His father had called in the family doctor and the dire look of him had been enough to encourage the normally intervention-shy Doctor Whitaker to prescribe a sleeping draught. It was during one of these visits from the doctor that Avery had had his epiphany.

"What's that?" Avery said.

"What is what Miss Silver?" Doctor Whitaker barely looked at him as he continued making notes in his small ledger. He was drawing up a prescription for another draught, his mind already on his next patient.

Avery reached across his bed and lifted a dullish red instrument from the doctor's case. It was a long and rounded tool, the thickness of an infant's arm but attached to a handle. Several wires were connected through the handle suggesting some further additions. Despite its presence in the doctor's kit and its obvious medical intentions the shape was undoubtedly phallic. Avery examined it and was instantly struck by the firmness but pliability. Doctor Whitaker looked up and a frown broke across his forehead. He delicately withdrew the instrument from Avery's grasp and replaced it gingerly back in his case.

"It is a Vibrating Massage Device Miss Silver. Not a nice looking instrument but nevertheless a useful one when it comes to dealing with feminine humours." Doctor Whitaker replied. "I quite hope that with your constitution and your own late mother's strong presence of mind, God rest her soul, that you will never have call to have the use of it."

"What is it made of?"

The doctor had looked at Avery in puzzlement. Evidently, this was not the usual sort of question from a young lady. Now standing, ready to close his case, he was keen to be on his way but he was also rather proud of his new instrument.

"It is a vulcanised rubber Miss Silver. It's a funny sort of material, softer and more malleable than ordinary rubber. They can mould it to almost any shape they want, a little like pouring hot wax into a mould. It's rather more preferable than the old metal ones which frankly were cold and less forgiving..." the doctors eyes strayed to Avery's and his face coloured as he realised the impropriety of his words.

"Vulcanised rubber," Avery repeated, his eyes bright.

In the intervening weeks, Avery noticed with a mixture of disappointment and relief that Kate seemed to have lost interest in his activities and she neither mentioned that odd fortnight or the clothes hidden within his dresser. He imagined she thought the whole scenario strange and had begun to forget all about the illicit danger he had placed them both in. She could forget but he could not. The thought of his clothes, the sound his boots made upon the street as he walked, the memory of the looks he elicited from people he passed made his heart race. He noticed that Kate no longer gave him a knowing look as opportunity after opportunity to continue his nightly excursions seemed to pass by. He wondered whether he had expected too much of the young girl and she had lost the courage. It was after one such perfect opportunity, a Saturday evening when the house was empty of all staff save for Kate and Jamieson who had retired early to bed (reportedly to work on some buckles of Old Mr. Silver's!), that an excitement seemed to rise up in her. He and Kate had been sat in companionable silence in the drawing room. Avery had been sullen all day; his mind was busy thinking about the device he had seen in Doctor Whitaker's bag, the girl from the alley, Connie and his tortured dreams of Kate.

He was hardly aware of her leaving the chair opposite him but he felt a draft as she opened the door. He glanced up just as she slipped through the door throwing him a wink. And then the door closed. It was such a welcome gesture after days and days of feeling adrift from her, he wondered whether he had imagined it. After a few minutes pondering its meaning, he was compelled to follow her. A few moments later, he opened the door to his own room and found her busy with a damp cloth polishing his shoes. Without being asked, she had prepared an evening suit for him which was now laid upon the bed like a shadow.

"Kate! What on earth are you doing?"

Kate spun round, her eyes dancing with excitement.

"Sorry, I know you didn't ask me but I thought if I made a quick start, you could be out before dark and...."

"Put it away."

His voice was sharp and Kate looked stung by the tone.

"Sorry?"

"You heard me. I'm not going anywhere." He tried to avoid her gaze but after a few moments in the silence, he eventually levelled his gaze to meet hers.

"But, this is a perfect opportunity!" Her tone was petulant and Avery detected a quiver in her arms that suggested she was struggling with self-control. "Your father won't be home for hours, we've the house to ourselves. What's stopping you?"

Avery stepped back from her, watching the rise and fall of her chest as she tried to draw her breath calmly. His dreams of her, far from abating, in light of the event with Connie had only grown clearer. Where before he had woken frustrated at the lack of satisfaction, now he woke in a sweat, shuddering with pleasure. Kate roused him from his sleep so softly that on occasion he had almost pulled her to him. The proximity of her at these moments, half asleep were his most vulnerable. So completely he believed his transformation in his dream and so vividly had he imagined the taste of her flesh beneath him as he moved inside her that for several waking moments he

130

was insensible to his own body. In some ways the realisation is more difficult to accept and harder for him to inhabit his female body. He had taken to avoiding her as much as possible, preferring to dress himself rather than have her eyes on his female form or her watching him walk about in a dress.

"Have you changed your mind, Sir?"

She watched him as he moved across the room and he felt more absurd than ever in his usual plain dress. Far from having changed his mind, he was more determined than ever to find a way to never have to feel as he did then. As he sat down on the end of the bed, he knew he would need her help in achieving the next step in his plan.

"No Kate. I haven't changed my mind. Of what I am about to tell you I have never been more certain in my life. Will you help me?"

He held his breath needlessly as Kate nodded eagerly, her fingers clenched around the fabric of her apron.

~o~

It had taken a few weeks to track down a medical manufacturer who would take a design and, at the time, Avery had noted with concern how readily the man had agreed to the unusual commission. He watched from outside the office door, straining to hear their exchange, as Kate negotiated with the proprietor.

"I will admit, Miss, that this is a most irregular request. If you could tell me more about the intended purpose of this...device...then perhaps I could...," The

131

man had looked Kate up and down before licking his lips salaciously. "…guarantee your satisfaction?"

Avery had insisted that he accompany Kate but she was unsure that the presence of another woman in such a transaction would add to the legitimacy of the request. He had objected at first but, having witnessed the outrage of the proprietors of two outlets, had eventually been persuaded that caution was best exercised alone. It was agreed he could accompany her but must wait outside in the guise of maid.

"I am afraid I cannot go into detail, Sir, but suffice to say that I would be extremely grateful of your help in matters of my delicate health."

Kate, dressed in one of Avery's finest dresses, looked like a wealthy lady of means and, furnished with some ready cash, the two had hoped to persuade this latest manufacturer with wealth alone, but evidently, he wished to negotiate his terms.

"I see," he nodded sagely. "And the straps?" He was seated at a desk and she noticed him slip his hand inside his trousers.

Kate, feigned interest and continued with her cover story, the details of which she and Avery had concocted a few nights ago. He had supplied some of the information Doctor Whitaker had provided and Kate had added some of her own detail.

"My doctor is quite unable to massage me to satisfaction and I am left feeling quite out of sorts after his visits. I have employed a young maid with the specific purpose of curing me of my ill humours." The implication was clumsy and Avery thought that she sounded a little foolish; however, the effect was instantaneous and he noted with disgust the tendons in the man's arm begin to flex.

"Tell me more," he whispered hoarsely.

~o~

As Avery Silver sauntered down the Tottenham Court Road, he felt at once both as conspicuous as a pelican but all the while more at home in his skin than he had ever felt in his twenty years upon the earth. The thing which had stoked Avery's flame was solid between his legs, the soft bump of it against his thigh as he walked and with every reminder of its presence, gave Avery two things. Firstly, it gave Avery confidence. The confidence to return the smile he had just been cast from a lady beneath her hat; the confidence to tip his own hat in acknowledgement and to stride more purposefully despite having no errand. Yes, the warm, hard shape Kate had collected that afternoon and had strapped to him, gave him confidence but it also gave him an appetite.

It was easy enough to find Connie, having returned to the same place albeit a few hours earlier. Avery had spotted her quite quickly. He watched as she pressed herself at passing gentlemen. By some she was rewarded with a wink but business was slow and she could not elicit more than that. Avery saw that others visibly recoiled from her, the mere proximity of her seemed to seep under their noses, like a foul smell curling up their features in distaste. She too seemed choosy with her clientele. Several times, she sensed the distaste before it was obvious and saved herself the effort of a wasted opportunity. Avery watched with interest from his hidden vantage point as the woman spotted a lone figure turn into the street. His presence seemed to cause her some concern and, although he was too far off to discern his features, it was obvious from his posture that he was dangerous. The whore drew her shawl up from around her elbows and covered herself, stepping backwards into a doorway. Hers was an ugly line of work and Silver recalled reading of a case reported in the press only a few months ago, of a murdered woman found brutalised. As the man passed her by, Avery noticed her close her eyes in palpable relief. He took the opportunity to cross the street.

"Good evening again, Miss," he said softly.
The woman visibly rose as she jumped at the sound of Avery's voice. She had spun around wildly but was clearly relieved to find her stalker had not been the dark haired man.

"Christ! What do you mean by sneaking up on people like that? 'ere don't I know you?" Her eyes narrowed as she recognised Avery's face but she failed to place him immediately. He stared directly at her but there was no moment of enlightenment. Caught off guard momentarily, the woman returned to her pitch at hand, a small swell of pride visibly making her hold herself taller at the prospect of a repeat client like the proper house girls got. Her eyes darted around and then she grabbed Avery by the wrist and led him across the street.

"I've a room only two minutes away. Come on," she said.

Though Avery knew he would not be making use of the services she offered within her room, he also knew that to discuss his proposition out in the open would be foolish and he allowed himself to be led, trusting only her discretion of a few months ago to prevent him from falling foul in this dark city. He followed the woman a few streets away to a run down side street off Helier Road, whereupon she stopped beside a tired wooden door that had once been painted a fresh white. The door had borne much abuse and was heavily scuffed, paint peeling from the scratches, the white faded to a dull grey like the fog which Avery imagined would lingered here in the winter.

She turned to check that Avery had followed and then gave a cursory glance around them both, to ensure that they were not to be followed inside. The door opened out into a narrow passageway which after a few steps led straight into a staircase. A single door ajar to the left gave Avery an insight into the occupations of the rest of the household. There was little to see, but from the sounds emanating from the inch wide crack, it was clear that the ground floor occupant was hard at work. The woman, noticing Avery's hesitation, had ascended a few more stairs and now turned above him.

"Come on, sir. There's more I can show you than you can see here."

She stepped down one stair and pulled him by the arm again, leading him upwards to a first floor landing. He was pulled inside another doorway and into the centre of a small room. The sound of the door being latched closed behind him caused Avery to turn, startled. The proximity of this whore, the airlessness of the room and the danger in which he may have placed himself became evident and he had a few moments doubt. The woman turned from the door and threw off her shawl towards the bed. She arranged her business face and walked towards Avery, unlacing her bodice as she approached him.

"How do I know you, sir? You look like you would be someone I should remember."

By the time she reached Avery, she had pulled her bodice loose and pushed her breasts up out of the corset so the nipples stood proud of the material. The slight chill in the air caused them to stand erect, the skin around them puckering. She reached down for Avery's hands and pulled one to her chest, massaging her own breasts with his hand. Avery had not intended for this to happen and he was about to withdraw his hand but he could not ignore the sensation it was eliciting from his groin. He took up a grip of one of her breasts and dipped his head to take the nipple in his mouth. He closed his eyes and was immediately transported to his familiar lakeside setting and, instead of a whore upon whose breasts he was suckling, he was stood over Kate. Kate's hands ruffling his hair gripping him tighter and Kate's thighs nudging up into his crotch. Kate's hands unbuttoning his trousers.

"Wait," he groaned.

Avery stepped backwards and away from the woman who was now stood looking at him in surprise. His withdrawal from her seemed to dislodge whatever had been preventing her from recognising him and her eyes narrowed as she considered him again.

"Hang on a minute. You're that tom?'"

Her face broke into a wide grin as if she was relieved that she would not be required to perform after all. Given how well Avery had paid last time for nothing, there was every chance that this could turn out to be another lucky night.

"I 'ave to tell you miss, I ain't ever been with a woman before," she paused before adding "I'm not so sure I would, normally, but for you, Miss, I'll only charge you double."

She regained her composure of what she should be offering her clients and stepped forwards more coyly than before. Evidently, she judged her sales pitch should be less forthright. However, her words had filled Avery with a heat far greater than his previous desire and he curled his lip as he attempted a civil tone.

"Madam, I am not here to avail myself of your services."

With this he took a step backwards so that his knees were met by the bed behind him. He straightened himself before her, composing his tone before adding. "I am here to discuss business of another kind."

The whore's face fell as she tried to fathom his meaning. She looked at him warily, freshly suspicious of this character from whom only a few moments before, she had had the promise of a lucky night.

"What kind of business?" She cocked her head at an angle and appraised Avery from tip to toe. "I told you, I ain't into girls, even if they do look like fellas."

A pulse at Avery's temple throbbed as he ground his jaw tightly on his anger before the woman remarked.

"And you do look like a fella, Miss."

Her eyes were narrowed again as if she was trying to seek out an optical illusion from Avery's image.

"Far better than those tom's up the West End."
Her gaze settled on Avery's throat where the shirt
collars clung to his neck. He was endowed with a small
lump in his throat which looked like an Adams apple.

"If I hadn't felt for your cock, I wouldn't have
known," she said this softly, as much to herself as
Avery and, as if trying to reassure herself, she stepped
forwards to Avery, her arm stretched out to his genitals.
Avery had been anticipating such a gesture and he was
quick to grab the woman by her wrist and he
sidestepped her, so her arm was twisted behind her
back. He pushed her arm upwards and stepped behind
her so his head was resting next to her's when he
spoke again.

"If we are to continue this conversation, you will
not try that again, do you understand?"

The woman was confused, at the small of her
back where Avery stood against her, she could feel
something firm pressing against her. Whoever this
person was holding her tightly, she could no longer be
sure whether he was in fact male or female.

Avery let go of his grip and stepped away from the
woman.

"I am not here to taste your wares, Miss..." he
paused, allowing a gap for the woman to introduce
herself formerly. She looked at him, holding her wrist
where he had restrained her and gave him a wide
smile, showing one or tooth gaps where decay had
begun.

"Constance Brown," she said, bobbing a wry
curtsey at her own introduction. "You can call me
Connie, Miss"

"Well Connie, you will call me either Mr. Silver or Sir, is that clear?"

"Sir or Miss, the price is the same for me and what you do with your time is up to you but by my reckoning you already owe me sixpence."

Connie had regained her sense of what was important and in her trade, time was money. Avery too wished to get down to the business of his errand.

"I will pay you for your time Miss Connie but I wish to make an arrangement with you for which I will also reward you well."

Connie's eyes flickered at the mention of reward and she walked to the makeshift nightstand beside her bed, an upturned crate, faded linen covering its surface. She drew some water from the ewer and poured a cup for herself. She sat upon the bed and withdrew a bottle from under its frame. Avery could see it was some sort of spirit. She added a dash to the cup and drank from it sedately all the while watching Avery from over its rim. She did not offer him anything. Stood before her, Avery began to outline his proposal watching her neutral face take in the details. Her eyes showed the only indication that she was hearing him as they twinkled at the sum of money he was suggesting. As he finished off, there was a silence and he stood rather nervously awaiting her response. Hearing the words spoken out loud had underlined the fact that the whole plan rather relied on both Connie's discretion and her willingness to place herself in a modicum of danger. Connie finished off her drink and then stood, the frame of the bed squeaking a little. She replaced her cup on the little crate and stepped towards Avery holding out her hand.

"You owe me half a crown for tonight and for another sixpence I'll give your proposal some thought."

Avery felt his shoulders fall in disappointment, he was all too aware of the risks required from Connie in assisting him but he had hoped that his money would be persuasive.

"Come back tomorrow an hour before six and I'll give you me answer."

He pressed the money into the woman's hand and turned to the door.

"I'll see you tomorrow," she smiled before adding, "Mr. Silver."

~o~

Connie's room looked exactly as it had the previous evening and Avery was pleased that she should have gone to no extra effort to accommodate him. The bed was still unmade and the little chest was still strewn with junk: the debris of an earlier meal and the cup, empty again. Connie had agreed to his plan and, having elicited twice the fee from him, had gone out on to the streets, reluctant to leave him alone in her room. As Avery stood in the doorway of the small wardrobe inside which he was to hide, he marvelled at what Connie thought might be worth his taking. The bottle under the bed, she had not entrusted with him, for she had taken this along with her. She had twice told him.

"It's what's between my legs what's worth anything in this room, sir," she spoke deliberately, pronouncing the 'Sir' as if Avery were indeed royalty or that she may be rewarded by using the term more frequently. There was no doubt that she was wary of him, as if she did were unsure of what he truly wanted from this arrangementm but the lure of the money was too strong and she had been tempted in before she could get cold feet.

After only half an hour or so, he heard a thumping down the stairwell indicating the front door being slammed. Had he not divined that she had got lucky, Connie made sure that Avery knew she was not returning alone by talking loudly, her voice travelling up the narrow stairs and slipping into the room, hardly muffled by the thin door.

"It's your lucky night, sir, my room is still warm from a fire."

It was true, Avery had insisted that the woman light a small fire before she left, promising to replace her meagre coal supply twice over. The room was not overly cold but it did not lend itself to nudity and that was part of what Avery was paying for. He pulled himself into the wardrobe and drew the door ajar leaving an inch crack through which he could see the bed clearly. A few moments later, the sound of Connie's voice nervously announced herself to the empty room.

"Here we are, sir, this is it. My room. Nobody but you and I."

Avery closed his eyes at the lack of subtlety of the woman but the strangeness of the woman announcing her arrival into her own room was lost on her companion. The sound of the door closing and then a man's voice followed.

"Bloody hell, it's hot in here." His voice was deep but soft. He didn't sound as confident as Avery had expected but rather he sounded a little nervous.

Connie backed into the room, leading the man by his wrists much as she had tried to with Avery the previous evening. She glanced at the wardrobe and thinking herself to be in the agreed position, she got to her knees and began unbuttoning the trousers of the man before her. He was a labouring man, Avery judged, his boots had tidemarks of dust and grime. His woollen jacket was patched several times over and he wore a cap. Avery smiled, self-satisfied, as the man took off his jacket immediately and threw it on the bed. Beneath his coat, his shirt sleeves were rolled up showing thick forearms, dark with hair. As Connie reached inside his trousers and drew out his furled member, the man pushed his hands through her hair. Avery was surprised by the size of the man's cock, it was much smaller than he had imagined and less imposing. The effect of it poking out of the man's trousers was at once both comical and absurd. He was disappointed when Connie took the entire thing into her mouth and he could no longer see the shape of it. The man was clearly not disappointed by this manoeuvre and rolled his head back with a moan, grasping the back of Connie's head as he did so. It was difficult to see with the man's arms obscuring the view but Avery could see her head bobbing as she sucked at him. A few moments later, the man took his left hand away and rubbed his chest and Avery was shocked to see the change that had occurred. Where before Connie had been sucking at a soft purple lump of flesh which barely hung from out of the front of the man's trousers,

142

there now stood a thick baton the size and length of an infant's arm bobbing slightly as it defied gravity. Connie's hand was inside the man's trousers fondling something else hidden out of Avery's sight. There was none of the nerves as the man's voice came again.

"On your hands and knees."

Obligingly, Connie dropped onto her hands facing the window and lifted her skirts up to her back. The man dropped his trousers, crouched over her, bracing himself with his hands on her haunches and, leading with his cock, he dipped down to position himself over her. Avery could see the moon of Connie's white thighs and buttocks between which a dark crop of hair formed a frame for two crescents of pink flesh. It was only visible for a moment before the man's own thigh eclipsed the view and all Avery could see was the back of the man's trousers. Avery heard the man spit and fumble with his cock before the sound of Connie's moan punctuated the air. There was stillness and an almost complete silence before the room seemed to pivot entirely on the scene in front of Avery. The man dipped and thrust on his haunches, slowly at first, building up a rhythm which rocked Connie forward. Her legs were set wide, the soles of her feet facing Avery, in his hiding place, bounced upwards from the wooden floor with every plunge of the man's hips. The silence had been broken by the rise and fall of the man's breathing, each time he pushed himself deep inside her he let out a grunt. From Connie too there was a corresponding sound as if the air was being pushed out of her from the inside and she exhaled loudly on each slap of flesh upon flesh. Avery was all too aware that he had been holding his own breath but now he joined in with each breath that the man took. His own hips began to twitch in time to the fierce rhythm. He was aware of his own desire as he imagined his own cock squeezing up inside Connie. He closed his eyes and imagined the tight feeling as he pushed his way inside. There was a scuffling sound and Avery's eyes snapped open, his breath held. The pumping motion had stopped and the man pushed harder into Connie, causing her to buckle under his weight. His buttocks twitched spasmodically. As he grunted, he thrust a final time and then his legs relaxed and he collapsed forwards, covering her completely. There was but a moments' silence before Connie's legs turned as she tried to move the man off of her. For a moment, Avery wondered if the man had fainted or fallen asleep before he seemed to stir. He rolled off Connie, beneath him and pulled himself to his knees. Connie sat back on her feet, the dark hair between her legs slick with a white deposit which had begun to roll down her thigh. There was a strange and uncomfortable silence as the man, now stood and ignoring Connie, pulled up his trousers and tucked himself in. There was a wet patch across the front of his trousers which he dabbed at with a rag from his pocket, cursing. Connie meanwhile raised herself to her feet and waited beside the door. The man collected his jacket from the bed and took out a coin. He tossed it on the nightstand and walked out of the door without looking at Connie. The final exchange took less than a minute. Avery was stunned at the intimacy of the act that had taken place yet the brutality of the parting.

"Get what you come for did you?"

144

There was a hard edge to Connie's voice which Avery had not noticed before and he held Connie's gaze as he climbed out of the wardrobe for some more evidence of this different side to the woman.

"Are they all like that?" Avery asked.

"Like what?"

"So...," he searched for a word "...perfunctory?" He noticed that she looked confused and he added, "So quick?"

Connie looked at him and shook her head incredulously.

"No Mr. Silver, some of them aren't such Gentlemen."

~o~

Avery left Connie's that night not ready for home. His fingers were burning with the desire to touch somebody. He knew that when he arrived home, Kate would be waiting to let him in and that it would take all of his willpower to resist the urge to pull her to him. There was a niggling frustration that he was unable to perform what he had just seen. Trying to delay that moment for as long as possible, he walked slowly down the main streets before flagging down a cab. When Avery finally returned home that evening, he was able to avoid a scene with Kate. He neither met her gaze or responded to her enquiries beyond a mutter. He fell into bed confused, visions of that evening played across his mind. In some ways, he was excited but in many others he was frustrated, he would be unable to accomplish the same act. He had not known what to expect and the reality had left him un-sated and more curious. He had seen in the alleyway chaotic and fervent fumbling and he had seen a short, animalistic coupling on the floor like dogs. The whole act had seemed without much pleasure for either party and was more like a transaction than any other sale he had witnessed. The word 'spent' seemed quite appropriate. The man had spent some money and spent himself. The exchange perfunctory.

When he finally fell asleep, Avery's dreams were mixed up. His own self became the man he had seen earlier. The whore, Kate. He plunged himself inside her but each time he thrust, Kate's face became that of Connie. Annoyed, he thrust harder at her body willing Kate's face to remain but with each stroke, her face would melt away into the ambivalent faraway gaze that Connie had adopted to ease the discomfort of her chore. It was in this confused state that Avery awoke the following morning. He had got back in to the house late and it was past three when he had fallen asleep. Now Kate was leaning over him, trying to rouse him and he was still half asleep as he put his hands about the real Kate's face and pulled her down to him. After a night spent dreaming of forcing himself between her legs the touch was tender and gentle. It was the only weapon left to him after the ferocity of his passion had failed to bring her any pleasure. He was quite unaware that this was no longer a dream yet Kate was fully awake as he reached out from the bed. His breath was hot and slightly sour from sleep but the kiss he laid was velvety on her top lip. It was a moment before he realized his waking world had collided hard with his dream and Avery felt awash with uplifting happiness. His eyes flickered open and he saw Kate's face above his own; her eyes closed and her lips slightly parted. Startled, he immediately began to apologise, the kiss still fresh on his lips as his words tumbled out.

"I'm sorry. Kate...I was still. What are you doing?" he stammered.

Kate recoiled from the bed, her hand pressed to her face where Avery's lips had been. She coloured immediately and he could see her heart hammering in her chest as she tried to catch her breath.

"Miss Silver. I'm so. Avery, sir..."

"Forgive me."

The position into which he had placed her seemed unforgiveable and he watched helplessly as her tears came readily. She ran to the door in a state of panic but in that moment, Avery had climbed out of bed and ran to prevent her from opening it. He too was panicked by the situation and was keen to keep Kate inside the room until he could convince her that it had been a mistake.

"Kate, please you mustn't go. I'm so sorry. It was all my fault."

"I'm sorry...oh God, I knew this would happen, it's all my fault."

Their words tumbled together.

"...all my fault," they said together.

Avery's hand covered Kate's over the door handle. It was larger than hers by some proportion. There was a moment's pause as they found each other's eyes again and a shiver of recognition coursed between them. Avery gripped her hand longer than was necessary and it was Kate who withdrew hers first, sure that this was not Avery's intention. She turned her face away from him. Avery's jaw tightened. It seemed like a harsh rebuke and he was ashamed of who he was. Ashamed too of who he could not be and his thoughts. How he had spent his dreams that night defiling the woman stood beside him and how one simple kiss obviously disgusted her. If she knew of the filth in his mind, she would be horrified and he was all at once filled with self-loathing. He turned, his face contorted in self-disgust. Kate's voice came from behind him.

"Please don't tell anyone about this. Please."

Avery snorted, hardly believing her ingenuousness.

"Kate, I shall hardly admit it to myself let alone another living soul." He turned to face her. If she was so disgusted by him, then at least the secret hope that she might feel the same was now settled.

"I won't tell anyone if you won't," he agreed.

Kate looked at him, slightly bewildered.

"Of course," she nodded. "Of course." She dropped her gaze and looked around the room. She shrugged her shoulders and stepped back in to the middle of the room.

"Best get your clothes ready," she indicated to the wardrobe. Kate looked relieved seemingly able to shrug the episode off. She bustled across the room, wringing her hands a little. Her nerves manifested themselves verbally as she busied herself in the room.

"Well, breakfast will be late this morning. Mrs. Druce has had a to-do with Mary-Ann again. You know how those two bicker. Not that you would 'cos you don't get down to the kitchen do you? But if you did, you'd know how those two bicker. This room won't straighten itself out. Oh, your father wants to see you when you're dressed."

Avery froze. His father very rarely wanted to see Avery at the moment, his time was roundly being monopolized by the widow Fearncott. When they did see each other, talk invariably got around to his father's wish that Avery become more 'sociable' as his father put it. The intention was clear, to find Avery a husband and the idea put a chill in Avery's heart that even winter alone could not.

"I don't think there's anything to worry over. It's about his fancy woman. Sorry, you know. Mrs. Fearncott. Sorry." She shot a grimace at Avery.

Avery snorted with laughter. His frustration was completely dissolved by the impropriety of her comment. Given all they already shared, the commonplace suddenly seemed so absurd. He stepped forward, sat on the bed and put his head in his hands before breathing a sigh of relief as Kate continued to bustle around him.

Chapter Nine - Imogen, 1911

The noise in the room grew steadily as the jurors whispered to one another. I watched the Coroner who rubbed his temples and called the Clerk across to the desk where he proceeded to direct him on an urgent errand. Beside me, John had taken up his hat once more, twisting the brim methodically round and round. He had begun to regurgitate the proceedings to me as if I had not witnessed them myself.

"Thank you, John. I have been beside you the whole time, have I not?"

He shot me a look and grimaced before continuing at a mumble.

"I tell you it's a sham, a waste of taxpayer's money." I smelled a sour odour from him that I hadn't detected before. He must have been drinking last night. "It's an excuse to drag this side show out for as long as possible. I tell you, there has never been such a clear cut case as this!"

I won't deny that his words made me flinch with their thunderous insensitivity but at that moment I was numb to them; all my energy instead was focused on breathing in, breathing out and remaining upright. After a short interlude, the clerk hurried back into the room carrying a glass of water into which the coroner now tipped a sachet of salts. He mixed the two with a silver stirrer, that he took from his inside pocket, and the room quieted in anticipation. He sipped from the glass, his face twisted in distaste.

"Ah. That's better. Now where were we?" He consulted the papers in front of him again and narrowed his eyes as he read the file. "Mrs. Imogen Bancroft?"

He looked up at me and I surprised myself with the confidence in my voice as I acknowledged him. "Yes, sir."

He indicated the chair which Leech had vacated and I stepped past my husband briskly to take my position in front of the jurors. I was aware of the Coroner's voice introducing me as I watched them appraise me.

"This is Mrs. Imogen Bancroft. Daughter of the deceased, wife of John Bancroft of Hampstead, London. Mrs. Bancroft made the third and official identification on the evening of 4th January."

There had been one or two wry smiles at the mention of John and I felt, rather than saw, the look of annoyance on his face at this remark.

"May I remind you that this is a difficult time for Mrs. Bancroft and would respectfully request that you keep your enquiries brief and to the point." Here, he levelled his gaze at both men who had already spoken. He then moved his gaze to me and raised his eyebrows, his voice softening slightly. "Mrs. Bancroft, thank you for your time today, if you are ready then could we begin with your own account of the deceased?" He indicated with his hand that I could begin but I had not been expecting such an open question and could not imagine where to begin. There was an uncomfortable silence marked with the coughing of the clerk and the scraping of a chair. My gaze skipped over all of the faces that waited for me to speak when one of them spoke for me.

"Perhaps you could tell us what kind of a father he was?" the man said kindly. I stared at him, his hair was dark and flecked with grey like the feathers on a starling. My mouth was dry and he smiled at me. The corners of his eyes crinkled with his upturned mouth and I knew he was a father too. I focused on him and no one else as I offered a cautious reply.

"A generous one."

The speckle haired man leaned forward slightly, his eyebrows opening his face into a question urging me to continue. I considered what he was asking, wary of what hidden trap I might be lured into.

"My father was generous with whatever he had to give." I licked my lips to lubricate the words as they formed. 'His time, his money, his love, he would give it all freely and without a scratch on a slate.'

"Hadn't you better say she?"

There were a few stifled sounds of amusement as the comment sank in. It had come from a man I had not appraised up to that point. He was young, roughly attired and slightly grubby looking. He wore an expression of distaste as though there were a smell emanating from his fellow jurors. It was an expression I had encountered before when John and I had visited the small church on the borders of his family's estate at Christmas. It was the look of envy and of disgust rolled in to one. This man was jealous of the wealth I displayed in my clothes, my simple jewellery, in the pallor of my skin, yet at the same time, he was superior to me. Was it not my father and not his that was being picked over in this way. Yet despite this, he would return tomorrow to his life of toil and I would return, in my grief, to my more privileged one. His words were

152

the only way he could, momentarily, redress this balance.

"I beg your pardon," I asked.

"I said, hadn't you better call her a she?" he enunciated each syllable carefully.

The words stung me and I felt my cheeks grow warm.

"No sir. I will never say she."

The young man sneered at me, his arms folded across his chest, a ready retort upon his lips.

"Now then, we'll have enough of that if you please." The Coroner flashed the young man a warning glare and gradually indicated to the speckle haired man to proceed

"You were close to your father?" he continued.

My heart skipped a beat and it was all I could do not to look at the shape of my father's body under the cover of the sheet in the centre of the room. Of course I had been close to him, growing up he was the king of our family castle. My mother ruled my world but father was king and how I loved him. Kind and strong, strict and funny, it seemed there was nobody he couldn't be. When John came into my world, I found John could also be many of those things and of course, when I married, my father's role in my life was diminished but not vanished. Contrary to John's belief, my father had still been king. As I pondered this, I wondered whether this was normal. Would the men before me see something in our relationship which was unsavoury, unsatisfactory. I looked to Geoffrey for assistance. He too wore an expression of mild benevolence and, instead of fearing the question, I allowed my answer come naturally.

"I always thought I was closer to my mother."

As I suspected, there was an audible acknowledgement and several of the men made notes in their matching notepads.

"My mother and I were more alike you see. As a child, she was more involved in my daily care. Whilst we had a nanny, it was my mother who brushed and plaited my hair at bedtimes. Of course, Father and I would play when he had the time but mother and I would talk about anything and everything. We talked of pretty shoes and of handsome knights from days of old. Whenever I think of her, my ears tingle with the memory of her voice. We would talk about anything. Anything at all. But with father it was different; we didn't seem to need to talk. We would weave hours of silence into an invisible shield, that even mother could not find us beneath. Mother and I spent most of our time together but it was a relationship we always worked at. Whereas father and I just belonged together, it is as easy as recalling a fond memory."

My eyes had been scanning the room sightlessly, as I had tried to put words to the strength of bond I never appreciated I had with my father, when I realised I was staring at John. He looked at me curiously like I had been describing a lover instead of a father and again, I felt guarded.

"Thank you Mrs. Bancroft." The Coroner broke the spell and I glanced at the speckled hair man who was still smiling paternally at me. "Forgive me for speaking so plainly, though for the record we must ask. Had you any notion that the deceased was ever in disguise Mrs. Bancroft?"

154

"None," I replied curtly. In contrast to the last question, I had been anticipating exactly this line of thought and even the raised eyebrows from the men in front of me that followed. I had expected even a snort or two of derision, from the young man at the end but not from John. Even the Coroner looked slightly incredulous as my husband shuffled uncomfortably to hide his outburst.

"No notion, whatsoever? There was no hint of a double life of which you were aware? No peculiar habits?" he added.

A double life! That struck me as laughable. When my father was usually up to his eyes in the day to day running of his one busy life? As for habits, this had taken me a little by surprise. How do you suppose one would know what a strange habit consists of? That John must take off his left shoe before his right has always seemed compulsive but not unusual? Did my father have any habits which may have indicated to us that he was hiding a dark secret?

"What kind of habits do you mean?"

The Coroner continued, "The details are a little delicate but of course what we are trying to establish is how this business came to pass and how..."

"What kind of habits do you mean?"

"Well, it was evident from the post mortem that....the deceased was.....er.... in possession of female reproductive organs and we can therefore conclude that she...er.....that the deceased would have had......." The coroner, so used to dealing with the dead, was struggling to communicate with the living. "...would have had.....monthly courses," he concluded eventually. Scanning the rest of the room, there were a number of men who looked blankly at one another. Rolling his eyes, he added, "The concealment of a monthly course from everyone in the household I would imagine to be very difficult."

I was aware that he was waiting for me to respond to this deduction but the thought was so peculiar, so alien to me that I simply could not acknowledge it. After several minutes of silence, he moved on to his next line of investigation.

"Mrs. Bancroft, I know that this is very difficult for you but you must understand that the records held by the Public Record Office must be irrefutable. In this room, we have several questionable facts that must be righted and it is the job of the men before you, and myself to record the truth."

My face must have shown some of the confusion I felt. Several questionable facts? That my father had concealed his gender was disputable but what else was being analysed here? The coroner removed his glasses and rubbed the bridge of his nose with a tired but practiced gesture.

"Mrs. Bancroft. If it is the finding of this inquest, and believe me, I find little to suggest that it would not be so, that the person you believed to be your father was female, then I am afraid, your own birth certificate must be considered void, as too, shall be the marriage certificate, both of which have been used by the deceased on a number of official contracts." He waited whilst some of the meaning penetrated my now spinning mind. "Mrs. Bancroft, have you considered who your real father is likely to have been?"

Of all the things I expected to be aired in that room, despite my utter acceptance of what was now

156

incontrovertible, I honestly had not considered that question. My father lay before me on that table. The thought that, in fact, he was a stranger to me, chilled me and I blinked into the silence, my face flushed.

"And your mother?" he added.

I jerked my heard around to face the man full on.

"My mother?" I repeated.

He looked apologetically at me and indicated the paperwork in front of him.

"Mrs. Bancroft, it is entirely plausible that if the deceased concealed her identity and that the woman posing as her wife was complicit in the deceit, which we must assume," he added as I opened my mouth to defend her. "...then it would not be entirely improbable that your own identity is in doubt."

"Now just hang on a minute!" John erupted. "My wife is not the one on trial here, she is an innocent in this."

"Thank you, sir. This is not a trial of any sorts. Please remain seated. We are merely trying, for good order sake, to unravel this mess."

"This is absurd!" Geoffrey joined in. He too was rattled by the methodical dismantling of the Silver family.

"Please. Can we please remain calm. Mr. Leech, you of all people must see the possibility of what I am suggesting?"

"I see exactly what you are suggesting and this is a rum show Mr. Barrowclough, a poor show indeed. Can't you see that the poor girl has just lost the only father she has ever known and now you are trying to take her mother away too. For shame."

157

There was some murmured agreement and interest from the group of jurors as Leech worked himself into a shrill pitch. His face was pink with the excitement and John was attempting to get him to take his seat.

"Thank you Mr. Leech. Gentlemen," he added more loudly as the murmurs rose. He waited for silence before continuing, his attention back on me. "Thank you Mrs. Bancroft. I can see the toll that this," he paused to find a neutral word, "this affair is having on you and I must confess, I am a little in need of a break myself. Gentlemen we will break for lunch and reconvene in an hour to go over the remaining evidence. Thank you again Mr. and Mrs. Bancroft, Mr. Leech, you are free to leave."

And that was it. There was murmuring as the jurors gathered their jackets or notes and filed slowly out of the room. I was aware that Geoffrey and John had come to my side to escort me from the room but when I tried to take my feet, I found all my reserves had been drained and I slipped sidelong to the floor. The last thing I saw, as my eyes rolled upwards and I slipped into darkness, was the flaking stucco ceiling painted in a scene from Genesis. There was a blue cloaked figure painted centrally, shrouded by a yellow aura of light; around him there were stars and planets as the heavens burst across a virgin sky.

In the beginning, God created the heaven and the earth. And the earth was without form, and void; and darkness was upon the face of the deep. And the spirit of God moved upon the face of the waters. And God said, "Let there be light": and there was light.

Chapter Ten - Avery, 1869

It would be a good few days before Avery could leave the house again. He had indeed met with his father that morning who had proffered what he had hoped would be good news. The widow Fearncott and he had plans to marry. Toby Silver was not surprised by his daughter's lack of jubilation at the news. Since his wife's death, his guilt had manifested itself as an over protective streak which kept the girl from gaining independence. As a result, he was left with a daughter who, so far as he knew, had no friends and only left the house to drop in on the needy or to visit the museums and who would, no doubt, remain a spinster under his care until his death. He had accepted this as his burden and only wished that she would find some joy in this new episode of his life.

"I don't expect that this is totally unexpected news and I hope that you will spend the remaining few months before we are to marry, to get to know Mrs. Fearncott a little better." Toby brushed a stray wisp of hair from his brow.

Avery observed his father neutrally, wondering how this turn of events could be factored in to his own fast changing plans for his future.

"I am sure your choice of bride is none of my concern father, how the two of you do together is..."

"For God's sake Alice don't be so damned sterile about this. Mrs. Fearncott is to be family. She is to be my wife and, if you allow it, she could become a close second to Mother."

He let the words hang in the air for a few moments before chasing them down, in another attempt to persuade his daughter of the benefits on offer to them both.

"Georgina is a charming woman Alice and she informs me that you are not too old to take your own place in society, hmm?"

The old man eyed his daughter hopefully but was met with a look of disgust on Avery's face. As the words fell from the air, the frost lingered. This had already been a topic of discussion. Toby had tried to press upon his daughter, the importance of her prominence on the society scene, in order to secure a husband, but had been met with such anger that he had failed to force the matter beyond an awkward conversation. Avery's silence was an improvement on the normal hostility with which such a suggestion was met and, foolishly, Toby was cheered a little.

"There now you see, perhaps you would like to attend the ballet with us one evening?"

Toby had already begun to bury himself in to the newspaper and was oblivious to Avery's contemptuous look.

Of course, Avery was far from pleased with the news and was dreading the fact that the Widow Fearncott wanted to get to know him better. Thus far, Mrs. Fearncott had not been a regular visitor to the Silver house. Evidently, it was more convenient for Toby Silver to visit her in her own home. According to Kate, they were also to be seen together most frequently at dinner, the ballet or the opera and Mr. Silver had spent a small fortune on the woman. Most of the social circuit upon which the two flitted would not be surprised about their marriage and many, Avery acknowledged, would also be hoping a woman's impression upon the household would bring changes to Avery's future. A lunch had been planned for the following day and Toby had insisted that his daughter be suitably presented for an introduction to his future wife. As the time of Georgina's arrival approached, Avery showed little sign of getting ready and had sullenly taken to his room. He was beginning to grow concerned that if this woman took too much of an interest in the way he was living his life, she could jeopardise the fragile plans which he was busy forming.

Kate too seemed concerned, but not about the future. The young maid dealt mainly in the present and she had looked at Avery that morning as if trying to appraise him as the Widow would later do. By the look upon her face she had seen much to disapprove of. Kate had therefore taken it upon herself to select an outfit that would neither impress the widow nor 'let the side down'.

"You'd best not draw too much attention to yourself" she had argued. "You don't want her thinking you can't look after yourself, do you? If she thinks that grey thing is the best thing in your cupboard then she might want to take you shopping for new clothes."

As her voice became muffled from within the huge mahogany cabinet, Avery suspected that Kate enjoyed busying herself with his clothes. The dresses, that caused him discomfort and forced him into facing the world as the woman he was not, were a source of great joy to her.

"Ah! Here we go. This one is perfect." She pulled out a navy blue dress, it was simple as all Avery's female clothes were but he knew Kate thought it an elegant outfit and he often caught her admiring it. He stood wincing as she helped him dress, prickling visibly as if the fabric cut into his skin where it constricted his body. Kate said nothing but just busied herself, affixing a hairpiece to adapt his unruly hair.

"Does she have any children of her own?" Kate asked.

This had not occurred to Avery and he was suddenly filled with a horror that the acquisition of a stepmother might also herald an extended family all of whom would, no doubt, busy themselves with his welfare and future prospects. The thought was a dire one and his growing sense of unease was all at once evident to Kate. She tried to make it okay again by answering her own question

"I don't think she does actually. Now that I think of it, I'm quite sure she hasn't. We would have heard already if she had."

She finished brushing through his hair and stepped back to appraise the job. Her face was unreadable but Avery sensed her forming a question.

"What is it Kate?"

She shook her head and turned away.

"It's nothing. Honestly...It's just…"

"Just what Kate??

"This won't change anything, will it?"

It was a clumsy question but Avery loved her for asking it. Just as he had begun to feel alone again with his concerns, she assured him that he was not. In reply he turned to face her.

"Everything is changing Kate."

162

The girl's face clouded with a confused look and to save himself from any further discussion, he swept out of the room to meet his father downstairs to greet Georgina Fearncott.

It was a mixture of a formal and informal greeting. Avery's father was barely recognisable as the dour, quiet man that Avery knew. He positively beamed with delight when introducing Mrs. Fearncott and he waited expectantly for his fiancé's approval of his daughter. The daughter he barely knew.

"Georgina my dearest, this is my daughter, Alice."

"Alice," he hesitated as if to add an affectionate term but did not, "this is Mrs. Georgina Fearncott. Your mother to be," he added in a boyish tone, delighted with his own wit. It was as if he had brought home a prize. He was obviously pleased with himself. He waited for Avery's expression to mirror his own delight. It did not come. Though Avery was genuinely moved by his father's delight it merely marked out his own unhappiness more acutely.

"A pleasure to meet you, Mrs. Fearncott. I would like to say that I have heard much about you but I am afraid my father has kept you rather a secret. If only I knew you a *little* better it should be an improvement."

Georgina Fearncott's eyes glittered with disapproval. She had taken in Avery's appearance from the moment she entered the room and now, at close quarters, she was able to study Avery more exactly. She was quick to respond to his cool greeting as warmly as she could, simply to placate Toby.

163

"Darling Toby, you never told me Alice was so," she made a short play of searching for the right word, "tall." She selected after a moment.

Toby glowered at Avery as if it were his daughter's fault that nothing appealing could be found to say. This was not starting off as Toby had expected. The three of them were saved from any immediate conversation as the arrival of Jamieson, to serve drinks, presented a welcome intrusion.

"I must say Toby, your home is quite beautiful. These sketches are very impressive." Georgina had wandered to the small bureau that had been Toby's wife's and had picked up some drawings. "Are these yours, Alice?" she did not look around.

"Sadly not Mrs. Fearncott. I do not draw."

"Indeed?" The older woman turned slightly and raised an eyebrow towards Toby before replacing the sketches and continuing her tour of the room.

"What is exactly that you do on your father's good will, Alice?" she still failed to meet Avery eye to eye. Avery was beginning to get the measure of how this woman's opinion was already being formed of him and he was not overly keen to dispel this immediately. Until he was able to more fully form his plan, he could not afford to waste his energy on turf wars with Georgina Fearncott.

"Oh, Mrs. Fearncott! There are a good many ways in which someone in search of self-improvement may usefully be employed in this city other than simply drawing! I could show you some of the charitable works I have been researching in some of the more deprived areas of our great capital?"

Mrs. Fearncott's slightly curled lip was reply enough for the time being to assure Avery that the woman had no intention of being friends.

"But of course. This will no doubt prove very useful to your future husband how?" she countered.

Toby waded in at this point, not to spare Avery any awkward questions but rather because his stomach indicated that food was being served in the dining room.

"Georgina darling? Shall we?" he offered his arm and led his fiancée through to the dining room.

Avery followed behind watching his father's neck flush red as Georgina leant close to him and whispered upwards in to his ear. He glanced behind him at Avery as they walked and nodded in approval to the widow. Although quite unaware of exactly what had been said, Avery was not expecting it to be good news.

After the first course had been served, the widow continued with her cross examination.

"Your father tells me you don't yet enjoy the finer entertainments that our beautiful city has to offer?"

Avery considered the most recent entertainments of which he had partaken and wondered what Mrs. Fearncott would have made of Bateman and Goodwin's idea of fun.

"If by finer entertainments you mean the ballet or the theatre then no Mrs. Fearncott, I am more inclined to reading."

"Really? What do you read?"

The last time Avery had read a suitable book which he could discuss with his father's fiancée, had been at least six years ago, being Gulliver's Travels.

Avery had been expecting just this and was pleased not to have been caught unaware.

"I am reading a fetching story by Elizabeth Gaskell at the moment, perhaps you have heard of it? Lois the Witch?" a faint smile played across Avery's lips.

His choice of reading material evidently did not meet with approval and was met with a cold stare.

"I am not familiar with her work."

"Why don't you tell Alice about your summer plans darling?" Toby started to help himself from the open tureen of sliced pork.

For a moment, Mrs. Fearncott considered Avery as if judging how best to frame the opportunity.

"Well, as your father may have already told you, I very rarely spend summer in the city. I find the heat in town quite oppressive," she flapped her hands around her face as if to illustrate the predicament she wished to escape. "Since your father has a lot of business between now and November, I had intended to go to my family home in Chalfont St Giles to spend some time in final preparation for the wedding." She made an attempt to look conspiratorially at Avery but the gesture lost a little something in translation. "I have invited my niece to come along with me for a break. You are about the same age. I am sure you would find plenty in common with one another."

"Georgina wanted to spend a little time getting to know you, Alice." her father interjected.

"Amersham has a fine, if small, society scene and I am positive your presence would be met with a good deal of ...interest."

"I am sure my father would rather I stay to help him here with any arrangements."

"Nonsense girl! You will go to Chalfont St Giles with Mrs. Fearncott and her niece and the three of you will have a marvellous time."

Avery's heart sank and he gritted his teeth as thoughts of a summer spent languishing in his newly acquired identity began to dissolve before his eyes.

"But father?"

"But father nothing," Toby Silver smiled benevolently as he tucked his napkin in. His life was falling in to place at last. A wife to fill his home and someone else to worry after his daughter. With any luck, this break could be the making of the girl. Could he even dare to hope that the child might find a suitor whilst in the country? He played down Avery's further protests with a shake of his head and turned his attention instead to Jamieson.

"Break out some wine man, this calls for a celebration."

~o~

As he stormed past Kate two hours later, Avery was in a foul mood. He was dressed and changed to go out within twenty minutes. Kate, alarmed by his mood, was concerned that he would not take the usual care in concealing his escape.

"Just wait why don't you? Your father only left a moment ago. What if he comes back?"

"I have to see someone," he growled as he paced behind the door. "Will you just please go and check the hall."

"Who do you have to see?" she ventured.

"For God's sake, Kate, please!"

"I just don't see what the hurry is that's all." She walked away from the door to look out of the window. "If you could only wait until it was dark..." she squeaked as he grabbed her from behind and pressed her against him.

"What are...?"

Avery forced his lips to hers. Taken by surprise, Kate struggled and pushed against his chest, moving her face from his.

"Avery!"

He was taller and stronger and easily pressed Kate back up against the wall. She turned her face upwards, as if to welcome his embrace, and he swallowed her lips in his own in a hungry kiss. His hands cupped her face and her heels were lifted from the ground, her back against the wall and her toes at a stretch to meet her tall mistress. Avery felt a powerful urge to push his hands up under her skirts and to grab handfuls of flesh to draw towards him and as soon as he thought so, he felt sick with fear. He knew that Kate did not choose for him to do this to her; that she was reliant upon him for her livelihood and that he was abusing her trust in him. He pushed himself off the wall, balling his fist at the anger that surged in him at his father, at Georgina Fearncott, at his own body. As the temper continued to rise up in him, he saw Kate, her beautiful face clouded with confusion. He knew he disgusted her and he turned on his heels, in a moment he had left the room. Discovery or not, he needed an outlet for his anger and he needed it then.

"The girl that was with you that night in the alley, who is she?"

Connie looked quizzically at Avery as he watched her re-dress. She was no longer as wary as she had been about his proposition and she found she looked forward to his visits. As yet, there had been no actual intercourse between them with Avery preferring to watch her touch herself and talk loudly of the things she liked and disliked a man to do to her. She had begun to grow comfortable around him and had taken a real pleasure in having him touch her for a change. He took instruction well and she had delighted in being at the centre of her own pleasure for once.

"Sarah?" she asked "Blonde, little thing?"

Avery coloured as her enquiring eyes latched on to the meaning of his enquiry. She laughed as she slipped on her blouse and leant across the side of her bed to retrieve the flask she kept her gin within. Her skirt was still hitched high and Avery looked away as he caught a flash of her dark pubic hair slick with her own juices. It was a pointless gesture as he had just watched Connie spreading them wide before pushing a thick dildo inside herself. For the last twenty minutes he had clambered on the bed beside her and taken the thick baton and continued to stir at her taking a nipple in his mouth and toying with the puckered flesh between his teeth until she grabbed him by the neck and forced him into her chest. He found himself so engrossed during the act that he forgot entirely that the woman was not Kate and the flash of her sex afterwards made him feel shabby. Far from satisfying him, these excursions were replacing his desire with something far more dangerous; ambition This evening he had been close to pulling out the phallus he had had fashioned for himself and placing this inside her but for some reason he was too shy to do it, despite his great urge.

"Sorry, Sarah, yes what of her."

Annoyed with the way her eyes danced in amusement at his discomfort, he threw the coins he had counted out on the bed beside her.

"I'd like you to arrange for her services. Here," he added.

The gesture was crude and Connie was insulted. Although fully aware of the role she played for him, she had felt less like he was a customer. There would never be any trust between them but she was not afraid of him. She was about to snap back at him but she was afraid of losing her meal ticket. Avery had paid double the going rate recently simply to watch her at work with another man, to take lessons or, like today, to simply bring her to a climax while she whispered the same old lines in his ear that she did with all her men. Connie was amused and intrigued by Avery but, most importantly, he paid her well. It was therefore a surprise that she felt a little jealous by his enquiry after Sarah. A far less experienced and sharper looking girl, it seemed like a slight against her and, for some reason, she felt it more keenly from this strange woman than any man.

"And what's wrong with me?" She felt hot as her cheeks flushed and she thought suddenly of all the instruction she had been giving him over the last weeks, she compared his inexpert fumblings with how skilled his touch had been this evening and she felt both proud but protective. She glowered beneath her fringe, ashamed at being slighted.

Avery stumbled over his apology not wishing to either offend Connie or threaten her loyalty upon which he depended.

"Nothing" he said "nothing at all. It's just...she..."

He was embarrassed that he should be asking at all and he combed his hair with his fingers waiting for Connie to say something. Though she wanted to hear some apology, some reason for his preference, she was also tired and wanted some time to herself for a change.

"Be here next week at 9. I'm sure she would love the opportunity to earn some extra cash."

Relieved, Avery gathered up the rest of his things and turned to leave.

"What shall I tell her?" she asked.

"Tell her nothing and it will be worth some extra cash for you."

As Avery turned and left, closing the door behind him, he did not hear Connie's words.

"Oh yes, you're a man alright. Arrogant pig."

~o~

As he woke up the next morning, he knew he would have to apologise to Kate for storming out as he had. He was embarrassed about how this would be received. He had expected his actions to have brought Kate's normally positive and cheerful disposition to a temper yet, to his surprise, she managed to act as if nothing had happened.

"Quite how you manage to get these clothes so grubby in only a few hours in town is beyond me. Why, your father could wear most of his clothes for days without so much as a brush down but then he doesn't kick them off all over the room like you do."

"Kate, stop folding those damned clothes and look at me for a minute."

The girl's shoulders tensed and for the first time since she had entered the room that morning, she stopped talking. She turned, clutching the trousers she had picked up from the floor tightly to her stomach. He noticed immediately the dark shadows beneath her eyes as if she had not slept for many nights.

"Kate? Are you alright?"

She looked surprised. This was obviously not the enquiry she had expected, nor was it what Avery had intended to say, but the look of her so drawn and tired had shocked him.

"Sit down. Here." He stood up and stepped forward to press the girl into a seat. He took the trousers from her fingers and noticed at once that she was trembling. He imagined she was scared of him and the thought made him sick to the stomach.

"It's okay." He tried to hold her gaze; to assure her. "Kate I am so sorry about yesterday. I don't know how to make this up to you. You must think me most shameful. I cannot think how much you must hate me."

Kate's eyes met his, fiercely and she reached out to take his hand in her own.

"Avery. I don't hate you. Oh, I could never hate you."

The tone of her voice took him aback and he felt his fingers tingle at her touch. He searched her face for a clue as to why she trembled so and he could only see his own desire projected across her trusting face.

"I don't know why you left so angry yesterday but if you would only tell me what you want I could help you.' She paused as he turned his face away but she reached up with her free hand and held his face in her direction. 'Haven't I shown you my loyalty already? Haven't I done everything you've asked of me?"

"Yes," his voice was quiet and he waited as she continued with her plea.

"Then tell me what you want?"

Avery was alert to the thudding in his chest as his heart quickened at the sight of her. He was also aware that what he wanted was far from what she had in mind and he chastened his lips tightly before stepping away from her in one swift movement. Whilst he trusted Kate implicitly, there was still part of his own mind that could not accept what it was he wanted. In order to have it, he would need to abandon everything he knew and face an uncertain future. He did not yet know whether he could ask someone else to face that kind of fate on his account.

"I don't know, Kate."

His eyes lingered over her for a moment and then he stood, smiling broadly, and declared. 'I want you to have the day off and I want kippers for breakfast!'

Though she smiled at him in return, it was a mechanical gesture and she offered him no complicity with it. It did not look like she wanted the day off nor to serve him kippers or porridge or devilled eggs, she looked for all the world as if she had not finished with the conversation. Avery, though, had finished and, clearly frustrated, Kate picked up the ewer of water from beside his bed and stalked out of the room without another word, the door closing with an angry bang.

~o~

When Kate returned that evening, though officially due an evening off, she came straight to the drawing room to talk with Avery. She entered the room, looked around to ensure they were alone, and closed the door behind herself, turning the key in the lock.

"We've been discovered!" she stated simply.

"What do you mean '*discovered*'? By whom?"

It was then that he noticed she was shaking a little, from fear or anger it was hard to tell, but he made her sit down in the chair opposite his own.

"Sit here. I will pour you a drink and then you shall tell me what has happened."

As Avery handed her a glass of port, she did not even flicker with any recognition of the impropriety that her own mistress be serving her a drink. Instead, she took a long gulp and began to recount her day.

"I knew Mrs. Druce wouldn't be pleased with you asking for kippers this morning. She hadn't planned it and she was in a foul mood. She has been trying to get information out of me for weeks about what you are up to. It's not gone unnoticed by the rest of the house that you seem to keep to your room most evenings when your father is out. I suppose some of them think you a little melancholic but I have been trying to reassure them that you are reading or having some of your 'headaches' again.

"*It's not as if I should be expected to keep kippers on hand for some girl's whimsy. If this is how she behaves, it's no wonder that she has no prospect of a husband. Sure enough how could he keep up?"*

Kate's impression of Mrs. Druce was quite canny and when she glanced up to see Avery's response, he looked only bemused.

"I know, I know but it's how she talks, but she held her tongue after that, muttering into her great big chest. I would have said something but I couldn't trust myself not to speak out of turn. So I just ignored her. The kitchen was full of people. Mary-Ann and Jane were at some chore or other and I could feel them looking at me. Their disapproving looks. That Mary-Ann has had it in for me since the minute I got here. She's jealous and she's been needling me about your 'headaches'. So she turned from the sink and gave me a proper look. I wasn't feeling in a good mood myself and I wanted to get out of the house. So I told them that you'd given me the day off and Oh Goodness, the stir that caused! I had thought about making something up, like an errand or something, to stop them being jealous but I felt peevish after you and I...."'Kate stopped and changed tack. "After the look that Mary-Ann had thrown my way. I was not surprised when she sidled up to me and said *"You must be looking forward to a day on your own for a change?"*

"Now, she is not the friendliest of creatures and something in her voice put me on alert but, not being in the mood for game, said nothing. I simply rolled down my sleeves, reached past her for a cloth to dry my hands and nodded. She stepped out of my way and, raising her voice to address the rest of the room, added *"Mrs. Druce, if you still need those cloves I could nip off*

175

with Kate, here and pop over to Wilsons?" Mrs. Druce barely registered her, still muttering as she was and just nodded. So Mary-Ann whipped off her apron and rounded on me. *"Hang about Miss Ward, I'll only be a minute and I can walk with you up to the Earl's Court Road."*

"To be honest with you, I had not really wanted to leave that morning but now that Mary-Ann was intent on tagging along, I was keen to get away quickly, and preferably without her following me. As we left the house, she kept looking at me strangely and, I'll admit, she made me feel quite uncomfortable. A few moments later we were shoulder to shoulder headed up the Gloucester Road. The whole way she didn't say a word but just kept looking at me as we walked. There was something in that silence that was more threatening than some of her sharpest retorts and I just wanted to get rid of her.

"I suppose you want to get on?" I said as we reached the junction with the Cromwell Road. I made to veer off left but Mary-Ann pressed alongside me again.

"What's the hurry?" she said. *"Old Mrs. Druce takes an hour to walk to Wilson's and I can make it in ten minutes so I figure I have at least an hour to kill before they'll miss me. What do you say to a little wander up to Mrs. Flatts?"* She flashed me a chummy grin and hooked her arm through mine. *"Unless you have other errands to run?"'*

"I couldn't see an easy way out of it so I allowed myself to be led in the opposite direction. I walked in silence, listening to Mary-Ann's stream of chatter about tourists before we arrived at the tea rooms. It all seemed so inane, I wondered whether or not I was mistaken about her. We ordered some tea and a moment later we were sat together with two cups. Horrible grey stuff it is too and I was just about to say as much when the mood changed.

"She treats you like an absolute skivvy you know"' she avoided my eyes and spooned a third sugar into her cup, slowly stirring after each one. *"I know, ours is a life or service but you haven't taken a day off in eight weeks."* Then she looked up at me and stared hard. *"It's almost as if she has something over you"'*

"It wasn't a surprise, she has suggested worse before now but it's usually been in passing or as part of her usual insults. Being so close in that room caught me by surprise and I found myself answering truthfully.

"And what if she has?" I said.

"Oh, Avery, the words were out before I had chance to catch them. She watched me for a while in silence then looked down to her cup which she stirred for a few moments before raising it to her lips. She spoke quietly before taking a sip. *"And where does her young man factor in all of this?"*

Avery's brows shot up in surprise. He had been listening to Kate tell her story and he had been expecting the worst but this line of enquiry was completely out of the blue. It was of course a nonsense and, for a moment, he felt he could laugh but Kate continued.

"I was as confused as you look now Avery so I said to her. "Young man?" and I tried to keep my face neutral but I barely had to fake my surprise. Trust me,

Mary-Ann is many things, but she is not green and I felt she was trying to play me again. Either way she did not try to stifle her amusement very well.

> *"'Young man? What young man? Only the young man you admit to the house three or more times a week!'"* She barely kept her voice down and I was forced to look around to see who might have heard.

"'Will you keep your voice down!'"

"Well, that was all she needed as confirmation and she leant in closer before adding *"I hope the young Miss knows what risk you take on her account and rewards you well?"*

Avery was stunned. Their secret was out, of a sort. He sat dazed for a few moments before it dawned on him that Mary-Ann had not discovered their secret but had misinterpreted the late night comings and goings for something else entirely.

"What did you say then?" he enquired of Kate who had fallen silent. Evidently, she was waiting for some sort of eruption from Avery but he felt entirely calm.

"Well Mary-Ann had leaned back in her chair and begun to sip her tea. She had a look about her as if she had struck gold. She knew it and she was going to wait patiently for me to make her an offer."

"An offer?" Avery interrupted.

"Of course! She isn't about to keep your secret for nothing you know. My head swam. I had to think fast. She thinks that you are entertaining some fancy man up here alone in your room."

The reality of the danger into which this news now placed them began to dawn on Avery and his face fell.

"Continue." He rose and walked to the window to watch the sun fade from the square beneath him.

"Well, you don't know Mary-Ann like I do, but she couldn't resist the opportunity to gloat, to sharpen her tongue on the situation.

'*"To be honest, I didn't think the young miss was capable of catching a man. I was half expecting her to end up like old Miss Beckett."* - The spinster who lives next door.' Kate added in case Avery did not know.

'*"I must say, she is certainly a dark horse, ain't she? What would her father say if he knew?'* She raised an eyebrow and cocked her head. '*Jus think of all that extra wear and tear on your feet running up and down those stairs an extra dozen times a day. I know I would want to be recompensed for that."* She had leaned back and started to count on her fingers. *"There's the price of shoe leather, less sleep, fewer holidays and the danger money."*

"'Alright!" I had flared. "I'll give you half a shilling if you'll keep your trap shut."

'*"A shilling and I will see what I can do."*

"And that was that, she took the shilling, smug as you like, and stalked out of that tea shop like a high class cat."

"A shilling?" Avery intoned quietly as he continued his vigil at the window.

"She'll want more, sir. Lots more."

He nodded as he tried to think of how to manage this latest turn of events. For the moment, he would fund Kate to pay Mary-Ann's silence but he would need to make a decision soon about his future.

~o~

The following week Avery retraced his steps to Connie's room. He knocked at the door and waited until Connie appeared. She looked pleased to see him, her hair was brushed and she was not dressed for the street. She seemed more relaxed than the last time. She was not working tonight.

"Come in, Sarah is upstairs."

She stepped back into the narrow corridor to allow Avery in ahead of her. Avery removed his hat and made his way up the, now familiar, staircase taking care over the steps which were rotten. He pushed the door at the top of the stairs. The room was warm once again. Connie could afford to take a few days off and it showed. The room felt a little more lived in. There were drinks and the remnants of a half chicken meal perched on an old table. This evening it appeared as though he had arrived uninvited.

He turned to watch her enter the room and recognised the surprise he had not noticed downstairs. The room was well lit and seated on the bed was Sarah. In the light of the room she bore very little resemblance to Kate after all. There were similarities, she was petite and her hair was worn in a similar style. The girls' skin was waxen and pock marked where Kate's was milky and smooth. She did not look very healthy and her eyes were cold. Still she smiled when Avery nodded to her. Where Connie had been dressed for warmth and comfort, Sarah was dressed for work. Though her shawl and bonnet had been discarded and she had taken the liberty of removing her boots, her feet tucked up underneath her on Connie's bed. Avery wondered how long she had been there and what they had been discussing? How well they knew each other? How well either of them could be trusted.

"As promised, one girl delivered to your service. Sir." The tone was unmistakably bitter but he didn't take his eyes from Sarah. He considered the younger girl for a moment before nodding.

"Leave us."

Avery moved to the window to look down on the street below as Connie collected her coat and hat, muttering all the while before leaving disgruntled. He stayed at the window listening to her footfall on the steps below until the door beneath him opened onto the street and she stepped out. He watched as she glanced upwards at the window whereupon she saw him watching her and she smiled, tipping her bonnet and giving him a wink.

"Well, sir, time is money." Sarah's voice brought him back in to the room. Avery turned to see what his money had bought him.

The girl had arranged herself on the bed. She had begun unbuttoning her blouse. Her breasts, more ample than Kate's, were pushed up by the lacing. At the swell of her chest, there were marks and Avery shuddered as he recognised teeth marks. He was momentarily frozen, as he considered what this woman was and what purpose she served. What other men she put her service to. The thought was a heady mixture of excitement, disgust and pity. For a moment, he considered leaving; discharging his debt and leaving. He turned his hat over in his hands and glanced over at the door.

"Connie said you was shy."

She stood up and moved across the floor to stand in front of him. She was clearly no stranger to this situation. It was not unusual for a man to become intimidated by a working girl but she had coaxed plenty of men into bed and Avery would be no different. Since he had first come into the room, her demeanour had changed. Having noticed that there was something awkward about Avery, she was now firmly in the driving seat. In her line of work, getting things over and done with was the golden rule. She lowered her gaze to his crotch, where Avery could feel the solid form of his rubber cock resting against his thigh. The nerves were exciting him and the anticipation was raising his ardour. Unlike Connie, she moved in a more sultry manner; it was a well-practiced gait that earned her way. Avery could see it as the device it was and it unnerved him, but it achieved its goals. As she approached, she reached to his trousers as Avery expected she would and he caught her hand as he had with Connie before.

"No," he said firmly. He wanted to control this situation and not be dominated. He drew himself up from his shy posture and spun her round so her bottom was nestling into his crotch, rubbing up against the firm shape at his groin. She could feel it, that much was clear and she gave a surprised intake of breath. She trembled a little at the turning of the tables and the shiver that went down her excited Avery. Had he a real cock, it would have grown twice the size. Not being able to see her face in this position he was better able to endow her with the one he wanted and he evoked Kate's image in his mind. He held on to her wrist with his left hand and roughly pushed his hands to her breast. He was immediately transported to one of his dreams where he had done just this to Kate. It seemed second nature to him as he squeezed her chest, a nervous pulse of electricity coursed from his fingertips straight to his groin and he sensed that if he was endowed like a man, he would have just spent his load into his trousers, a sticky mess to be dealt with by Kate hours later. The sensation was overwhelming and perhaps Sarah sensed his release too and she gave her own sigh of relief. Perhaps her own night was over and she had not needed to even lift her skirt? He let go of her wrist and pulled back the hair at her neck, inhaling deeply. There was an unclean, sour smell beneath the overpowering rosewater she used but beneath this was the familiar smell of warm flesh. Hungrily, he reached around and cupped both her breasts. Her anticipation of an easy evening being over, Sarah resigned herself to playing the full works. She put her head back against his shoulder clawing at the back of his neck.

"Oh sir, yes sir," she breathed huskily. These words, whispered so, were her stock and trade. It was what Avery wanted. Was this was what he wanted from Kate? With Sarah before him, he found he was fighting an urge to sink his teeth into her neck, he wanted to be inside her, stirring her, on top of her, making her cry out in delight.

He noticed one of her hands slipped away from his neck and grab his buttocks. She pulled him at the neck and his thighs, closer to her. His groin was grinding against her behind and she could feel something hard prodding her. Instinctively, he grabbed at her wrists and this time spun her to face him. He held her face with the other hand and he forced his mouth onto hers. This time the taste was only sweet. Despite her poor health and marked skin, her lips were soft and, as they parted, her tongue was silky. He had never experienced anything like it. Their mouths entwined, he again felt a surging between his legs and he stumbled forwards until he felt the edge of the bed behind them. When he opened his eyes, he was instantly perturbed not to see Kate's face and his head swam with indecision with what he was about to do.

"Get on your knees," he said quietly.

"I don't take it up the arse, Sir," she stated moodily, her expression clouding over again.

The spell was almost broken but the situation was already so intoxicating, she could have spoken of her mother's prayer mat and Avery would still have pushed her on to the bed. As she slumped forward on to her hands and knees, he lifted her skirt throwing it over her head covering her face so he could unbutton himself. In haste he gripped his member and, following, Connie's instructions, he eased himself gently inside the young girl knelt before him and began to rock slowly. As he varied the length of his stroke, he leant forwards and slid his fingers to the source of the girl's pleasure. Connie had shown him how to please her and she had promised it would be no different with Sarah and, as his fingers slid over the little mound he recognised the moan. After a few minutes they had found a rhythm together and he found himself transported once more to his dreams. Distant at first, a wave of intense pleasure began to grow in his own groin as the straps rubbed across his own sex, bringing him to an unexpected climax. The shock and pleasure was too much and he slumped against Sarah bringing them both to a heap upon the bed.

After a few moments, Avery raised his head from her back and brought himself back to the reality of Connie's room. He was full of a euphoric feeling of pride but also embarrassment. The girls face was turned to the wall and a shadow obscured her features but he could see that her eyes were closed. He was spared further embarrassment as he withdrew himself from between her legs. He swung himself off the side of the bed and hurriedly stooped to compose himself and arrange his clothes. The fronts of his trousers were crumpled and damp and he pushed the wet shaft of his cock back into his pants where it rested warm and heavy. He brushed at his lap, moving in to the candlelight to see better. Behind him he heard the rustle of skirts as Sarah put her own attire in order. Bound by an unexpected intimacy, he felt softer towards her but uncomfortable with himself so exposed. He longed to know if he was adequate, if his performance was believable. If he passed. After a moment, he turned to face her. She was staring at him curiously.

"Con did tell me," she said bluntly. Where before her face was pale, the exertions had put a glow about her and a little warmth in her eyes. "That was your first time weren't it?"

He felt naked beneath her gaze and he nodded

"Well it weren't mine," she added, "with a woman I mean."

Avery's jaw tightened as the unintended insult of her words washed over him like a poisonous draught of air.

"Believe me, I've 'ad plenty of this, that and the other," she added misinterpreting his withdrawal for shame.

She stood at last and busied herself with her laces, tying up the bodice under her ample cleavage.

"When Con told me to come over. She said you was a Tom. A good one mind but a Tom. So there I am expecting a bit of this," she mimed with her little finger, "and you give me some of the other." She groped at the front of his trousers and clutched at the hard rubber cock.

"When you first stuck it in me, I thought I'll kill that Constance Mayweather. She's lied to me but it weren't until I felt it with me hands that I knew you was a Tom and even then I would only have known cos Con told me. I knew a fella once whose cock was so hard and white it was like a bone." She continued laughing and pinning her hair and talking about a good number of men she had 'had' and their cocks.

For her, it was a few throwaway comments, but for Avery it was as if he had just been christened.

~o~

"Your ears must have been burning, Silver."

Bateman's broad grin was becoming a familiar and welcoming sight as Avery swung himself in beside his two friends in the cab. As the door latched behind him, the cab lurched off from their regular rendezvous point at the corner of Flood Street.

"So why is life so dull for the two of you to make me a centre piece of your conversation?"

186

Avery leaned forward off his coat tails and took the hip flask which Goodwin now proffered him in the gloom of the cab.

"Ha! Of course you are right Silver. If we had more interesting news we would accept your chide but, sir, we have heard some tales about you that would make your hair stand on end."

Avery was swigging heartily from the flask but the words choked him and he spluttered into his gloved hands. Bateman, seated beside him took the flask away and beat him on the back.

"Steady man! We can't be wasting good drink now, can we." Bateman did not find Avery's reaction unusual and continued without breaking stride. Goodwin's eyes however settled on Avery's and there they remained as Bateman spoke again.

"So, do you remember that whore we met up with a while back? You might not remember but if my memory serves me correct you got on rather famously. I was surprised Goodwin remembered at all, he was two sheets to the wind that night!" Bateman nudged Avery and winked at him, jeering at Goodwin as he spoke. "That young blonde I had, you had your eye on as well."

"Sarah," Avery whispered.

"That's right!" Bateman acknowledged. "I knew you'd remember her."

The cheer which had accompanied Avery from leaving the house that afternoon immediately dissipated.

"Well, I was ...er....at a loose end last night. Old Goodwin here had to stay in with mummy." Bateman pulled a face at his friend. "And I found myself around the seven dials with some spare cash and I don't mind if I do, but this girl comes over to me and at first I don't recognise her. She spins me the line that she's seen me before and, believe me Silver, I was sold without any of the extra talk. Why I didn't notice it that night but she has a finer figure than Connie."

"Get on with it!" Goodwin urged. Avery noticed that Goodwin was still staring at him hard, his expression a little strange. His stomach was knotted tight around a ball of fear inside him.

"Alright, alright. So anyway, I was sore tempted even without a few jars to have a quickie in the alley but she said she had a room so I followed her. It wasn't the Halcyon by any standards but I was hardly paying first class rates. Anyway, anyway," he continued noticing Goodwin's impatient face. "She tried talking to me again but frankly by this stage, I was damned near to bursting and I had her on the floor. Twice," he added leveling a frank stare at the both of his friends.

Avery had a vivid picture of the route which Bateman had taken to Sarah's room having become a regular visitor himself. He could imagine the way Sarah's hips swayed as she preceded him up the narrow staircase to her room and he could sympathise with the limited staying power Bateman had possessed once the door had closed behind them. He could even see now how she would have been positioned on the floor, her skirt thrown over her head as Bateman worked his, now stiff cock, in between the lips of her cunny, pushing his way hard inside her. She would have let out a muffled cry which she had worked on. Connie had shared with Avery how noises often helped the girls bring men on more quickly to their climax.

188

Within a few strokes, her own juices would have started to flow and, well greased, Bateman would have spent his load quite quickly. Whether he had managed to achieve this twice was doubtful but Avery was not concerned with his friends' stamina. What he was interested in was why Goodwin was looking at him so keenly and what Sarah might have told Bateman.

"As I was getting dressed, I noticed she was watching me. Can't blame the woman of course! She said she knew me again and then brought up that night. Said she knew a friend of mine. I thought she was talking about Goodwin of course and I apologised on his behalf. Unfortunately, not all men were created equal."

Goodwin rolled his eyes and aimed a cuff at his friend from across the cab before leaning back, a blush on his cheeks but all the while watching Avery still. There followed a silence as now both men watched Avery for his reaction to this story so far.

"And?" Avery finally spoke.

"As if you didn't know!" Bateman exclaimed. "So the truth is out and he still claims ignorance." Bateman threw his hands in to the air in mock exasperation before leaning in conspiratorially. "So it seems our young Silver has made himself a new friend and do you know what your friend told me."

Avery's hand was gripped tightly around the door handle of the cab, one eye was on the door as they slowed at a junction and one eye on Bateman and Goodwin who now loomed at him from the half-light.

"Turns out you are a dark horse indeed sir." Bateman nudged him hard. "Miss Sarah tells me that you are the '*biggest*' customer she has ever had!"

With that, he cracked his own leg hard with his palm and began to laugh. 'Don't look so surprised Silver, why she told me that you nearly poked the back of her throat when you took her on the same rug I did!' Bateman slapped Avery on the back again and congratulated him. 'You old dog!'

Avery was confused, in between the relief and shock, he felt his face form into a smile and he heard his own chest rumbling with laughter but his eyes remained impassive as he tried to take in his narrow escape. He owed Sarah a sharp rebuke and a reward in equal measure, certainly the admiration which Bateman now bestowed upon him seemed worthy of a few extra coins but on the other hand, Goodwin continued to regard Silver oddly and Avery wondered why she had mentioned him in the first place.

As the bravado of the three men reached a crescendo, the cab pulled up at last to their destination in Cleveland Street. The three of them stepped out of the cab, dressed smartly in evening wear all of a similar height and broad slim build.

"Gentlemen! Enough talk of the cheap seats, tonight we are hunting a more exquisite prize. I will wager that by the end of the week, I will have finally persuaded Miss Greenwood to have her wicked way with me."

Goodwin snorted loudly and threw his eyes into the air. Avery knew he would take Bateman's money and Bateman would be no closer to securing the object of his attention for the fourth week running.

"You will never manage it," Goodwin rebuked. "She sounds completely out of your league."

The three men swaggered up the steps to the building in front of them and within a few moments, the door had opened and the three of them had been swallowed inside an orange glow.

Chapter Eleven - Imogen, 1911

In the following weeks, John was proved to be wrong about a lot of things but in one thing he was absolutely correct. By the evening following my father's death, most of the newspapers had run some story about him. True to his word, John had managed to keep the details from permeating most of the headlines but all of them carried the story in some form. When John met with the undertaker the following day, I managed to read one of the less lurid reports.

January 5th 1911, London
Evening Argos
SILVER REVEALS A CLOUD IN LINING
Dead man, Silver found to be a woman. 'Daughter' unaware of Fathers' deceit.

Avery Silver of Hamble Gardens, Parsons Green, magistrate, father, widower and reputable gentleman was reported dead by his housekeeper in the early hours of yesterday morning. An unremarkable man whose demise, whilst sad, would hardly seem noteworthy were it not for the news which followed this bland announcement.

When called upon to verify the death, Doctor William Stevens of

Hatton Hill found that Avery Silver had been hiding more than a tidy inheritance for his daughter to discover. It transpired that Mr. Silver was in fact a woman and had been living undetected as a man for many years. This extraordinary news has been met with disbelief and shock by all that knew this otherwise unexceptional man. The writer has learnt that Avery Silver 'married' a woman and the two had a daughter together who is now in her thirties. Avery Silver survived his 'wife' of 30 years by eight years. Of the two, Silver's neighbour, Mrs. Victoria Phelps, had this to say:

'They were always such great company to have at a dinner though she (Mrs. Silver) was a fiery one. She had a quick temper and was always very defensive of Avery but they were both such fun. I hadn't seen much of him for a while. He has suffered her death more than most. Died of a broken heart, I expect. Avery, a woman, they say? I don't believe it. Not for one minute.'

So complete was Mr. Silver's deceit that there has been a similar response at every enquiry *made by the writer to get to the bottom of the matter. Of the deceased, Mr. Arnold Quick, proprietor of local book shop 'Mayfair Books' was full of praise:*

'He was a gentleman. I don't know who stands to gain by the vicious lies but I'll be damned if I'll let anyone repeat it in my earshot, and that's what they are. Lies. Oh yes, Avery Silver was a regular client in here. He paid his accounts in a timely fashion and could always be relied upon for a decent conversation. He wasn't a tattler or a gossip. He always had something decent to remark upon matters of importance. It'll be a pack of lies. All of this will be to sell papers.'

Doctor Stevens was unwilling to officially comment on the case until such time as he has provided his report and full statement to the Coroner but was able to say:

'This case is most extraordinary. There is no precedent of required protocol. I am afraid I am unable to comment any further.'

Avery's daughter, one Mrs. Imogen Bancroft, married to John Bancroft of Worcs., Chairman of

Brindlecome Estates, has been informed and reportedly was unaware of her 'father's' secret. Mr. Bancroft himself was also unavailable for comment this afternoon but it is supposed that he too, was ignorant of this deception. The coroner, along with the local magistrate's office, has launched a full enquiry to determine the legalities of this singularly strange revelation.

As I read the words, two truths seemed to leap about the page. My father was dead. My father was a woman. At the time I suppose, I must still have been in denial as I remember now very clearly that the newspaper report, rather than upsetting me, seemed only to make the situation all the more absurd. Of course, the words were sensible enough but the meaning of them still did not seem to penetrate my mind.

When I woke in the morning following my appearance at the Coroner's Enquiry, I was insensible to how I had got home. I recalled with shame the Coroner's words and how they had, in one fell swoop, stripped me of a father and a mother. The sense of falling returned to me and I assumed I must have fainted in the Coroner's Court. Given the fuggy headedness I was feeling, I assumed John had called Doctor Jonas to administer a sleeping draught. John had already left the house some time ago. He had left word with Stokes that he would be busy at his office in town and that meals should be served without him.

Evidently, he was inclined to keep me at an arm's length and I had preferred it that way. Being alone felt preferable to being treated like the enemy. With the boys at their grandparents and the staff appearing to avoid me, the house was uncommonly quiet. John had started organising God only knew what that needed organising and, though I was sorry not to be a part of the process, I was also thankful not to be dealing with all of the people. The reporters had mercifully left us alone, directing their attention instead to the Coroner or to John's office. Instead of the press hounding us, there had been an almost constant stream of visitors or calls to enquire after both John and myself. I had not thought myself so well acquainted but word, it seems had begun to spread amongst our inner circle. I had admitted only one such caller and immediately had wished that I had not. A woman, Martha Doone, the wife of one of John's business partners, whom I had always got along reasonably well with had called by with the sole intention of dropping a social ultimatum; either I distance myself from the whole situation or I could say goodbye to bridge club. Though I preferred to distance myself, I was not about to be given such a directive by Mrs. Doone, so was careful to ensure she did not mistake my meaning when I offered to show her the door.

After her visit, I was glad of the cool of the glass pane against my forehead as I watched her carriage lurch away from our door. The window afforded a good view of the square to the front of our house. In the winter time, the low slung branches of the maples and beech trees turned to skeletal fingers and one could just make out the houses across the square. I watched as the world beyond the chill glass went on as normal, as if my own had not been destroyed. Birds still flew, one or two carriages drew past as sedately as before and people seemed to mill about on their usual errands. A large woman dressed in a dour brown dress, cloaked against the bitter winter air pushed an infant's carriage across the gardens; a pair of gentlemen in hats and woollen coats walked across the gardens deep in conversation and a cab, pulled by a sturdy bay horse, rounded the corner of Upper Terrace. It was at once both reassuring and alarming to see the world an unmoved place, but I watched with growing ease, as I imagined that my life could once again return to some level of normality. All of the figures within my view were breathing out miniature clouds as their warm breath crystallised in the cold air and seemed to converge above them to form the dense white sky that hovered above them; it shrouded all of London with its damp breath. The sound of the bay horse's hooves on the street outside grew louder as the cab drew alongside my window and stopped. My heart froze as I realised that the cab was delivering someone else to our house. The driver hopped from his seat and opened the door and folded down the steps before assisting a woman from the cab's interior. Her face was obscured by a hat as she concentrated on stepping out of the cab. She had accepted the drivers' assistance with a gloved hand. Her clothes were very elegant but not modern and the additional support she required from the driver suggested that she was a woman of some years. I glanced across the square where both the two gentlemen and the nanny had stopped in their tracks to note the arrival at my house. The two men were now gesturing to the house and talking rather animatedly; the nanny had frozen in her tracks making an effort to conceal her stares by fussing over the blanket in the pram. My heart sank as I realised that my world returning to normal had been subterfuge for a square full of busy bodies desperate to catch a piece of gossip. My attention returned to the woman who ascended the steps to my front door. Her face became visible and I did not recognise it. As I cast my mind back to all of my husband's extended family gatherings and social functions, I found I could not place her. No doubt, she was the wife of one of John's business partners.

"Mrs. Bancroft?"

"Yes Stokes."

"There is a Mrs. Evesham here to see you. Shall I show her in?"

Evesham? The name brought me fresh confusion and I looked to the sombre butler for some assistance.

"Mrs. Evesham?"

"I do not recognise the name I am afraid, Mrs. Bancroft. Do you wish me to show her in?"

I frowned, suddenly struck by the thought that this woman could be a journalist or a gossip-monger come for some sport.

"Ma'am?"

"Yes," I replied. "Show her in."

The butler turned from his post.

"But don't stray too far Stokes, she may not be welcome."

Stokes nodded with grim authority and returned after a few moments followed by the woman from the cab. The woman stood on the threshold of the door, evidently undecided about her errand and she looked at me with a mixture of apology and fear.

"Mrs. Evesham, Madam."

Stokes' voice seemed to bring action to the woman and she stepped forward to allow for the door to be closed behind us, Stokes inclining his head to me as he did so.

"I would ask you to sit down?" I gestured to the chairs, walking around the small table "But I am afraid you have caught me at rather a bad time."

I looked at the woman's face, waiting for an answer to this statement, some explanation of her unannounced arrival.

"Thank you," she said, simply and walked to the chair I had indicated and settled herself in it avoiding my eyes as she did so.

I supposed she must have misunderstood my gesture and was about to ask her directly who she was, when a knock came at the door announcing the arrival of the tea tray I had ordered when Mrs. Doone had shown up.

"I was just about to take some tea, would you care to join me?"

"Thank you. That is very kind."

Mrs. Evesham watched in silence as Maud carefully placed the tea tray down and I took the opportunity to examine this woman a little more closely. As I had noted from the window, she was dressed in an elegant dress of dark grey satin and her blonde hair was shot with white. Her face was well made up and showed very little sign of her obviously advanced years. Her hands now removed from their gloves were lined and speckled with dark spots..

"Will there be anything else Madam?"

"Thank you Maud. That will be all."

I waited until we were alone before stepping forwards and taking a seat opposite this mysterious stranger and began pouring the tea. There followed an uncomfortable silence and it was obvious that Mrs. Evesham was waiting for Maud to leave us before she would begin. The click of the door in its latch prompted us both from our silence.

"I must apologise..." she started.

"Mrs. Evesham..." I began, our voices colliding in an effort to break the silence. I looked at her and indicated she should finish.

"I must apologise for my coming unannounced. I didn't know if I should come at all." She added almost as an aside to herself.

"Forgive my bluntness Mrs. Evesham, but how should I know you?"

She gazed at me. I felt uncomfortable and not a little annoyed.

"Have we perhaps met before?" I volunteered, trying to assist this woman to some recollection of her business with me

I watched as she scanned my face seemingly searching for some recognition. There was something familiar about her which I could not place. Her eyes took me in, watering a little without blinking, a slight smile creeping in to the edges of her lips.

"Yes." She nodded, still keeping me under her scrutiny. "We have met before.....Imogen."

The familiar use of my name seemed improper under the circumstances and I blushed.

She leaned forward and continued to stare deep into my eyes, willing me perhaps to remember her.

"I…I'm afraid I don't recollect our meeting Mrs. Evesham?"

I began to grow a little flustered that I had forgotten who this woman was and she seemed to sense this and looked away. Her attention now on the tea tray, she began lifting sugar cubes into her cup.

"I suppose, I didn't think that you would. You were so very young."

I continued to stare at this woman, confused by her intrusion and a little miffed at her vagueness.

"Mrs. Evesham, I am afraid that this is rather a difficult time…."

"Of course," she nodded, her hands, which had been resting awkwardly in her lap began to fidget with the material of her skirt. "I must apologise again for my intrusion….it's just I…."

I was still waiting to find out what this maddening woman wanted and I began to grow rather irritated.

"Mrs. Evesham. I must insist that you state your business. I am afraid I do not recollect where I should know you from. I am sorry to be so very blunt but we are a family in grieving and I haven't the time to entertain strangers."

She watched as I delivered my tirade and she nodded at me solemnly.

"I know. I am so sorry about your father, Imogen. He was a good man."

The hairs on the back of my neck prickled in warning, expecting some barbed comment.

"A good man," she repeated, holding my stare.

"You knew my father?"

"And your mother."

"Evesham? How is it I've never heard of you? Who are you?"

The woman cleared her throat and picked up her cup of tea.

"My name is Elizabeth Evesham," she paused before adding, "nee Greenwood?"

The name still didn't mean anything to me and she paused, seemingly expecting some recognition. As none came, she continued.

"I thought perhaps your father had mentioned me?" She spoke quietly almost to herself, a little disappointed it seemed. She glanced around the room nervously as if expecting someone to assist her. A brief silence followed before she found her inspiration on the mantel behind me. She stood and her sudden movement caused me a little alarm, the cup and saucer I had been sipping from clattered together. She walked to the fireplace and reached for a frame in which a studio photograph of my mother and father stood.

"May I?" she glanced at me, her hands already stretching to the picture.

The photograph had been taken several years ago at a studio. My mother was seated in an upright chair, my father stood behind her in his finest suit. The image was the only one I had of my mother and I suspect that fact alone had kept John from removing it from the parlour. I nodded as Mrs. Evesham took up the frame.

"The last time I saw your father was almost forty years ago."

I was about to insist that Mrs. Evesham state her business but I was taken by the fond look she had in her eyes as she studied the photograph. If she had known him forty years ago, she may be the only person who could help me understand his deception.

"I can't believe he is dead," she said.

The bluntness of this statement was muted by the emotional outburst which followed. Mrs. Evesham replaced the photo on the mantel and extracted a handkerchief to cover her eyes.

"Mrs. Evesham? How did you know my father?"

Chapter Twelve - Elizabeth, 1869

"I hope you feel better soon, Miss Elizabeth."

"I am sure I will, Cribbs. I think I shall just sleep for now. Be sure, I am not disturbed."

With a brief curtsey, Cribbs closed the door behind her with great care and Elizabeth allowed a smile to creep across her face. Listening intently, she could hear the maid's footsteps fade into nothing as she made her way back downstairs. The picture was so vivid in Elizabeth's mind that she might well have had two glass floors beneath her feet. If she did, she would have seen through to her older sister Agnes' bedroom below. It would be as neat and as prim as she kept herself. If she could peer secretly inside this room there would be little of interest within. Agnes would probably be sat in front of her looking glass, thinking nothing and seeing little more. Beneath Agnes' room was the parlour where their father would be seated in a large winged-back chair, still in his suit, stiffly waiting to be called to dinner. A man of habit, he would not be pleased to be kept waiting and would be less pleased further to learn that Elizabeth was too ill to come to dinner. He would nod his head solemnly when told the news and, fearing something sinister had befallen her, would begin to ask for a doctor. Cribbs would politely interrupt to advise him that she was merely in pain with her monthly course and that there was no need to trouble the doctor. His face would colour at first with such delicate information but lighten to hear his youngest daughter was not at death's door, and he would settle himself instead with just Agnes for company.

Elizabeth was pleased not to have to listen to Agnes drone on and on about her fiancé, Richard. Instead, their father would have the task of nodding in the right places and seeming to appear interested. She waited a few minutes to hear Agnes' door opening and closing below her. The sound of lightly placed footsteps descending the staircase assured Elizabeth that she was now alone upstairs. Pulling back the bedcovers, she stepped carefully onto the rug, the bed creaking as she leant across it to the clothes stand upon which her dress had been hung. Straining to hear any sounds above her own breathing, she pulled on her clothes and stockings before silently tiptoeing off the rug and onto bare boards. Her boots were beside her dressing table and, stooping to pick them up, she caught sight of herself in the mirror. In the soft glow of the gaslight, her eyes were alive with sparkle and were a perfect replica of her late mother's own eyes. Were it not for the colour of her golden cherry wood hair and the fuller mouth, she could be a young version of her own mother and she knew this both grieved and pleased her father in equal measure. At seventeen, Elizabeth was not yet a woman but she was no longer a girl. She had also inherited her mother's long neck and high cheekbones, and she was a striking beauty. This was something that had not escaped Elizabeth's attention and she smiled at herself in the mirror, pleased with what she saw. Elizabeth, amused at Cribbs' stupidity, or perhaps impressed by her discretion thought of the girl's dull face and smiled.

A distant clatter from several floors below hurried Elizabeth in her tasks. Pausing only to apply some powder and lipstick, she clumsily laced up her boots. She was unaccustomed to the task and she silently cursed her own soft fingers. Having simply knotted the laces, she picked up her coat triumphantly before slipping soundlessly onto the landing. A faint and distant rumble assured her that her father was enlightening Agnes with the day's events at the office and she tiptoed across the landing to the back stairs. The stairs led to the basement kitchen and the smell of dinner drifted temptingly up the stairwell and almost made her change her mind. Feigning being ill with cramps had meant that she had not eaten all day and she felt quite weak with the hunger. Noiselessly, she descended one flight to the first floor and waited. The clanking of pans and pottery sounds seemed close but the muffled voices reassured her that she were safe. Another flight down and she was at the back of the corridor leading to the front door.

"Cribbs!" The loud voice of the cook from the bottom of the stairs startled Elizabeth as he called out for Cribbs. Quickly, Elizabeth ducked inside the open study door as the maid scurried past. The girl muttered bad-temperedly as she passed and Elizabeth caught the words 'Old Trout' before Cribbs slipped down the stairs. For Elizabeth, it was the all-clear that she needed. With the house staff downstairs, and her father and sister waiting in the parlour to be called for dinner, she took her chance. Slipping from the shadows of the empty room, she hurried into the entrance hall, skirting the parlour door until she was standing before the front door, her hand upon the knob.

"Elizabeth?"

The suddenness of her father's voice calling her name made her jump.

"Good heavens, Agnes! How could you even suggest such a thing?"

His voice came from inside the parlour and Elizabeth was half torn between staying to listen to why he should call out like that and what on earth Agnes had suggested, but the fright made her jumpy and instead she slipped out into the fresh, spring city air. Despite the earlier heat of the day, the evening breeze from the river some streets away was chill and Elizabeth was glad of the coat she drew around her. Hurrying down the front steps, she walked quickly up the King's Road heading towards Victoria. She kept her head down, casting sideways glances about her. She was fuelled by adrenalin but her nerves were making her skittish. As she crossed a side road, an elderly gent bumped into her, apologising profusely as he did so. Her heart thundered as she thought for a moment that she recognised him. She pulled away from his apologetic hands but he was insistent, checking that she was okay.

"Going somewhere in a hurry like that, Miss, and you will be sure to meet with something eventually. A sticky end perhaps?" He chuckled at his wit and smiled good-naturedly at her. She drew her hands back from his and, apologising for her haste, she bustled off, leaving him shaking his head. A few streets away, she began to slow down and her sense of dread was quickly replaced with excitement as she instead took pleasure in the feeling of freedom and anticipation of the night ahead. The fading light of the evening sun, setting behind, threw a long shadow before her. After twenty minutes or so, the number of passing carriages and cabs diminished as she turned into Elizabeth Street and the relative calm of Belgravia. Her steps faltered and she paused at the corner of Chester Row, looking left and right. She was not stood for long before a voice from close behind her startled her.

"Miss Greenwood!"

Elizabeth spun round to face the direction of the voice and, from the growing shadows of the tall houses and prim hedges, she made out a familiar outline. A young man of about twenty, dressed in evening wear stepped from the gloom on to the pavement and into the glow of the evening light beside her. He swept her a bow with the tip of his hat and appraised her fully as he drew himself up again. His hair beneath the fine silk hat was pale and cropped neatly. He sported a tidy but thin moustache that looked as though if it has taken a great effort to cultivate. The rest of his face was smooth and his complexion was as sallow as wax. Stood before Elizabeth, he gave off an air of quiet confidence and high self-opinion. He touched his moustache with a smug grin before taking the hand she offered him in greeting. His eyes did not leave hers for a moment as he planted a soft kiss upon her gloved hand.

"I was not sure if you were in earnest, Miss Greenwood. What luck that I decided to wait another few minutes for you. I had all but abandoned the idea for one of your whims."

"Mr. Bateman, I do believe you are pleased to see me." Smiling at him, Elizabeth turned and began to walk away from the young man. He hurried to accompany her, his cane flailing for a moment whilst he measured his steps in time with her quick and purposeful gait.

"I'll hail us a cab quickly, we can't have little Miss Greenwood spotted out at this hour can we?"

Elizabeth considered this for a moment but despite the implications, had to agree that this was a wise precaution. The short walk to Chester Row was dangerous enough, a young girl out late on her own, but to be seen by one of her father's fogeys in the company of this particular young man, and unaccompanied, would be a disastrous scandal. She raised an eyebrow at the young man as if she were considering his slight and found his wit wanting. The young man laughed at this gesture and turned to stride ahead to the King's Road, where he raised his topper to a passing hansom. Stepping back as the horse pulled up beside him, he opened the door and held his hand out for Elizabeth's.

"Cleveland Street," he called up to the cabbie before jumping up behind her. "And there's an extra shilling if you can make it before ten," he added. The latch of the door barely clicked before the cab lurched off, causing Bateman to pitch forwards. He steadied himself on the seat back before settling himself opposite Elizabeth.

"Nothing like a keen start, Miss Greenwood. I very much like how the stars are aligning this evening."

Elizabeth smiled to herself in the gloom of the cab and turned away from the cool gaze of her companion. The breeze from the darkening sky was refreshing after the unseasonal heat of the day and she closed her eyes, offering up her chin to the draught.

Beyond the window, another side to this city was beginning to wake up. Elizabeth's head rested on the frame and she watched as the familiar sights were replaced by versions of themselves she had not seen before. As the cab drew up past Park Lane towards Marble Arch, she could see Hyde Park alter before her very eyes. Beyond the boundary of the iron fence and the privet hedges, the well-travelled Broad Walk - by day a smart passage for ladies to traverse - was all but abandoned, the shadows already proving too much of a danger to a gentleman and his wallet. The greenery, so peaceful and inviting during the day, repelled by night, as under its cover may lurk any number of assailants. As the carriage rolled on slowly in the heavy traffic, lights from the gas jets of Park Lane glimmered across the fence, and Elizabeth saw a furtive flash of white and spotted a pair of eyes from under a bush. A girl, not much older than Elizabeth, was relieving herself in the undergrowth, the dirty white of her petticoats hitched up behind her back, her thin grubby legs camouflaged in the evening light. Their eyes met for an instant and then a shadow fell across the girl's face and the carriage had moved on.

As they approached Marble Arch, she heard the driver cursing. His hopes of an extra shilling seem to have vanished as the traffic slowed to a stop. She leaned across the upholstered seat to the far window and peered down Oxford Street. A crowd was gathering and she could barely see beyond them to where two carriages had collided. A loose horse, causing a nuisance, was rearing up. There seemed to be a body on the road and Elizabeth tried to make out if it were moving. As the crowd moved away from the horse that had shied to one side, she could see the body was that of a woman. Her neck was broken awkwardly and her dislocated head was twisted to her back. Elizabeth turned away in disgust and nausea rose up in her stomach. Her companion watched her take in the scene then laughed at her discomfort.

"Come now, Elizabeth," he joked, "surely you have seen worse things? As a lawyer, your father must have picked over some thoroughly rotten corpses in his time!" He appeared amused at himself and leant back chuckling, as Elizabeth composed herself to stare once again out of the window. Although it made her feel sick, she could not help but be drawn to stare at the unfortunate scene. The face of the head was turned away from her but she willed its features to reveal themselves to her and she found herself imagining the face of the poor creature. The body was shabbily dressed and the visage of an elderly crone appeared in Elizabeth's mind. She imbued her with a nose half eaten away with disease and lips crumpling into a dusty and dry hole where a mouth should be. She imagined that the skin would be drawn tight across a misshapen skull with dark sockets for eyes. She shivered and was pleased when a cry came from the cabbie and the horses lurched forwards again, leaving the recovery of the corpse to be seen from another window.

The scene had taken some of her bravado away and she was glad that the young man remained silent. Her empty stomach and light head contrived to send her slipping to the carriage floor but she managed to focus and stay in her seat. After a few minutes the carriage drew to a stop and her companion, checking from his window that they had arrived at their

211

destination, alighted from the cab, turning to escort Elizabeth safely to the ground.

"Here we are, Miss Greenwood. The Chapel of Iniquity!" He flourished his hand towards the building behind him.

An unimposing frontage offered Elizabeth very little promise of interest inside. The bricks were a dark sandy colour and the several large windows were bordered with fresh white paint. It was a prim building, indistinguishable from much of Fitzrovia. The smart, black door was raised from the street by just a few stone steps and even this detail made Elizabeth's heart sink. The place seemed so ordinary; she had at least expected to descend into debauchery!

Elizabeth was disappointed that there was nothing strange about the building; from the outside it promised very little of what Mr. Bateman had described to her over the last few months. Giles Bateman was the son of a rich client of her father's. Elizabeth had instantly disliked the young man but had been curious about him. She recalled their first meeting when, finding her father occupied and Agnes out with Richard, she had walked into the parlour to find a curious looking man asleep in her father's chair. His head rested against the upholstered wing, and the lace antimacassar had slipped to his shoulders and looked like a shawl arranged to keep him warm. His hands were tucked between his legs and his mouth was half open. She was both offended and amused to see a strange gentleman so arranged and was about to call for Cribbs to remove the offending person, but instead chose to consider him a while. He was about her age though perhaps a little older. She guessed about nineteen or twenty. The moustache he sported was fine and patchy and gave him a slightly scruffy look. His fair hair was well oiled and he wore a well cut suit with an expensive watch-chain hung about his pocket. As the young man moved in the chair, his expression changed to that of a grimace and he stretched one of his arms, opening his eyes briefly to check his whereabouts. His eyes flickered momentarily before alighting on Elizabeth, sat opposite him at the other end of the mantel.

"Forgive me!" he spluttered, standing hastily and brushing away the lace from his shoulders. His face had grown quite pink and Elizabeth raised her eyebrows at him in response. "I must have fallen asleep," he added sheepishly.

"Indeed!" she exclaimed. "I had not realised my father had extended his services to provide lodgings. Do you wish to use the bathroom also? I can arrange for shaving implements to be brought to you."

The young man brought a hand to his moustache and considered Elizabeth for a moment before smiling. Her eyes were twinkling with amusement and he gambled on her being in jest. He laughed and stepped forward to introduce himself.

"Giles Bateman," he proffered. "And at a guess, you must be Elizabeth."

Having not heard the name Bateman before, the advantage was now most certainly the young man's and Elizabeth reverted to her usual defence in such situations and feigned boredom.

"Well, Mr. Bateman, you will excuse me if I do not rise but I am feeling rather tired myself."

"Yes, us night birds often are," he winked at her.

213

Awake, Giles Bateman seemed much older than she first had thought and she now put his age at around twenty-five. The gesture on a younger man would seem impertinent but now seemed rather flirtatious. She found his comment curious and pressed him.

"I confess, Mr. Bateman, to being no such thing; rather, I am merely an early riser. Might I enquire what task you would expect a young lady to occupy her past sunset?" She cocked her head innocently.

The young man's eyes had twinkled as he had tapped his finger to his nose and winked at her. The arrival in the parlour of their respective fathers had saved any further indiscretion on his behalf at this meeting and Elizabeth had been left feeling a little annoyed by his forwardness, but also curious as to what illicit entertainment he could be referring to. Her world was a narrow one but she sought to broaden it at every opportunity. That very evening she had pressed Agnes about where Richard took her of a rare occasion when his maiden aunt could chaperone an evening.

"You know where we go, Bess. Always to the same place."

Elizabeth knew but pressed her sister again in case there was some hidden excitement that had eluded her.

"Tell me again," she cooed at Agnes, feigning girlish delight. She hardly needed to press Agnes to talk; it was her singular delight in life, believing her courtship with Richard was the only thing worth discussing. And so Agnes went on.

"Richard always insists that we have the best table in the restaurant. It is exactly in the middle of the room, thus we are at the centre of everyone's attention as we take our seats. Of course, Richard is always so courteous and seats his aunt first and then myself. He doesn't allow the waiters to do it, of course. They know him very well and they serve us a bottle of the good wine. The wine they keep for their very best customers. Of course, Richard tries it first to make sure it is the good stuff and the rogues aren't trying to pull the wool over his eyes. His friend Eddie was thoroughly fleeced a few months ago by a Semillon, with them pretending to serve him fine claret and actually giving him some watered-down reject. That would never happen to Richard."

Elizabeth could barely keep her eyes from watering as she stifled a yawn with the back of her hand and prayed she could keep from glazing over as she usually did. It was usual for Elizabeth to become so tired of listening to her sister that she slipped into another, more interesting world. Agnes was always furious when she didn't elicit the correct oohs and ahhs at her stories and Elizabeth thought this must be the secret to why she had not yet heard anything of interest in Agnes' stories. She had not reached the end of any of them and thus she determined now to try to stay alert to hear the end of one.

Sadly, after an hour of her sister's full attention, she was unable to keep hers from wandering off and she had once more retreated to another place. As Agnes droned on and on about Richard's exquisite table manners and his impeccable taste in neckties, Elizabeth was recalling how the young Mr. Bateman had winked at her. She didn't think he had either good manners or a particularly well-judged taste in neckties, but she did think he knew about having a good time.

215

How she longed to taste a little of the life on offer outside her own four walls. She read books about convivial gentleman and the whirl of a dance floor. She dreamed about being adored by all of society, of being the toast of each season, of being the centre of all that is fashionable in London. It would be several months before she could plan her big debut but she felt she had been ready all her life. Elizabeth Greenwood, who had been born two weeks prematurely, could wait for very little in life and she was determined that she was not going to wait any longer for fun either. She knew enough to know that Giles Bateman could offer her none of this but she also knew that he could be a step on her ladder. As she sat watching her sister's lips move, seemingly without stopping, she resolved she would persuade Giles Bateman to show her some of the London she longed for. As she pondered her decision, she began to smile broadly, a hint of mischief on the edge of her lips. The timing of this was unfortunate as it coincided with Agnes detailing a recent account of Richard's aunt's back troubles.

"What are you smiling about, Bess? You weren't listing to me at all were you?" Agnes threw up her arms in exasperation and began berating Elizabeth for her lack of attention. Whilst she whirled around the room, exasperated by her sister, Elizabeth finally gave in to the yawn she had been resisting and stretched backwards, falling on Agnes' bed.

She had to wait a few more weeks before she had the opportunity to question Mr. Bateman on what he had meant, but he had been elusive and had only roused her curiosity further.

"Miss Greenwood, I am afraid that such entertainments are beyond even your imaginations and, might I say so, your sensitivities," he had added, with a raised eyebrow. Their liaison was interrupted by one of the domestic staff and she could not press him further. However, he clearly wished to court her interest and behind the stooped back of Cribbs, he had stepped his way lightly across the rug to the door in the manner of a waltz. All the while, he kept his eyes on Elizabeth. She had burst out with laughter at seeing him so and Cribbs had stood to find out the cause of such mirth. But by the time she had looked around at the young gentleman, he had composed himself by the door and, tipping his hat, had taken leave of them both. The next time they had met, Elizabeth had feigned disinterest in his tomfoolery and had remained quiet as he had tried to tease her.

"I admit, I am quite tired today, Miss Greenwood. I was kept from my bed a long while last night in the most energetic of pursuits."

Elizabeth, having settled herself in a chair with a book, had not glanced up but had casually turned a page.

"Mr. Bateman, I am not in the least interested in your fantastical stories. I do not believe for one moment, that you even leave your house of an evening, let alone engage in anything more energetic than creating hot air."

Taken aback, the young man had sat down opposite her and had played with his hat for a few minutes. He had been enjoying these meetings and was a little crestfallen that Elizabeth took him for a liar.

"I will have you know that I am a regular member at a most diverting dance saloon and I that have my pick of partners."

He sat sulkily for a few more minutes before adding, 'I have received many compliments on my footwork. If you were to come to the club, I would prove it to you.'

Elizabeth's face did not betray the pleasure she felt at having secured the information she needed. She merely looked up at the young man and smiled.

"How kind of you to invite me, Mr. Bateman. I would be delighted to join you."

Mr. Bateman's face had coloured and he had tried to undo his invitation, but Cribbs had arrived with a tea tray.

Over the course of the next few meetings, Elizabeth had managed to encourage the young man to speak more freely with her about the dancing club and on one such occasion, she had pressed him on when he would take her with him.

"My dear Miss Greenwood, I had not realised you were prone to gallivanting," he had remarked with a grin. Wiping his fingers across his fluffy upper lip he had added, "When you are as mature as your sister, perhaps I will enjoy the pleasure of a dance."

Elizabeth was furious at the comparison to Agnes and had made it clear to Mr. Bateman that she was no shrinking violet.

"My sister, Mr. Bateman, may be three years older than I, but has the skill of a walrus on the dance floor. You blow more hot air than Mr. Gladstone. I do not believe that this club of yours exists. If it did, you would take me there as you promised to."

Shaking a little with anger, Elizabeth now leant to the task of pouring some fresh tea in her cup and felt her face grow flush. After some moments, the sulky tone of the young man had caused her to look around.

"Perhaps I will."

"Then perhaps I will come", she had added.

"Perhaps if you were to meet me outside my house on Thursday next at eight o'clock, I might escort you."

"Perhaps I will be there," Elizabeth had concluded, smiling to herself as she brought the cup to her lips.

And so there she stood on the threshold of what had become a magical club to her in her mind. Knowing very little about its whereabouts, she had relied upon her own imaginings to bring the place to life, and so well-known it had become to her over these past weeks that seeing it now, she felt let down over its seemingly innocuous appearance. Although careful not to let the young man see she was downcast, it was obvious and amusing to him that she was disappointed.

"Come, Elizabeth. I have not brought you here to mope. I have brought you to dance."

With this hushed intonation, he swept up the steps to the doorway and knocked a series of taps. The door opened and a doorman greeted the young man by name.

"Welcome again, Mr. Bateman! Is your companion joining us this evening?"

"Yes, Wilkes. This is Miss Greenwood. She is interested in joining our little circle. Elizabeth?" Here he extended a hand down the steps to where Elizabeth was hesitating and he smiled encouragingly. "Shall we?"

Driven by curiosity and intent to show Bateman that she was made of sterner stuff than he believed, she mounted the stairs, passed the doorman and swept into the foyer beyond. At once the place seemed to come to life. A buzz of excited voices mingled with the sound of music, all muffled by the great number of people within. A grand marble entrance hall opened up before her, rising to all three stories of the building and crowned at the peak by a dome of glass. Hung from the iron work were several chandeliers, the lamps casting curious shadows on the glass above. It seemed that stars were coming home to roost in the roof of Number 17, Cleveland Street. A dazzling staircase swept upwards and melted on to a first floor gallery around the entrance hall. To her left, the hall continued under a grand archway and into a larger room, from which she could hear the strings of a band, playing a lively number. There were many people in both the music room and the entrance hall. Waiters circulated with trays laden with glasses of wine and snacks.

The sound of laughter and merriment was interspersed with the clink of glasses and soft shoeing from the dance floor. Elizabeth's face lit up in delight as she turned back to Giles Bateman, who was holding out his arm, gesturing with his head to the archway leading to where the music was coming from. She handed her coat to a nearby waiter and placed her hand through the young man's arm. As they made their way to the dance floor, Bateman was greeted by several faces and Elizabeth was acknowledged at once with an agreeable mixture of curiosity and approval.

The dance floor was highly polished and resembled the surface of a lake; as the dancers whirled around in a quickstep; their reflections looked like falling leaves in an autumn sky, never landing, only hanging in the air. She placed a hand on Bateman's shoulder and allowed his arm to coil around her waist, and before she had a chance to catch the beat of the music they were off. She felt a giggle rise in her throat and there it remained, tickling her until she was giddy with delight. Whirling around the room, the music rose and fell as they passed other dancers. Whilst she had danced before at many a dull family occasion with cousins and young boys, she had never danced with a man before and she felt the firm hand of Bateman quite exciting. Elizabeth imagined her father's face if he could see her. His eyes would be bulging, and his lips screwed up as tight as the piano lid at home had been since her mother died and she laughed out loud at the image.

"Perhaps you believe me now," Bateman crowed.

"Oh, I believe this place alright," she replied.

They stayed on the dance floor for three more dances before, unaccustomed as she was to the energy required, she needed a break. Bateman was joined almost immediately by several other gentlemen, all eager to know with whom he had been dancing. Elizabeth caught the eye of a waiter and beckoned him forward but before she could take a glass herself, a man had taken one for her and placed it in her hand, introducing himself as he did so.

"Silver. Avery Silver. And you are?"

"I," Elizabeth returned promptly, "am very pleased to meet you." She raised her hand and watched as the man pressed his lips to her gloved fingers. He seemed amused by her coy reply.

"Would you care to dance?" he asked.

Throwing back the contents of her glass, she raised her eyebrows and shoulders heavenwards to Bateman in a gesture of defeat and allowed herself to be led back to the dance floor. She noticed Bateman's look of both amusement and jealousy and she was delighted with herself. Silver was a much more accomplished mover than Bateman and she struggled to keep up with him, cursing her own lack of expertise as, twice, she trod upon his feet.

"You will forgive me I am sure, Mr. Silver, but I am quite out of practice."

"Then you must come more often to our little club and get some."

Whirling her to a stop, they stood applauding the band as it was announced that the musicians would take a ten minute break. Bateman was watching from the side of the dance floor and his face turned darker as Elizabeth placed her hand upon Silver's arm and whispered to him.

"Why don't you show me around this palace of yours, Mr. Silver."

"It would be my pleasure." Offering her his arm, he escorted Elizabeth from the dance floor and beyond the watchful gaze of Bateman. Elizabeth knew herself to be fairly tall and she was pleasantly surprised that Silver stood a few inches taller than she. As they climbed the wide staircase, it was too busy to pass arm in arm and Silver took her hand to lead her to the balcony above the grand hallway.

"Do you know Mr. Bateman?" she asked, raising her voice so she might be heard more clearly. At this level, the voices from the ground floor had risen to form an almost impenetrable fug.

"Giles? Of course. I should say everyone knows Bateman." She noticed how soft his voice was in contrast to the hard angle of his face. "I might ask you the same question but I fear I know exactly who you are Miss Greenwood. Bateman has told me much about you."

So, Bateman had been talking about her, had he? The thought that he and this Silver had discussed her both annoyed and intrigued her. Far from taking any offence, her curiosity was roused. As they passed on the landing towards the minstrel's gallery overlooking the ballroom, Elizabeth leaned over the balustrade and picked out Bateman from the crowd.

"You know, he told me a lot about you too Mr. Silver," she ventured, turning to face him and arching an eyebrow.

"And if that were true, what do you think he may have told you Miss Greenwood?"

She admired the way he leisurely leaned alongside her and she suspected that he too was trying to pick out Bateman from the crowd below them.

"Ah Mr. Silver, I think Mr. Bateman would have first told me of your confidence." She waited to see if he had any reply. "That you are a fine dancer is nobody's secret. So what would Bateman have wanted me to know about you? Surely any young man would wish to have warned me about anyone who might be dangerous. Are you dangerous Mr. Silver?" She waited as Avery merely lowered his gaze to watch her from under his brow. He licked his bottom lip and waited for her to continue. "He would have warned me about your charm, I think. That you are a collector of fine things, perhaps? Maybe you use your charm to collect fine ladies?"

Silver punctuated her suggestion with a snort of laughter but he continued to gaze down at the rest of the party. She looked at Silver sidelong and took in his features as the noise of the band tuning up below mingled with the hum of the rising conversations. His thick dark hair was worn in the longer style and framed his angular jaw. In comparison to the straw haired, flush faced Bateman, Silver was indeed the finer figure but the 'something' less ordinary about his features was the one thing that she could not place. After a few moments of silence between them, Silver smiled and, without turning to face her, addressed her again.

"I would not trust him anyhow. For a matter of fact, he told me that you were rather plain."

Despite herself, Elizabeth smiled.

"If he had not told me any of these things, how would you have me think of you Mr. Silver?"

Silver cocked his head to take in the young woman before him. Elizabeth had stepped in front of him, one hand on her hip, the other thrust towards him, her pale skin flushed from the heat coming from the dancers below. Her full lips were parted and her eyes were shaded with a sultry gaze.

"How would I have you think of me? Miss Greenwood, just that. I would be well satisfied if you did indeed think of me?" And with that he placed one arm behind his back and offered his other to Elizabeth. His confidence was different to Bateman's. Giles' tone was

224

self-assured but it struck her as cocky. Silver's self-belief was intimate and it plucked curiosity deep inside her, making her resonate with intrigue. She stepped forwards and placed her hand over his arm and as she did so, the firm muscle in it tensed causing a shiver to run down her spine.

"Shall we?"

~o~

Heady with the intoxicating buzz of the champagne and the taboo of the evening she had just passed, Elizabeth was a little worse for wear as the cab deposited her and a cross looking Bateman on the Kings Road. She lost her footing as she stepped down from the carriage and fell heavily upon the young man.

"Miss Greenwood, please take hold of yourself!" He cast a sullen look at Elizabeth and she could tell that what had seemed a good idea to him several hours ago, now looked to be a very bad lack of judgment. He had not anticipated her getting so drunk and he wished to be rid of his young charge, without any blackening of his own character, at the Greenwoods' house. Whilst he did not wish to be implicated in her sorry state, neither did he wish to abandon her on these mean streets. In her state, he didn't reckon on her making it home without interference and although he was vexed at her behaviour this evening, he was not insensible to his public duty.

"Come along, Miss Greenwood." He put her arm around his shoulder and escorted her along, the now darkened street, towards the house. Before he had decided where best to try to deposit Elizabeth, whether to chance upon the servants' entrance or brazen the front entrance, the front door had opened and the thunderous face of Mr. Greenwood had appeared. From behind him, the face of a police constable and a sour faced old woman appeared, taking in the sight of Elizabeth returning home.

"Bateman!" Mr. Greenwood thundered. "What the devil is the meaning of this?"

"Hush, Frederick," the old woman counselled, casting glances towards the darkened windows neighbouring them. A twitch at one curtain revealed that news such as this would spread if they did not keep their voices low.

"Brown! Help my daughter inside and have Cribbs escort her upstairs," he hissed. Bateman stood helplessly as Elizabeth was escorted inside the house and out of sight. Relieved as he felt to be delivered of her, Bateman felt the more pressing matter of Mr. Greenwood's ire. The old man stood aside whilst Bateman trudged inside the house for his grilling.

"If all's well, sir, I will conclude my report at the station." Nodding at Mr. Greenwood and the old woman, 'Madam', the constable took his leave, shaking his head as he passed Bateman. As he walked away from the Greenwoods' house, the constable heard the click of the front door followed by the unmistakable sound of Mr. Greenwood's shouting. He shook his head and walked off into the night.

Chapter Thirteen - Imogen, 1911

I can't deny that as I listened to Mrs. Evesham talk, I was riveted. It is not very often that any of us catch a glimpse of our parents as they were in their youth and certainly in the circumstances of my own father, his youth was the only key I had to unlocking the secret of who he really was. On the other hand, the picture Mrs. Evesham was painting made my head spin. So, my father was a charming flirt! He had met this woman, Elizabeth Evesham nee Greenwood at a dance. The idea of him gallivanting around London at some private club, charming ladies and being mysterious was not so strange. I will admit that it was an image that was at odds with my own of him; a quiet and studious man who was the centre of family life. Albeit incongruous, it was at least imaginable. I gather from many of the wives I have spoken to, that their husbands have had access to more 'colourful' opportunities in their lives than perhaps we would credit them.

"I can see this is a struggle." Her voice, still strong was a little hoarse. She had not stopped in over two hours and her lips looked ready to crack. I rubbed my own neck, stiff from holding it in tension, listening and waiting for another shock. But it had not come. I had the feeling Mrs. Evesham had not finished her story and was bracing myself for another revelation.

"I'm sorry," she blurted, all at once a flurry of nerves. She walked away from the fireplace where she had wandered and collected her handbag from the chair.

227

"I shouldn't have come here," she said softly.

"Mrs. Evesham, you knew my father. You are probably the only living soul who knew him properly so how come I don't know of you?"

She stepped towards the door, an explanation forming on her lips, and scanned my face, her eyes full of tears.

"I shouldn't have come here," she repeated and with that she turned the door of the parlour and stepped outside.

I was shocked by her sudden outburst of emotion. It was the only genuine grief at my father's death I had yet seen. Her abrupt departure took me by surprise and before I could collect my thoughts the sound of the front door closing indicated she had left. I hurried to the hallway calling for Stokes.

"Yes madam?"

"That woman, did she say who she was? Did you know her?"

"I am afraid not madam. Shall I call after her?"

"No," I replied quickly, the thought of giving the vultures beyond my walls another scene to feed them with was enough to stop me. I turned to go upstairs. I had gone but a few steps when Stokes' added.

"I took a calling card before I presented her."

I turned to face Stokes, his face looking up at me gravely. He was obviously torn with the decision of with whom his loyalties lay. John would no doubt be informed of my visitors today but the butler held out a small white card:

Mrs. Robert Evesham
4 Brown Square, Mayfair

"Thank you, Stokes," I said taking it from him. "Thank you."

228

Chapter Fourteen - Elizabeth, 1869

"Did you sleep well, Frederick?"

Frederick Greenwood looked up from the breakfast table at his elder sister Georgina Fearncott. His eyes were dark with shadows and he still looked as thunderous as he had done at 2 o'clock that morning, when he had finished his interrogation of young Giles Bateman.

"Don't be ridiculous, Georgina. Of course I did not sleep well," he barked. "My youngest daughter has been gallivanting around London half the night without a chaperone and in the company of the son of a man I am defending for a rather shocking breach of the peace."

Frederick Greenwood rubbed his forehead with finger and thumb, pinching the bridge of his nose, stifling both his rising temper and a yawn.

"Is she up yet?" he asked more pleasantly.

"She is ill. With the drink, Frederick that is all." the older woman added as Frederick looked up with concern. "Cribbs is attending to her. I have told her to wait until she has been sent for."

Georgina sat opposite her brother in the chair his wife had once occupied and began spooning Kedgeree onto her plate.

"Have you decided what to do with her yet?" she ventured, watching him as she replaced the lid of the serving tureen.

Her eyes barely blinked whilst she watched him agonise over how to handle the situation. The anger he had felt towards Bateman last night was still there but he knew he would not be able to use this to any effect with Elizabeth. He was never any good at dealing with the girls. It was something his wife had always handled. How would she have dealt with Bess? He racked his brain trying to imagine her seated where his sister now was and he tried hard to hear what she would suggest. But nothing came. How much simpler would it be if he had boys. He could have dealt with a son in this matter. Would it even have been such a fuss or would he have been proud of a son's adventurous streak? His sense of daring and a bold will to seek out pleasures wherever they may be found. Feeling his head begin to ache, he rubbed his eyes again and saw Georgina still watching him.

"What should I do, Georgina?" he asked wearily. "When Agnes told me last night that she had seen Elizabeth dressing up and planned to leave the house in secret, I refused to believe her. I am a poor judge of character to have disbelieved one daughter and been tricked by the other. I am a poor father for always favouring Bessie and now I see that she plays me for a fool. Whatever I do, it won't be right. Help me, Georgina. What should I do?"

Georgina lifted her teacup to her lips, her saucer held just below, and drank long from the pretty china cup. She continued to watch him and, without any consideration of the matter, she replaced her cup and placed the saucer on the table, replying steadily, "I wonder if you would consider my help, Frederick. As you know I am to leave for the country over the summer. The heat in the city is becoming quite insufferable and I have to make some changes to the furnishings at Juniper Hall before my wedding."

231

Frederick waved his hand, urging her to come to a point; his patience was thin and he was eager for a resolution to the matter. Fond of his daughter as he was, he had very urgent matters to deal with at the office, particularly now in reference to Mr. Bateman senior.

"I think perhaps the change of scene and a woman's influence may be good for young Elizabeth. I think perhaps she would learn a great deal in my charge and I have a particular job in mind for her." Here Georgina paused, rearranging her napkin in her lap. "There is another young girl who shall be accompanying me who is in need of a good role model. I believe they would make perfect companions for one another."

Georgina watched her brother as this information sank in and she leaned back, allowing him room to digest the information. She knew him well enough to offer up only the basics of information and allow him room to breathe. He was a slow but deliberate man and liked order. Despite his obvious love for his youngest daughter, her continued disruption in his house was not acceptable to him and this would offer him the perfect solution. Out of sight, she would not entirely be out of mind, but he could trust that Georgina was taking care of the situation. Georgina refreshed both her own and her brother's cups, stirring her own with several lumps of sugar. Although she already knew that Frederick would accept her suggestion, she had to play this tired old charade of his being in charge and she sat impatiently, awaiting his approval. It took a little longer than she had thought and a good ten minutes had passed before Frederick eventually gave the idea his blessing. Once agreed, Frederick got fully behind the idea, taking some of the credit for the good sense of the matter. Keen for Elizabeth to continue some form of education, Georgina could tutor her in Pianoforte, being an accomplished player herself. Before Georgina could remind Frederick that this estrangement was in fact a punishment as well as a lesson in how to behave, he had rung for Cribbs to bring his daughter downstairs to his study.

"Come, Georgina. I want you to put this task of yours to Elizabeth. Who is the young ward you had in mind?"

"Alice Silver."

"Silver? Toby Silver's daughter? I've not heard you speak of a daughter before. Tell me about her."

Georgina was not keen to share her thoughts just yet on Alice Silver. Part of her early exodus from the city was to spend some time getting to know the curious girl. They had met on only a few occasions and, since her first introduction, had barely spoken more than two words to one another. There was something about the girl that caused Georgina not to want to seek out her company. When she visited Toby Silver at his home and Alice was in the parlour, she felt uncomfortable in her company. The girl seemed not quite to fit her own body and this made her awkward and ungainly. She seemed too large for a room when she was in it. That she was tall could be accepted but her hips were narrow, her shoulders broad, and she had too thick a waist. Her hands were large and the girl didn't seem to know where to place them. These habits did not grate on Georgina the way they should. And when she had first spoken! The girl had a voice a tenor would be proud of. It was not so much deep or unrefined, it was just....coarse. Had the girl been her own, she would have been irritated by her clumsiness and reprimanded her. As it was, something about Alice made Georgina's skin prickle and she wanted to find out why. She usually spent some of the summer at her country home and she had determined to get Alice out of her father's care to get to the bottom of her. When she and Toby were courting early on, she had found it easier not to ask about the girl as it was clear that father and daughter were not close. Now that she was to be Mrs. Toby Silver, it was Georgina's duty to sort this matter out. The sooner she knew what made the girl tick, the sooner she could get rid of her.

"Alice is most awkward, socially. I had hoped that Elizabeth would be able to help me with the girl's finishing. I know how accomplished Bessie is and was rather hoping some of her grace would rub off on Alice, and perhaps some of Alice's shy nature on Bessie?"

Frederick considered this for a moment, rising from his chair, his folded napkin in his hand.

"It sounds the very thing, Georgina. An in-built chaperone and a gooseberry at that! Why ever did we not think of this before?" He cast his napkin down upon the table and strode out of the door, Georgina swept away from the table behind him with a wry smile upon her pale, dry lips.

Chapter Fifteen - Avery, 1869

Avery awoke from his dreams with no shadow of guilt or shame. It was true that as Kate had roused him from sleep, he felt the awkward nearness of her and he was as conscious as he ever was as to how he held his breath as she leant across him to collect up a scatter cushion from beside him. All the same senses and feelings were aroused that morning but for the first time, he had woken from sleep not having dreams of pinning the slim form of Kate beneath him; instead he had relived the previous evening he had spent with Elizabeth Bancroft. There was no doubting the young woman had been handsome but more than that, she was bold and arrogant. Every time she looked at him, her eyes searched his face defiantly as if daring him to touch her. And oh! he had wanted to touch her very much and judging by the faces of many of his companions at the club, he was not alone, including a very peeved Bateman. As his thoughts turned towards his friend, he frowned. Bateman had been talking of little else for a few weeks and had been visibly proud to have finally persuaded the young Miss Greenwood to venture into the nightlife. He had been even more visibly perturbed by her spending most of the evening on Avery's arm instead of his own and his parting comments to Silver had been more than flecked with warning.

"You would do well to remember that, whilst I am happy to have you share that back street whore, I mean to make Miss Greenwood my own. Do you understand?" The look which he levelled at Avery was, unmistakably, angry. As he recalled it, Avery groaned and rose to wash. Kate stopped midstream in her daily bustle to bring order to Avery's room and watched his clumsy attempts to tame his hair.

"You were back late last night," she ventured. "I mean, I don't mind waiting up for you. I just worried that you...." She allowed the thought to linger in the air before she brought it home to roost. "I worry every time you leave this house that someone might recognise you or that you'll be found out."

Her normally calm voice rose and Avery hushed her. Her uncharacteristic nervousness worried him and he turned to face her, smiling to try to lighten the mood. Kate was not so easily distracted and having taken the opportunity, she continued.

"It's all very well for you Avery, you are off, God knows where, and I am left here with an empty room and an empty bed to account for. I tiptoe past Mrs. Druce's room and in to the kitchen and sit in the cold. And it is cold in the kitchen at night you know. Not that I mind that but there I sit silently, all alone in the dark thinking about how many ways you could have come a cropper before you knock for me to let you in. And then the knock comes which always makes me jump half out my own skin. I don't know how my heart can stand it, even when I open the door, I never know if it's going to be you or a policeman come to deliver bad news and then there's the thought that on your way back up the stairs we are going to meet someone from the house. Arthur, Mary-Ann, your father!! And there I am! Swanning up before you as if it's the most natural thing in the world to have your mistress follow you up the servant's stairs after midnight dressed as a man!"

The stream of consciousness poured out without her taking any breath and Avery stood before her, shocked. Not at the fact she was saying any of it but that she had not told him before. Whilst he had known there was risk on her part, she had assured him so many times and, foolishly, he had not considered it again. Kate stood before him and, wrung out by her outpouring, she looked at her feet.

"Kate." He offered his hand to her and she took it but did not look at him.

"I'm sorry." He pressed his finger to his own lips to silence her as she looked up at his words. 'And I should be sorry too. I had not considered any of what you have just told me. I had thought the dangers all to be my own and that is not true. I am more grateful to you now than I have ever been because I know now what loyalty you afford me.' He watched as her eyes rose to meet his, the hint of a blush forming upon her pale face. 'But I do not know how to repay you.'

"Repay me?" Kate looked at him searchingly.

"Please, let me finish." He dropped her hand and walked to the window. "I fear that you think that what I am doing is for sport or for pleasure." He wheeled around and clapped his hands. "And do not misunderstand me Kate, much of this gives me enormous pleasure but I need you to understand that this is no whim."

He dropped his gaze to meet her own and she nodded.

"I know, sir."

"I mean to leave this life behind Kate," he gestured at himself and the room around him.

237

"The house?" She narrowed her eyes, not understanding him.

"The house, the life I lead within it. This!" He picked up a discarded dress from the stand beside him and dropped it to the floor. "Whilst I am here, I cannot be myself and whilst I cannot be myself, I cannot be happy."

Kate watched him warily as he tried to make his meaning clear.

"But what about your father?" she said. What about me, she wanted to add.

Avery sat down on the stool beside the dressing table and put his head in his hands. "I don't know, but we must leave this all behind, Kate. Don't you see?"

"We?"

"I mean...I need you Kate, far more than you realise and I cannot do any of this without you. If you would only see how much this all......"

The knock that came at the door made each of them jump far higher than they both imagined was possible. Avery was roused to a standing position and instinctively, given the recent comings and goings within the room, he darted around the room looking for any clues which may give his double life away. Kate, busy doing the same, scurried to the door and, acknowledging the young scullery girl, scurried off without another word to Avery thus not finding out what her mistress had been about to say to her.

~o~

The slightly serious tone of the conversation with Kate had unnerved Avery and, after such a frivolous

238

evening as the previous nights, he was not keen to hang around to discuss the matter again. He knew that he would have to face her again soon and the question of both their futures was becoming a pressing one but whilst he could avoid it, he would. As his heartbeat returned to normal his thoughts turned to Elizabeth Greenwood and the parting invitation she had cast at him as it became clear that Bateman was taking her home.

"You look like a man who enjoys nature Mr. Silver?"

"Indeed?" he had inclined his head with a questioning look.

Bateman had gripped her tighter and given Silver a sharp look.

"I hope I will bump into you again sometime. Perhaps I have seen you already? Do you walk in Hyde Park of an afternoon?"

"Yes, a walk always lifts my mood in the afternoon Miss Greenwood."

"Particularly after one is feeling rotten," she offered finally. The young woman, now slightly worse for wear had smiled suggestively at him before being wheeled away by Bateman.

It was less than subtle and Avery expected Bateman, having heard the exchange, would also be found in the vicinity of the Hyde Park area. Yet, as he strolled along the edge of Rotten Row, he was surprised to see Miss Greenwood, seemingly alone. He watched her for some minutes before noticing a young maid several feet behind keeping a sluggish pace with the languid steps of her mistress. He smiled to himself as he recognised the delicate way in which Miss

Greenwood moved. The day was not particularly bright and the air was already beginning to become warm with a thick haze settling in the air between them and the high sun. Elizabeth Greenwood wore a hat, tilted to shield her eyes a little and even at this distance, Avery could see that she kept her eyebrows knotted as if the bright light pained her. He chuckled to himself wondering if she would even remember suggesting that he meet her here and whether he would find her as disarming as he had found her last night.

"Miss Greenwood?" He stepped out from the edges of the sandy pathway and raised his hat to, the now stationary, Miss Greenwood.

"Mr. Silver! I declare! What a coincidence!" The words were delivered flatly but with a smile that assured Silver she had full recollection of the previous evening. As the young maid drew up behind her mistress, her eyes rolled at the advent of Silver upon their afternoon's stroll. The gesture was not entirely lost on Silver and he wondered how it was possible that this girl was able to gad about one of the most public thoroughfares in London with only a naïve young maid as chaperone greeting young men so gaily. He was full of admiration for the young woman but more than that; he was intrigued by her confidence.

"What a surprise indeed!" Avery returned loudly, his own tone matching hers for mock incredulity. "You have brightened up what was threatening to be a very dull day Miss Greenwood."

"I was just remarking to Cribbs here the very same thing. Wasn't I Cribbs?" Elizabeth did not look at the maid stood behind her and in return the young girl did not glance at her mistress or Avery as she returned, monosyllabically. "Yes, Miss."

"Do you care to join us?"

"I would be delighted." Avery offered up his arm and felt her gloved fingers, at first light upon the sleeve of his jacket, press purposefully upon his forearm as they began to walk on. Elizabeth set the pace and they were soon many paces in front of Cribbs who, in turn, had cut her stride to allow her mistress the distance she obviously was seeking for this interlude.

"How do you do this morning Miss Greenwood?"

Elizabeth Greenwood rolled her eyes and threw her head back, the veins on her neck rippling. It was a vulnerable pose but showed great strength.

"Oh Mr. Silver. I am afraid you will find this amusing but I feel quite unwell. There! I knew you would be unsympathetic." She pushed out her bottom lip and tried to look cross as Avery chuckled. "I am afraid I have not built up the constitution that you have." She smiled and pressed his arm again.

"Yet!" he countered.

Flashing a quick glance behind them to ensure they were well out of the earshot of Cribbs, Elizabeth whispered. 'I hope I did not get you into any trouble with Mr. Bateman last night. He could not fail to lift his mood all the way home and I feel I am much to blame for his dour spirit having spent most of the evening with you instead of he.' She had leant in to deliver this and her breath was warm upon Avery's neck making his jaw clench in response to the current of pleasure she had sent down his spine. "No trouble, Miss Greenwood. I can assure you that Giles is quite alright. I am sure he was simply tired."

241

"Merely tired you say? I suppose that would explain the dark look he gave you but what do you think he meant by you and he sharing a woman when we left last night?"

Avery felt his cheeks colour a little. So she had heard! It was awkward but he felt sure she had been in such a heady state that he could convince her she had heard incorrectly.

"You must be mistaken, Miss Greenwood. I do not know what you mean."

She leant away from him as they walked, considering him with a raised eyebrow, questioningly.

"Mr. Silver, if I have given you the impression that wool may be pulled over my eyes then I am sorry to disappoint. I hope you will credit me with the truth more frequently than I am at present intending to meet you again."

Her tone remained utterly charming and her eyes danced mischievously and Avery felt a little dizzy at the speed of her tongue. Bateman had spent many evenings recently recanting to both he and Goodwin at how the girl dazzled and lashed at one and the same time.

"Which is?" he ventured.

"At the moment, never," she replied. "You have ten minutes to make me change my mind." With that she broke her grip on his arm and turned to face her maid, who had been left behind a little and was panting a little in the heat of the afternoon sun.

"Cribbs? It's awfully warm, would you be a dear and run and fetch us some lemonade whilst we take some shade over there?" She indicated to a broad sweep of trees on the easterly bank of the Serpentine

242

beside which several wrought iron benches had been positioned to take advantage of the view. It was an area Avery knew well, for he had spent several evenings taking in a promenade amongst his fellow Londoners. Even the bench that Elizabeth now led him to was familiar. He had sat and watched many sunsets across the long lake after an early evening. It was a great place to watch people as they passed by. He would take note of how gentlemen greeted each other, how they tipped their hats, clasped each other firmly by the hand and then the elbow effusively. How they fumbled with their trousers when they thought they were not being watched or, when the shadows began to lengthen, how they approached one another, gauging the other's intent. He himself had been approached by another man on one such evening. He had been caught in a bit of a reverie and found himself staring too hard as a man had stopped to adjust himself when he noticed Avery watching him. The man was short but his clothes were well tailored, if a little crumpled. Avery suspected the man was a city gent but the faint whiff of alcohol as he approached warned him that the man was a little the worse for wear.

"You like to watch do you? How about you give me something in return for my troubles?"

For a moment, Avery had thought his disguise had been rumbled. The man's face was glazed with want. He had seen the same face come across Bateman or Goodwin and Connie's punters. It was a face he fancied that even he possessed. The evening was drawing in and, although the sky was still shot with blue, the light was fading fast. He had glanced up the road and seen only a few solitary gentlemen some distance away.

"It's alright, I know a place we can go. We won't be seen. Come on, sir," the man had continued.

Sir? So the man wanted Avery as he was. He was about to respond when he noticed the man reach into the front of his own trousers and withdraw his member. The flesh colour against the dark of his trousers was stark and Avery could not help but stare and the man took this as a sign that Avery was game.

"Come on, take a hold."

There was not time enough for Avery to register his surprise at being approached in this way, and by another man too! It would be later when he could process the absurdity of the situation. A man in want of another man only to find that man was not quite what he had in mind! At the time, Avery was too shocked to consider the danger he could be in and could only laugh and walk away.

"Oi! You can't do that!" The man's voice was loud. Too loud and one of the distant figures turned to see what the commotion was. It was growing too gloomy to see what was happening but it was enough to disperse the man quickly and Avery had walked briskly home.

Now, as he took a seat beside Elizabeth, he watched only Cribbs hurrying across the vast green towards the pavilion where refreshments could be purchased.

"You have until she returns to change my mind back again Mr. Silver. It would be a great shame if you cannot. I was beginning to think we could be friends."

Avery cast about in his memory trying to remember exactly what Bateman had said to him. At the moment, Elizabeth was in danger of believing that he and Bateman were complicit in some way. To win her attention? To share her, even?

"Miss Greenwood, I fear that you may be much mistaken by what you may have overheard."

"Do you think me a *"backstreet whore"* Mr. Silver?"

The phrase Bateman has used came thundering back and Silver responded immediately.

"Good God no! Miss Greenwood, how could you think such a thing? I can assure you that you are indeed mistaken."

"So you do not think me a whore Mr. Silver but do you intend to share me like one?"

Avery snorted with incredulity. "Of course not! I would sooner eat my own head than share you." The words had come out wrong but the sentiment was entirely genuine.

"Good," praised Elizabeth. "Then at such a rate you shouldn't have to. I much prefer your company to Bateman's."

As she delivered this, she squeezed his thigh before standing to turn and greet the returning Cribbs.

"Good girl, Cribbs. What took you so long? Oh don't say you didn't bring any sugar? Oh be a sweetheart and fetch us some, won't you? You would like some sugar wouldn't you Mr. Silver?"

Cribbs looked as if she would sooner strangle her mistress than do her bidding but she made no sound as she turned on her heel and skulked back across the grass. Elizabeth turned and lowered her gaze at Avery Silver.

"I wonder if you could change my mind back again before the next time she returns?"

She sat down again beside him but this time a fraction closer. Their thighs touched and she pressed her knees towards him, her hand once more upon his thigh. Silver leaned back against the bench, his arms outstretched across the back of the bars and discretely placed a finger in between her shoulder blades and firmly drew a line up to the nape of her neck where the curl of her hair lay tightly coiled. The sensation it invoked within Elizabeth caused her to once again squeeze Avery's thigh and the two felt a concordant shiver of desire pass between them.

"Have you changed your mind Miss Greenwood?"

"Oh yes," she replied, her eyes shut tight.

Chapter Sixteen - Imogen, 1911

The afternoon of Mrs. Evesham and Mrs. Doone's visit were, thankfully, devoid of any further unexpected visitors allowing me some small respite in which to quietly grieve and to try and order the many disordered thoughts that buffeted inside my mind. It was the third day following my father's death and a note had been delivered from the undertakers requesting a set of clothes in which to dress my father for burial. The coroner had concluded his examinations and had released the body for the funeral three days hence. I was grateful of the task as I had been putting off a return to Hamble Gardens fearing what I would unearth there; nevertheless, I found I was relieved of the excuse to go. John had already set Heston about clearing the house ready for sale and I wanted to see the place before the desiccation was complete. I knew Heston well enough to know that he would keep safe such personal effects of my father's as he would have wanted and I looked ahead with trepidation at the task. Such proximity might bring me closer to understanding this mystery but, at the same time, reveal more than I was willing to learn.

The city had conjured up a cold, so sharp, that I thought my lungs were being ripped apart as I made my way by cab across London. I was raw by the time we reached my father's house and grateful to step inside the warmth. The door was opened by a young parlour maid whom I did not recognise but, so glad was I to be out from the bitter cold, I forgot to raise the matter immediately. I had been so mindful of staying warm in the cab that I had not had time to think on the journey about how I might feel being back inside that house.

The moment the door closed, the familiar warm smells of floor wax and oak, sandalwood and oil coiled their way into my mind releasing powerful feelings of comfort and happiness. As the young girl took my hat and gloves, I noticed that the roses on the console table had been refreshed. They were my mother's favourite flowers and my father had always insisted that there be fresh roses every week even since she had passed away. She had believed that roses were not so much a romantic but an optimistic flower; their many layers of petals opening daily to reveal a new face even when they began to die and shed their bounty, she collected the fallen petals and had them to dried to demonstrate their eternity. Before I had time to soak up the familiar feeling of home, I was struck by the changes that had occurred in just three days. The long-case clock had been covered by a white sheet and, even from under its shroud, I could hear that it had not been wound. Many of the paintings which my father had collected were now removed from the wall, squares of pale wallpaper indicating where once they had hung.

Heston appeared in the hall from my father's study and his countenance lifted from one of great heaviness as he took in the sight of me. I smiled and inclined my head towards him.

"Madam," he self-consciously indicated to the bare walls. "As per your husband's wishes, I have begun compiling an inventory of the house. The paintings have been collected in the parlour where

248

Messrs.' Webster and Round have started to catalogue them."

He looked at me in a wretched manner which told me he was loathed to undertake this dismantling of his master's home, his own home. I could imagine his disgust at having the auctioneers inside the house, picking over the collections of my parents in both a detached manner but also barely disguising their appetite for the sensation that occurred under this very roof. There was an unfamiliar air about Heston which put me at unease as if he wanted to discuss something with me but his sense of propriety forbade it. If my own uneasiness had abated, I would probably have tried to wrestle it from him but the strangeness of the house looking so bare stirred up a sense of dread and I was trying only to concentrate on not weeping or ranting.

"Thank you Heston. I am come for some paperwork and to collect a suit for my father."

"I will see to it madam." He stepped aside and I walked directly to the study. He followed me to the door.

"I will get Lottie to bring you some tea Madam."

"Lottie?" I called to mind the face of the young girl who had let me in a short while ago and remembered that I did not recognise her. "What happened to Florence?"

"She was dismissed, Ma'am." Heston said simply, his face utterly neutral.

"Dismissed?" I repeated. "Why?"

"Mr. Bancroft understood that the press was informed as a result of a leak within this house Madam."

I understood perfectly. Neither Heston nor Mrs. Rooksmith would have spoken to a soul about what went on under this roof. They were of a different generation of domestic staff believing the upper echelons of society had a right to behave differently than theirs. What limited gossip must have occurred between the staff of one house or another was little more than worthless prattle. Such a revelation as my father being a woman, quite aside from shocking them to silence, would have certainly been kept confidential. Florence, a young girl of twenty or so, of the new generation would certainly have weighed up a good reference from our family as having little currency in light of the revelations and would therefore throw her lot in with the press without so much hesitation. The news depressed me a little, as I once again doubted who I could trust. I looked at the smart form of Heston stood waiting for a dismissal or an order and I felt a small glow of affection for him in his steadfastness. Could I rely upon him as I once had my father or could he also be concealing something from me?

"Very good. Thank you Heston."

Heston nodded and left me in my father's study. As he drew the door closed behind him, I realised I had never been alone in this room before and a curiosity awoke inside me. From my earliest childhood memories this room had held a charm that only forbidden places can. My father would emerge from hours inside its confines, doing I could not imagine what, to earn our modest fortune. My father had been a keen investor and had selected wisely a number of trades and had profited greatly from their success. He advised others on their own finances and portfolios and was rather well regarded at it. As a result, he spent many hours in this room with many clients and acquaintances discussing business and, by all accounts, not one of them ever guessed his secret. I was surprised to feel a small swell of pride at the idea that my father had been so clever. I shook my head and rolled my eyes. It was an absurd feeling but the warmness it brought to my heart gave me the first feeling of tenderness and I was not ready to feel thus so.

Slowly, I walked to the large desk upon which the police inspector had been sat when I had last been in the room and, upon which, there still lay the volume of poetry that he had been perusing. I ignored it and continued around to my father's side of the desk and took a seat in the captains' chair which sat before it. The wood creaked and the leather sighed; the noises instantly sending me back to another time when it had been my father eliciting those same sounds. I looked across the desk, the room unfamiliar from this angle and I could see myself stood in the centre of the rug which covered the floor. I must have been eight or nine; my hair was tucked behind my ears and I am looking at my feet. From what I can see of my face, I am burning bright red and I can feel the heat of the memory as I cast my mind back.

"What have you got to say for yourself, Imogen?" *My father's voice is low and expresses only disappointment. There is no hint of anger; there is no space left in the room for any after my mother's outburst. She stands behind him, her back to the room, looking out of the tall window. She has one hand to her*

mouth clasping her lips between thumb and forefinger as if sealing them from uttering anything further.

"Well?" he says, after it is clear I will add nothing to the shame filled silence.

His voice is distant and I know that I have grieved him far greater than my mother's harsh words could ever have allowed me to realise.

"I'm sorry," I manage to mumble.

I can hardly remember how the whole incident had come about. My parents had kissed me goodnight as usual and I had insisted on keeping a light with which to read by. Nanny Owen usually extinguished it, a while late,r when I was weary and nodding. As soon as my bedroom door had closed, I had taken it in mind that the long shadows being cast by the candle light were more sinister than usual and I had taken up the candlestick and set it closer to me. I knew it was wrong but I was a sensible and careful child and I didn't expect any accidents. The closer I drew the candle towards me, the darker the corners of the room seemed and I eventually managed to prop the candlestick deep in between my pillows. Of course this had been a stupid plan and I am lucky to be alive at all. Needless to say, the light bobbed and caught the edge of my bed linen. I was so shocked by the ferocity of the blaze that I was momentarily struck dumb. Afraid of the fire but also knowing that it was my fault, I tried ineffectually to solve the problem. I had tried in vain to blow out the fire but this only served to further ignite the blaze and, leaping from my bed, I had let out a scream. The scenes that followed would be rather comical had it not been for the seriousness of them. In my own head they seem to be recalled only in double speed, rather like the spinning optical wheels where the movements are jerky. Nanny Owen appeared and screamed. She flapped and lunged for me, pulling me to her. My father rushed in to the room, his shirt was unbuttoned at the neck and he was not wearing a tie. It was the least clothed I would ever see my father alive. He shouted and grabbed for my ewer on the nightstand, he snatched it up and threw the water over the flames. A younger Heston ran into the room, carrying some container or other of water which he also threw at my bed. I remember the grotesque, spectral flames licking and curling through the cloud of jet black smoke. My father pushed me out of the room into my mother's arms. Heston returned with dripping wet linen and he and my father re-entered to wrestle with the flames to bring them under control. It is over in my head in a few minutes. I told my mother what happened and she was instantly thrown into a temper. She thrust me from her, screamed out in fury and marched me downstairs to the study. Two plump teardrops blossom at the corner of my eyes and one falls across my cheek and I bite my lip. "I'm really sorry," I say again quietly.

"There is no-one sorrier than we are, Imogen. Tonight we have all had rather a shock, the greatest of all being that we came so close to losing you."

My mother turns from the window and tears are streaming down her pale face and I notice for the first time that she is shaking, not from anger or chill, but from fear.

At the time, the scene seemed so horridly unfair and their response such an overreaction but as I sat thinking about that night I considered how I should feel if Sebastian or Thomas had ever been so near death and a cold, sharper than the bitter air outside, swept through me and I shuddered. Yet, though I am brought closer to them by the memory, I find myself wondering again whether they could feel the same way for me if neither of them were my real parents. A knock at the door brings me back to the present and I am surprised to see the face of Lottie as she brought in a tea tray to the study.

"Over here ma'am?"

"Yes, thank you."

"Can I fetch you anything else ma'am?"

"No,..er yes. Actually, can you ask Mrs. Rooksmith to come and see me in half an hour please?"

"Certainly ma'am."

She curtsied and left me alone once more. I made a start on the desk drawers. Half of them were full of well labeled envelopes, receipts and dockets relating to the finances of the house. There was a drawer full of keys, all labeled with meticulous care. *Clock, hall. Clock, mantel (parlour), Pantry* etc. There was an order to these drawers which I found comforting. I don't know what I was looking for but after a few moments of searching, I found nothing. There was a knock at the door again and I jumped.

"Ah yes, Mrs. Rooksmith," I gestured to the chair. "Won't you have seat?"

The old woman smiled at me and sat awkwardly in the seat opposite my own. The desk between us seemed suddenly to be wider than the Thames and I felt quite distant to the old woman.

"It's good to see you, Miss Imogen," she started. "I'm so sorry for your loss. Your father was a good man."

There was conviction in her sentiment but her voice tailed off as I looked away uncomfortably. I was not yet ready to discuss the matter and denial seemed far more appealing.

"Heston will have told you the plans for the house and that we shall have to let you all go at the end of next month. Of course, you shall all have the most excellent of references. John and I have always regarded your services very highly and my father would want me to reward your loyalty. Accordingly, I have made arrangements for three months extra salary to be added to your final pay."

There was a loud snort and I glanced across at Mrs. Rooksmith to note that she was blowing her nose, her eyes were red. The desk between us grew even wider as I felt the gap in our emotions. She was a woman grieving for her employer in abundance whilst there I sat, numb to her tears and still quite unable to shed a tear for my own father. I felt strangely outside of myself as I watched this woman, whom I had known for many years, compose herself. I was unable to offer any comfort but instead I remained seated behind my father's desk, my face impassive and my hands still. I was saved any further discomfort by a knock at the door.

"Yes?"

The door opened to reveal Heston.

"I have prepared a box with all of the clothes, ma'am. Do you wish to see them before I pack them away?"

255

I looked to the cook opposite me.

"Do excuse me Mrs. Rooksmith," I searched for some words I could offer to replace my own lack of emotion but could find none. "I am grateful to you for your loyalty to my father."

She rose from the chair and, without another word, she left.

I returned my attention to Heston.

"I will be up presently."

I waited until he was gone before I opened the drawer to my father's desk again. I looked through the same contents but, finding nothing, I followed Heston out of the room and mounted the stairs once more, disappointed. It was not until I was at the top of the stairs that I realised that I must enter my father's bedroom again in order to view the suit. As I stood in the doorway, I was grateful to see that the curtains were drawn wide and the room was already showing signs of being packed away. The bed has been stripped and there was no sign of my father within it. I walked into the room, my head angled away from the bed, ignoring the ghost of the image in my mind in which my father is sprawled like a science experiment. Heston was hunched beside my father's wardrobe against which he has hung a smart black mourning suit. On a dress horse he has pressed a shirt. He was just putting a touch of polish to some already shiny black shoes as I approached him from behind.

I noticed with surprise that the shoes Heston held in his hands were smaller than I remembered. My father was tall, as tall as John in his prime although more recently he had begun to take on a slight stoop. John's shoes were much bigger and it fazed me that I had never noticed before. Heston did a double take before rising to attention.

"Ah, Mrs. Bancroft, I hope that this is in order." His knees clicked loudly in the expanse of the near empty room. The lack of personal effects did little to deaden the creak and I remember again that Heston was quite old himself. It struck me that Heston had been close to father. His personal butler, his dresser, his aide. Surely Heston of all people should have known my father's secret.

"It is your father's best suit. It is fairly new...."

He stopped. It was new because it had been brought for my mother's funeral.

"Thank you Heston." For the second time, I was compelled to reach out and touch his sleeve. It was out of character for me and I sensed immediately that he was uncomfortable with the gesture. Yet it was the only thing I could think of to do or say.

"Will that be all Madam?"

I withdrew my hand and nodded, looking away from him; eager to ask him what he knew but not to hear his reply. I waited to hear the door close behind him before I screwed up my eyes with my fingertips rubbing away the images of my father. The way he looked at my mother's funeral, so vulnerable and shaken by the loss of her. I took up the sleeve of the suit hanging limply in front of me and held it to my face. I was instantly transported into my father's arms and there, in the comfort of his scent, I wept for the first time since his death.

Chapter Seventeen - Elizabeth 1869

As the trap pulled away from Amersham Station, Elizabeth felt her mood darken yet further. The dull train journey alongside Cribbs, who could barely contain her excitement about leaving the city for the first time, was an endurance of her patience. The fact that the scenery passing them by showed little promise of excitement, further deepened her sense of despair at such a forced exile. She had endured her father's lecture about reputation and order with a sense of boredom and, of course, had expected some form of punishment. Knowing that she was his darling, she had been confident that whatever he had had in mind she could escape, by means of her expert persuasion. This was something she had cultivated since she was a little girl and Agnes, no matter how hard she tried to emulate her, was unable to exert the same influence. She had therefore been rather shocked when, on the matter of her punishment, her grim faced aunt had been ushered to the fore, and Elizabeth was less impressed when she found out what the old girl had in store for her.

A summer break at the Fearncott country finishing school and, no less, she was expected to babysit for the runt of some man the old woman had her claws into! The nerve of her! Who did she think she was? As unlike her father as was possible to be, Aunt Georgina was a sly and vindictive woman who clearly resented Elizabeth. She had never been a fan of her mother, that much was clear. Choosing to either criticise her or ignore her completely, their relationship had always been strained. Despite being a ridiculous notion, Elizabeth chose to blame her aunt for her mother's death. It was unfair, but Elizabeth despised her aunt for the obvious hold she had over her father.

Elizabeth's face was contorted into an ugly grimace as, eventually, the trap made a turn off the main road, through an entrance gate and up a long, cedar-lined driveway. The warm sunshine that dappled through the tall canopy could do little to lift her mood. On the contrary, the play that the light made in the dusty air before them reminded her of only a few days ago when she was seated alongside the strangely enigmatic Avery Silver. As the long drive swept beneath them, she thought on that afternoon and tried to recall the way Avery had looked at her, and she instantly felt the same rush of heady breathlessness he had imbued her with. She was curious about how he made her feel and had been hoping to feel it again. When she had left with an irate Cribbs later that afternoon, they had pledged to meet again very soon and she was furious to find herself here in the country, with no way of sending him word. There was to be no pleasure for her this summer and would do her utmost to make life miserable for everyone.

"Cribbs! Do wipe that ridiculous smile off your face. You look like a halfwit," she snapped. The face of the young maid fell immediately and she turned to look in the other direction, as Juniper Hall appeared through the foliage at the crest of the drive.

The sandstone house, reflecting the bright light of the summer sun, appeared as though it were ablaze. The many windows sparkled like diamonds set in a great golden casket and Cribbs couldn't stop herself from exclaiming out loud.

"It's beautiful, aint it!"

Concealing her own admiration at the wealth of her aunt's estate, Elizabeth merely breathed a sigh of disdain and returned to look the way that they had come, imagining London at the end of the long drive. As the trap rattled to the bottom of the grand stone steps, a stable-hand took hold of the lead horse and drew them to a stop. The driver leapt from his seat and readied the steps, standing back to allow the two women to step down. At the entrance to the house stood Georgina Fearncott, dressed in a pale lilac dress imprinted with delicate spring flowers. As was usual, her silvery hair was pinned tightly and, despite the gentle breeze, remained perfectly in place. In the drab surrounds of their London home, Elizabeth always felt Georgina's large and colourful presence out of place. Here, Elizabeth noted with displeasure, she seemed entirely congruous.

"Elizabeth!" her aunt called abruptly, barely concealing her dislike of the girl. "Don't dawdle, dear. Come on."

Turning on her heel, she disappeared into the house and Elizabeth stalked after her, followed by Cribbs. Leaving the warmth of the day and stepping into the house, Elizabeth tried to take in her surroundings. The dark wood floor was well polished and led up to an impressive first floor galleried landing. The long walls were adorned with elaborately framed oil paintings and each frame contained a similarly seated portrait of a dull-faced man, each possessing a hooked nose of varying proportions. No doubt, these were ancestor's of the late Sir Fearncott. Glancing at them, Elizabeth thought what good fortune it had been that her aunt had never managed to have a child with him. With her crumpled face and his ugly beak, the poor thing would never have faced daylight! Smiling to herself, she climbed the stairs after the fast receding shape of her aunt.

"I have put you on the second floor above my own bedroom. Our guest will be in the room beside yours." The old woman turned to see Elizabeth meandering up the stairs behind her and Cribbs still standing in the hallway below.

"You, girl!" Georgina bellowed. "Fetch Miss Greenwood's bags and follow on!" She turned a cheerless smile on Elizabeth and admonished her on behalf of the dawdling girl. "We haven't all day, have we, Elizabeth?"

Elizabeth matched the shallow beam of her aunt and nodded her agreement.

"Quite, Aunt Georgina."

As the old woman turned to proceed along the second floor corridor, Elizabeth poked a tongue at her back. The room, to which she was shown, was twice the size of her own and larger even than Agnes', the latter point giving her cause to feel somewhat smug. She wandered to the large windows to see what view she had been given. The room was at the back of the house and faced South and Elizabeth could see only the kitchen garden and a sunken walled garden, at the bottom of which there was set a wrought iron gate. Through the thick summer foliage of the trees, she could only just make out the rooves of a handful of houses in the distance. Compared to London, the green space and the beautiful countryside, erupting with colour, should have been refreshing, but Elizabeth saw nothing in the view but a long and dull summer ahead. She turned from the window, her aunt watching her carefully.

"It's beautiful," Elizabeth enthused, her eyes staring coldly into Georgina's. "Thank you for inviting me to spend the summer with you, Aunt Georgina."

The old woman cocked her head to one side and considered her niece.

"This is no holiday, Elizabeth," she started. "This is a punishment for your ill-chosen excursions and, though your father may not see what you are about, I certainly do." She paused, allowing the frankness of her words to sink in. "I, for one, know what you seek, Elizabeth, and you will not find what you are looking for here. I will be keeping a close eye on you, my girl, and if you want to find your way back to London, you had better watch your step. I had forgotten how the country air agrees with me and I may consider staying longer than the summer."

Elizabeth's unblinking stare was met by a cold smile from her aunt as she added, 'And I fancy I may prefer some company, if I intend to stay.'

Elizabeth's heart sank as the meaning of her aunt's words sunk in.

"Ah, there you are." Georgina broke off her stare and stepped to one side, allowing Cribbs to deposit two of Elizabeth's cases at the foot of the bed. A butler followed close behind with a large trunk.

"I will let you get settled in then." She turned and bustled out of the room. "Tea on the terrace in one hour, Elizabeth," she threw over her shoulder. The butler closed the door behind him and Cribbs started to open the cases.

"Well, she don't get no happier does she?" remarked Cribbs, and the first genuine smile of the day played on Elizabeth's lips before she sullenly undid her bonnet and flung it at the bed.

"Don't unpack everything, Cribbs. I don't intend staying for very long."

~o~

Just over an hour later, Elizabeth prowled out on to the terrace where Georgina was waiting. The girl's lateness, albeit slight, had not gone unnoticed by Georgina but for the time being remained unchallenged. Their relationship would be about gaining ground from one another, little by little. For the moment, Georgina was prepared to let Elizabeth win the smaller battles.

"Well, I am pleased to see you are changed into something a little more suitable for tea than the last time." Now they were equal. "Your father probably told you the reason why you are here, Elizabeth. Accustomed as I am sure you could make yourself to a period of leisure in the country, I need not remind you that this sojourn is not a holiday." Georgina raised an eyebrow daring Elizabeth to speak or to argue. Elizabeth stared defiantly at her aunt but kept silent. At no sign of any interruption from Elizabeth, Georgina continued.

"Yes, well. Ahem, we have a little job for you. You will recall the widower that I was talking to you of a few months ago, Toby. A fine man. Lost his wife ten years ago. He is a partner in a law firm and is highly regarded and well thought of. Since the death of

Walter, I have been quite lonely. This estate is quite large and troublesome. It is not something a woman should manage alone."

Elizabeth managed not to speak up. Her aunt's ability to outstrip men half her age in both acuity and wit was widely recognised. The running of this estate was well within her capability.

"Toby is endowed with his own wealth and a proven business man. He is well suited for my needs and it is likely therefore that we shall be wed in the autumn."

Elizabeth wondered whether the poor unsuspecting Toby was aware of his future with Georgina and if he had yet posed the question. Her eyes twinkled mischievously. She was as amused at her aunt's portrait of herself as a widow of poor means as she was intrigued by the prospect of a wedding. This had not gone unnoticed by the astute Georgina who immediately added.

"It will be a small affair and unlikely to hold any interest for you."

Elizabeth enfolded her arms back into the confines of her lap and within her perfect ladylike posture there lurked a sulky child.

"So," Georgina continued "Have I spoken to you of his daughter?"

Elizabeth feigned interest and considered the question pretending to recollect any such mention.

"I don't believe you have, Aunt Georgina," she responded, politely

"Alice Silver? I must have told you of her."

Elizabeth frowned trying to recall if she had heard mention before of the girl. Her immediate thought was of Avery and she wondered, hopefully, if this girl might be a sibling or a cousin.

"You know her?" Georgina asked.

There was little that got by the old woman who had noticed the flicker of surprise register across the young girl's face.

"No, Aunt Georgina. The name is merely familiar but I do not know any Alice Silver."

Satisfied, Georgina continued.

"Who you know, Elizabeth is of no consequence to me. But in this instance, what you know is of great use. Alice, sadly, has been without female influence for many years. She is beyond the brink of womanhood and has very little etiquette. If she is to form part of this family, which of course is my wish,' she inclined her head towards Elizabeth, it was a gesture that included Elizabeth, 'she will need to learn to behave in a more refined manner."

Elizabeth almost choked on her tea. Was she right in thinking that her aunt was asking for her to teach someone else how to behave? Given the conversation of a week ago, this indeed seemed rather farfetched. This girl must desperately require some finishing if she was being engaged for the task. Georgina too, paused to see what effect these words would have on Elizabeth. Consummately educated, the girl merely raised one eyebrow and inclined her head in ascension

"You will find that this is an altogether appropriate situation for both of you. Alice is in great need of the right sort of tutelage if she is to find herself a husband and you," she raised her voice and glared at Elizabeth pointedly, "are in great need of responsibility and censorship. Of course, much of this I would undertake myself but I have a wedding to organise and an estate to manage. You will find, within these grounds and these walls, Juniper Hall is a perfectly adequate space to undertake this task."

Having satisfied herself that Elizabeth had not objected to the plan nor had shown any great enthusiasm, Georgina allowed a disdainful smile to creep out across her face. Elizabeth watched in silence, as her aunt then reached across the table and took a slice of cake.

"Aren't you having any? Quite right, too. I suppose you can ill afford any more weight around your hips."

Elizabeth flashed her aunt an acidic smile and drained the last of her tea.

~o~

The days that followed blurred into one, as her aunt's routine dragged each minute into an hour and Elizabeth could find no way to entertain herself. Her aunt had a great many books but all of these were many years out of date, classics whose titles revealed very little interest for the young girl. The History of Tom Jones, A Foundling! Why ever would she wish to entertain herself on the story of a deprived Welsh child? The music room did not want for much by way of instruments but Elizabeth, barely able to force herself to the piano at the best of times was even less inclined to do so in this particular room. An internal space, there were no windows which made the room far more chill than any other in the house. At the peak of the summer, retiring to this dark and cold space was like an exile from all that had made London pleasurable. Her aunt took her meals at certain times and was seemingly glad of the company which Elizabeth afforded but took no pleasure in. Enjoying the opportunity of an audience, Georgina talked incessantly about her first husband and how Toby was superior to him in most ways. After only a few days, Elizabeth was rather looking forward to the arrival of her young charge, if only for a break from the tedium of the routine. She nodded serenely as she and her aunt took yet another tea on the terrace and, is if reading her mind, Georgina brought the subject up.

"I believe we are to expect Miss Silver after lunch tomorrow."

Despite herself, Elizabeth perked up. Perhaps she and the girl would have much in common. At very least, she would be an ally against her sour old aunt. Cribbs had proved useless in this regard, preferring to place her hands over her ears whenever Elizabeth spoke ill of the old bag, lest she be accused of badmouthing the old woman.

"That is good news, Aunt Georgina. Shall I arrange for some flowers to be cut for her room?"

Georgina smiled at her niece a little more benevolently. She had high hopes for how this summer was to turn out and she praised herself again for her clever plan.

"Why yes, Elizabeth. That would be lovely."

The following day, Elizabeth was on edge awaiting the arrival of her aunt's future step-daughter. All through lunch her aunt's chatter grated most horribly and she was unable to keep her annoyance in check.

267

"Toby tells me that his daughter is quite unaccustomed to any sort of social scene. Can you imagine Elizabeth?" her aunt scanned her peremptorily before adding. "It doesn't bear thinking about does it?"

"No, Aunt Georgina." Elizabeth pulled a face and pushed her plate from her and replaced her napkin over the half eaten lunch. "I am afraid I have rather a poor appetite. The change of air is still rather unsettling; I am going to take a walk on the lawn. Please, will you excuse me Aunt Georgina?"

The older woman waved the younger girl away and smiled to herself smugly. She had no further plan for Elizabeth than to inconvenience her and hope that, between the two of them, they could break down the defences of Alice Silver. Georgina Fearncott was very pleased with how things were going.

A few minutes later, Elizabeth descended from a quick change into some walking shoes and was out of the side door and on to the terrace; a miffed Cribbs scurrying afterwards with a parasol.

"Miss Greenwood?" The young servant caught up with her in several strides and tried to position the shade above her mistress. This proved more difficult at the pace Elizabeth was keeping and, after two close calls with the edge of the parasol and Elizabeth's head, the mistress stopped dead in her tracks and, rounding on the girl, she snapped. With a quick whip, she held the other girls wrist, tightly in her hand

"For God's sake, Cribbs. Will you leave me alone?"

The younger girl trembled slightly, a look of panic on her face. She had not expected her good intentions to deliver such a rebuke.

"Miss Elizabeth. You're hurting me." She tried to wrest her arm from the tight grip but Elizabeth held firm, her fingers squeezing a little harder.

"Just leave me alone." She thrust the girl's arm far from her and, after levelling a warning stare, she stalked off down the sloping lawn away from the gaze of the house. She had been in her Aunt's charge for little under a week and already she felt her liberty had deserted her forever. The effect of her aunt's constant attention was like being placed between the pages of a book and pressed like a precious flower. To top it all off, she had dreamed of Silver last night and she had been disconcerted to find in her dream that he and Bateman had been plotting after all. The two had made a gentleman's bet to see which could woo Elizabeth first. Whilst it was only a dream, it had served to further dampen her mood. It was likely a result of her guilt at not being able to get a message to Silver before she left and she was determined to find a way to send word to him before the week was out. Perhaps the arrival of her step-daughter to be, would divert her aunt long enough to allow Elizabeth to get a letter out somehow.

She walked for over an hour before her mood could be considered improved at all. She was a little embarrassed about how she had spoken to Cribbs and she resolved to speak more kindly to her. As she returned within view of the house, her heart lifted further when she saw the sight of a carriage upon the gravel. So she had finally arrived! Elizabeth did not have many close female friends and, in normal circumstances, she would not have been overjoyed at the prospect of another girl with which to share her time. However, her confinement here and the promise of some more exciting excursions made the arrival of Miss Silver very promising. Her aunt had indicated that this girl was in need of an '*airing*' in polite society and Elizabeth was determined that she should make this sooner rather than later. If the girl needed manners and a more refined disposition, then she was keen to get started. She picked up her pace and hurried to the terrace where she could now see her aunt's frame silhouetted against the pale walls. She was taking a seat and another figure had joined her, stepping from the wide open parlour doors and casting another long shadow across the facade of the house. As her feet crunched on the gravel and she climbed the steps, her aunt spun around announcing cheerily.

"Ah, here she is. Elizabeth?" she called out. "We wondered where on earth you had got to. Oh my dear, you will want to change your dress, you have soil upon your hem. I must apologise Miss Silver, my niece had a mind to take a stroll after lunch. You will see we have quite the space for it here. Not quite Hyde Park but at least it is more private." The old woman's voice tailed off as she turned around to face Elizabeth.

Elizabeth walked towards the seated figures with the sun at her rear. The figure seated beside her aunt was shielding their eyes, trying to examine the approaching Elizabeth. From what Elizabeth could see of the face beneath the hand, it was clouded not only from the shade but also with something else; it was a look of horror as they recognised each other.

"Elizabeth. This is Alice Silver, my future step daughter." She attempted a maternal smile which achieved something rather more menacing. "Alice, this is Elizabeth Greenwood, my niece."

270

There was a smile of recognition and a flash of white as her eyes grew wide for a moment but otherwise nothing about Elizabeth's demeanour betrayed the fact that either of them had met before. There was a lengthy pause and Avery could only watch in horror as Elizabeth coolly surveyed him from top to toe.

"I'm delighted to finally meet you, Miss Silver." Her manner and expression was perfectly neutral, as she offered her hand delicately in the air between them.

Georgina, satisfied with her niece's start, turned to examine Avery, whose face was somewhat less neutral. His face had fallen and his eyes were flickering, as he tried to gauge what Elizabeth might say, if anything.

After a moment, Georgina brought her hand to her mouth and gently coughed to encourage the introductions along.

"Miss Greenwood," was all that Avery could muster in his shock.

Evidently, this was enough and, well satisfied but oblivious to any discomfort, Georgina clapped her hands together and continued with her overly loud ambitions for the summer.

"Elizabeth, will you show Miss Silver to her room and then let her settle in to get freshened up from her journey. We shall take tea in an hour in the blue parlour."

She turned on her heels and, spotting Kate begin to gather the bags at her feet, she clapped her hands at the maid as if she were shooing away a cat.

"You girl! Leave those, Brown will take them. Sally, have Miss Silver's maid installed in the side room. Where is Brown?" Her voice did not diminish as she bustled off through to the adjoining room but rather seemed to grow louder still.

As Kate followed the young housemaid up the stairs, she cast a glance behind her towards Avery. She had not made the connection yet between the two of them but Avery's ashen face and racing heart had not gone unnoticed. Avery and Elizabeth were left looking at one another rather awkwardly. Afraid to put words to the fear rising in his throat, Avery's jaw was tightly clamped shut. Elizabeth did not look at him directly but instead turned on her heels to precede him to his room.

"This way Miss Silver, do watch the bottom step. My aunt has a penchant for shiny things and this house is no exception. If it were any more polished, one could use it as a looking glass." She laughed; a hollow sound that gave Avery a chill but he relaxed a little. Although Elizabeth was clearly unnerved by his arrival, she was clearly not going to give him away. He hoped that they would get a chance to talk when they got to his room. As they rounded the top of the stairs however, Elizabeth, several steps ahead indicated a doorway to one side.

"This will be your room, Miss Silver. I hope you find it comfortable. I am sure your maid will be with you shortly to unpack."

And with that, she turned on her heel and disappeared down the corridor.

"Elizabeth!" Avery hissed, trying to call her back.

"Is everything alright, Miss Silver?"

Avery spun around in surprise to hear Georgina's voice. Had she not been downstairs only moments ago? As he wondered on this, the widow bustled into the room past him pointing out the view from the window and issuing instruction.

"As the sun looks so fierce, I thought we would spend the afternoon getting acquainted with one another in the house. I could show you both my pottery. I suppose your father has told you all about my collection? I am sure Elizabeth would be delighted to show you."

Before he followed Georgina into his room, Avery looked down the corridor after Elizabeth, but she had gone.

Chapter Eighteen - Imogen, 1911

As I came down the stairs, Heston took one look at me and suggested that I return home and twenty minutes later he had deposited me inside a waiting cab. He confirmed that he would continue with his task of setting the house in order but that he would arrange personally for my father's suit to be delivered to the undertakers. It was a scant gesture but one in which I found some consolation. As the cab rolled off, I found his eyes and nodded to him in thanks. Whether Heston was astute enough to recognise I had been crying was not in doubt. I had my suspicions that he was well versed in turning the other cheek. My tears had exhausted me. When I returned home, I sat in silence for a few hours with only my own dizzying thoughts for company. Shock had given way to anger and, in turn, the anger had become confusion. I had begun to

273

accept that my father could not have been my father and if my mother was not my mother, then who was I?

The sound of the telephone ringing in the hall startled me. It had only been installed last year and the noise was still so unfamiliar. John, of course, had been thrilled with it at first, making unnecessary journeys to another exchange just for the sheer delight of calling home. I had yet to get used to the contraption and felt vaguely uneasy whenever I was called to listen to the strangely disembodied voices crackling from the earpiece. Far from being curious about who was calling, I had grown used to the way the fractured tones interrupted other peoples order as one call or other was taken by the staff and directed to John. I was surprised therefore when the door to the parlour opened and Amy stepped in to the room with a bob.

"Pardon me madam but there is a caller on the telephone for you."

"Who is it?"

"It is a Mr. Evans. The undertaker," she added as she was met with my blank expression.

"Did you tell them Mr. Bancroft is dealing with all of the arrangements?"

The girl coloured slightly, her hands playing nervously with her apron.

"Yes Madam but he said it was urgent."

I closed my eyes and composed myself with a deep breath. I stood with mild irritation, not at Amy or John or even Mr. Evans but more with myself that I was not involved with the details. I suddenly felt like I had abandoned my father and I felt a rush of energy as I was given this task. I brushed past the young maid and out into the chilly hallway. The telephone, a dark ebony candle stick style handset with ivory embellishments was stood on the new purpose bought stand, waiting like an unannounced visitor. I took up the earpiece and lifted the stand to my mouth.

"Mr. Evans," I questioned into the receiver.

"Mrs. Bancroft?" came a distant voice.

The voice was nasal and I began to imagine the face to whom it should belong.

"This is she," I confirmed.

"Ah. Mrs. Bancroft. I am so terribly sorry to trouble you but under the....er... circumstances I thought it necessary to interrupt you at home. Your husband was not available at his office and I must speak to either one of you directly."

His tone was a peculiar mix of affected subservience and deference but with a hint of smugness and I took an instant dislike to this man. His face swam into my imagination as that of a rodent. One of the sole delights of speaking via the telephone is, of course, that one does not have to hide any such feelings and I rolled my eyes as I interrupted him.

"What is the matter Mr. Evans?"

"Of course, forgive me. You received my note requesting clothes for... um...the deceased?"

"Indeed. Mr. Heston, my father's butler, is to deliver them this afternoon."

There was a pause before he drew out his response.

"Ahhhhhh,'" another pause, "Yes. Mr. Heston...."

His tone suggested a superiority towards Heston which I found more than a little abrasive.

"Has he been?" I asked

"Ah, yes. That is to say, he is still here Mrs. Bancroft."

I could feel my forehead crumpling as I sought to comprehend the point of this man's call.

"If Heston is there, then what on earth is the problem?"

I was met with a silence.

"Did he forget the suit?" I volunteered.

This time, the silence was so pronounced I took the phone away from my ear to look at it.

"Mr. Evans?" I tried to coax the man into telling me the problem.

"Ah, yes. The..er...suit. No, Mrs. Bancroft, quite the contrary. Mr. Heston has indeed delivered a...a...a......suit."

He placed an emphasis on this last word which suggested that, at last, we had come to the point of this conversation and I relaxed my shoulders a little. I could of course deal with such a trivial matter. Perhaps when I had cried over the sleeves this morning, I had left some salt stain or other.

"What is the matter with the suit, Mr. Evans? Is it not clean? I must confess that when I saw it this afternoon that I did not notice any problems, but of course you will have had greater opportunity than I to inspect it. Surely Heston could arrange for it to be...."

I was so relieved the matter was of such inconsequence that it was a few seconds before I realised Mr. Evans was trying to interrupt me.

"Mrs. Bancroft, you will forgive me for interrupting you. The suit is both clean, and very fine, but quite unsuitable."

"Unsuitable?"

276

His interruption had taken me aback and I was so confused that momentarily I wondered what he meant.

"We are aware that there are some peculiarities surrounding the death of the deceased and we are further aware that there has been some misunderstandings but I am afraid it is quite improper to bury a woman in gentleman's clothing Madam. I can quite understand your wanting to...."

A hot wave of shock flushed over me as I at last understood what this odious man was trying to tell me. The heat made me glow, at first, with shame that I should have failed to interpret his stuttering and then it turned to anger. Both feelings left me momentarily stunned and at a loss for words. I listened, my mind whirling, whilst he continued chattering in an endless stream of idiocy. He made no apologies but only continued to express his own dissatisfaction. I could find neither the words nor my own voice to interrupt him, as he continued with his lecture.

"...I happen to know that we were the third partnership to be offered the body for burial after two refusals from other firms, and of course, we can continue to provide full discretion but I must insist, Mrs. Bancroft, that alternative provisions be made as to the attire of... erm....the deceased."

They were the third undertakers? John had not told me any of this.

"Heston," I managed at last.

"I beg your pardon Mrs. Bancroft?"

"Heston. You said that he was still there. I would speak with him."

There was a brief pause and then Mr. Evans cleared his throat.

277

"I am afraid that won't be possible Mrs. Bancroft." He dragged this last sentence out in a tone of self-importance. I could sense his chest puffing out in triumph.

"And why not?"

There was a kind of amusement in his voice as he answered.

"That was the other matter about which I wished to speak with you. Mr. Heston is being detained by the police."

~o~

The last time John and I had ridden in a cab together was on the drive to my father's house on that fateful night when our worlds were turned upside down. That journey had been markedly different from this one in many ways but in one it was blissfully similar. On that first journey before the discovery, John had been my rock of support. Having only too recently supported me through the death of my mother, he had plunged himself into action. He had held my hand in his and kept his arm around me, protecting me from the cold and the gaze of the bystanders outside my father's house. I was afraid that if he withdrew his support, I would start shaking and not be able to stop. Since that night, he had withdrawn his arms from around me and become cold. Although I had started to shake at first, I already knew that I could stand alone. John was seated opposite me and, far from being someone upon whom I could lean, I considered him to be someone I no longer knew. Could I rely upon him as my mother had my father? But, despite the difference in the reasons, we were united in our anger and outrage with the undertakers. A few minutes after I took the call from Mr. Evans, John had arrived home to find me putting on my coat and gloves and I had recounted the conversation.

"Why didn't you tell me there had been a problem appointing an undertaker?"

For a moment, he had stared directly at me and tried to take both the measure of me and of the situation. Evidently, entering ones' house and finding one's wife riled up and dressing to leave was enough to make one proceed with caution. His tone was calm as he had followed me outside.

"Imogen. What has happened?"

"I have just taken a call from Mr. Evans of Evans & Sons. They have detained Heston and called the police," I added and John's face fell.

"What?" he blustered. I turned and swept into the waiting cab. "Imogen!" he had hissed, trying to keep his voice down. "What the blazes for?" The cab lurched as he pulled himself in behind me, pulled the door to and knocked on the roof with his fist.

"Evidently there has been some..." I hadn't wanted to use the same word as Evans but without knowing exactly what had transpired I had no choice but to repeat it. "...altercation between Heston and a member of Evan's staff."

John's eyes flashed at me and then at his pocket watch.

"This is nonsense! Imogen, I can deal with this. You really should have stayed at home."

I considered him for a moment, in his anger and his pomposity before responding.

"Why didn't you consult with me over the funeral, John?"

He had been about to respond curtly, a ready response on his lips but something about the way I had looked at him made him hesitate.

"Imogen, please. You must see that however you felt about...,' he levelled his gaze at me as he grasped for the word least likely to embarrass us both "...Avery."

"My father."

He raised his voice over mine, his eyes indicating he was not prepared to listen

"The fact remains that this is a precarious position for us. If the investors get a whiff of this then be sure and understand that we will..." his voice had begun to rise and he bit his lip.

He lowered his voice and tried to explain. "Imogen, reputation is everything and you have to understand that this is a bad business, and we should get rid of the evidence as quickly as possible." He immediately regretted what he said and tried to cover his poor choice of words. "I just thought that we should probably get the funeral done with quickly and you being so...distraught...I wanted to..."

"The evidence?"

"I didn't mean..."

"The evidence? That evidence is my father, John!"

"For God's sake Imogen," he leaned back quickly and tipping his head backwards, he blew out his breath towards the roof of the cab.

"I am trying," he spoke slowly and deliberately as if keeping his temper was a struggle for him and I once again marvelled at this unfamiliar side to my husband. "I am trying to understand all of this mess but I cannot comprehend your loyalty!"

"Can't you, John?" I leant forward and tried to take his hand but he refused to let me. "Can you really not see?"

He looked at me and, shaking his head, he expelled an audible sigh and looked out of the window instead. When we arrived at the undertakers, there were a good many people in the parlour's entrance but I could pick out Mr. Evans without an introduction. His sallow skin sagged around his fleshy face. His posture was tall but he held his hands furtively about him in an affected look of servitude. It was evident from John's expression that he also found this man to be loathsome. I wondered how difficult Evans had made it for John, knowing of the undertakers who had turned the service down.

"Mr. Bancroft. Mrs. Bancroft." Evans stepped forwards and it was his turn to colour a little as evidently, he had not expected both of us to arrive. The interior of the office was sparsely decorated and was fittingly sombre. A simple desktop of heavy oak was laid bare except for two large catalogues to assist with the sale of coffins and monuments. The room was by no means large, yet we were the eighth and ninth occupants.

"Can I offer you a drink?"

"No damn it, you may not," John had snapped.

The room, already hushed, fell silent. It was clear that conversation had been about Heston.

281

"What the devil is going on, Evans? Who are all these people?" John indicated the other people. "You promised me discretion," he hissed.

John glared around the room, eyeing each of them was a fiery gaze. There were two young men and dressed in uniform black but were not wearing their jackets. I guessed they must have worked at the parlour. A third man at the back of the room stepped forward, his uniform immediately identified him as a police constable. He was young and looked around awkwardly before addressing John.

"Sir? I believe you are the employer of...," he glanced at the notebook he had been clutching "... Mr. George Heston of Hamble Gardens."

John looked fazed before he replied.

"Well... I am one of the executors of my father in-law's...," he opened his mouth wildly. "... That is to say... er... Yes."

The constable looked relieved and he lowered his voice.

"Very good, sir. Come through to the office." He turned and made his way past the hushed crowd to the far end of the parlour where there was a side door which he knocked on before stepping inside. Whilst we waited for a response, my attention was drawn to the rest of the room's occupants. I could see now that there was someone sitting down behind the group. Evidently, it was this man that the young constable had been questioning as we arrived. He too was dressed in a sombre uniform of black and grey, an employee. Where he differed from his colleagues was that his nose was swollen and bloodied and his white shirt collars were wet with crimson blood. I looked at John who had just seen the same thing and his eyebrows drew together in confusion. Seeing my horror, he clutched my hand tighter. Before we could really take in any more of the scene or discern anything from the hushed whispers which had begun to escalate around us, the constable opened the door and beckoned us forwards.

"Mr. and Mrs…," he looked back to us as he shut the door.

"Bancroft." I finished.

"Mr. and Mrs. Bancroft, sir," he announced to the room.

The second room seemed equally as crowded as the first. A back office, there was a desk and drawers and too few places for anyone to sit. I barely registered the response from his superior, instead my eyes took in the sight of Heston, seated at a table, his head hung forward. The familiar posture was evident. His back was straight, his hands were regimentally clasped on top of his knees. He looked less like a smart butler but more like a small boy who had been caught truanting. At the sound of my voice, Heston rose from his seat and caught my eye before staring neutrally as before. The sudden movement of the old man caused some alarm and the senior policemen stood.

"Please stay seated, Mr. Heston."

Heston remained standing and the constable was visibly annoyed at being ignored. I stepped forwards into the room past John and took Heston's hand in my own.

"What is the meaning of this?" John's voice was unsettled.

283

He was addressing the inspector but he appeared ruffled. The events of the last week had disturbed his core such that he was unsure upon whom to rely except himself. It had brought out an insecurity in him I had not noticed before. If we were still on fond terms, I would have reached for him to assure him. The truth was, I could not be sure of anything myself.

"Mr. Bancroft. I am sorry to have disturbed you, sir….."

The inspector had stood to draw my husband to one side so that they may speak in hushed tones. I was growing used to this isolation and instead I took the opportunity to talk to Heston. Heston, still rigid in his seat, looked pale and drawn, the fallout of my father' legacy was weighing heavily on him. A pulse in his temple throbbed with the tension of clenching his jaw and he looked beyond me.

"What has happened here?" I whispered to him, still holding his hand. He said nothing. The mumble of the inspector's voice filled up the space above us.

"…….by all accounts, it was an unprovoked attack Mr. Bancroft. I am afraid I won't be allowed….."

The vein at Heston's temple bulged, as he re-doubled his efforts to remain impassive; I felt a tremor in his hand.

"Heston? Did someone attack you?" I drew his hand towards me and turned it upwards. His palms were dry and cold but showed no marks. I turned them over.

"Heston?' his knuckles were raw and bloodied. The fresh rose of a bruise and the dried scarlet were a stark contrast to the grey, almost blue of his hands.

Heston's eyelids closed briefly and as he re-opened them, it was as if he had just returned to the room. He focused on me for the first time and he seemed surprised to see me. He looked down at his hands in mine and he recoiled ever so slightly. His fingers curled back and he drew his elbows in to his body. It was the slightest of motions but it drew John's attention.

"Just look at him!" John's voice joined the fog above us and he indicated to where I was crouched before Heston. "He is an old man, Inspector!" John sounded incredulous "I have no doubt that some affray has occurred but as for assault, Heston is twice the fellows age and half his size. I am surprised your man is not ashamed to have this trouble caused on his behalf!"

There was a murmured assent from the constable guarding the door and there followed a brief silence, broken only by the distant voices from behind the wall to the shop. There were people still feasting on the details, no doubt there would be enough to dine on for some weeks yet.

"Heston?" I whispered.

"Mrs. Bancroft." His voice was low and I guessed that he was feeling ashamed at being at the centre of the commotion in which we were now caught.

"Tell me what happened."

Over my shoulder, I caught the muttered sound of the constable as Heston began to talk.

"Wouldn't say a word before the lady arrives and now he's the regular singing Joe!"

"It was a fairly new suit Madam. I had pressed it carefully before you came and cleaned his shoes too." I nodded "After you left, I boxed the clothes up with good tissue. It keeps the folds crisp," he added. "Then I told Mrs. Rooksmith where I was going and I caught the next regular bus to the address Mr. Bancroft had given me.'"

Here he nodded behind me towards where my husband was standing but he kept his eyes on my own as if to make sure I was listening to his account carefully.

"I must admit that I had not heard of the name, Madam. I had assumed it would have been the same directors as Mrs. Silver." Here, he had looked down at his feet and nodded his head. "Mr. Silver had been very pleased with how it had all been handled, I had felt sure that it would be the same company."

John mumbled something behind me but I didn't catch it.

"When I stated my business to the clerk, I was asked to wait until Mr. Evans himself could attend to me. Having no other business that afternoon, I was obliged to wait. I wanted to make sure that Mr. Silver's suit was left in good hands," he added quickly. "I was shown to a corridor in the back, for privacy the clerk had said. After about ten minutes, one of Mr. Evan's colleagues came out to see me. He told me that Mr. Evans was busy and asked to take the package through. You will think me foolish madam, but as the last service I could perform, I wanted to make sure Mr. Evans himself received the package and I said that I didn't mind waiting. The gentleman seemed a little amused but allowed me to do so. I suppose I waited another ten minutes before the same man appeared. He told me that Mr. Evans was still rather busy, I could leave the package with him and he would see that Mr. Evans received it. Not wishing to become an irritant, I said I would prefer to wait than hand the man the package and said I would need to hear from Mr. Evans that the clothes were suitable before I left."

Heston spotted my quizzical expression.

"Sometimes clothes no longer fit you see Mrs. Bancroft. It has been several months since that particular suit had been worn and I wanted to save Mr. Evans the bother of sending a boy to the house later if it didn't."

I indicated for him to continue, drawing up a chair myself to sit more comfortably beside him.

"So, he said I could wait and as I did, two young chaps went about their business down the corridor. They had been moving a long, empty wooden coffin from one room to another. I tried not to stare Mrs. Bancroft but I wanted," he paused and a blush broke across his cheeks. "I wanted to see Mr. Silver one last time. I had tried to see beyond them into the room where they had ferried the coffin through." His lips had grown dry as he had spoken and he paused to moisten them before continuing in a lower tone. "I'm sorry Mrs. Bancroft."

"What did you see?" the thin voice was mine but I hadn't realised I had spoken.

My voice took Heston by surprise too and he glanced up at me.

"'What did you see?" I repeated in more even tones.

"It was Mr. Silver."

I had known that this was the case and whilst I felt a pang in my stomach that somewhere in this very building my father's body lay I also knew that Heston had not told me the worst.

"What did you see?"

"At first, I wasn't sure it was Mr. Silver but for some reason I found myself unable to look away."

Heston coloured again not looking directly at me. It was an admission of weakness that he had succumbed to that most human of emotions, curiosity.

"I thought it was another person. I thought it was another body," he paused to gauge my reaction but if I had one it did not stop him. So steeled was I for this, that I must have wiped my expression clear. Despite Heston's hushed tones, John stepped forward.

"Steady on Heston. I am sure Mrs. Bancroft doesn't need to hear all this. Can we talk about this more privately?" John continued in a quieter aside, presumably to the constable. I kept my eyes locked on Heston's. He had not glanced up at John's intrusion either.

"The body was already half dressed in a long black skirt; the legs demurely placed together."

I shuddered as the image of my father returned to me.

"A man was working on the clothes as I watched. I suppose when I had readied Mr. Silver's clothes, I had not considered how it must be to dress a dead person and I was astonished to see how skillfully the undertaker performed the task. The un-biddable limbs seemed to respond to him as he skillfully fed them into the sleeves of a heavily laced blouse and he rolled the body to one side to carefully tie the fasteners at the neck. As I watched, I felt suddenly sure that Mr. Bancroft had chosen Mr. Evans with great care and I was well pleased that Mr. Silver would be so well attended in his final preparations. I took another look at the body which the man was clothing and felt sure the family of the dear woman would also be well pleased."

I felt growing unease as Heston continued.

"I was about to look away, almost forced to look away as the fellows in front had finished putting their coffin away and one was about to close the door when I recognised the body. At first the head had been obscured by some box or other from which the undertaker had been selecting the clothes and as he removed it, the face was Mr. Silver's. There was no doubt. I pushed past the fellow at the door and he in turn tried to block my way. The box of clothes getting pressed in between us. One of them tried to stop me.

'Hold on there Sir, you can't just go walking in to any room you like. This is a restricted area.'

"At his words, the chap who had been dressing Mr. Silver looked up with a fright. *'Now look here'* I had said. *'Now look here. There's been some mistake. Those are not Mr. Silver's clothes.'* The man had looked confused and after a small pause, his face lit in recognition and he appeared to make an apology. *'Of course they aren't the right clothes, we have been waiting for the deceased's daughter to provide us with some. You aren't Mr. Bancroft. Are you a relative, a friend?'* I had shaken my head. I suppose now, that's why he must have assumed I was merely a delivery man. *'Are these the clothes?'*

"He had reached me in a few strides, still standing beside the door and had prised the box from my shocked fingers. He had grinned at me as he took

289

them and then he had stepped away to the nearest bench to open the box. *'I'll just check sizing before you go in case I need to get another set.'* Though I was still shocked at the attire of Mr. Silver, I was relieved that the man knew there had been a mistake and had the good foresight to check the contents before I left. I was about to say something to the man when he roared with laughter. *'Have you seen this?'* I didn't know whether he was addressing me or one of the two young men, still stood behind me. Though no longer eyeing me suspiciously they had not left. The undertaker lifted the garments I had so carefully packaged and showed them to us. *'Evans was telling the truth then! Seems the old girl was into a bit of this, that and the other then.'* He had winked at me as if I were complicit to his chain of thoughts and then turned to take the suit over to where Mr. Silver lay in a skirt and a blouse. *'I saw it in the paper a few days ago and I didn't believe it at first. Some woman dressed like a man had half the town believing she was a man. I wouldn't have been taken in. You only have to look at her to see.'* As he spoke, Mrs. Bancroft, I could feel a temper rising up in me but if he hadn't have continued, I might have just walked out and made a complaint to Mr. Evans and Mr. Bancroft."

He was imploring me with his eyes. He didn't want to finish his story but I needed him to and I told him as much.

"Tell me what he said."

"Mrs. Bancroft, there is no need...." Heston's voice was filled with concern all of a sudden. In imparting the scenes to me, he had returned to his quiet and mannered self.

"Honestly, Imogen. Haven't we heard enough?" John was quieter than I had heard him all day.

"Tell me," I repeated forcefully.

"He grabbed the skirt that he had dressed your father in and lifted it up declaring 'If you don't believe me, there is always an easy way for me to prove it."

"Good God," I barely registered John's voice.

My own vision was obscured with a mist as I imagined the scene and I could see the ensuing cacophony as Heston lurched loose from the men at the door and raged towards the man stripping his employer of the last of his remaining dignity. I tasted the visceral anger and my own knuckles throbbed with the impact his own made when they connected with the man's jaw.

The room in which we now sat was silent but voices from the adjoining room pervaded the charged atmosphere and my skin began to crawl with the proximity of the real culprit of the evening.

"I'm taking George home," I announced baldly.

As I turned to address John, the constable made to object to Heston's leaving. I flashed him a warning look which I hoped conveyed the determination I had to remove Heston and he nodded before declaring it had been his intention, based on good character to release him without charge anyway.

"I want my father's body moved from this place. Tonight," I added in a firm tone as John sought to contradict me. "If his body is not moved then I shall remain here to guard it personally."

Despite his prior reluctance to assuage me, I will give him his due that he too was astounded at the behaviour of the undertaker and thought it best, on balance, to remove my father to another location. As I escorted Heston to the cab, I left John dressing down Evans.

It was a half an hour or so before John, Heston and I were on our way back to my father's house. In the cab, the only sound was from Heston himself apologising to us both, over and over until I placed my hand over his again. It had the desired effect and he remained silent for the rest of the journey. It was all I could do to stop myself from thanking him for his actions which, far from bringing me shame, as John so obviously perceived the matter, but rather filled me with affection for the old man.

Once again, I found myself watching John from the corner of my eye as the shadows rolled across his face from the street lamps we passed along the route home. His face was fixed in an unfamiliar grimace, his nostrils flared as he fought to keep his composure. It was obvious his mind was racing, his eyes flickered in the dark, punctuating each of his hidden thoughts. I tried to remember his face as it had been over Christmas but it seemed too long ago to recall. As we drew up to the familiar house, a silent tension mounted in the cab. I realised that John had not been back here since that night and I could see his body go taut.

"John, I will see Heston in. You may go on without me. I won't be long," I added as he failed to make his mouth form any words.

He nodded then coughed, jumping down to allow Heston and myself out. As he climbed back in to the carriage, he glanced up to the second floor window and I saw a flash of guilt cross his face. He looked slightly ashamed as he ducked back in to the cab and he lingered between staying and going. There was a moment's indecision and he raised his face to me. His expression was softer; his mouth half formed on a question. I waited for the beginning of reconciliation but there was a noise behind me as the door was opened by Mrs. Rooksmith and the moment was gone. John closed the cab door, knocked on the roof of the cab with his cane and then he was gone, without a further glance at me.

I turned to face the house and watched the figure of Mrs. Rooksmith come bustling out of the house. She was wearing two overcoats; with just the remaining staff in the house, the fires were not being lit. Heston was still stood by my side watching the street, as the cab in which my husband was being carried had turned from sight. The square was quiet and for the first time since this episode began, there did not appear to be anyone lurking to stare; I suspected that the vultures had already found some fresh story upon which to feast. I turned to face Heston.

"I'm afraid my husband is having difficulty with....," I considered what left I had to hide from Heston before I relinquished my thoughts "....the truth."

"If you would judge, understand," he said simply.

I half smiled at this, torn between the men I thought I knew. My father and my husband had become like strangers to me in this last week. And there I was, side by side with old Heston, someone I never presumed to know but who seemed so familiar to me then, I felt he could be both of the men I was missing, husband and father. Friend.

"A man who asks questions cannot avoid the answers," I retorted and with that, I steered the old man up the steps towards the waiting housekeeper who noticed our proximity with a wary eye. She had had quite enough impropriety for one lifetime and, in deference to her blood pressure, I forged forwards to allow Heston the liberty of following after me.

Chapter Nineteen - Elizabeth, 1869

To the outsider, tea had been a successful, and seemingly pleasant, affair. Georgina would later remark to her maid that the girls had seemed to have got along very well and that she hoped, very much, that each would serve as a good influence to the other. Elizabeth, usually so sullen had appeared very animated, quizzing Alice over and over about her interests. In fact, so pleased with the way in which Elizabeth had behaved and how much less bold the awkward Alice had appeared, Georgina had retired to her room to write a small note to advise Toby. Elizabeth had professed an urge to go for another walk and, having accepted her aunt's advice about sun spots and taken a parasol, agreed to show Alice the formal gardens.

As Georgina mounted the stairs to the first floor landing, she watched curiously at the view of Elizabeth striding out across the lawn, her tall frame carried upright and perfectly poised underneath her parasol. By contrast, the angular shape of Alice Silver, trotting behind to keep pace made the girl appeared ungainly and clumsy. Georgina was cheered by the good turn she was accomplishing this summer. She had a good feeling about the outcome and felt deserving of the praise both Toby and her brother would surely give her after this episode. Contentedly, she broke off her gaze and continued to her room, humming to herself.

~o~

"Miss Greenwood, wait."

Elizabeth didn't turn, nor did she wait, but only slowed her pace slightly to allow the form of Avery to draw level with her.

"Miss Greenwood, I must apologise. I don't know what you must think of me," Avery began awkwardly.

Elizabeth snorted derisively, quickening her pace and turning sharply off the path towards a small summerhouse. The speed at which this was executed caused Avery to overshoot the path and he had to hurry to catch Elizabeth up again.

"Miss Greenwood, please I want to explain!"

"I don't pretend to understand why you have deceived me, Miss Silver," she stopped and made a big show of looking Avery up and down. "Or is it Mr. Silver? I barely know where your duplicity starts!"

"You wouldn't understand if I told you," Avery said.

"Why don't you try?"

Avery thrust his chin to the sky, searching for inspiration from the heavens to try and put into words the feelings he had, until now, not been asked to describe. He tried to remember what he had explained to Kate but he could not recall her asking him to. Avery had told her and that had been enough. He wondered now whether even she actually believed him. He saw Elizabeth lose patience and it was obvious that she felt this whole thing had been some kind of joke at her expense and he needed to make her understand. Above them, the canopy under whose dappled shade they now stood, wavered in the breeze and a few early acorns fell. Avery stooped to collect one, all at once an idea forming in his mind and he pressed it into Elizabeth's hand.

"What?" she asked, her brow furrowed.

"What is it?" Avery nodded at Elizabeth's open palm and the seed she held upon it.

"And now we are to have a nature lesson? Really Miss Silver, this is quite ludicrous."

"Tell me what it is, please," he added.

"Okay, if you are intent on making this difficult as well as awkward. It is an acorn."

"And when you plant it, Miss Greenwood, what will grow from this acorn."

Elizabeth rolled her eyes before uttering in a sing song voice. "Great Oaks from Little Acorns Grow."

"An oak tree! Correct." Avery grew more animated. "So we are agreed that inside this little seed; in this tiny acorn are all of the elements to grow an oak tree?"

Elizabeth raised one eyebrow and was about to retort before Avery continued.

"So when I plant this acorn, the shoots will come from the ground and divide. Two leaves will grow and spread and slowly the sapling will take the form of an oak?" he earnestly held his arms aloft, stiff inside the pale grey dress. Elizabeth's head hurt to watch him so attired. "But what if, when the leaves formed," he continued, "instead of the familiar rounded seven eared oak leaf, instead they were more like my hand, like green fingers, like a chestnut tree? What would it be? Would it be an oak because it had come from an Acorn or would it simply be what it was?"

297

He looked at her with desperation, he was struggling to make himself plain and he willed her to understand.

"Would it be any less a chestnut because it had grown from an acorn?" he asked.

"Miss Silver, I hate to interrupt this riveting nature lesson but I am quite sure that what you are suggesting would never happen?"

"Why?"

"Because how trees grow is God's divine will and what you are suggesting is to presume that God could make a mistake."

"But what if He did?" Avery asked.

"Who? God?"

"Yes"

Elizabeth looked at Avery uncomfortably. It was clear she understood the implication of what he was suggesting and she needed time to think. Where before she had assumed that Avery's disguise had been some elaborate trick, a wild joke played on unsuspecting girls, here was something else entirely. Elizabeth had not been prepared for this but she felt sure she knew what her sister, Agnes would do. In that moment, she was the only guide Elizabeth could summon.

"God doesn't make mistakes," she stated coldly before wheeling around and returning towards the house.

But Avery knew that He already had.

~o~

298

A perfunctory and cool dinner followed and it was breakfast the next day before Elizabeth was drawn to Avery again. Having retired to his room after breakfast, Georgina encouraged Elizabeth to invite Avery to accompany her with some studies. The weather was good and she fancied Miss Silver might find some interest in drawing. Unable to explain her reluctance to her aunt, Elizabeth knocked lightly on Avery's door and stood waiting. There were hushed tones from behind the door and Elizabeth could make out Avery's voice and that of a girl. Elizabeth froze for a moment. She wrinkled her nose in annoyance. She had wanted to speak with Avery directly and now she may have to wait. She listened and their conversation continued. The volume was low but a hissing urgency beckoned her to lean against the cool door, but she could make out nothing. The closer she pushed her ears to the wood, the less she was able to determine. She was about to knock again when she was startled by Avery's sudden call.

"Come in."

So her knock had been heard! Elizabeth's initial fury rose again. The rudeness to have left her waiting! She gripped the door handle with renewed vigour and erupted into the room. Avery was seated at a desk and a girl, the serving maid he had brought with him, was stood close beside him. Too close. Elizabeth had not noticed the young girl before but was instantly struck by their proximity, the hushed rowing a moment before and now the look upon the girl's face. Elizabeth could not place why, but the girl was uncomfortable and she immediately sensed an awkward tension in the room. The young girl did not look away as Elizabeth appraised her but, rather, she raised her chin slightly, proffering her best side for inspection.

She knew immediately that there was something unusual in the relationship between Avery and his young maid. The girl seemed uncomfortable with Elizabeth's presence in Avery's bedroom. Her gaze was direct. Elizabeth was amused by the sense of guarded jealousy that she could feel emanating from this young girl and her lips twitched at the corners, suppressing a smile.

"Miss Silver? I wonder if I might have a word with you." Elizabeth did not break her gaze from the maid's. "Alone," she added after a pause.

"Of course. Thank you Kate. That will be all," he said simply.

The girl looked like she could spit and, for a moment, Elizabeth was afraid that a scene may break out. She neither moved nor spoke and it was Avery who began to look most afraid of a scene. After a few moments the young girl collected herself.

'Of course, Miss Silver.'

She emphasised her address a little and Elizabeth saw Avery flinch at her words. The young girl scowled as she took her leave from the room, remembering only to nod her head courteously as she left. Elizabeth did not watch her leave but merely waited until the click at the door indicated they were alone.

"Elizabeth, I," Avery stuttered.

"I haven't come here to listen to any more of your explanations"

"But Elizabeth, I must explain. Please."

"Please?" Elizabeth repeated, one eyebrow raised. Her tone at last familiar and he was momentarily struck dumb. She stood with the same assured confidence that he recognized. It was only he who now differed from their meetings of a few weeks ago. His attire and his situation put him at a great disadvantage. He felt without wind to his sails, quite shipwrecked entirely. "I came to talk to you about my Aunt Georgina," Elizabeth said.

For a moment, Avery looked as though he might continue with his protestations but, unable to find anything to say, he remained silent. Elizabeth walked over to the window, her back now to the room and to Avery, still sat at his desk. He was afraid to stand, ashamed to show the full length of himself before her. He wanted to remain small. He wanted the floor to open beneath him and swallow him whole.

"You know if this all wasn't quite so absurd, it could be rather funny." She turned. She was smiling. It was a strained expression. Avery's face was confused.

"Oh for pity's sake. You remember why I am here?"

He looked puzzled.

"What happened in London....I don't want to talk about." She held out her hands to stop Avery interrupting her. "I hardly understand what has happened myself but the extraordinary circumstances are that my Aunt has become engaged to your father. We are to be cousins Avery. Isn't that wonderful news?" Her face was set with the same grim smile. It did not look like it was wonderful news to Avery. When Elizabeth had mentioned she did not want to discuss what had gone on in London, Avery looked crestfallen but Elizabeth pressed on.

"And if that in itself weren't such marvellous news, I have gainful employment,' she continued, a small laugh escaped her and she looked around, gesturing to the room as if the whole place amused her. "I am to be your mentor and guide!"

Avery looked up. He no longer looked confused. He was scowling. Of course he knew why he was here. His father and Mrs. Fearncott had already told him of their hopes for him this summer. He could find neither the words nor the expression to match the grimness of his mood.

"Now don't look at me like that! The way I see it, you and I have much to gain from one another and you owe me."

She continued to talk into the silence he was affording the room.

"Now, my aunt is expecting us to spend a good deal of time with one another in the hope that the best of our respective virtues," here she counted on her fingers and looked at Avery.

"Clumsy, bookish, shy, modest, prim....' She indicated to herself. 'Graceful, charming, feminine, alluring..."

"Elizabeth," he tried to interrupt.

"Whilst I am sure that much of your tutelage will be closely monitored here at the house, I am quite sure that in a week or so we can be trusted to venture into town together. We shall be each other's chaperone."

"Elizabeth," he pressed.

"Whilst I have no wish at the moment to spend any more time with you, the diversion into more civilised company will be reward enough."

302

"For God's sake, Elizabeth!" Avery erupted. He could not understand such a cool reaction. If the shoe had been on the other foot, he was sure he would be furious. He had been waiting for an opportunity to speak with her and now they were alone again, she was refusing to acknowledge him or what had passed between them in London. He watched as she took a measure of him again. Her long gaze took in the drab dress, the sleeves of which he tugged at uncomfortably. He could see that it made her as uncomfortable as it did him and he sat down again behind the small desk to conceal some of himself. Whilst he hoped she would rather not see him dressed this way, he could see that she was not entirely unsympathetic to his discomfort. As if she could read his mind, she offered quietly.

"It gives me no pleasure to see you squirm so."

"Then let me explain..."

"Oh, for pity's sake. Please! No more seed stories." She threw her arms to her sides and stalked across to the foot of the bed where she sat down, a little defeated. He waited whilst she closed her eyes. Her chin was thrust upwards and her neck was pale above her high collar. He tried to push the image of how, only a week or so ago, he had pressed his lips to that same flesh. Before he had time to consider his urges, he stood and was beside her in a few strides. He sat awkwardly beside her, the dress clinging about him in ungainly folds. Elizabeth opened her eyes.

"What the? What are you....?" she had a panicked look as Avery leant in to kiss her.

Elizabeth stood, pushing him away, and stepped to the side of the large bed frame. For the longest of minutes, there was nothing but the sound of Avery biting back his frustration in angry breaths and Elizabeth chewing her nails. She eventually stepped away from the bed and in two long strides was beside the door.

"I can see we will have to start with a lesson on personal space. My aunt wants to see you at eleven in the drawing room." She opened the door as Avery said softly.

"Elizabeth. I truly am sorry."

"So am I," she muttered, closing the door.

Chapter Twenty - Imogen, 1911

When I arrived home a few hours later, I felt energised. Though I had slept little over the last few days and eaten even less, I felt that my real emotions were finally beginning to come to the fore. Where before I had only felt a shock that had numbed me, I now felt alive with indignation. Listening to Heston in that room and how he had shown such loyalty had made me cringe. I had watched as John shrank in embarrassment as the story unfolded. I was not ashamed of Heston and I was not ashamed of my father. I was angry at him. I was angry at him, not for deceiving me but for not trusting me. I was grateful that only Stokes was waiting for me upon my arrival home, and as I walked upstairs to my bedroom, I felt relieved that I had managed to avoid a confrontation with John. All the way home, I had rehearsed what I would say in response to any one of his, by now, predictable statements and, though fresh on my lips, I lacked the physical energy for an argument. I mounted the stairs and tiptoed cautiously past the bedroom in which he had been sleeping those last few nights. There was no light from beneath the door to his room and I hurried to our marital bedroom. It was empty and the last of the strength I had felt on the journey home dissipated with the sigh of relief, I exhaled as I slumped on the pillows.

"Immy?"

I started with surprise.

"Is that you?" John's voice was slightly slurred and I gripped the sheets with stifled anger.

"I'm tired John. I just want to go to sleep."

The form of his shadow loomed out of the dark from the chaise longue in the bay window from which he now roused himself.

"I hoped you would come home." His voice was needy like Thomas when he could not sleep. "What time is it?" he added.

"It's late John. Go to bed and let's talk in the morning."

There was a clump as he stood up and he stumbled a little.

"I hoped you would be home Immy."

There was a rustling as the sheets lifted beside me and he slipped in between them. I rolled away from him, turning my shoulder towards him, hoping my back would signal my intent to sleep. Instead, he moved closer to me and propped his head on my shoulder. His heavy chin dug into my clavicle, the sharp fresh whiskers on his chin scratching my flesh.

"You're cold Immy! Here, let me warm you up." His voice was thick with a smile and he inelegantly ran his hands over my thighs, rubbing harshly. His breath was sour with alcohol and I tensed from his touch, trying in vain to prevent his large hands from pulling up my nightdress.

"John! Please!" I turned on to my stomach, hoping he would quit but he rolled along with me and I was suddenly pinned under his weight against the mattress. He moaned with delight and slurred once more into my ear.

"Oh Immy!"

With the indelicate hands of a stranger, he leaned on me and raised himself up to begin tugging at my nightclothes, drawing the fabric up to reveal my naked bottom, as he did so I could feel him grow hard against me and I cried out again.

"John! What are you doing? Stop!"

My pleas went unheard and unheeded, and he fumbled with the drawstring of his pyjamas, and his hot member fell firm against my buttocks where he rutted for a few moments, his fingers trying to prise my thighs apart.

"John! No!" I screamed out. The pitch was high and it shocked even me. Had anyone within the house heard, I expected them to immediately rush to my aid. Whilst time would prove that no-one would spring to my defence, it had reached inside John's foggy head and he appealed to me one more time.

"Imogen! I am trying to help you!" he slurred angrily.

He had lifted himself off me to examine my face, evidently surprised that I was not submissive to his advances. It was enough and I rolled out from underneath him, landing indecorously in a heap beside the bed. He leaned over and his expression was of great amusement.

"What are you doing, Imogen? Come back to bed."

He pulled back the covers, his pyjama bottoms loose around his thighs and his eyes danced over my half naked form. He smiled at me and held out his hand to pull me back to bed. I took his hand and drew myself back up and slipped beside him whilst he caressed me clumsily.

"I'm sorry Immy. I've not been gentle have I?"

"No," I agreed, not tonight, nor this week. As he slipped an arm beneath my head and drew himself above me, I cast around for a recent memory of John being gentle or supportive. The night my father's death had been announced hadn't he been protective, hadn't he held me close? But that was before the scandal. Since then, he had treated me like a problem, like a conspirator, like a foe. The man, who eased himself between my legs and slipped inside me so intimately, was like a stranger to me, and I felt ashamed of him. The effects of the drink wore quickly and he was finished much sooner than was normal, and I breathed a sigh of relief, as he rolled his weight from me and fell into a deep stupor. Despite my relief, I found I could not move and remained, as he had finished with me, legs spread wide, a wet slick forming on the sheets where I lay; his scent upon me like an animal.

As I lay there in that way, the image of my father swam before me and then without warning, my mother in the same position. I frowned and drew my legs up towards my chest, turning on to my side, away from John. Had my mother lain beneath my father in the same way? How could she have? How could they have shared what John and I had just experienced? Surely, they were never Man and Wife if they had not? Again, I thought of how my mother's role in all of this was diminished and yet surely she was just as much, if not more, guilty? They had always seemed to me to be a paragon of happiness and, with John, I had tried to emulate them. The fact was, they had never been able to share such intimacies and surely as a result, they could never have been truly intimate. Or had they been? I wondered where their intimacy came from. Did they experience one another's bodies like John and I had done once? The thought confused me and I could not imagine ever feeling desire for someone who had a woman's body, no matter how much I loved him. Against my wishes, my mind lingered on an image of my own mother lying stiff under the body of my father as he laboured above her but I could not imagine it. I screwed up my eyes and tried to shake the thought from my head. Eventually, a troubled sleep came over me and I thought only of my mother and I could not see her anything but content, happy and whole.

~o~

Breakfast the following morning was awkward. John avoided looking at me and spoke monosyllabically. It was not only inconvenient, it was almost impossible and I eventually abandoned any attempt to talk to him about what I had thought after leaving Heston yesterday evening. As he quit the table for work, folding his newspaper as he did so, he leant down from habit to plant a kiss on the top of my head but as his lips came close he was unable to make contact. Instead he rose stiffly and left the room without a word. I was unaccustomed to considering the staff around me but the abruptness of his departure left me feeling embarrassed in front of Stokes and I, too, rose and left the room.

"Ready a cab for me, Stokes. I will be downstairs in ten minutes."

"Yes Ma'am. Where to?"

I hesitated. Stokes was a good twenty years younger than Heston and of a different generation. I had never considered whose man he was, as John and I were always of one accord. Though he had shown some discretion with Mrs. Evesham in recent days, I felt I wanted to have some space to myself.

"I haven't quite decided yet. Have him available for a few hours and I will decide en route."

"Very good Mrs. Bancroft."

If he thought it unusual, his expression did not betray him and, as I left a short while afterwards, he saw me out of the front door with no discernible opinion. As the cabbie saw me into the cab, I offered him our destination.

"Where to Ma'am?"

"Brompton Cemetery, please."

Within a quarter of an hour, we were drawn up outside the North gate, farthest from the small church. The cab rolled off to wait for me and I walked down the central avenue in the quiet of the winter's morning. There were already several mourners fresh upon the day and I was careful to avoid eye contact; their raw loss was palpable and I needed to keep my own at bay for what I needed to do. After a short walk, I found the avenue of headstones which I had come for. It had been a while but I was drawn to my mother's grave as if she herself were sat upon it. Though it had been several months since last I was here, and so much had happened since, the familiar feeling of her presence washed over me as reassuring, and I forgot that I was angry with her and tears rolled down my face. I could almost feel her draw me to her, her small frame enveloping my adult self as if I were a small girl again. Though I had steeled myself to remain strong, my shoulders shook with the lonely grief I had been carrying. For several minutes, I stood weeping, the headstone blurred through my tears.

"Why didn't you tell me?" I sobbed.

Time seemed to melt away and I could imagine her face before me. Where only a few months ago I had been upset because I found that could not remember the turn of her mouth when she smiled or the shade of her eyes, here was her face pristinely in my mind's eye. She was looking at me without shame and she refused to avoid my eye. I closed mine in order to see her more clearly.

"Why didn't you tell me?"

And what would she have said to me? And when would she say it? As I thought of my own two children, what age could she feasibly have told me? When I was twelve? When I was sixteen? Could I imagine myself telling either of my sons something so important and so devastating? What if there was a secret about their own father, one so monstrous that could change their relationship with him forever. Would I be able to take that from them? From him?

I could imagine her dilemma. The truth that started so small but with every day that I believed it, it became larger and larger until it was too big. *'Your father isn't your father Imogen, he's a woman.'* The absurdity of it struck me and I laughed out loud. My father had been the most wonderful father I could have wished for. Wasn't that the only truth?

I stayed for a further half hour allowing all of my mother's reasons and love, but not apologies, seep into me before I finally understood. I laid four roses beside her headstone. As I read her name and pondered the blank beneath her own, which had been left for my father, my heart surged with heat as I remembered with horror the conversation I had overheard John having at the undertakers.

The church had refused to allow my father to be buried with my mother citing reasons of decency. John had begun proceedings to secure a more secluded, 'private' plot and the thought made me feel distraught. I walked back to the hansom and the driver, pleased at the opportunity to move in this cold and opened the cab door.

"Will you please drop me at the vicarage?"

Chapter Twenty One - Avery, 1869

A few weeks ago in London, after he had heard about Mary-Ann blackmailing Kate, Avery had found himself wandering aimlessly around the city. Unusually, he was not dressed in the disguise of his suit but instead a recent acquisition that Kate had convinced him to purchase to avoid the attention of Georgina Fearncott. It was a compromise of sorts, a dull and plain dress with a well-cut short jacket. A hat and veil enabled him to keep his face well hidden and his hair could be clipped up into a bun. Kate had been the first to point out that he needed to be careful when he was abroad in his dresses, in case he were to meet someone from is evenings. Though he had doubted his two worlds could collide in such a way, he had appreciated her concern and merely accepted her assistance into whatever clothes she saw fit.

That morning, Kate had proffered this outfit and he had obliged her. His father has been entertaining some clients at the house and Avery had taken to the streets to avoid the usual presentation at the close of business. *'Have you met my daughter, Alice?'* Toby Silver wasted no opportunities to fish for some matrimonial prospect on his daughter's account. Usually, if he were taking a stroll, he meandered around the familiar streets of Kensington and Piccadilly but on that particular day, he had found himself thinking about Mary-Ann and how her obedience and silence could so easily be bought. The girl imagined Avery was entertaining a young man in the house like some bawdy tart; like Connie. The idea both amused and annoyed him. In truth, the lack of loyalty riled him when he compared the young girl to Kate. He could not help but wonder what Mary-Ann would have done had he confided in her that day instead of Kate. As he continued on his walk, he could not help but extend the comparisons and he tried to imagine Mary-Ann in Kate's repose within his, by now familiar, dream but found he could not. The thought had caused him to shake his head to dispel the image and he had stopped in his tracks, looking around for a clue as to where he had found himself. He was in a park but it was not a familiar one.

"Excuse me? Where is this please?" he asked a woman wearing much the same garb as himself. The girl's voice was thick with an accent and she rattled off at length, gesticulating up a main thoroughfare, and then smiling at Avery proudly. He only managed to catch Zoo and Regents Park but that was good enough for him. He returned the smile and walked up in the direction the girl had indicated. Plenty of other visitors were also heading in the direction of the tall brick walls that he could now see were indeed the buildings of the Zoological Society of London. He had heard that there were strange and wondrous creatures but had never wanted to visit. He stepped closer to crane his neck around the entrance booth and there came such a sound of merriment and excitement that he was not hesitant at all when the lad offering tickets simply held one outstretched to him and named a price. Once inside, he attached himself behind a large group of tourists; a group of out of town couples who were drably dressed and he was able to blend in without drawing any attention. In this mode, he was able to meander around the zoo, staring at each of the unusual creatures whilst receiving a running commentary from the group he was shadowing.

"It's so ugly, Matthew! Why does it look so?" The young woman's voice was shrill.

"It says here that they are a beast of burden much like our mules but in hotter climes, Diana. Far from being ugly, they are rather majestic. Why I have seen uglier women in Plymouth, eh John?"

"And this one. They're like goats horns but the thing is more like a horse!"

"Well, God's creatures are indeed unique," came the reply from a solemn looking lady.

"You can't tell me that is one of God's creatures! Look at it for heaven's sake."

The woman shrieked and the room in which they all were now standing fell silent.

They had stopped beside a cage inside a vast house within which there was a creature three times larger than a dog but with the face of an oversized cat. It was slender and muscled and reminded him of carriage dogs. The coat was striped and matted and gave a look of both being in shadow yet at the same time in the full glare of sunlight. The woman had shrieked because the creature had roused itself from a sleeping position and had now begun to pace the front of its cage. In doing so, its eyes danced jealously over the growing crowd.

"It's looking at me like I'm food," whispered the woman, Diana.

As he watched the tiger's beautiful face, Avery was inclined to disagree. Its glittering eyes were not focusing on the people but rather the spaces in between. The animal was surely hungry but not for meat, for freedom.

Over the course of the ensuing days at Juniper Hall, with bad weather keeping all its occupants within the confines of the house, Avery was reminded of that day and felt a sense of great empathy with the beautiful cat. After Elizabeth had left his room, Kate had returned to find him in a state of great frustration and, for once, he would not share with her any of his thoughts. Though she seemed to have guessed that Elizabeth and he had met before, she had not yet realised that Elizabeth knew his secret and the danger this placed him, and indeed herself in. After several attempts at rousing his spirit, he had snapped and bid her leave him alone for the rest of the day. Now she watched warily, and with growing suspicion, as he avoided Elizabeth's gaze and Georgina's hospitality. On the third day of their arrival, Kate had cornered him before breakfast. He was seated on the corner of the bed, his feet placed apart and one elbow resting on his knee, his look about as thunderous as the ever deteriorating summer sky.

"I don't pretend to know what's going on between you and Miss Greenwood," she stood before him "but if you ask me, which you won't I'm sure," she placed a cautionary hand on his shoulder as he raised his head to speak. "But if you did, I'm sure this situation won't be improved by your being so sullen." He scowled at her and turned his face away, shrugging her hand from his shoulder. The gesture was insolent and childish and she could have walked away. Instead, she grabbed his chin and turned his face to hers. As she did so, his scowl melted into surprise and he opened his mouth to say something.

"Last week, you spoke of release, of freedom and I have not seen you so trapped as you seem now. Whatever it is you need to do, do it or else I cannot stand by and watch you stifled this way."

She kept her hand fixed around his face as his eyes searched hers. There seemed to be no words willing to come to his defence and her words suspended around him. Yes, trapped. That was how he had felt, even in his own body as he had always felt, he now felt surrounded by barriers. His father was to marry Georgina then he and Elizabeth would be bound together forever. Elizabeth would always know his secret and she would surely tell someone, if she had not already. How had he hoped to get away with this? Surely the taste of freedom he had already had would be his last? As he thought it, the idea sank in his heart like ice from a thawing roof. How could he live the rest of days trapped inside himself? He watched Kate's concerned face opposite his own and felt the pulse from her heart race through her fingertips against his cheek. The words dissolved in the air around them and what was left was charged with expectation. After a few minutes, Kate withdrew her fingers, bringing them to her chest where she fiddled with the buttons of her uniform nervously. She seemed anxious. Her breath was tremulous and she looked emotional. She had just given him, what was tantamount to an ultimatum and now, in the absence of him accepting her help, the moment seemed a little foolish.

"I can see I've spoken out of turn." She stepped backwards away from the bed. The distance she created seemed to break him from his reverie and he closed and opened his mouth several times before finally breaking the silence.

"I should get dressed," he said simply.

Kate closed her eyes, her hands gripped in silent frustration and she wheeled around to the wardrobe in which hung the several similar drably coloured dresses she had grown accustomed to dressing Avery in. She reached inside and reluctantly withdrew a dark grey dress and hung it on the outer door whereupon she reached for the velvety clothes brush. It was a mechanical action and, as her fingers deftly swept the fabric, she felt she could be doing this with her eyes sewn as tightly shut as her own mouth now felt. She chewed on the insides of her cheeks pondering what else she could offer up instead of this mute assent.

"Come now Kate. I think something a little less drab will be more suitable today."

She turned on the spot, the proximity of his voice startling her. His eyes were sparkling again and he reached past her to the trunk within which they had so secretively stowed Avery's few suits.

"Ah, yes. Here we go."

She stepped aside and took receipt of his fine dark navy walking suit. As she gripped the cloth, her eyes twinkled. It was as if the material were imbued with an energy which swept both of them along on a breeze of danger. She shivered and smiled at him.

"What shall I tell them?"

"Tell them whatever you like, only make it quick before I lose my nerve." He grinned at her, his face pale in the grey of the dreary morning light.

~o~

It had been curiously easy to leave the house. There were only two other maids within the staff who were attending their duties with their heads down; two scullery maids safely ensconced within the airy kitchen over which presided Mrs. Green the cook, and of the gardeners and stable hand there was no sign. Avery scuttled past the perimeter of the walled garden, beyond the view of the main house into open fields within ten minutes. Over to the south of the house when they had arrived a few days earlier, he had noticed the tall spire of a church, no doubt from the neighbouring larger town of Amersham and it was in that direction he headed, his heart hammering in his chest. Where in London, the number of people who might discover him afforded him the luxury of anonymity, here, the relative solitude was exactly what could reveal him. It was half an hour before he found the narrow lanes widening to a broader thoroughfare upon which a signpost indicated a further three miles to the town. He was not used to walking such distances over such uneven ground and, after another half an hour, his boots began to rub and he knelt by a fence to take one off and rub at his sore heels. As he lingered, welcoming the pleasant arrival of blue sky, he heard the approach of a trap from the direction he had just come. His heart leapt and he looked around for somewhere to hide. He glanced at the approaching dust before the horse and determined that he was already spotted, so his furtive hiding would be judged yet more conspicuous. He prayed it was not Georgina

319

and, replacing his boot, began to walk in the same direction with the hope they would pass him by. As the trap drew nearer, Avery's ears began to throb with the sound of rushing blood and he felt his face colour with tension. He was holding his breath. A few moments more and it would draw level with him, he felt sure he could sense the horses reigns being drawn in. He held his shoulder up to protect some of his profile and then the trap passed by. He kept his eyes fixed downwards until it was safely passed and he glanced up under his fringe to see the fast retreating form of Elizabeth peering round the side of the trap's canopy. From the rear window he could see that she was not alone. Was that the back of Georgina's head or her maid? Could it be Kate? Whoever it was, they were not looking in his direction but even at this distance, and with the receding dust from the road, he could tell that Elizabeth was smiling.

~o~

Kate was not surprised to see him return so early having failed to discourage Georgina and Elizabeth's trip into town a few hours previously. Once she had safely smuggled him unseen back into his room, she rattled off an account of the morning.

"Oh! You won't believe how hard I tried to stop them Avery. I told them you were feeling poorly and that you had kept to your bed with a stomach complaint. The old lady wasn't in the least troubled by this but that Miss Greenwood, she kept on asking me questions. All the while insisting that she come and tend to you. Well Mrs. Fearncott was pleased by that I can tell you, she insisted Miss Greenwood be allowed to keep you company." Kate's fingers worked nimbly at Avery's buttons as she spoke, she had dropped to her knees in front of him working on the buttons at the front of his trousers.

"I thought fast, mind. I pressed my own hand to my stomach, right here."

She balled her fist and placed it on Avery's waistline. It made him flinch. "And then I grumbled about feeling poorly myself and how it might be catching. You should have seen her recoil at that. I thought to myself, that's done it. But she still looked at me strangely. I don't know how you met her sir, but she's a one to watch. Sorry." She had pulled his trousers down and had caught her nail on the back of his leg. "So she skipped over to the old widow, keeping her eyes on me the whole time and begs for a trip to the town. I couldn't help it but I jumped right in when she said that and then she knew she had caught us. She narrowed her eyes at me, like the cat that got the cream. She wouldn't let up until the old woman lamented. Of course she dressed it up as an errand to buy barley water or some such tonic, all to help you of course. I saw through it as clear as I see you standing before me now. She's up to not good."

Avery listened in silence and wondered whether Elizabeth was truly a threat to them both or whether she was biding her time. Surely, she could have revealed him right there at the side of the road, humiliated him in front of the old woman, yet she had not. Of course, that wasn't to say she had not discussed the matter with the old woman on the journey. As Kate put him into his nightdress and hustled him into the bed to complete the pretense, he knew it would not be long before he found out and if he stayed put, something told him his patience would be rewarded very soon.

Kate left him alone for the rest of the afternoon and being resigned to bed, he slept a little. When he woke, he could tell from the fading light that the day was drawing to a close. He started in bed, immediately aware that he was not alone. He sat up and peered into the gloom around him expecting to see the familiar face of Kate bringing him news.

"The country air can make one rather tired can it not, Silver?"

Elizabeth was seated by the dressing table. She was fingering the silver vanity set that had been placed there so carefully by Kate that very morning. Though Avery never thought of them, he had noticed how delicately Kate always handled them. She was almost reverent with them yet Elizabeth handled them with a quiet disdain. She held the small mirror into which she now gazed, appraising her reflection as she spoke.

"Though you may not believe me, Silver, we have a lot in common." She swept a finger over her eyebrows, smoothing the fine hairs flat, keeping her attention on her face in the mirror as she did so. "We both hold stock with appearances." She looked towards him where he had sat up in bed to watch and listen. He held his breath. "And we both seek to be delighted with danger." She casually tossed the mirror back on to the dressing table where it clattered. Avery waited.

"I had been wondering whether you had been brave enough to bring along your...disguise. And whether you would be bold, or stupid enough to seek danger under our noses."

"It's not a disguise. It's who I am."

Elizabeth closed her eyes and flapped a hand in his direction, indicating she was neither interested nor ready for explanations.

"Regardless, I am right am I not Silver? You cannot deny what you are...what you want and you cannot stop yourself from seeking it?"

There were many things he could have said to try to explain or to put it better than she had but it had not gone unnoticed that he not yet called her Miss Silver, only Silver and instead he nodded.

"Then, if we are of the same spirit, you will also agree that this..." She looked around them both and made a shrug to indicate the entire room, the house and its occupants. "....this situation is abhorrent and you will no doubt wish to find a way to make it more appealing?"

He nodded again.

"Good. Then here is how I propose we make it so."

~o~

"I must say, Miss Silver, you have made a remarkable recovery. You look almost passable this morning. Will you take some breakfast?" Mrs. Fearncott indicated the vacant seat to the left of her, opposite Elizabeth. "The weather also seems to have made a turn for the better since yesterday. Elizabeth was just wondering whether you and she might wish to take

323

your watercolours to the river? That is if you feel up to it?"

Avery took his seat and allowed one of the maids to serve him some kippers and egg.

"I believe I do feel up to it Mrs. Fearncott. What a lovely idea Miss Greenwood."

"Call me Elizabeth, please."

The two young ladies chattered pleasantly over breakfast about composition and light and Georgina Fearncott was not too proud to allow a self satisfied grin to break over her face, at the relative ease with which she appeared to have broken down Toby's daughter.

It was just as easy to persuade the old woman a while later that two maids would be quite too much, as they were prone to chatter in pairs and that Kate would be quite sufficient to carry their equipment of which there seemed a lot.

"We have packed our overcoats in case the weather turns again Aunt Georgina."

"Take some lunch with you as well, there is no sense in rushing your composition for the want of sustenance," the old woman added.

Kate began to look like a pack mule with the bag, picnic basket and sketchbooks and Georgina was about to insist on Cribbs coming along when Kate insisted she was '*Quite capable, Mrs. Fearncott.*'

Kate's accent was enough to convince her that she would be ill advised to press another maid to the service. She muttered to Elizabeth as they left.

"They do breed them stronger in the North but they have never quite managed to temper their sullenness."

Elizabeth smiled and nodded in agreement, rolling her eyes to effect. With a last fluttering wave to her aunt, Elizabeth skipped down the steps to join Avery and the two of them joined arms and sauntered down the lawn to the bottom gate, Kate stoically trudging after them. Georgina felt her spirits rise, as she envisaged her plans bearing fruit at last, and she embraced the opportunity to catch up with her own correspondence. Once they were out of view of the house, Elizabeth pulled away from Avery and he in turn strode back to help Kate with her load.

"I don't expect to know what she is up to, but be careful," Kate whispered to him, as he took the heavy bag from around her back.

"Hush Kate, there are many means to the same end."

She frowned at him and repositioned the picnic basket across her arm scowling ahead at the fast retreating figure of Elizabeth.

"Yes, and there are just as many ends to be met," she added quietly.

~o~

It took them just over two hours to reach Amersham having found a quiet place by the river for Kate to stay with the easels and paints, and for Avery to change his attire. Crossing the Harewood Downs at a trot, Elizabeth had let out a great snort of laughter.

"What is it? What's so funny?"

She had thrown back her head, her hair trailing down her back in curled tresses and laughed even more deeply. It was infectious and, without knowing the reason why, Avery began to laugh as well. He was less self conscious now he was dressed in the comfort of his trousers and boots again. The clothes gave him a confidence he had failed to muster in the last few days. He had caught up with her and had asked her again, a little guardedly in case he were the reason for her mirth.

"Elizabeth?"

She stopped and looked at him, her lips trembling on another outburst.

"Can you just imagine the look on Aunt Georgina's face when she sees poor Miss Ward's attempts at a watercolour?" She burst out laughing again and walked on. Avery had felt a little ashamed to leave Kate at the river all alone and the thought that she should be mocked for her efforts to assist them made his face grow pink. Elizabeth had walked ahead, still giggling and he followed, his light mood darkened slightly. After a while, and both perspiring in the heat, they arrived on the outskirts of Amersham just before midday.

"Is this it?" Elizabeth could barely hide the disdain from her voice. Though she had traversed the street in a cab from the station, she had expected the town to herald more but upon closer inspection, they were able to walk the length of the town within ten minutes. It was a thriving market town but, in comparison to the bustle of London, was sleepy and dull. Avery indicated a smart public house on the approach to the station and escorted Elizabeth across the street. They decided to eat some lunch and from their window seat, they watched the comings and goings of the town come alive, like a symphony. There was a stream of grey looking people arriving from the station and milling towards the town. Just as many were returning with brown packages tied up. They provided the rhythm of the street. There was a mixture of high-class ladies stopping to chat, their brightly coloured dresses punctuating the grey like a timpani. A baritone of well suited gents strolling about with purpose and elderly gentleman inspecting their pocket watches moved like percussion; the organised chaos of grey and brown scurrying servants seemed to weave a melody around them all dizzying in their speed, Avery was reminded of the sound made by bumblebees in their frenetic scourges for pollen. Slow as it was compared to London, Avery was somehow mesmerized.

"Oh good God!"

Elizabeth's voice startled him and he knocked his tankard of ale, spilling a portion across his lap.

"Oh Lord!" Elizabeth continued to exclaim.

Avery stood up and began to mop at his trousers with his napkin. As he did so, Elizabeth also stood up and peered more closely out of the window.

"It is. It's him!" she cried.

Avery was caught between intrigue and irritation. The barmaid had scurried to his assistance and was now arranging the plates before them to mop up the spill whilst at the same time flapping at Avery's trousers with a beer sodden rag which smelled like an open toilet.

"Who? For goodness sake, will you please stop!" He grabbed the rag from the girl and threw it on the table. The girl muttered at him and, grabbing the cloth, scurried back behind the bar.

Elizabeth's face was like a child's as she both tried to peer out of the window yet drawing back from the light to do so discretely. She looked like she had been caught playing truant from school yet something about her made Avery think that she wanted to be caught. He leaned across the table and tried to follow her gaze. The summer had finally dawned in the country and the bright light of the sun reflected from the pale buildings opposite so that Avery had to squint to see the faces beyond the window. As he scanned the scene, he was about to draw back when he recognised Bateman stood directly opposite. He was looking in the direction of the tavern. Avery's first reaction was one of shock and he pulled his face away from the glass. He had to double check himself. Involuntarily, his hand shot to his thighs where his hand met the reassuring feel of his trousers. He had considered Bateman a friend but here in the company of Elizabeth and in the vicinity of Georgina's home town he recognised the risk and immediately began to panic.

"Do you think he has seen us?" Elizabeth's voice was calm and he glanced down at her anxiously. She seemed remarkably calm and had a strange look on her face.

"I hope not! Come on, we should be leaving." He pulled Elizabeth up by her arm and marched towards the door.

"He does not know about you does he?" she pulled her arm from Avery's grip and the two were stood looking at each other. He tried to grab her arm again to draw her away to the door which exited to the side.

As he did so, the main door opened wide bringing a warm gust of summer air and with it the familiar figure of Bateman. He stood for a moment, allowing his eyes to become accustomed to the gloom. Avery spun around and turned his back on his friend. Elizabeth, however, exclaimed loudly.

"Bateman! Is that you? It is! What a pleasant surprise!" She stepped from behind Avery and grabbed his arm. "Avery. Look who it is."

Avery, his back still to Bateman stared hard at Elizabeth, his jaw tightened around words he could not form. The pause was too long to be polite and Avery turned slowly to face Bateman. His reluctance had not gone unnoticed and Bateman's expression was one of suspicion and jealousy in equal measure yet his manners forbade him to betray himself.

"Miss Greenwood! And Avery? Well, what a surprise!" His tone suggested otherwise. "What a pleasure?" he repeated.

He had stepped towards Elizabeth and taken her wrist to place a kiss on her gloved hand. As Avery watched, it gave him some pleasure to note that they were slightly soiled from their earlier walk on the downs.

"What on earth are you.....both...doing here?" he asked.

Elizabeth looked between the two men lingering with some thought as she considered Avery's stony face. Her eyes lit up with a raised eyebrow as she

329

stepped towards Bateman and took his arm genially and placed her hand over his.

"You won't believe this but I am staying nearby with my Aunt for the summer and I…..happened upon Avery here on a chance visit to town.'"

Avery stepped in, unable to keep his tone even.

"And what are you doing here Bateman? Isn't this a little off your usual track"

"Now, now Silver, I could say the same about you," he winked at Elizabeth to neutralise some of the menace. "Would you both care for a drink?"

Avery had taken breath to decline when Elizabeth accepted, a mischievous smirk on her lips. She returned to the window seat which had been cleared of plates and waited.

"It looks for all the world like you are following a scent Silver," Bateman growled.

"And you Bateman? What brings you this far from town?"

"What will it be gentlemen?" A barman had appeared in place of the timid barmaid and he smiled amiably at the two young men. He hoped they would stay and boost his takings. Glancing across at the well-dressed Elizabeth, it had not gone unnoticed that the trio clearly had some money to spare.

"Three of your finest ales if you please. And one for yourself my good man!" Bateman stated cheerily. Avery sighed and eyed him warily.

~o~

It was a few hours later when Elizabeth and Avery re-traced their steps over the downs and found the hollow in which Avery had hidden his dress. The walk had been tiring and, after a few drinks and the heat of the afternoon, they had felt drained and had fallen into a sullen silence. Avery had broken up the party with Bateman by taking his leave and indicating discretely that he would not, could not wait for Elizabeth. Knowing she would not be able to find her own way home she was able to excuse herself at the same time.

"Avery, will you walk with me until I am collected?"

Bateman's look had been thunderous and he had clamped his jaw shut on some impolite exclamation. Taking their leave, they had been careful to ensure that he had not followed them as they slipped out of town via the main road and away across the common lands. The last they had seen of him was as he raised his hat to Elizabeth with a small bow and a smile and then, standing up, he had nodded to Avery with narrowed eyes. As he watched the retreating form of Elizabeth crossing the road, the glint of the high sun had caught his eye and Avery was reminded of the wolf in Grimm's fairy stories.

Now, as Avery hid from view to redress himself, he thought of how that expression would morph into something far more sinister if he were to follow them to Georgina's. He shivered in the cooling shade of the oak as he shrugged on the dress over his bare arms.

Chapter Twenty Two - Avery, 1869

By the time Avery, Kate and Elizabeth were within sight of home, the last light of July was fading from the sky and they were met by an anxious party from the house. The faces of Cribbs, Helen and Peter, a sullen boy from the stable, were unmistakably peeved at having found the three of them so soon and come to no harm. Peter had half been hoping all three of them had fallen in the river and been washed away to sea. The quiet suburbs were devoid of any such headlines and, though miserable and wet looking, Avery and Elizabeth were very much alive and well. As such, all three of the search party looked as though they had found a penny but lost a pound.

"Thank heavens," exclaimed Helen dryly. "The mistress has been alive with worry for you all." She fussed directly to Elizabeth who stalked past her and off towards the house. Cribbs went scurrying after her and the stable boy, throwing up his hands, shook his hand and padded back behind the house. The older maid raised an eyebrow to Kate and Avery, who between them were carrying the load of equipment and bags. She went to Avery's aid, casting Kate a frown.

"It's alright. I've got a good hold. I think Kate needs a hand."

"I can manage," Kate snapped and Helen shot her a look.

"Well. If you can both '*manage*', I will see you back at the house shortly. You have both missed dinner. If cook can '*manage*', I will see that something be left out for you." With that she rounded on her heels and strode back to the house.

As soon as the gathering dusk took her from view, Avery dropped his bag and turned to Kate.

"Kate! We need to get back to London."

The urgency of his tone was all too evident and Kate still looked cross with having been left all day on a damp river bank to swelter, painting two lots of the same scene. She seemed to have been doing a good job in the first few hours but then her inexperienced enthusiasm had altered the paintings beyond recognition. By the time Avery and Elizabeth had shown up they were little more than a child's daubing. The paper, thin beneath her brushstrokes, had begun to wear and Elizabeth had mocked her ruthlessly. Avery too had smiled and, in her anger, Kate had finished packing the bags rather carelessly. As she had pulled the easel shut, the paintings slipped from their stand and fell to the mud of the river bank.

"Ha! In one fell swoop you may have managed to improve them tenfold!" Elizabeth had crowed.

Avery had shot Elizabeth a scowl as he had rushed to help Kate try to rescue them from the waters edge.

"What? Can it be helped that she is as clumsy as she is useless at landscapes?"

As Elizabeth spoke, one of the watercolours slipped further down the bank and Avery had to step into the shallows to retrieve it. It was a step too far and his footing, inside the unsuitable dainty boots beneath his skirt, slipped on the riverbed and Avery had half sat in the water. It was too much for Elizabeth and she roared with laughter. Kate and Avery's moods had darkened.

"Well, at least we don't have to show Aunt Georgina one of those awful pictures. We can say the remaining one is your effort and the wet and spoiled one could pass as my own which got ruined. It makes it far more believable. Don't you think?"

She had not waited for a response but had strolled off leaving Avery and Kate to finish packing the supplies and hurry after her. No-one had said more than a few words to one another all the way back to Juniper Hall. Avery had been deep in thought. Running into Giles Bateman had unnerved him and now he offloaded his thoughts to Kate.

"We must think of a plan and we must think of one soon. There is a chance we will be discovered," he continued.

In the fading warmth of the day, Avery's face was pale and he pulled on his lip nervously.

Kate did not seem to be roused into any kind of panic, her voice totally steady.

"Who did you see in town?" her voice was calm.

"Bateman," he said simply though he knew the name would mean nothing to her. There followed a silence which he could not resist filling. He trusted Kate and he was now in a position where he needed to share his worries. "He's a friend of mine. Someone I know from town. We go out together, a group of us."

He looked at Kate to discern her reaction but her face was full in shadow. He glanced towards the house where windows were blazing into life as rooms were lit for the evening.

"So this Bateman, he's a friend?"

"We go out drinking and dancing and making entertainment. It's how I met Elizabeth. Bateman had his eye on her and I think I may have overstepped the mark and now he is here. He has followed her here and now he knows I am here and...Oh God Kate, do you think he knows? What if he knows?"

"Calm down Avery!" she railed, moving into the light. Her eyes, first on his and then behind him towards the house, narrowed as she considered their dilemma.

"You don't understand Kate. If he knows she is staying with her aunt, he could turn up at any opportunity. He will only have to make some enquiries as to her whereabouts and he could be here at any time."

"Miss Greenwood is here in disgrace is she not?"

Avery nodded.

"And why is she in disgrace? Cribbs mentioned something about her mistress sneaking out and being brought home by a man in the small hours. Would that be you or Bateman? Or could it be that Miss Greenwood is to be found by any number of young men out of an evening?" she added waspishly. The comment went unnoticed by Avery and she waited whilst her words sank in.

"It must have been Giles. That night after we met. It was late when she left."

"Giles?" Kate asked.

"Bateman."

"And if it was Bateman who was caught bringing her back late," she continued.

"Then he will be persona non grata!" Avery finished.

335

"So we should stay. If you stay here at the house, he can't discover you?"

He was about to add something else when a voice called to them. It was Georgina. She was closer than they had realised and the sound of her voice made both of them jump.

"There you are." Her tone expressed irritation and she flashed a scowling smile in the fading light across Avery and Kate in turn. 'Both of you.'

Avery's skin crawled as he wondered how much she had heard. He recalled glancing at the house a few moments before and the route had looked clear. How had she managed to creep up upon them so suddenly and so soundlessly. A heavy set woman, she could hardly have kept from making a noise across the gravel path at least.

"I can't imagine what you can both be thinking of to remain outside a moment longer. Elizabeth has informed me of your accident by the river. I expect you wish to have a bath and get changed?"

She stepped aside and indicated for Avery to precede her back to the house. Avery bent to collect the equipment, which he had dropped to talk to Kate. Georgina snapped at him. "Leave that. She said she could manage. If she needs help, I will send Cribbs back down."

Avery ignored Georgina and scooped up his bags and indicated to Kate for her to follow him. Seeing the steely glare with which the old woman fixed them both with Kate didn't hesitate.

~o~

The following day was just as searing and, along with dry heat, the air was oppressive with tension. Elizabeth had acted quickly to return to her aunt's good books and had taken great delight in elaborating over the details of their 'day out'. Georgina's ill humour had been dismantled entirely when Elizabeth had produced Kate's 'effort', attributed entirely to Avery. After the laughter had died down and Georgina's face had returned to its usual dour expression, she lauded.

"There is no doubt in my mind, Miss Silver, that your father has dealt you a great handicap in neglecting your education. There is certainly nothing in your artistic palette that warrants pursuing." She almost looked sympathetically upon Avery, as if such a creature should deserve pity rather than piety. She considered Avery, sat sullenly before her, and saw for a moment the child that had lost its mother. Avery glanced up and glared. He reached behind his head and stroked his neck. With that simple gesture, Georgina almost put her finger on what made her uneasy around Avery. He had a masculine presence and it unnerved her. The sympathy had been a brief interruption in her austere façade and instead a grim flash of malice flickered across her narrowed eyes. "I still hold firm that your talents must lie somewhere Miss Silver. Perhaps a spell indoors working on a frame or two?"

Avery's face fell hard and the old woman was well satisfied that this new chore would diminish some of the spirit which she was beginning to see, and disapprove of.

"You do know how to embroider?" she added incredulously.

After Avery had been set to the task of working on some childish sampler, Georgina grew bored of watching and retreated to her study where a cooling breeze swiftly lulled her to sleep. The opportunity to throw the task aside was taken up and Elizabeth scorned from the corner in which she had been observing his efforts.

"Come now Avery, how do you imagine you will ever be married if you cannot offer your husband any of these '*charming*' skills?"

"How on earth do you think any of '*this*', would impress a man?" he lifted the sampler and indicated to the watercolours around him which Georgina had shown him to inspire. "All of it. What does a man want with it? What is it for?" He grinned at the absurdity of it and began to undo the stitches he had so carelessly been working on for the last hour. Elizabeth laughed out loud.

"And so what do you imagine a man would want from a lady if not her needlework?"

She picked up a ball of thread and cupped it in her hands.

'If you were in want of man, what do you think you would wish for?" she asked.

Avery's face twitched as he considered the comment. He knew that he would never be in want of a man. It was as inconceivable as a hen falling in love with a fox. Without warning, he imagined himself like Connie, on his hands and knees, being forcibly rocked by a man thrusting at him and he felt violated by the thought but smiled despite himself. He felt sure that

Connie had no great talent for turning a pious scene to a sampler or committing a still life to canvas but he knew that she was far more in demand than many women he had impressed upon. He ignored her question and answered his own.

"Any man in want of a wife would surely know that such facile tasks must surely dull the mind. I am sure such women are in high demand for exactly that reason."

Elizabeth sported a wide smile as she welcomed the return of some of Avery's former wit.

"However," he added quickly, interrupting a ready retort. "any man in want of a woman would do well to remember that ladies who make such light work of such fiddly tasks would surely be deft in other areas."

Elizabeth watched Avery with rising interest as she took in his awkward form. Stood behind the armchair, the odd skirt which he was wearing was disguised and he only looked slightly incongruous in his laced blouse. His hair had worked loose from a shabbily tied ponytail and he looked slightly wild and out of place. He seemed too big for the room.

As she watched him, she became aware of a familiar feeling and she closed her eyes until she could feel his hand upon her thighs that day in Hyde Park. She took a breath before she spoke again.

"What makes you think that any woman would wish to be wanted in any way but as a wife?"

He smiled at her with a curious sidelong look.

"There are many ways to be hungry Elizabeth but sating one's appetite is not always enough to staunch the craving."

339

Avery made to step out from behind the armchair but the sudden glimpse of his skirt broke the fragile illusion which Elizabeth had been sheltering within.

"Stay where you are!" Her tone was more stern than she had intended and some of the atmosphere was torn from the room and Avery too seemed to become aware of his dress and he grew awkward again. She wanted to retrieve the moment and cast around for something to draw him back to her.

"And what about you Avery? What is it that you desire?"

She was earnest and her voice lacked the slight mocking tone with which she usually seasoned her enquiries. Avery was taken aback both by her direct question but also the sincere way in which she seemed to wait for his response. As he looked at her standing before him, he could think only of the recurring dreams he had which night by night took different forms. From one day to the next he could wake from the same dream buoyant with pleasure at the shivering form of Kate or Elizabeth as he dominated either one. The scene is the same each time, the warm summer day beside the lake. Each time he starts with a caress so fragile that each of the women dares not breathe lest he disappear. In his dreams, he grows to such a state of arousal that he begins to grow breathless with desire, he becomes more urgent and with Kate, she pushes him from her, rolling him to one side. The rejection seems insurmountable and it takes his breath and ardour away. The exquisite feeling when she then leans across him and begins to dominate him is nothing short of ambrosial. On the other hand, when he and Elizabeth are beside the lake, she is alluring but impenetrable and just as it seems he cannot seduce her, she submits and he has her pinned by her wrists, beneath him as he explores her breasts with his hot breath. He of course cannot tell her either of these things and instead he asks her a question.

"What of you Elizabeth? What do you crave in a husband? What is it you want from a man?"

She snorted and, feeling free of the conversation, she put a hand to her head and looked beyond Avery to the window behind.

"I do not crave a husband, Avery but I do need one. You may object if you like," she added noticing his look of incredulity. "Oh, I am sure this will not surprise you and do not try to hide your distaste but what I want from a husband is money."

She stood and walked to the window without passing Avery.

"I want a large house, bigger than this one and I want status. I want my sister to envy me. I want her to want my life. I want a husband who will give me all of these things. I want a husband who bends to my will."

It was Avery's turn to snort derisively. "Well, I can tell you now that Bateman will be none of the things you desire."

"Of course not," she agreed. "My father has someone in mind for me, that much is clear."

She turned to see Avery's reaction. He was silent and looked stunned. She turned back to stare out of the window.

"He is a very high ranking and promising politician. Not so young as you or I but not so old as you might think. It seems he has a need of me, like I have a need for him, and it has been agreed that he

341

and I will be married in time for my 19th birthday. He has one more tour of Europe he wishes to conclude before we make it official. I am quite sure that the places he will visit will not be somewhere he wishes to share with a new bride on our honeymoon." She turned to Avery again. "That should not sound so odd as it does but I am afraid it is as it is."

She waited but Avery had not yet found his voice. "Needless to say, this is not something which I wish to be repeated. To anyone," she added.

Avery's pulse began to quicken as the old frustration within him was wakened. Whilst much of the recent ground he had gained had allowed him the freedom to explore a life outside of the one he was born to, he knew also that he was not able to fully complete any such transition. As Elizabeth spoke, he felt removed from her and he imagined how he could ever fool a woman completely enough to make a life like the one, or unlike the one she was describing. It was one thing to fool a woman for a night but what about a lifetime.

Elizabeth stared from the window and considered what she had said already before adding. "I need a husband who will give me a position. I need a husband that will give me a family."

He would of course never be able to be a father a child and Avery felt his freedom being taken away.

"You are a woman many men would find difficult to please Elizabeth. I should say that such a man would find you cold. I hope this gentleman you are betrothed to may find warmth at someone else's hearth for I do not envy him."

342

Elizabeth did not turn around. She did not want to see Avery dressed as a woman whilst he spoke to her like this. She enjoyed the tone of desire that he could not help but infuse his words with when he spoke. The words were not meant to be encouraging, nevertheless she found herself drawn to him.

"I am sure my husband to be has given this as much thought as I have. I consider him a man of the world and he will be under no illusion as to exactly what I am bringing to this bargain. He craves a trophy to bring respectability under the guise of a happy home and in return he will provide me with the status I require."

"And how can you be sure he will not bend you to his will in time?"

Elizabeth laughed a little crudely and pressed her hands to her lips to stifle the abrupt change in tension.

"I am sure it won't be any great shock, once you have met him, to understand that I shall not be the only one in our relationship in want of a good man!"

Avery was stunned but he too wanted to laugh.

"And so, after you have married your *respectable* man, you will be happy?"

Elizabeth shrugged. "Of course not. Who is ever happy, Avery? Show me anyone who is content with their life and I will show you a liar."

Avery considered Connie and Sarah. He was sure they were not content with their squalid life. Would they choose a steady and proper income over the dangerous and dirty work that came with such high rewards? What of Kate? Didn't she seem happy? Wasn't she at peace with her lot in life? He thought so but considered how jumpy she had been recently and wondered whether she was truly content with the dangerous game he was playing. And what about Bateman? Yes, Bateman. Wasn't he content with his circumstance? He was young and he was wealthy. The years had not yet eroded the youthful looks and slight but firm figure. No doubt in time, he would begin to resemble his father and his cheeks and stomach would begin to fill out, his face crumple under the weight of years. For now though, wasn't he content? Perhaps not. Didn't he want Elizabeth and hadn't she denied him, in favour of Avery? At least, she had done as far as he was concerned.

"I crave a man who will deny me everything, who will fight with me all day and love me passionately whilst still furious with me. I want a man. A real man."

There was a silence in the room and Elizabeth wondered whether Avery was still there. She thought perhaps she had gone too far. She was about to turn around when a creak close beside her indicated Avery was directly behind her.

"Do you hate me?" she asked.

Avery lowered his face to her shoulder where she could feel his breath upon her skin. She began to turn around but he gripped the base of her neck and held her firmly facing forward. He slipped his hand forcefully around her waist and pressed his lips to her ear.

"Yes," he said.

Chapter Twenty Three - Imogen, 1911

The house was larger than I had imagined. By no means did I consider myself to be an aristocrat or gentry but I was aware that along with my husband's wealth and business there also came great privilege. It was therefore a surprise to find that Mrs. Evesham's home was considerably larger than our own. She had given no impression of being so wealthy. Her clothes had been no finer than my own, in fact they were old fashioned and perhaps a little shabbier. She had arrived in an ordinary horse drawn carriage. She had been austere but by no means plain. I checked the calling card again to ensure I had the address right. 4 Brown Square, Mayfair. The house was right. I was about to call up to the cab driver to check when one of the large doors to Number 4 opened and a liveried man nimbly approached the carriage door. He called to the cabbie and swung the door open in a flash.

"Mrs. Evesham is expecting you madam," he flashed me a well-practiced, shallow bow and I accepted his hand as I stepped down from the cab. I walked slowly up the steps wondering for the tenth time that morning whether I was doing the right thing. Should I have told John where I was going? It suddenly seemed absurd that I was out at all given my state of mourning. Yet strange things were happening in the city. I can remember as a girl when a death in a friend's family heralded new wardrobes and routines. Black crepe abounded. The lack of any family, distant or otherwise meant I watched most of these routines from afar. The first taste of any of it was when my mother died. I was of course living in my own home by then and so I continued to watch the arrangements at a distance. My father was a close follower of the old etiquettes but since the death of the Queen, there seemed to be a change in attitudes. I had not seen so many modes of mourning. I reflected that these last few days had been the strangest yet and could not be made stranger by my not adhering to some outmoded code of conduct (of which I was probably unaware anyway!). I was feeling more resolved by the time I had handed my outer clothes to the maid in the entrance hall and I was satisfied that Number 4, Brown Square was not a dangerous place. To ease my conscience, I remembered that Stokes of course had taken the address.

After being advised that Mrs. Evesham was engaged on a telephone call, I was shown to a very plain but smart drawing room. The decor was very *a la mode* and I noticed at once that the room had been freshly decorated, the smell of turpentine and fresh paint lingered behind the mask of dried roses. The floor was laid with parquet and was well lacquered, electric lights hung from the modern pendant reflected in the sheen. The walls were a pale green, upon which were hung a few simple pictures framed in ebony. At first glance, they appeared to be drawings but on closer inspection they proved to be photographs. I kept my hands clasped together as I gazed around the rest of the room taking in the simplicity of the space. It had been discussed at Christmas with John's family that the display of knick knacks was becoming rather outdated and that the current fashion was for simple art; statement pieces, sculptures and so forth. Whilst I had made a mental note at the time of the change in fashion, my preference was always to surround oneself in the clutter from holidays, gifts from friends and pictures of the familiar. Just as paintings were being replaced with photographs so too was character with convenience. My eyes lit upon some photographs which were on display including a rather informal shot of a slightly younger Mrs. Evesham stood beside a motor car. She was wearing a light coloured dress and her unpinned hair was blurred as if lifted by a wind which the camera could not capture. She was stood formally waiting for the camera to expose her image yet she remained relaxed. She was smiling, a captivating expression which made me mirror it almost immediately.

"Gosh don't look at that frightful picture," came a voice from behind me.

Startled, I turned to find Mrs. Evesham bustling forward to take the photo from me. She wore a well fitting dress and moved with a practiced ease but with an awkward tension. I sensed that she had indeed been expecting me. As she swept past me to take the photograph, the scent of jasmine was rich. As she took the frame from me, there followed a silence. The carefully placed conversation starter was clearly not serving its purpose. She didn't expand on the photo and I did not ask any more about it. After a brief pause where she considered the image herself, she replaced it on the sideboard and walked around the settee playing with her wedding ring nervously as she did so.

"Won't you have a seat?" she offered, indicating a choice of several. "I've ordered some tea."

She glanced at the door, a nervous smile ready on her lips.

"Gemma won't be long," she said.

As if rehearsed, a young girl appeared at the door, dressed in a similar livery to the footman, a deep jet black shot with emerald stripes. Her uniform was as stark against her pale skin as the surrounds of the room. I suspected the clothes were also new.

"Ah, here she is."

Mrs. Evesham settled a little as the young maid busied herself with a tea tray. The diversion allowed me a brief interlude in which to study Mrs. Evesham again. She was not a tall woman but she held herself proudly which added an inch or so to her average frame. It was difficult to put an age to her. In my mind, I had rather settled on her being around fifty but on closer inspection there was more evidence of aging at the corners of her eyes. Her neck too was lined and I imagined she was more likely to be around my father's age. As was. The thought of him brought me back to my reason for business and I shuffled forward on my seat, both anxious to interrogate this woman but also to be gone from her pristine new home. The gesture was enough to nudge Mrs. Evesham from her own reveries and she looked at me and then the maid.

"Thank you, Gemma, that will be all."

The young girl retreated from the room, pausing only to acknowledge her mistresses last order with a nod.

"Ensure we are not disturbed please."

I watched with a growing sense of unease as the door slowly closed to leave the two of us alone. I was suddenly afraid of what I may learn from this woman.

"Forgive Gemma she has brought the old service. It is rather fine but it does not match the new decor."

Mrs. Evesham picked up her cup, examining the perfectly acceptable floral pattern carefully before replacing it on its saucer.

"I would like to say she is new and didn't know any better but alas she is simply a careless girl."

She smiled and pulled a face as if to say, such is life and she shrugged.

"She is however the daughter of the woman who makes the finest pastries this side of Paris," she looked at me conspiratorially, her eyes twinkled and she gestured towards a strand of fancies. I noticed her hand shaking slightly as she spooned a sugar in to her tea. She lifted a cup and saucer and began to pour.

"Not for me, thank you'," I said.

She looked a little disheartened and it was as much for her benefit as mine that I added, 'perhaps in a moment'.

"Mrs. Evesham..."

"Please, do call me Elizabeth."

"Mrs. Evesham," I tried to plough on but she fixed me with a pleading look. "Elizabeth..." I conceded. "You knew my father." All of my well practised words seemed useless and I cast around searching for the phrases upon which I had decided.

She didn't seem to have heard me or else she had her own version of how this conversation should begin. She set her cup and saucer down upon the table and sat forward on the edge of the chair seat. She looked at me searchingly.

"I had thought perhaps that if we ever met, you would remember me."

She had caught me off guard and I was at once aware that I was gaping. I narrowed my eyes and looked at her again. I tried to cast around in my mind for any memory of the woman but there was none. I rested my head on one side and considered her. As I did so, she looked at me regarding her and, with an amused tone, she added.

"Ha! There is no reason you should Imogen. I thought I would have recognised you, even after all these years but of course I don't." Her eyes searched over my face. "Do you know........I can see Avery in you." Her eyes narrowed and my skin crawled with the intimacy of her tone.

"Tell me the rest?" I uttered slowly.

She rose and stepped behind the chair upon which she has just been sitting. It was a series of movements that she made fluid and my heart leapt at the suddenness of it. She braced her hands on the back of the chair, her head down.

"Mrs. Evesham?" I asked but she held out her hand to quiet me.

"If I don't get this out, I am afraid I never will." She looked me straight in the eye and I nodded.

"I don't know what your relationship with your father was like," she continued. "or what you know of his past. I don't know how valuable you will find what I have to tell you but for my own part I feel a great injustice on his part being done to him. Imogen, your father was a wonderful man and there is no doubt in my mind, none whatsoever, that he was a man. There is nothing any Coroner, Newspaper or Doctor could say

350

to convince me otherwise. I have no intention of being base about this Imogen but we are each more than the sum of our bodily parts. There are men I have met who had been born blind but could see things more clearly than any sighted man, crippled men who stood taller than my own husband ever could and your father who was twice the man than many believe themselves to be.

"In the years since I last met your father, I have met and regarded many men with interest and respect. I have known eminent actors, skilled surgeons, doctors, lawyers and politicians. I have even met with Royalty.' She gave a flourish with her hand. 'I have met this country's finest minds...and some of the not so fine." she added with a smile.

"In all those men, I have never come across such a paradox as your father. That he was born a woman, I suppose, is the crudest and most obvious but more than that, he was a truly intriguing person. Forgive me Imogen but you look like a woman of the new century so I will speak plainly with you. There are very few people in this world that are truly original, who can provoke within others genuine fascination. Most people have access to a great quantity of words which they can organise into a modicum of intelligent conversation but having listened to them you realise they are saying very little.

"When I first met Avery in the sweeping halls of Cleveland Street, I was drawn to him instantly. True, there was something unusual about him but, more than that, he looked at me as if he had the answer to a question I hadn't even posed. I hope I do not embarrass or upset you but I am not ashamed to admit that there was an instant attraction. He had such a beautiful face, which was a paradox in itself, of strong jaw but soft skin. He had a quiet confidence that normally attractive men exert in an unattractive conceit. As we talked, it became obvious that he had much more to offer than just a fine looking face. He surprised and intrigued me. That night and the next day, when I met him in Hyde park, I will admit I was excited at the prospect of his being in my life. By the time I had left him a second time, I felt truly alight."

Elizabeth cast a glance at me to see how I was taking the story. Ordinarily, I might have felt uncomfortable at this acknowledgement of my father's private life, particularly from a woman that was not my mother, but I found I was pleased. I found I was desperate to hear more. She went on.

"Meeting him was doubly difficult as I was due to be married the following year. It was not a match for love but one that I wholeheartedly advocated for position and wealth. I was a cynic about love and of affection and had not met a man who had made me question that. I wanted to spend more time getting to know Avery but of course my family had different ideas. My father thought the city was a bad influence on me and was concerned that my reputation would become tainted and jeopardise my marriage prospects. My aunt offered to take me under her wing for some *'guidance'*. If that wasn't the worst of it, they had decided to couple me with the daughter of her fiancé who herself was in need of tutelage. When I found out that I was to be sent to the country for the rest of the summer, I was furious, but there was little I could do to send word to Avery. We had arranged to meet in a few days time but I did not know where he lived. So I sent word by the only way I could think of; via a mutual acquaintance, a man by the name Giles Bateman. The following week went terribly slowly. The seclusion, the silence of the country and the company of my miserable aunt could have been borne under normal circumstances but I couldn't help but think of Avery. You know what it is like when you are young and you find someone who is rare, you cannot help but think of them. By day and by night I thought of him, hardly giving a moments thought to the young charge who was arriving for my help."

The old woman paused and closed her eyes and I felt she was herself transported back several decades to when her heart beat fast with the yearning.

"You can't imagine the blow I was dealt when I arrived back from a walk in the country air one day and found Avery seated beside my aunt, taking tea upon the terrace wearing a dress. It was.....," she searched for a word, her cheeks flushed with embarrassment. "........absurd."

"He was lucky I could remain so composed and frankly, the shock must have played a hand. There was no doubt though that it was entirely absurd. The last time I had seen him, he had been dressed in a well cut suit, he had been charming, he had made me tremble and then there he was sitting in a dress with, and this was somehow worse, a demure and lifeless demeanour.

"I was furious with him, of course, but more than that, I felt cheated. Yes, cheated. He had stolen himself from me and the woman that had replaced him made my skin crawl. She was insincere and awkward and yet possessed him so utterly. I am not sure that this makes

353

any sense but that is how it felt. It is entirely down to my upbringing that I managed to remain in role but the moment I was in my room, I am not ashamed to admit that I screamed into my mattress, I thrashed and kicked about with a pure rage. At first I felt foolish, that his dressing as a man were some elaborate game to keep himself amused or could it be the other way around and at that very minute, Avery was dressed as a woman to entertain himself. I will admit that this thought fuelled my anger and in my anger at him, I was surprised to feel desire. It was my desire for him which confused me the most. Was it him I desired or was it her? I have to admit that part of me was disgusted at the idea but another part of me was intrigued and I had to find him to put my disordered mind at rest. I went to see him and I knew as soon as I saw him that I desired him and the incongruous costume only made me feel sick. Don't look at me like that Imogen. You would feel the same, I am sure. I am a woman of the world and I have known many a woman fallen foul of Sapphic pleasures; from the tidiest of housemaids to the haughtiest of dignitary's wives. I also know that I am not in the least bit interested in taking my pleasure with a woman."

I had to interrupt her. There was a boundary that was dangerously close to being crossed.

"Please, Mrs. Evesham...Elizabeth. You said that you knew my mother."

She looked at me awkwardly, the remainder of her speech drying up on her lips and she appraised me as if only just seeing me in the room. It was an odd moment and I understood that this was probably the first time she had retold any of the story and I felt sorry for having interrupted her train of thought.

"Forgive me, please continue," I said.

It was too late and, though I was sorry for interrupting her, I was relieved when she started her recollection from a new narrative.

"It's taken me many years to admit but your mother was much the prettier of the two of us which, at the time, piqued me. I wasn't jealous of course but it irritated me how she could look so resplendent wearing only her drab uniform. Her hair was always tied away under a cap but an innocent curl here and there would work loose during the chores of the day and it would frame her perfectly clear complexion like a work of art. On its own, her natural beauty would not have bothered me but she also had this perfectly adorable little figure and, whether she knew it or not and I suspect she didn't, she knew how to make it work to her advantage. Forgive me, Imogen, but some women have a natural understanding of how their body moves and others can work for many years on achieving the same thing and never come close. Your mother was petite, beautiful and confident. I saw immediately the effect this had on your father even though, at the time, she could not.'

As Mrs. Evesham spoke, I think I was so confused about what she was saying that I initially passed over some of the detail. My mother in a uniform? I listened as she continued with her story.

Chapter Twenty Four - Elizabeth, 1869

The following day, Elizabeth could not forget the shiver that ran down her spine when Avery' lips had pressed to her neck. As she watched him across the breakfast table passing over a salt cellar to Georgina, she could not decide whether she had been relieved or disappointed when he leapt away from her as the sound of the door handle being unlatched indicated the arrival of Kate. The sudden movement had not gone unnoticed from the young maid and Elizabeth had noticed the flush of blood upon the girl's clear cheeks and the rushed manner with which she hustled around the room. Avery had been almost apologetic towards her and Elizabeth's curiosity had been stoked so that now at the table she ventured a sly enquiry.

"Avery. I noticed that young Miss Ward was looking very drawn yesterday. It seems the country air does not suit her. I would be happy to have Helen wait upon you if you would think you could do without her?"

Georgina raised an eyebrow at this out of character concern for domestic staff. Avery's reaction was not so calm.

"There is nothing wrong with Kate. She is to stay here with me."

His tone was curt and he immediately saw the reason for her concern as Elizabeth received his flapped admission with a secretive smile. She flashed him a gracious smile and sat back in her chair. Elizabeth did not have to wait long to see how far she could push her advantage. After breakfast, Georgina announced that there would be a visitor to the house.

"Mrs. Rutherford is an old friend of mine. She is interested to find how you girls are taking to the country. It should only take her a few hours from Enfield so we should expect her sometime after three o'clock."

Avery barely heard. He was as uninterested in Georgina's world as she was in his. He was already ruminating on how to resolve the issue of his double life. The run in with Giles a few weeks ago had made him uncomfortable and although a return to the town had not repeated the incident, he was not keen to return home without a plan. He and Kate had been discussing a few variations of the same scenario and his choices were growing narrower. He was therefore only half listening as Georgina continued.

"She has had an unlucky couple of months by all accounts. Her household has diminished since her husband's death and she has now lost two maids in quick succession. Poor thing. We will probably spend much of the afternoon alone. You girls will wish to occupy yourselves in the music room no doubt?"

"How dreadful Aunt Georgina? Is she staying long with us?"

"It hasn't been agreed Elizabeth but I expect she will stay a few days at least. I had promised to look over her finances. She has not the capacity that I have for running such an estate and I hope to educate her."

Elizabeth smiled at the look of contentment with which this was delivered. If there was one thing which Georgina loved more than sheer meddling, it was being able to patronise and to boast. This offered her both such opportunities.

357

"Well, if she is in need of a maid for the next few days I am sure that Miss Silver's girl could stand in. Cribbs has pretty much been ministering to us both this past week anyway."

Both Avery's and Georgina's heads snapped upwards in unison but for different purpose. Avery flashed Elizabeth a warning glance unaware of quite what she was intending. For Georgina, it had not gone unnoticed that Avery's maid had not been performing her own duties but had had someone else doing it for her. The questions this alone begged would be stored in the old woman's mind for future reference.

"Well, that is a very practical solution. I had just been thinking how I could manage without Helen."

Avery was about to argue but a crash of glass in the corridor signaled an abrupt departure for Georgina and Avery was left gawping at Elizabeth.

"Why did you just do that?" he demanded suspiciously.

"Come now Avery. Don't be so uncharitable. You heard how the poor woman has no help upon which she can rely. After all, its only for a few days." She smiled at him and passed out of the doorway through which Georgina had just bustled. Avery was about to drop his guard when Elizabeth's face reappeared, a coy smile upon her face.

"Unless, that is, young Kate prefers Mrs. Rutherford's employ…"

She had slipped away before Avery had managed to expel his annoyance at her and when he found Kate ten minutes later in Elizabeth's room, she had already been briefed of her change in role for the next few days. Away from the context of this having been Elizabeth's idea, Kate was perfectly quiescent.

That afternoon, Elizabeth had indeed ensured that the two of them were to be found in the music room despite the weather being glorious. As the door latched closed behind them, the reason for her insistence became clear. Avery was about to complain and suggest that they take a walk to the summer house when Elizabeth brought out a key and locked the door. An internal room, there would be no way anyone could interrupt them without their knowing.

"Whilst Kate has an opportunity to get to know Mrs. Rutherford a little better, I thought you and I could do the same."

Though he felt manipulated and his annoyance had not abated, a wide grin spread over his face. Elizabeth, unsettled by the sight of him once more in his dress, had her doubts but sat down at the piano and began to play a simple tune.

"Will you accompany me, Avery?" she asked. "Something sombre perhaps, to suit your humour?"

Avery walked up behind her and placed his hands upon her shoulders. Elizabeth jumped a little nervously but continued to play softly on the keys. She closed her eyes and tilted her head to rest upon one of his hands, aware of how her heart beat wildly in her chest.

"I prefer something a little more lively," he whispered, pressing his lips to her bared neck.

~o~

The following days were marked by the same chain of events. The morning brought a mutual stand off where Elizabeth would tease, cajole and push him. Avery would grow annoyed and sullen. By the afternoon, the air between them had become charged with frustration. Avery wanted to find an open field and stand and shout. Elizabeth was desperate to get to that final point that made him snap; that moment where he touched her. Inevitably it came, one way or another. They would pass in a corridor and he would finally break and pull her to him in an embrace. It was a mutually unfulfilling way to get to a fulfilling moment. She would not simply ask him and as soon as the moment was over, she grew confused and thus would start the evening where she would push him away entirely. By the time Mrs. Rutherford had left, four days later, the two were causing enough friction to start a fire. Georgina had witnessed this from a distance and, as soon as her friend's carriage had rumbled off in a cloud of dust, she summoned both Avery and Elizabeth to follow her.

"Ladies. Walk with me."

The two of them cast uneasy glances at each other. It was obvious that Avery's first thought was for his secret stash of clothes. He had told Elizabeth that he had hidden them from Cribbs but in doing so they may been discovered by one of the other maids? Elizabeth's first thought was for the afternoons they had spent in the locked music room, the sneaked embraces in the darkened corridors or the previous afternoon in the summerhouse. They reached the terrace, where Georgina stood, surveying the formal lawns; two gardeners bent at work

"I am grateful to you both for keeping yourselves to yourselves whilst I have been otherwise engaged but I think that you have both been kept within these four walls long enough. I think the time is right for a small sojourn into town."

She looked at each of them before continuing.

"'I am going shopping this afternoon in town and I think you might both welcome the opportunity to join me?"

"Aunt Georgina! That would be lovely. Isn't that kind, Alice?"

But the look with which Avery received this news indicated it was nothing of the sort.

~o~

"'Miss Silver? Is there something wrong with your head? Your back?"

It was the third time Georgina had snapped at Avery since they had arrived in Amersham and Elizabeth had started to regret teasing him about this trip. He was clearly unnerved about running into someone who recognised them from their last visit. As a result, he was walking with a stoop and had been covering his face at every turn. Georgina had a pet hatred of poor posture and was being driven to distraction by this very public show of slouching.

"Then perhaps you would be so kind as to stand up straight. I don't wish the town to think I have brought you along from some crippled home." She tossed her head and stalked off, indicating that they should both follow. It was obvious that she was annoyed at having thought that the outing could have been a treat for them both when clearly there was much work still to do on Avery. Perhaps she had hoped that she could use this shopping trip as an excuse for getting Avery to wear something more feminine. She had commented to Elizabeth only the previous morning that the drab colours Avery wore were, at best, neat but made him look more like a missionaries wife than a potential wife (if Georgina had anything to do with it). Elizabeth was of course demonstrating better social graces, Georgina had remarked, and whilst she would never be a timorous girl, she was certainly behaving less impudently. As if on cue, Elizabeth followed her aunt, swiftly without a further word. Avery sighed and followed his father's fiancée inside the small department store trying to turn his head towards the busy street whilst holding himself upright. The three of them were met by a salesman primed for the very eventuality of three such obviously moneyed characters chancing upon his store.

Within five minutes, Elizabeth was leaving by the same door having skillfully extracted herself from the chore of persuading Avery into different clothes. Though she would normally have enjoyed some of the sport in deriding him so publicly, she had also spotted another opportunity she could not let pass.

"Aunt Georgina! Will you please excuse me? I need to find a WC. Ladies business." She added under her breath as Georgina raised her eyebrows. "I will meet you at the carriage when you are done."

As she slipped out of the doorway, she hurried down the broad main street towards the green strip of grass where the figure of Bateman stood chatting with two other men.

"Miss Greenwood!" His surprise was genuine. Though he had only seen her disappear into the department store a few moments ago, he had been caught off guard by two other familiar faces who now stood appraising Elizabeth.

"Forgive me. Miss Greenwood, this is Mr. Havers and Mr. Tremain. Gentlemen, this is Miss Elizabeth Greenwood."

She smiled at each of them as they raised her extended hand to their lips.

"A great pleasure it is too Miss Greenwood," said the older of the two. A sallow looking man with ruddy cheeks, she did not know whether he was Havers or Tremain nor did she seem interested to know. "You look very well since last we met, the country air must agree with you."

Elizabeth looked directly at Bateman.

"Mr. Havers is a regular at Cleveland Street," he explained.

"Yes, it is not only yourself who quits London in the heat Miss Greenwood. So few of our number remain in the capital that we have decided to take the remaining stalwarts on a tour."

"Yes, it seems there are a great number of us who choose the cooler country air. Why, even Silver has not been seen in a number of weeks. I was just telling Tremain that he had been spotted roaming these parts only a few weeks ago." Bateman did not break his gaze from Elizabeth's and she could not glean from his tone whether he had spotted Avery earlier when she had herelf noticed Bateman.

"Where Mr. Silver does or does not roam is of no consequence to me," she ventured but Bateman remained impassive. The ruddy faced Havers continued, unaware of the growing unease which crept over Elizabeth

"We were just telling Bateman here about a small shindig we are having tomorrow evening. It's not too far from here if you are interested."

Despite herself and the misgivings she felt, Elizabeth leapt at the chance.

"'Gentlemen, though it would be my absolute pleasure, I am not inclined to be wandering around the countryside on my own in the evening. There are any number of ways I could meet my end but falling in a ditch or being trampled by a cow is not one of those I entertain."

Bateman was quick with a solution.

"Why don't you see if Silver can accompany you?"

Elizabeth eyed him closely, desperately trying to make up her mind if he knew. She had to probe further.

"I am sure he would be delighted to. Why don't you pick us up from the turnstile on the London Road at 10 o'clock?"

Bateman's surprised face told her everything she needed to know and as she spun on her heel to return to the department store, there was a spring in her step at the prospect of some fun on the horizon.

Chapter Twenty Five - Imogen, 1911

As rapt as I was becoming with Mrs. Evesham's recollections, I had noticed the mantel clock approaching the hour and I had to interrupt her. Though the picture she was painting of my father both honoured and framed his life, I had not yet come to hear about how my mother and he became involved nor what Mrs. Evesham had meant by a uniform.

"I'm sorry. You must think I had forgotten what you had come to hear. I have not thought about that period of my life for such a time its all coming back to me as if it were only a few years ago."

The older woman shook her head a little sadly and considered me for a moment before beginning again.

"Mrs. Evesham, tell me about my mother."

"Your mother. Yes."

She continued looking at me, her eyes flickering over mine as she pondered the next words she would use.

"It would be a lie to say that your mother and I were friends. She did not like me nor I her. However…," she raised her voice as I tried to interject, "by the time we parted company, I think it is fair to say, we had a mutual respect for one another and I, for one, owed her a great debt of gratitude.

"In the first instance, I admit I thought her rather proud and above her station and once I knew that she had an affection for your father, I will admit that I was rather more 'unfriendly' than I would usually have been."

My face must not have concealed my confusion but Mrs. Evesham took this for disdain.

"My dear, things may be different in this new century but in my day, being overly familiar with one's maids was not to be encouraged."

"Maid? I am not sure that I follow."

Mrs. Evesham looked as confused as I felt.

"Kate," she said simply.

"Katherine," I corrected out of habit. John had always used her more formal diminutive.

"Katherine. Kate. Your father's maid," she added when I continued to frown.

I suppose I had been expecting her to say as much but it was still a shock. Yet, it was such a fitting skeleton in my mother's closet that I could not help but laugh. Though a surprise revelation, it seemed such a trivial thing in comparison and despite the fact, I felt a small disappointment that my mother had hidden this from me, it threw so much of her character into context that this was quickly eclipsed by a sort of relief. Images of her raced through my mind. She had her own maid, always a useless young girl who would only stay a few years at a time. What had seemed a reluctance to be waited upon, I had always attributed to her being unable to sit still, a sort of nervous agitation. Now I could see that it would have made her uncomfortable.

"Forgive me," I pressed my lips together. "I had no idea. Please continue."

Mrs. Evesham seemed oblivious to my shock but continued.

"Though I had no great regard for her at first, I did not go out of my way to make life difficult. It was Avery who bore the brunt of my plaguing. So I did not know much about her until Avery returned to London after the death of his father." She placed her hands upon her knees and began the next part of her story.

"'It was the end of the summer and things had been," she paused and looked at me without meeting my eyes before shaking her head. "Things had been difficult," she decided upon. Though interested in the details I let her continue at her own pace.

"The news about Toby Silver had come as a great shock to all of us. Though I had never met him, I had envisaged him as a great bear of a man quite the opposite of my late uncle whom I had once heard aunt Georgina describe as being the runt of the Fearncott litter. Avery took the news very well and though terribly upset, he managed to organise for Georgina and himself to return to London that very day. Georgina on the other hand was in a terrible shock. If Avery had not managed the arrangements, there is no doubt she would have remained at Amersham. He came to find me to say goodbye and was surprised to find Kate in my room with me. She had found me an hour earlier in ...." Her voice trailed off and she looked directly at me and blushed. Shaking her head, she stammered for her train of thought.

"She found me in a...a...a state of upset...and had seen me to my room whereupon she had proved to be a very good listener. You may find me selfish Imogen but there was a lot going on around that time. Toby's death was sad news but my tears were entirely for myself. Avery had assumed that Kate would return with him and was very surprised when she volunteered to stay. There was not the time for a conversation about it and within a few hours, Georgina, Avery,

Cribbs and Helen had left to catch the last train back to London.

"With Georgina gone, the house seemed diminished but without Avery it seemed cold. As I retreated to my room, I wondered whether I should have insisted on Kate going with them. Some of my usual resilience had returned and I was beginning to regret having opened up to someone, let alone a maid. However, when I opened the door and saw Kate sitting waiting for me on the blanket box, I was filled with a rush of gratitude.

"She was a good friend to me that day and that I had done nothing to deserve made it much more rewarding. It was a full week before we heard again from Avery and he advised that there was much to be done with his father's business interests and would therefore not be returning for the foreseeable future. He did not send for Kate and I sensed that this piqued her.

"Georgina on the other hand, had only been Toby's fiancée and she was therefore without a role in the proceedings. This did not suit her sense of purpose and she was trying her best to appear the distraught widower-to-be whilst investigating any claim she may have to the Silver estate. My father was no doubt very helpful in assisting her with this.

"By my usual standards, the following weeks were very dull for me but I was out of sorts and feeling unwell, so it was a welcome relief from being constantly on display. In that time, your mother and I spent quite a bit of time together. Some of the staff had been called to my aunts' London home and, inside the house at least, we were left only with the housekeeper and a few scullery maids.

"Though we were far from being friends, we became inseparable, by choice rather than duty. Of course, being the only lady's maid she tended to my dressing room, my wardrobe and kept me company on walks but she had such an easy and familiar way about her, I often found myself forgetting entirely that she was staff. Oh, I see how that makes you uncomfortable but it was true my dear. We lost contact over the years so, sadly, I do not know the woman she became, but even as a domestic servant she had character about her. I realised very quickly that I had never had someone within whom I could confide. Agnes, my sister, and I had never been close and we betrayed each other's confidences as a matter of such course that we had not trusted anything of interest to each other since childhood. My father had no time for matters of little consequence and I had kept other women at an arm's length viewing them as competitors. With Kate, she had nothing I prized and yet I was always conscious of my own jealous nature around her. Avery clearly had feelings for her and I could see why. She was sweet, quick witted, kind and caring beyond her station. More than that, she made me laugh despite myself and I could not help but like her.

"So, we made an unsuitable pair for the weeks before Avery returned. When he returned, he returned alone. My aunt Georgina had decided to stay with a friend to escape further attention and where she could 'recover from the shock."

Mrs. Evesham fell silent and I was still waiting for that moment where she pulled the rug from beneath me but it did not come.

"I don't know what more that I can tell you, Imogen." She glanced at me and then at her fingers which she had been twisting for the last five minutes. It was a nervous gesture and quite at odds with the confident and charming woman she appeared to be.

"When was the last time you saw them both?" I asked. I wanted to ask what she knew of me, about who I was. If my father was not my father then who was? I wanted to ask but was afraid to know.

"After the death of his father, Avery was the sole beneficiary of a not insubstantial sum of money. Whilst setting some of his father's affairs in order in London, he had also been setting some of his own plans in motion. When he returned to Amersham something about him had changed, he had lost a little weight and become more angular in the face through lack of sleep and he had probably not been eating either. As a result, the clothes that ill-suited him, now ill fitted him too and he was more at odds than I had seen him with his own body.

"His inheritance allowed him more freedom than ever before and that first evening after dinner he spoke to me in detail. He had laid plans to travel and of course, he had purchased tickets for himself and Kate. He was planning a journey across Europe and along the way he hoped to shed a part of himself. He would start the journey as a woman and return as a man, permanently. As he described the route by which he planned his tour; Ostend, Paris, Lausanne, Barcelona, Seville, I imagined him as a dark field snake coursing across the map, sloughing his old skin as he went, I will admit that I was intensely jealous. Not of Kate but of Avery. Travelling was something I ached to do and it was one of the things that made my imminent marriage more bearable. When he told me the news, I snapped at him and retreated to my room. I could not trust myself to say something I would regret.

"That evening, he came to me room and I was calmer but no less envious of the position he had found himself. It will seem cruel in the extreme but I would have traded Agnes and my father at that point to have half of the freedom he had access to. He was kinder to me that evening, we had left on such hostile terms it did not sit right with him and he was not inclined to hold his grudge. He listened to me and though I did not beg passage with him, I let it be known that I was open to the suggestion. No doubt your mother had some hand in what followed and by the morning Avery was offering me the chance to travel with him. At first, I could not see how I could but the more I considered it, the more possible it seemed. Why would my father and aunt object to a trip across Europe. Had I not proven, if not falsely, that I could be trusted?

"And so, we did. There were some objections from my father of course who insisted on a chaperone accompanying us. Avery threatened to abandon the trip and my father, really thought the idea a wondrous opportunity, was quick to agree some terms with Avery. Firstly, we would be required to send regular word as to our progress. Secondly, I was to be home before the beginning of April so that my wedding plans would not be interrupted. Lastly, we could not travel without a man. This could have been my undoing as Avery was beginning to tire of the conditions. Fortunately though, he found someone very quickly, a young man by the name of George Heston. I do not know where he found him but they were already well acquainted. Heston was introduced to my father as a scholar and though he had his concerns as to Heston's suitability he reluctantly agreed. Within the fortnight and into October we were crossing the channel. By the end of May, I was returning alone having left Avery, Kate and Heston in Milan.

"By the summer, I was Mrs. Evesham and her I have remained," she finished simply.

I looked at the old woman's hands which she had, by now, begun to almost turn into knots. For somebody who seemed to revel in the telling of a tale and had so far not been mean with the richness of details, I was surprised that she was so reluctant to fill in the gaps. By her own admission, she had spent almost eight months travelling throughout Europe with my mother and father and, to my delighted surprise, Heston too. Had she also not arrived home a month later than planned and barely in time for her own wedding? So, my mother and father fell in love whilst in Europe? Where did I factor in all of this? I was buzzing with questions. Not just for Mrs. Evesham but for Heston.

There was a draught as the door opened cautiously and the face of Mrs. Evesham's young maid appeared. She was trying to remain unseen and when her eyes lit on mine she coloured and tried to withdraw. In her haste, she hit her head upon the doorframe behind and let out a loud yelp.

"What on earth?"

Mrs. Evesham turned abruptly in her chair, knocking the table with her foot and causing the teacups to clatter angrily.

372

I had been holding my breath and it was such a comical end to the tension that I could not help but let out a laugh. Having seen nothing at the door, Mrs. Evesham spun around to look at me and, noting my laugh, her own eyes twinkled and she let out her own chuckle.

"Was that Gemma?" she asked quietly, bending forwards.

I nodded, a fresh wave of giggles rising up in me.

"What impeccable timing! More tea?" she asked me before standing up and going to investigate how the girl fared after her run in with the door. Glancing at the time, I reluctantly declined.

As I turned to leave a short while later, my eye was taken by a framed drawing; a portrait of the woman before me obviously sketched some time ago. It was a fair resemblance and no doubt sketched by a skilled hand but whoever had created it had failed entirely to capture the fierce intelligence in her eyes and sensuousness in her mouth. In doing so, the image could have resembled any number of younger women and I fancied I saw something of myself in the same pose.

"Oh, don't pay any attention to that. My first husband drew it when he was going through his, what I call, *'fanciful'* period. He tried his hand at sculpture you know but I am afraid not much survived in our last move. Thankfully," she added with a smile.

"I should love to have a copy of that photograph of your father and mother," she asked, her tone modest. "I have thought of them both often these past years and I do so wish I had had a chance to thank them for saving me."

I raised my eyebrows but she flapped her hand at me quickly.

"Don't mind me. I am an old fool and grown quite sentimental."

She was not so old nor was she anything of a fool but I said nothing. I sensed already there were some things that I would prefer not to hear from her. I was keen not to spoil the feeling I was leaving with and agreed readily to have a copy made. In the meantime, I was keen to digest what she had told me and reassemble what I had just come to know about both of my parents.

Chapter Twenty Six - Elizabeth, 1911

As she watched the face of the woman standing on the step in front of her, Elizabeth was surprised to see something of Avery staring back. She knew, of course, that it was absurd to think such a thing but she found herself wondering if perhaps something of Avery had been transferred to the young woman.

"Goodbye Mrs. Evesham," Imogen said politely and proffered her hand genially.

She remained as formal as she had arrived and Elizabeth had to suppress a smile. It seemed as though the older woman had shocked the younger woman with her directness. Though they thought themselves a more liberated generation, the new century had much of a whiff of the old one and Elizabeth thought that she was perhaps too forthright for either. She watched the young girl leave and then returned to find Gemma clearing away the debris of their meeting.

"I am going to take a nap I think Gemma. I feel I have a headache coming on. Can you please see that it is quiet."

There was no pain in her head as she lay on her bed but rather an ache where memories had begun to flood in from years of being locked away. Whilst she had been wholly honest with Imogen on every matter of which she spoke, there was of course much more that had happened that summer and as Elizabeth lay upon her bed she slipped into a deep sleep and was immediately transported back to that fateful night with Bateman.

~o~

Elizabeth had watched with a peevish mixture of jealousy as Avery had allowed the back door to be closed against the darkening night sky and the face of his maid had slowly slipped from sight. Kate had been drinking in the grateful look in his eyes as he reminded her he would be back well after bedtime. For the second night in a row, she had agreed to wait up for them and permit re-entry to their rooms after the rest of the house had gone to sleep. The first had been a dry run for that night and, all having gone well, they had elected to meet Bateman as agreed. Though Elizabeth knew that Cribbs would do the same (what choice does a girl in service have?) she also knew that Cribbs would certainly not do so without objection nor with any such pleasure.

"Do stop dawdling, Silver!" Elizabeth hissed.

He turned and flashed her a scowl. He had been hungry for a night out of his skin for a while and he was not about to let her spoil it. The night was still and the light coloured gravel was lit by a welcome moon so they had no difficulty in finding the road. They walked in silence until they had past the Gatehouse by some distance and then Elizabeth began to tease.

"Bateman is very much looking forward to seeing you I think, Silver. Of the two of us, who do you think he wishes to see more?"

He made no reply but she could sense that he was growing irritated. There was another minute of silence marked only by the scuffle of their shoes across the road. After a moment, the sound of a horse and carriage wheels came from up ahead and the distant outline of a carriage with a lantern swinging against the shot grey evening sky.

"I wonder when he came to Amersham whether he had hoped only to find himself one lady. What shock do you think he got when he stumbled across two?"

She had gone too far and he took her hand and dragged her roughly from the path.

"Swear to me that Bateman knows nothing."

"A lady shouldn't swear to anything she doesn't know."

"Stop playing games Elizabeth. Does he know or not?"

"Silver. When you manhandle me like this I quite forget that you have nothing to manhandle me with!"

She could sense his anger growing but it was not in her nature to relent.

"You know, you could be a very attractive woman if only you tried Avery. Perhaps Bateman might still be interested in you after all?"

It was too much. Elizabeth knew it but she was surprised when he grabbed her so tightly. She threw an arm out to push him away but instead her elbow connected with his head

"What's the matter Silver, don't you want to be Mrs. Bateman?"

He slapped her. Her face rang with the sting of his fingers across it and Elizabeth felt a hot rush of anger as she lashed out to hit him back. He caught her arms and tried to prevent her from hitting him. She was furious with him but the closeness of his breath upon her roused that same something in her that she was desperate to deny. She grew still in his arms and when she felt the tension in his arms begin to subside she pushed herself against him and pressed her lips to his. He recoiled from her and she caught at his arms and stumbled into him. It was an awkward movement and she was at once embarrassed by the unrequited gesture.

"You would do well to remember that I am the key to your freedom whilst you are here at Juniper Hall." Elizabeth snapped. She had felt a little humiliated at the rejection and wanted to gain the upper hand.

He looked at her in the greyness of the evening and then shook his head, turning as if to leave the way they had just come.

"Going so soon, Miss Silver? You prefer a quiet night with that slow creature of a maid?'

He stopped in his tracks and Elizabeth's ears burned with a quiet rage as she waited for a response. He turned slowly and with a contented smile he threw back at her.

"Miss Greenwood. I would rather a lifetime with Miss Ward than a moment longer with you."

"Fine!" she shouted, enraged. "Then I shall enjoy spending an evening with a real man. I expect even Giles Bateman's touch will feel magical after your own."

Elizabeth was still shouting the last words as an open top trap pulled up alongside them.

"Miss Greenwood? Silver? Is that you?" Bateman peered through the gloom.

His voice was amiable enough but he looked at them both guardedly as Avery continued to walk away from where Elizabeth stood. She could not be sure how much of the conversation Bateman had heard and she took his hand quickly as he passed her into the seat beside him. The way his cool fingers lingered over her own made her shudder but she kept her chin held high and looked into the distance as Bateman hopped down to chide Silver. He strode after the retreating form of Silver and Elizabeth caught most of the exchange.

"Not coming with us Silver?"

"It doesn't look like it."

"Don't worry, Silver I shall look after her." He lowered his voice and Elizabeth heard a scuffle in the dirt as he drew Avery closer to him. "Rest assured I will look after her very well indeed. As you fall asleep this evening just remember who she is with and whose hands are upon her."

"And you remember just who she will be thinking about as you do."

There was another shuffle as Avery shrugged himself free and retreated back towards the house. A few moments later, Bateman had pulled himself back into his seat and the trap moved on. Elizabeth hardly knew what Bateman talked of all the way to Tremain's house but she was glad of the mindless chatter or else she may have brooded over what had happened with Avery. As she watched the grey shadows of the hedgerows roll past, she felt badly about having provoked him but she was hopelessly confused about how she should feel about him.

About an hour later, the carriage pulled up outside a brightly lit house from which there was the sound of great gaiety and she was pulled from her thoughts to the matter at hand. Bateman had drawn close to her in the dark of the evening and his leg was pressing her own; his hand upon her arm, the knuckles of which she could feel against her bodice as he fingered the lacework. Now that she had arrived, she was in two minds about the evening. Her initial plan had been to make Avery jealous and to spend the evening dancing, making merry and playing Bateman for a fool. No doubt this was still very much on the cards but without Avery's presence this would be a less than fruitful evening. The proximity of Bateman was beginning to make her uncomfortable. She wondered if he had heard more of their conversation and had taken her angry comments as consent for something more. Before the trap had even come to a halt, Elizabeth stood and began to descend to the ground.

"Miss Greenwood, I have never seen you so eager!"

Her anger at Avery finally got the better of her and Elizabeth decided that with or without him she would have some fun that evening. Even the dreary and unsettling Bateman would be better than another evening trying to disguise her contempt for her Aunt's library.

"Then you have never seen me so dulled with life before Bateman, now hurry up and escort me inside won't you?"

True to his word, the place was densely populated with faces she instantly recognised from the building on Cleveland Street several weeks before. She knew none of them of course but there was a band again around which dozens of couples were dancing energetically. In a through parlour, there were lounge chairs in which a few men were sat talking and over which a few women were draping themselves. Elizabeth was quietly taken aback. Though she was always annoyed when her father banished herself and Agnes from the company of the men after dinner, she was still surprised to see this reversal. It did not escape her attention that many of the women were behaving in a more than winsome way. She also noticed that some of them were showing off more of themselves than was ladylike but at that moment in time she was too heady with her own sense of rebelliousness to consider the implications.

A young girl of Elizabeth's own age was seated in the centre of the room and, instead of fawning over a man like the rest of the women, she had two men courting her attention. She was at the centre of their affection and between the two of them she looked blasé but content. One of the men had his hand upon her shoulder and was talking softly at the side of her, his eyes locked on the side of her head. By contrast, the man to her left was comfortably seated close to her, his hand upon her waist, he was blowing softly on her neck.

As soon as Elizabeth saw her, she felt desperately disappointed that Avery would not see her in a similar repose. She wanted him to see her with a gaggle of men around her. Within less than two hours she was exactly where she wanted to be with Bateman beside her and another young man trying to divert her attention. For the first half an hour, Elizabeth found their ministration both flattering and sensuous and she was intoxicated with the abandon with which everyone around her embraced the evening.

"Miss Greenwood, you are the brightest flame in this room by far." Bateman's voice was husky with desire and she felt herself shiver with annoyance at his arrogant and assured tone.

"Then that must make you and Mr. Castle here the biggest moths?"

381

The young man to her right chuckled but Bateman merely glowered at him and laid a hand across Elizabeth's shoulder, his finger encircling a curl of her hair. He was closer than he had ever been and she felt the warmth of his breath, soured with drink, on her neck. She shivered as she saw the same look in Bateman's eyes that she recognized from Silver. She suddenly felt aware of the atmopshere within the room and, glancing to one side, she noticed one of the young women being led from the room by an older man, his face clouded with lust.

"Miss Greenwood. You give the impression of a woman lacking in pleasure when all around there is much to amuse."

"You are quite mistaken Bateman. I am a woman who knows great pleasure but there is nothing here to amuse me."

With that, she stood up and walked to the door. Bateman did not follow but merely looked at her from the comfort of his seat. A few men looked over at them from their own enclaves and Elizabeth was able to appreciate just how much the mood had changed. The room was darker and the air was thick with hedonistic promise as the women in the room were being tempted to more brandy. Elizabeth had grown uncomfortable and wanted to go home. In her opinion, the point of the evening was lost without Silver to witness it.

"I wish to leave," she stated baldly.

Bateman watched her from under a heavy brow before rising to follow. Before he did so, he winked at Castle and mouthed something that Elizabeth did not hear. She left the room, Bateman at her heel. The air was cool when they mounted their seats and even with the roof of the hansom pulled over Elizabeth was cold when they pulled away into the moonlit night. It was only twenty minutes or so that they had travelled in silence before she felt his hand come underneath the rug over their legs and grip her thigh. Elizabeth was not surprised and merely pushed him away. He laughed but removed his hand. Elizabeth shuffled in her seat to the far side of the bench and rested her head against the window frame, her eyelids drooping and her head beginning to loll. What seemed only a short while later the cab slowed down and the driver leaned in to the window.

"We are a five minute walk from the gatehouses sir. Do you wish to walk the rest of the way so we aren't heard?"

"Of course. Elizabeth?" he hopped down from the cab and turned to take her hand as she slipped out into the cool night.

"I can manage from here," she said.

"Oh Elizabeth, please," he said in exasperation and he turned to the driver. "I will walk Miss Greenwood to the boundary and be back within twenty minutes. Turn the cab and, for God's sake try to keep the horse quiet will you."

Elizabeth began walking away from the two of them and Bateman had to hurry to catch up with her. They passed around a bend and, once shielded from view of the driver, he pulled her to him. Elizabeth had been expecting some sort of attempt but she was still surprised. She had hoped that the hand on her thigh would be all. She pushed him hard on the chest but the gesture made him more amorous and he pressed his arm around her, his face close to her ear. He was strong and, though she struggled, he held her firm.

"Mr. Bateman! Please!"

He said nothing but only gripped her more tightly, pushing his face into hers.

"Giles! Please,' she said firmly. Her tone wasn't panicked and she did not scream but the volume alarmed him and he pushed his hand hard into her face covering her mouth whilst he pulled her down to the ground. The shock of his strength and the recklessness of his actions took her breath away. She could not have screamed even if she wanted to. He fell on her heavily pushing the wind from her lungs so that she struggled to draw breath. She had jarred her hip awkwardly and a pain seared up her flank that brought tears to her eyes. Her heart began to race as fear began to rise up in her throat and she tried to roll away from him. She turned onto her front and began to scrabble on the ground, his hand was hard around her mouth and the full weight of him on top of her crushed the air from her chest. She was going nowhere but her arms and legs thrashed helplessly. With his other hand, he had begun to pull up her dress and she let out a terrified cry. *He could not do this. He would not do this.* She thought and she still did not believe that he would do anything to her. *How could he? Why would he?* She thought to herself, over and over.

But he did.

~o~

Even thirty years later, as she lay recollecting that time, Elizabeth could feel the same shame and disgust that overpowered her in the days that followed that terrible night. When he had finished with her, Bateman had simply pulled her to her feet and, brushing down her skirts, had tried to kiss her goodbye. Afraid that he may try something else, she flinched as his wet lips touched her own and as soon as he had loosed his grip, she ran from him as fast as she could. Her hip was sore and as she got within sight of the house, confident that he had not pursued her, she allowed the pain to get the better of her and she limped to the back door. It was easy enough to gain entrance to the house without Kate being too suspicious. Elizabeth would find out later that her appearance had shocked the young maid, but at the time, Kate didn't say a word as Elizabeth swept past her through the kitchen. The following day, she faked being ill to avoid seeing anyone. She had woken early and examined herself in the mirror. The ordeal had left her eyes puffy and the lack of sleep made her skin pale. Her hip was bruised badly and there were marks all around her stomach and thighs which made her sick to look upon. It was not hard to convince Cribbs that she was unwell and, after a short visit from Aunt Georgina, she was left alone for a day to reflect on what had happened. It did not go unnoticed by Elizabeth that Silver made no attempt to seek her out. In the gloom of her room, she tried to sleep but could not. Unwillingly, her mind was bidden back to the previous night and she began to wonder if what had happened had actually occurred. A quick touch to her tender thighs and the sore ache in her stomach assured her that her recollections were entirely accurate. Her head was spilling with thoughts but she had no-one to talk to. Though she knew that what had happened was wrong, she began to wonder if what had happened to her was not entirely her own fault. Had she implied her consent somehow? Had it started many months ago before that first visit to Cleveland Street? No matter which way that she looked at it, the same thing had happened to her that night and she could not shake the heavy feeling in her gut, nor could she simply close her eyes and forget.

She was able to keep to her room for a few days more before Georgina grew impatient. Elizabeth sensed that her aunt found occupying Avery by herself an arduous task. She knew that her aunt found Avery's company unnerving and this alone almost kept Elizabeth from rising until the fourth day.

"At last Elizabeth!" Georgina called from the breakfast table. There was a look of genuine affection and enormous relief. The atmosphere into which Elizabeth had walked that morning was palpably flat. Avery had his back to her and she could not discern any such delight at her return to health.

"Have a seat, my dear. You do look very drawn; though on you it has the advantage of improving your cheek bones."

Elizabeth gave a hollow laugh and sat in her usual seat opposite Avery and though she itched to look at him, she resisted the temptation. As she helped herself to a few morsels of food, she could see from the corner of her eye that he was looking equally as furtive. He had balled his napkin up in his fist which was now on the table. He was glancing at the door and she knew that he was wondering when it would be polite to make his escape. Georgina, however, was so delighted to have someone else to talk to, that the awkwardness between them went completely unnoticed.

"Well I must say Elizabeth, that Miss Silver and I are very pleased to see you back to health. I expect you will want to keep to the house today until you have your strength back. I imagine a spell on the terrace may do you some good. Perhaps you could arrange for some flowers to be cut from the garden so that we may arrange them, Miss Silver. Miss Silver?"

Avery had stood up and was taking his leave.

"I will ask Helen. Mrs. Fearncott. Miss Greenwood. If you'll excuse me."

And with that he left. Elizabeth felt her stomach fall. She had not expected much from Avery right in front of Georgina but his attitude towards her was a double blow. That he had not forgiven her for that night was one thing but his rebuttal felt like a hard kick to the stomach when she needed someone the most. Elizabeth felt teary as her aunt leaned forward to whisper loudly.

"I don't mind telling you Elizabeth that Miss Silver is quite the most sullen and awkward woman I have ever met. I doubt whether she will ever find, let alone keep, a husband. Why she makes even you look quite appealing."

There was no hint of apology as she said this but, far from make her sad, Georgina's barbed comments lacked the power to hurt her and Elizabeth merely smiled at her in response.

"I am sure that Miss Silver's life will be the richer for it."

Unable to stomach the food or the company any longer, Elizabeth rose and left the table. Though unappealing as the flower arranging had sounded, the prospect of a morning on the terrace in the warm late summer air

387

was quite tempting. Elizabeth sat alone for an hour or so enjoying the feel of the early morning sun upon her face. She had her face turned away from the house as the sound of someone's approach came across the gravel. She was glad of the company as being alone only made her think of her recent troubles and she had resolved never to think of Bateman again. She was surprised that she had managed to go so long without Avery or Georgina seeking her out. The footsteps were slower and less deliberate than her aunt and she assumed, or hoped, that it would be Avery.

"It's not too late for an apology, you know," she called out without turning.

"Miss Greenwood?" came a thin voice.

Elizabeth spun round to face the figure of Kate looking at her with a shocked expression on her face. Elizabeth turned away from her with total indifference.

"Oh Miss Ward, what is it?" she was irritated that it was not Avery and more so, that she had been made to look foolish in front of his precious maid. There was a pause and then there came a sound like the girl had burst into tears. Elizabeth spun around to see find Kate weeping; her eyes already red rimmed and her face glistening with tears. Elizabeth was stunned, and rather than feel curious as to the cause of her tears, she found that she was disgusted.

"Miss Ward, what on earth are you doing? Will you take a hold of yourself?"

Her words were delivered sharply and without any pity and the girl managed to stifle her sobs as she delivered her message.

"It's Mr. Silver. He's dead, Miss."

Elizabeth's head swam and she glowered at her again.

"Avery?" she asked.

This made Kate laugh in a sort of relief.

"No, Miss. Toby Silver. Avery's father. The messenger has just arrived from London. Your aunt and Avery are going back to London right away."

Elizabeth was struck by the tears this serving maid was weeping for her employer and, though shocked by the sudden and unexpectedness of the news, it did not make Elizabeth sad. On the contrary, she was rather disappointed. She supposed that this would mean that she too would be returning to London and, where a couple of days ago she would have jumped at the chance to return to the city, she felt she could not return home just yet. She was disappointed too that Avery would be going. The young maid waited in front of Elizabeth as if she should say something and eventually she found her voice.

"What dreadful news."

Her voice sounded flat and without any emotion. She sat back heavily in her chair as she imagined returning to London and bumping into Bateman in her father's house; not seeing Avery ever again; being married to a man she knew she did not like let alone love. It was as if the news of Toby Silver's had slit across her stomach and the heavy feelings of dread she had been carrying now spilled out across the terrace. Before she knew it, she too was weeping heavily. Tears entirely of self-pity but Kate, taking them to be for Toby, hurried to Elizabeth's side and, kneeling down, began to stroke her hair and hush her. For Elizabeth, it was the worst thing the young girl could

389

have done. Since her own mother had died, no woman had ever taken Elizabeth to her breast like that and dealt her such kindness. By the time a few minutes had passed in that position, Elizabeth was drained of all the energy her meager breakfast had provided her and she hung limply over the side of her chair and in the arms of a maid. For a few moments, she took in great gulps of air as she struggled to bring her emotions back under control and when she finally fell silent, Kate asked her.

"What happened on Tuesday night?"

Had she asked a few moments later Elizabeth would have angrily rebuked the girl for daring to ask her but as it was, she had caught her entirely off guard and she simply blurted it out.

"Though you will probably think it entirely my fault, I was taken advantage of."

"Avery?" Kate returned immediately, a confused look upon her face.

"Bateman." Elizabeth countered immediately. The name upon her lips caused her stomach to knot and she looked away from the intense gaze of the young girl before her.

"You mean he...."

"Yes. Bateman. Yes. He raped me," she said, the words making her feel sick again.

Her voice cracked and though she had tried to brazen the statement out with nonchalance, she could not and instead, the words hung in the air and she found she could no longer meet the young girl's eyes. Kate knelt in silence, waiting for Elizabeth to look up again and when at last she did Kate brought her face in close.

"Have you told anyone?" she asked. Her jaw was tightly clenched and she looked a lot older than her years and Elizabeth was glad of it. It made talking to her easier. Elizabeth shook her head.

"Of course not," she retorted. "Whom could I tell?"

"If not your aunt, then Avery?" Kate tried to coax.

"Avery isn't even looking at me, Miss Ward, let alone speaking with me." Admitting it aloud made her feel twice as alone and she began to cry again.

Kate stood up and pulled Elizabeth with her.

"Come on, Miss Greenwood. It will do you no good at all for your aunt to see you like this."

But it was too late, Georgina had emerged from the doors just as Elizabeth had got to her feet and she too looked shaken, though Elizabeth noted her aunt's eyes were completely dry.

"Elizabeth! What on earth is wrong with you?" She eyed her niece and the young maid who was holding her up, suspiciously. "Why on earth are *you* crying? You never met Toby."

Kate was quick to reply.

"Please Mrs. Fearncott but Miss Greenwood and Miss Silver have grown so close, I think Miss Greenwood feels the loss more strongly for my mistress."

Georgina looked incredulously at her but the lie evidently was believable enough.

"Then, I suggest you go and help Miss Silver with her packing. Helen has almost finished mine and Peter has the carriage ready. The next train leaves in an hour so we must leave soon. Elizabeth, you will stay here at Juniper Hall until you are sent for. I think in the circumstances that your father will understand."

Elizabeth was dizzy from the lack of food and, along with the release of her emotions, her energy had dwindled so that she could barely walk up the stairs. Kate, escorted her to her room and sat down beside her holding her hand. Elizabeth was unaccustomed by the kindness and she felt quite overcome. She felt raw and, afraid at being left alone, she asked quietly.

"Will you stay with me?"

Kate paused to think for only a moment and then simply said, "Yes."

When Avery left for the station less than twenty minutes later, he seemed only to half hear what Kate was telling him when she said that she was to stay. He was distracted of course and he simply nodded as he was shepherded to the carriage. And then, he and Georgina were both gone.

~o~

It was upon Avery's return to Amersham several weeks later, that Elizabeth noticed the first real change in him. The absence had made his features less familiar and as she watched him step down from the cab, she could see, at once, that his face was leaner and his jaw more angular. His eyes were dark, suggesting he had not been sleeping well. The change was an improvement and only enhanced his masculine face. Kate has gone to town with one of the scullery maids to collect some supplies. Although she was proving to be a blessing to Elizabeth, her positive spirit and good natured way had been beginning to get on Elizabeth's nerves and she was only too pleased to encourage her to be gone. She was therefore able to meet Avery alone. As she watched him from the window of the bright day room to the front of the house, she hurriedly arranged herself for his arrival, fussing over her dress.

"Avery? What a surprise. You should have sent word ahead so I could have arranged for dinner. Come inside and sit down, you look dreadful."

He shook his head and looked past her towards the window.

"Where is Kate? Is she here?"

She said nothing but watched as he stood uncomfortably and paced a little at the doorway before deciding he would stay.

"I have come to collect Kate and the rest of my belongings and to say farewell." He glanced in her general direction and indicated towards her with a wave of the hand. "Is she here?"

He didn't look directly at Elizabeth and his concern for Kate over herself made Elizabeth cross. *So he was going?* She thought. She was under no illusion that things could not simply pick up as they had left off but his admission that this were to be the end threw her current predicament into sharp relief. In the weeks that he had been gone, she had felt changes in herself she could not explain. Her breasts were swollen and tender and she felt thick headed in the morning where she normally leapt at an early start to a day. Most mornings, she had felt nauseous and she had been trying to ignore the high likelihood that she was pregnant. In less than a year, she would be wed to a man twice her age that she barely knew and had been violated by one that she had known. The only other man she held affection for was now abandoning her too. She felt an anger rise up within her, they had not spoken properly since the night when she had been raped and part of her blamed him for what happened. She had been beginning to think that if Silver had been with her, then Bateman could not have done those things to her. Silver waited for a response but where Kate's nature was kind, Elizabeth's was not and she took no small pleasure in replying.

"No. She isn't and I am glad of it. Frankly, she is a pain."

He looked at her directly and for the first time since he arrived, he took a long look at her and as he did so, his eyes narrowed questioningly.

"What is it?" she asked.

"You look different," he said simply.

Elizabeth touched her stomach instinctively. *Surely she could not be showing yet?* She thought. Kate had been tying her dresses more tightly every day.

"Really? How?" she ventured.

He did not hesitate.

"You have lost a certain charm Miss Greenwood."

She agreed that it was probably as much as she deserved but the loss of his admiration hurt her pride and tears pricked at her eyes. With that he turned his back on her and meant to leave.

"And your clothes fit more snugly," he added.

This last comment, though childish, was of course designed to hurt and brought ready tears to her eyes.

394

Without him, Kate or, God forbid, even Aunt Georgina, Elizabeth was utterly alone. A dozen thoughts clamoured into her mind. *Could she return to London and have Agnes assist her in concealing this pregnancy? Would her father be understanding? Would Cribbs be a friend to her like Kate had been?* The wretchedness of her circumstances hollowed her of all hope and she fell into a great mess of tears. The noise arrested him and he turned to look at her again, more closely.

"Just go!" she shouted through the tears. "Don't look at me!"

He hesitated, considering whether to follow her directive, before seating himself beside her, an awkward hand upon her shoulder.

"Elizabeth?"

She tried to shrug his hand away but the gesture was halfhearted and she was relieved when he gently pulled her to him where she could collapse into silent tears.

"'Elizabeth?"

As she lay her head against his chest, she heard the door open behind him and from her vantage beneath his arms she saw the now familiar face of Kate appear at the doorway. Kate looked surprised, confused and then embarrassed as she took in both Silver's arrival but also their clinch. Albeit an innocent embrace, this time, Kate no doubt mistook it for something else entirely and, contrary to her usual devilry, it gave Elizabeth no pleasure in seeing the young maid look so grieved. Kate turned and left the room before she could pull herself up. Avery did not notice the intrusion and Elizabeth chose not to mention it.

"Elizabeth? What on earth is the matter? Has something happened?"

It would have been so easy to have told him everything right then. After all, she was utterly convinced that Kate would fill him in despite her assurances of secrecy. Though Kate did not yet know Elizabeth was pregnant, she was no fool and Elizabeth didn't know exactly how long she could keep it a secret from her. In the circumstances, Elizabeth reached for the only lifeline she had available to her, escape.

"Oh Avery! Forgive me, I have missed you so very much and now you have come back only to leave me again." She watched from the corner of her eyes as this registered with him. He said nothing but merely waited. "In less than a year, I am to be made little more than a slave. I know, I know," she hastened to add as Avery made to interrupt her. "This is partly my own choosing. I know but I had thought that we could spend the rest of the year here in Amersham. I am quite sure Georgina would be agreeable."

He began to shake his head and she continued to press him, almost desperately. Fear rose up within her as she considered the alternative of returning home.

"We could have a grand Christmas here. Perhaps have a party. A dance then?" she added quickly as he began to back away from her, still shaking his head.

"Elizabeth. It's out of the question."

His tone reminded her of her father's and, despite her need of his alliance, she found herself petulantly arguing with him.

"Why not? What on earth is so important that could stop you from enjoying yourself here for a few months? Without Georgina to watch over us, we are at liberty to take our pleasures where we will Silver. Does that not sound diverting enough for you?"

He looked at her for a moment and, though she was afraid he might refuse at any moment, she was pleased to see some spark of interest still flashing across his face.

"Elizabeth," he shook his head slowly looking from her to the floor, "I cannot stay here. I cannot stay at Amersham or in England for that matter. Just look at me." Elizabeth opened her mouth to argue but he raised his voice as he repeated. "Look at me."

He had stepped back and was presenting himself to her, his arms spread low and wide as if he were about to fall backwards upon soft earth. "Look at me."

Elizabeth could do nothing else and so she took him in as he had asked. He was wearing a black dress, in keeping with his father's death. His shoulders were rounded forward to disguise the slightness of his chest. His large feet were awkwardly crammed into scruffy lace up boots barely hidden under the hem of his skirt line. And atop all of this was Avery's perfectly masculine face. It was as though, she thought, a child had taken the body of a doll and placed the head of a tin soldier upon it. Though she had come to grow accustomed to him in this form, this fresh appraisal caused her to truly consider him once again. *He was a woman. Wasn't he?* She thought. *A woman as ill-suited to her own body as she was growing to find her own. He wanted something more than he was born to be but did that not make him the same as many women malcontent with what chance and circumstance had bestowed upon them?*

"I cannot live this way. I cannot explain to you how it feels to wake up each morning expecting a great injustice to be set right and yet find that, when I look in the mirror, I am still trapped inside this body. There is nothing I can do that will change that but the best that I can do is to stop pretending I have a future as a woman. I would rather die than live another day like this."

"Don't be so melodramatic, Silver!' Her tongue was sharp. As she spoke, she registered a reciprocal gnaw in her stomach about a destiny that she too would prefer to avoid. "You talk as if you have choices! What choice do you have? You are what you are and you must accept it! As I must accept my own lot in life."

"We all have choices Elizabeth. You have a choice whether you marry or not and you have a choice about how to enjoy it. I have no doubt that you will continue to enjoy your life as Mrs. Evesham almost as much as you have enjoyed being Miss Greenwood. I have a choice about whether to continue the charade that is my life or whether to reinvent myself. I am now a man of means and it is within my means to travel."

He paused and levelled a look at her. He knew how much she wanted to travel and Elizabeth, sensing his news, wondered how he would break it to her.

"I need to escape my past and to find my future."

She laughed. It was so ridiculous a statement but she felt sure that he would achieve it and her laughter was more to hide her disappointment and rising panic that she was to be left behind. He glared at her.

"I am leaving England."

Elizabeth was still smirking. "For how long?"

"Forever."

He had not blinked and she realized that he was serious.

"Forever?" Her tone was slightly shrill, as she realized that she would have no choice but to return to London and face her father. *What would happen to her?* She thought. *Could she still be married? Would her future be at stake because of the thing growing insider her?* Her eyes stung with ready tears but she refused to let them fall as she snapped at Avery.

"If England is so terrible for you then I shan't keep you a moment longer." In one swift movement, she had stood and swept from the room. A moment later she was in her own bedroom, her back to the door and her heart racing fast as she realized that she would have to return home.

~o~

When she woke the following morning, there was a moment before she remembered what had happened the previous night. When she did so, she was swept again by a dizzying feeling as she contemplated her fate. She was young and had really no idea what would happen to her if she had to face her family with a pregnancy. There was no doubting there would be horror and shock and a heavy punishment but Elizabeth could imagine more than dishonor and had begun to paint herself a bleak future as a spinster. *And worst of all*, she thought, *she would have a child.* By the time she had risen, dressed and descended for breakfast she was resigned to her fate and was

399

determined to put on a brave face before Avery left. Avery was already seated at the head of the dining table, a newspaper folded beside him. Though he was wearing a black dress, he looked for all the world as paternal a figure as her own father. As usual the quirk of his ensemble made her confused and she had to shake her head to clear it.

"Good morning," he offered and Elizabeth smiled thinly back. "Did you sleep well?"

Braced as she was for an exchange of the usual morning platitudes, Elizabeth found she could not stomach them.

"When shall you leave?" she asked bluntly.

He put down his coffee cup and looked up at her, the beginning of a smile upon his lips.

"Kate thinks we can have everything packed by late morning."

"Well, I don't think I will be able to have everything packed by then, so you shall have to go back to London without me. I will send word to my father that I shall return in a few days and perhaps you would be so kind as to organize my passage to Marylebone."

The smile on Avery's face grew and the wider it spread, the hotter she felt her cheeks burn. The anger and disappointment from the previous evening was beginning to well up inside her again.

"It's all very well for you, Silver, but I am returning to London with nothing. Less than that. You have everything and I am owed something." She balled up the napkin she had been carefully unfolding and threw it back down on the table, blinking away angry tears. The room was silent save for her own heavy breaths and she waited for him to say something.

"Why don't you just ask?" he said eventually.

Though surprised, Elizabeth knew exactly what he was suggesting and quite aside from the fear of a refusal, it was not in her nature to ask for anything. However, she could not ignore the spark of hope he had lit inside her.

"I don't know what you mean," she uttered, petulantly.

"Ask me."

"Ask you for what, Avery?"

He stared hard at her, his smile had faded and he seemed to be searching her face for something. After more than a minute, he pushed his chair back from the table and put his napkin beside his plate.

"Temper gets you into trouble, but pride will keep you there." And with that he stood and turned to leave.

His superior tone infuriated her but more so because he was right.

"Oh for Heaven's sake, fine then. Will you take me with you?" she shouted gracelessly at his retreating back.

He turned with a broad smile and said simply, "Of course."

Chapter Twenty Seven - Elizabeth, 1869

Though Avery had granted Elizabeth her heart's desire in letting her travel with him, it was a good few days before she forgave him. Unaccustomed as she was to having to ask for things she felt a little put out by being teased so. Nor did it improve her mood by being back at the family home, albeit a temporary measure.

"Elizabeth." Agnes's tone was formally neutral. Elizabeth could almost feel the temperature around her sister grow chill at the very sight of her. Time had done nothing to strengthen their relationship but rather put them at greater distance.

"Bessie!" Her father's welcome, on the other hand, was effusive enough and she felt momentarily elated at the hearty response her presence had evoked. As ever, it was to be short lived and within the hour, he was closed within his study and, Agnes had retired to her room. Elizabeth was left to haunt the rooms of the family home alone.

By the following afternoon, having endured only two meals with her sister, Elizabeth was desperate for some escape and it was therefore with more than great pleasure that she received a visit from Avery. As he was permitted to the drawing room, Elizabeth's face registered great surprise. Unusually, he was dressed in the most smart and fashionable of dresses. In keeping with his state of mourning for his father, the whole ensemble was black but Elizabeth was surprised to find that she admired the style very much. He wore a jet black bustle dress with lace applique accents. Obviously new and exquisitely finished, it must have been very expensive. She had never seen him wear any such outfit before and she was confused as to why he had gone to so much effort to visit her. For a moment, she wondered if he hoped to impress her perhaps with his newfound wealth and then she remembered that it was not her he hoped to impress.

"Is your father home?" he asked as soon as Cribbs had left the room.

"Of course. He is in his study."

"Have you spoken with him yet?"

"Of course not. Aunt Georgina had been sending him good reports and he seems more than best pleased that this summer has been both a diversion for me and that you have been a good influence."

This last comment caused Avery to smirk. He wondered if Frederick Greenwood could have any idea just how much of an influence the two had had on each other during their time at Juniper Hall.

"That is good news Elizabeth. This may be easier than we imagined. I would suggest we make the most of my being in good favour and ask that we be introduced."

Elizabeth wasted no time and whirled out of the room herself to interrupt her father's afternoon. Frederick was reluctant to break from his work but wished to set eyes upon the peculiar young woman that his sister had thought so in need of help. It would also be rude to deny an audience with the young woman after she had so recently lost her own father. The three spent an easy fifteen minutes in polite conversation and Elizabeth's father seemed very pleased with how he found Avery. After a further fifteen minutes however, he seemed keen to return to his work and the decision to have interrupted him proved to be most advantageous to Elizabeth and Avery.

"Mr. Greenwood, I can't thank your family enough for their support. Mrs. Fearncott has been like a mother to me and I owe her an enormous debt of gratitude for her taking an interest in my finishing."

Frederick seemed pleased that the conversation was drawing to a close and stood to leave but Avery continued.

"And Elizabeth has been my bedrock during this difficult time. We have become just the best of friends."

Glancing at his pocket watch, Frederick beamed in pleasure.

"Miss Silver, I am thrilled that Elizabeth has found such a friend as you also. My sister informs me that Elizabeth has been much more content these last few months. Well, perhaps I can look forward to seeing more of you soon? Well, if you will excuse me."

"I simply don't know how I shall manage without her?" Avery interjected.

"Without her?" Frederick had barely stepped one stride from his seat before he glanced back at Avery. "What do you mean, Miss Silver, without her?"

"I'm sorry Mr. Greenwood. I am leaving in a week or so and I shall miss having a friend like Elizabeth. As you know my mother died when I was young and I have no sister. Elizabeth has come to mean a lot to me over the summer and I shall miss her dreadfully."

Elizabeth watched her father's face as Avery mentioned his mother dying and she recognised the pained expression that her father wore when people spoke about her own mother and she silently praised Avery for getting this in quickly.

"Leaving?" Frederick asked.

"Forgive me. It's all happened rather quickly. It's just that it was my father's greatest wish that I undertake some travel before I get married..."

Elizabeth smirked and had to hide her face behind her sleeve to avoid laughing out loud.

"....and he had made plans for me as a surprise." He paused for a moment as if gathering the strength to finish his sentence. "I feel as though this is a last gift from him. I'm sure you understand?"

With this Avery looked at Frederick with a pained smile and Elizabeth could barely keep herself from crying with laughter.

"Of course. Of course. Well that sounds a splendid plan."   Frederick stated. He seemed keen to leave the room again and Avery looked meaningfully towards Elizabeth as the older man began to head for the door. "Well, I am sure that Elizabeth will miss your company equally but it will give you two young ladies that much more to chatter about upon your return."

"Avery is to follow the Grand Tour, Father," Elizabeth offered. "Avery, did you know that my father has travelled extensively in Europe?"

"I did not," Avery answered simply. "I would love to hear his opinion on Florence. My father thought the place entirely devoid of culture and suggested I leave it from my itinerary."

The effect on Frederick Greenwood was instantaneous. If there was one thing that Elizabeth knew her father enjoyed more than his work was talking about his time around Europe. She had told Silver as much and that Florence was the highlight of his own tour experience many years ago. Her father had returned to his seat in a state of some animation and begun a chastisement of the late Toby Silver's taste in tourist destinations. Avery sat, looking rapt, and Elizabeth thought he looked genuinely interested. She rolled her eyes and began the arduous but necessary task of listening to her fathers, seemingly endless, recollections of the Europe he had found in the 1830's. After more than an hour, he started at the sound of the doorbell and he stood, abruptly drawing out his pocket watch and exclaiming loudly.

"Heavens! I am very sorry Miss Silver to cut short our fascinating conversation but I am expected elsewhere."

"I should be the one apologizing Mr. Greenwood I have been monopolising your time. I should so love to finish hearing about your thoughts about the Swiss."

Again, it was a magical word and Fredericks eyes twinkled like Elizabeth had rarely seen them.

"Elizabeth, perhaps Miss Silver would like to join us for dinner this evening and we can continue this then."

And with that, Frederick left the room far more merry than he had arrived and in better cheer than Elizabeth had seen him in many years. Avery, though pleased, seemed annoyed that he would have to return again that evening. He tugged at the bodice of his dress and pulled a face at Elizabeth before disappearing after Frederick.

"I will see you at seven," Elizabeth called, a wide grin spreading over her face.

~o~

Over dinner that evening, Elizabeth barely had to interject a single word. The charm, with which Avery had enchanted her, worked just as well on her father and Agnes. As she watched the two of them dance around his conversation and trip over themselves to answer his questions, she again felt the soaring headiness of adoration. It was a curious emotion and she fought to preserve the feeling before it shifted to the bleak disappointment that he was a woman and this moment would not be replicated by her own choice in husband. By the main course, Avery had managed to elicit from her father what was tantamount to agreement that she could join Avery on his trip.

"Of course, in my day, it was not the thing for young women to be found on the Tour unless accompanied by their husbands. Your father sounds the very epitome of a modern man, Miss Silver. Of course, I should like to meet this chaperone you have in mind, whom did you say he was? A tutor?"

"Oh yes, I quite agree, Europe would be a dangerous place without a man. Yes, Heston. He is the son of one of my father's closest friends. He was a tutor in Bristol and has agreed to be my guide and to keep us from harms way. Of course you must meet him Mr. Greenwood."

"Oh please, call me Frederick!"

"Frederick it is. I shall have Mr. Heston come to see you. How does tomorrow suit?"

The old man frowned slightly.

"And that's the only thing, Miss Silver. Must you race off so soon? I have barely had Elizabeth home for a few days and she is to race off to the continent. I feel a little uncomfortable that this is all happening a little too quickly."

Here at last was where Elizabeth could be of use. She noticed the faltering of her father's resolve and she seized the moment.

"Oh Father. I will miss you dreadfully of course but I shall have so much time in London over the next few years when you will wish me away in Paris or Turin in an instant."

Frederick Greenwood acknowledged the meaning of Elizabeth's comments and considered his daughter for a moment.

"And if Miss Silver were to travel any later than October we would miss the best of the weather for the crossing," she added.

As if this, rather than his daughters blackmail, were the final piece of encouragement, Frederick Greenwood nodded his approval and scowled in mock defeat as his daughter rushed to thank him.

~o~

The following few days were a blur of activity as Cribbs and Agnes took charge of packing for her trip. Though jealous, Agnes was pleased to have something to divert her attention and she seemed keen for Elizabeth to accompany Silver having enjoyed her father's attention to herself. However, being trapped with her sister brought out the worst in Elizabeth's mood and she found that after a single day, she could suffer no more and took a cab to Silver's home. She found he and Kate performing much the same scenes that she had escaped from in her own house. Many of the regular staff had been dismissed and it was the young man, Heston, who was organizing the storage of valuables.

"What on earth is all this for?" she asked, fingering the chests and sheets covering the furniture.

"You forget Elizabeth that I am not planning to return to England for some time. I have employed a firm who shall rent the property for me whilst I am abroad. I am having the more valuable effects either stored or sold. Mine and my father's tastes are very different indeed and I would rather enjoy the money they release than the few poor memories they evoke."

Elizabeth yawned and draped herself atop a packing case that was full of his clothes. She pulled the first thing she could lay her hands, a heavy grey skirt. She shook it out and lay it beside her. Kate, busy folding shirts into one case and blouses in another, eyed her cautiously. For a few moments, Elizabeth simply stared whilst Kate and Avery continued at their tasks. Absent mindedly, she pulled out another item, an ivory blouse with mother of pearl buttons and a lace neck; she laid it above the skirt carefully pressing the fabric with her hand. The clothes lay like a shadow beside her.

"You know Silver, you should take us both to dinner or something. To celebrate," she added.

Avery looked up and, seeing the clothes, frowned and looked to Kate.

"I don't think so. There is much to do still."

"Oh come on Avery, if you are not to return to London then we should make the most of the time we have left."

Avery frowned again and looked between the two women.

"I just don't think we shall have the time."

Kate, who had been watching the exchange, spoke.

"If Miss Greenwood were to stop undoing the work we have already completed and lend a hand then we could be done in half the time."

Though unused to being spoken to like that by domestic staff, Elizabeth had grown used to Kate's frankness. She opened her mouth to speak but Avery got in first, smiling broadly at Kate.

"I've an idea. We should all four go for a meal this very evening?"

"Four?" said Elizabeth. "You don't mean...?"

"Heston and yourself, Kate and I...the four of us," said Avery. 'If we are to make this work Elizabeth, you must be willing to play your part. Why not start this evening?"

"But surely Avery, you are not thinking of starting here in London? What if we are recognized?"

"Don't tell me you have cold feet Miss Greenwood. If you would prefer, you can always stay safely at home with Agnes?"

Elizabeth scowled at him and slid from the packing case, pulling the clothes from beside her as she did so. She folded them up untidily and stuffed them back in the case in which she had found them.

"I confess that I am as hungry as a wolf," Avery declared. "I could clear the table of fowl, venison...."

As Avery reeled off a list of the food he could eat, Elizabeth felt herself grow nauseous and she had to dash from the room clutching a hand to her mouth. A

410

few moments later, Kate found her in a spare bedroom, sat upon a bed.

"Are you okay, Elizabeth?" Kate asked.

"Never better," she replied and standing up straight, she felt herself grow bilious once more and she rushed to the washstand and vomited.

As the days had turned to weeks, it had become harder to ignore the changes that had been happening to her body. At first she had thought the sickness was a result of the violation and that she simply felt sick thinking about it. But then her breasts had begun to hurt and she had been finding the smell of certain things repulsive. When she missed her course, Elizabeth knew there was something up and now so did Kate. As she wiped her mouth on a towel, Kate's voice broke the silence.

"You're pregnant," she stated, confirming Elizabeth's fears. "It's Bateman's?" she asked and then apologised immediately. "I'm sorry," she said. "Please, forgive me."

"You think very little of me, Kate," Elizabeth stated matter of factly.

"I've spoken out of turn. I'm sorry," she said again. "I don't think little of you. Honestly." She repeated and she coloured.

"Then what is it?" Elizabeth asked.

"For a moment, I thought it might be Avery's," she said with a shy grin.

Elizabeth laughed out loud and found herself clasping her sides with delight. Absurd and impossible as it was, it was not such a ridiculous notion. She half hoped it were true.

411

"Kate. Please, you must promise me that you won't say anything to Avery. I cannot let this stop me from escaping London, from escaping Bateman. Do you understand?"

She could tell that this was asking for too much and Kate looked very uncomfortable but she nodded her assent.

"What will you do?" she asked.

But Elizabeth had not thought that far ahead. Acknowledging that she had to do something meant acknowledging that the sickness in her stomach was '*something*' in itself. All that she knew was that she had to leave London. She smiled at Kate.

"I will get dressed and have an entertaining evening out. Come Kate, we must find you something to wear."

And with that, she began to rummage through the clothes that Avery had laid out to be sent to charity.

~o~

Several hours later, the four of them cut an unremarkable group as they descended from a cab and made their way through a busy Covent Garden to the Irving Music and Supper Rooms. It was a place that Elizabeth knew her father did not frequent but it was somewhere Avery had visited and found to be anonymous and safe. It was the perfect opportunity for Heston and Kate, unaccustomed as they were to being treated as equals, to practice their roles.

"Not so near the stage. Do you have a table nearer the sides?" Avery asked as the maître d' tried to place them at the front of the room towards the edge of the stage. Elizabeth noticed that Kate was quite relaxed although she seemed unable to allow the waiter to wait upon her. At the door, a man had held the door for her and she tried to take it from him and even now as a chair was drawn back for her, she seemed quite flustered as she sat upon it. On the other hand, Heston, who was a complete stranger to her, seemed quite uptight. It was almost comical how ill at ease he seemed around this whole scenario. She had thought to herself what a treat this must be for someone of their status, to experience a taste of a life that was not normally within their aspirations. On the contrary, you could have mistaken Heston's discomfort as superiority. He wore an expression of what seemed to be disdain but it was only because Elizabeth had seen his look of horror when Avery had suggested the trip that afternoon, that she could see his look was one of fear.

"That's better. Thank you," Avery smiled around the table as they all took their seats. Kate seemed to be enjoying herself, looking about her with the eyes of a child at Christmas. Avery, in turn, couldn't take his eyes from her, she was overwhelmed by the world into which she had found herself and it was obvious to anyone watching that she enchanted him. It was unlike Elizabeth but instead of directing her annoyance at either of them, she dropped a napkin carefully beside her chair and turned to Heston instead.

"Heston. Be a dear and pick up my napkin won't you?"

Of course, he leapt to it and it was the only time that evening that she saw him at ease. To do someone's bidding was as much in his blood as it was in a hounds to follow the hare. As Heston scurried to her far side, dropped to his knee and collected her napkin, Avery caught her eye and narrowed his gaze. Elizabeth threw a bored glance back at him and, taking the napkin from Heston, she looked around him at the room. The room was filling nicely and there was a good assortment of old and young, rich and the not so rich. She was vaguely aware of Heston excusing himself from the table but, as he did so, her gaze was distracted and her eyes fell upon a few familiar faces. Despite Avery's wish that they remain inconspicuous, it was not in Elizabeth's nature to be such a wallflower and she was hoping to find some entertainment. She preferred Avery's company when she was the focus of his attention and the evening promised little of that. At such a distance, she could not at first see exactly who it was that she recognized but by the time that she had it was too late. Bateman had seen her too. She felt herself grow cold before a searing heat crept across her chest and neck. Her reaction made him smile and he kept his gaze upon her as he leaned towards his dining companions and excused himself. She watched with horror as he rose from his seat and made his way to their table. Avery and Kate had not seen the exchange and when Bateman drew up at their table, they both looked surprised.

"Miss Greenwood. What a pleasure to see you back in the city. I had been afraid that you would be quite lost to us. Some say the country has such a charm but I for one have never seen it."

He had stopped between Elizabeth and Heston's empty chair and he now stooped to collect Elizabeth's hand upon which to place a mannered kiss. She remained stiff and it was an awkward gesture. The tension was not wasted upon Kate who was immediately cautious of the stranger, unaware of who he was.

"And Silver, I see that you too are returned to us. And I see that you are keeping some new company since your return?" His gaze fell upon Kate who was looking to Elizabeth to confirm her suspicions.

"Miss Ward. This is Giles Bateman." Elizabeth spoke flatly.

"A pleasure to meet you, Miss Ward." He bowed his head politely. Kate glared at him. "And who is missing from your company?" he indicated the empty space which Heston had vacated and it was Avery's turn to colour.

"Just a friend," he mumbled. "I don't wish to be rude Bateman but we were in the middle of discussing a private matter and...."

But Avery did not have the chance to finish his sentence as the return of Heston stoked Bateman's interest tenfold. Heston was at the disadvantage as, returning to his seat, he did not recognize Bateman from behind and by the time he had drawn level it was too late to conceal himself.

Bateman recognised him instantly but did not acknowledge it. He smiled broadly and then, chuckling to himself, he caught the arm of a passing waiter.

"Will you bring us some wine, and you might as well make up another place here for the moment." With that, Bateman took a chair from an empty table and swung it between Heston and Elizabeth. "Well, well, well," he breathed. "Goodwin told me he had lost a good valet in you, Heston but I didn't know it was

415

become you had gone up in the world." Bateman indicated the suit which Heston wore and the dinner table at which he sat with Silver and the two ladies. Heston said nothing but stared straight ahead. Elizabeth kept her eyes on Kate and watched as the young girl struggled with an instinct to say something. This was unfamiliar territory for Kate and no doubt she was chewing on what she would have said to Bateman in a less public setting.

"So, Silver, do you have to hire friends now or is young Heston here on his own purse?"

Silver said nothing and the table fell silent for a moment whilst a waiter set up a place before Bateman and placed a bottle of wine before him.

"Will that be all, sir?"

"No. If you can tell my party that I will be indisposed for a short while and they must start without me. Thank you."

A moment later and they were left alone again. The noise around the room had begun to grow as more people filled in for that evening's entertainment. The handbill they had found on their table promised a variety of acts including a few comic singers. As the waiter left, a burst of applause began to fire around the room as one such act arrived on the stage. Elizabeth, Avery, Kate and Heston sat quietly, looking around the table but not at each other. Bateman was clapping loudly and he wore a smirk across his face as he noticed the grim mood.

"Now, now. It's almost as if you aren't pleased to see me? Silver, tell me what I have done to deserve this treatment. Am I to be sent to Coventry with no explanation?"

416

Elizabeth turned to see Silver's face. She knew that he and Bateman shared no love but it was unlike him not to meet him head on. She suspected he was nervous for Heston or Kate or indeed both. If anyone that she knew fed back to her father that Heston was no man of education but a valet, then the closest she would come to Europe was listening to her future husband's recollections of his own travel. It was not just Heston whose disguise she suspected that he feared would be uncovered. It was Kate's. As she watched him now, she saw Avery move his hand across the table cloth and place it over Kate's own. She had been shaking slightly as though she might cry at any moment. Elizabeth recognized at once that this was not from fear but from anger. Avery's gesture was protective and it did not go unnoticed by Bateman who laughed out loud.

"Aha! I see! Forgive me Miss Greenwood but I had thought that Silver here was your dinner partner but it looks as though he has a new focus for his affection." He laughed again and she felt her insides twisting. She was not afraid of him but she was feeling the pressure both to keep Heston and Kate concealed but also to protect Avery. She still had no idea if he knew anything about Silver's true identify. Surely, he would also have heard of the death of Toby Silver or enquired after Elizabeth when she was at Juniper Hall. The way he was staring at Avery threatened something and she was scared that all of their carefully laid plans would come tumbling down.

"So you and Heston are Chaperones? Gooseberrys? Or..." he paused and then, looking between the pair of them, he laughed again even more loudly. His eruption caused several people to turn and stare. The act on stage, though moderately amusing, had not elicited more than a quiet chuckle. Bateman held up a hand as he tried to choke back his laughter.

"Don't tell me that you and Heston here are partners also?"

It was Avery's turn to speak and he did so calmly but firmly.

"Bateman. You have not been invited to join our party but I have not objected. Nobody has any interest in how you know Mr. Heston but I do know that you will not insult my friends. Now, if you would be so kind," he indicated the food which was being laid before them, "we would like to continue with our meal."

Bateman and Avery locked stares with one another and unblinkingly, Bateman downed his glass and, standing to leave, said. "Of course. Miss Greenwood. Heston and, forgive me but we have not been introduced?" He lowered his gaze in what he intended to be a seductive gaze and extended a hand towards Kate.

"I'd rather touch a viper," she muttered but Bateman did not catch it.

"Pardon?" he said but Avery pressed her hand again and she said nothing else.

Bateman smirked at Avery and then turned to leave. He was greeted at his table with raucous cheers and Elizabeth noticed that she recognized a handful of faces. She glanced over at Avery and one look from him told her that he too had noticed.

"I think it unwise to rush off. I don't think that he will be back any time soon. We have paid for this meal so let's eat and try and enjoy the rest of the evening."

418

It was easier said than done and though nobody looked directly in Bateman's direction, the sensation of his gaze however real or imagined made for an uncomfortable night. The entertainment was a little distracting and at least made up for the lack of conversation at their table. As soon as the meal was cleared, Avery was about to suggest calling it an early night when three men arrived at the table. Elizabeth did not recognize them but Avery clearly did.

"Silver," the taller of the three stated. He was smiling broadly, his cheeks were crimson and his eyes danced around the table. A rounder man, also well on his way to merry, was effusive and clapped Silver around the shoulders with a warm hello. By far the shorter of the three was less inebriated and considerably cooler with his greeting.

"I thought it was you. Bateman said it wasn't but of course I had to see for myself. We have wondered where you had got to over the summer but I can see now just how busy you have been." His eyes danced over Kate and then Elizabeth.

Avery was cautious but he was less guarded than with Bateman. He stood and shook the round man's hand.

"Lloyd, it's good to see you. Well, Miss Greenwood you know. And these are my good friends George Heston and Miss Ward. This is Lloyd Frensham, Jack Kent," he indicated the taller man, "and James Cox."

"A pleasure," uttered James not taking his eyes from Avery but nodding towards Heston. He ignored Kate and Elizabeth.

The taller man, Lloyd, threw a bow in Kate's direction and shook Heston by the hand. Heston looked uncomfortable but Elizabeth was suddenly pleased of Heston's presence. What little she knew of him she approved of. He seemed a stolid character and she felt sure that Silver had chosen his companion well.

After a few minutes, the three men had drawn up seats alongside Avery and Heston and had begun talking loudly. Silver flashed Elizabeth a look and mouthed the words "Ten minutes". Without the full attention of Silver or Heston, she felt vulnerable and her neck prickled as though Bateman were watching her from afar. She had glanced around a few times but had not seen him and she hoped he had left already. She noticed Avery, Heston and Lloyd stand as Kate pushed her chair from the table. By the time he had realized, Jack was too late to attempt to stand and by the look of the short James, he had no intention of showing any respect for either Kate or any of her dinner guests.

"I'm going to the lav," Kate whispered to Elizabeth. "Are you coming?" she asked.

"The lav? To powder your nose no doubt?"

"Eh?"

"Don't worry," Elizabeth added, rolling her eyes. "I think I shall wait here."

The comment didn't go completely unnoticed and Kate blushed a little as she left the table. For a few moments, Elizabeth sat alone on the periphery of the evening, watching Avery's smile fall upon the three men in turn as he calmly answered questions about his summer. Heston also seemed to be following the conversation and Elizabeth eventually allowed her eyes to wander around the room. She lit first upon the table at which Bateman had been sitting and, seeing it empty, she breathed more deeply and she felt herself relax. With the freedom to gaze around she turned to consider her fellow diners. As she did so, she saw Kate at the far end of the room squeezing behind chairs and between tables. Elizabeth rolled her eyes and smiled. '*Typical*', she thought, Kate was trying to leave unnoticed like a housemaid. Elizabeth would have made herself as large as possible so people would see her coming and have time to step out of her way. As she chuckled, she noticed a face close to the door that she recognized. Bateman. She was not the only one watching Kate's slow progress from the table and, as she slipped from the room, Elizabeth noticed, with a feeling of unease, Bateman following Kate out. She looked across at Silver who was deep in conversation and she opened her mouth to interrupt but she could think of nothing to say.

"Is there something wrong?" It was Heston, he was so attuned to waiting upon others that it was only natural he noticed Elizabeth's pause for attention.

"Miss Greenwood?" he asked softly.

She considered him for a moment and something about his quiet strength made her feel ridiculous and some of his calm flowed to her. Bateman could not hurt her here. In a few days time, she would be free of London and free of him.

"It's nothing," she replied. "Will you excuse me. I think I will join Miss Ward after all." And with that she rose, excusing herself from the table.'

True to her earlier observations, she swept down the centre of the room so that chairs were drawn back in advance of her passing. She had crossed the room in a matter of a minute. As she exited the main hall, a wide staircase swept back down to the street, or upwards towards the ladies room. Elizabeth was just about to ascend the stairs when an impulse made her take the stairs down. When she levelled out on the ground floor, she followed the stairs down another flight to a darkened corridor. As she stepped from the bottom step, she could make out the muffled sound of a woman's voice and a scuffling from around the corner. Elizabeth's heart began to pound and she felt her mouth dry up as she felt her instinct drag her onwards. She stepped lightly to peer around the corridor and, as her eyes adjusted to the gloom, the outline of a man struggling with a woman came into focus. The man held the woman by the wrists and had her pushed against the wall. As the man bent his head again to the woman, Elizabeth was not surprised to see Batemans's face against Kate's. In the split second it took for Elizabeth to be filled with rage, she found she could feel the hot breath of Bateman upon her own face as he had pushed himself upon her over the summer. She would not remember lunging at him but Kate would tell her that evening how she seemed to come from the walls themselves. Elizabeth flew at Bateman's head, grabbing his hair, his cheeks and his eye sockets. She hissed words at him furiously that she had never heard orated before. Words that seemed to come from another tongue and Bateman was knocked to one side, reeling. He drew up his arms to protect himself, hardly knowing what had hit him.

"Keep off! Keep off you devil!"

In the flailing gloom, he caught sight of Elizabeth and began to laugh. She felt her anger rise and her attack became more fierce.

"Get off her! Get off her! Get off her, you swine. You reprobate!"

He had grabbed hold of her own wrists and though she struggled he was far superior in strength. Kate had been knocked to the floor in the scuffle and she now began raining blows upon Bateman. In one swift motion, he knocked Kate away with a blow to the side of her head. She fell to the floor once more and there she stayed. He had Elizabeth pinned for a moment against the wall in much the same position in which he had just held Kate. Elizabeth shook with fear and anger that she could be overpowered like that. She managed to bend her head to where he held her wrists and bit his hand hard.

"You little bitch," he shouted though his face showed that same dark excitement that she had seen in the lane that night and she began to scream. There came a rush of cold air then a loud thud accompanied by Bateman yelping.

The next moment, she was free and Bateman was sprawled on the floor clutching his nose. Heston was stood over him, his fists balled and his shoulders rounded forwards as he shadowed Bateman. Kate was warning him.

"Careful Mr. Heston, be careful."

Bateman shook his head and then lunged for Hesston's mid riff, the two of them staggering backwards into the opposite wall. Fists flew and, as they connected, there followed the sickening sound of bone on bone.

Elizabeth's own rage was far from dispersed and she tried to pull Bateman from Heston. As she did so, Bateman whirled round and pushed her to the ground. She clattered into a packing case and Kate shouted out.

"Be careful. She's pregnant!"

Both Heston and Bateman stopped. Heston was torn with an urge to assist with Elizabeth and to pummel the remaining daylights out of Bateman. He opted instead to stand still and wait.

"You're pregnant?" said Bateman.

Kate groaned and whispered to Elizabeth over and over. "I'm so sorry Miss. I'm so sorry. Oh Lord. I'm sorry."

Bateman began to laugh.

"Oh this evening just keeps on getting better! And you the dutiful bride to be Elizabeth! I am appalled! What kind of woman must your fiancé think you to be?"

Elizabeth was numb with rage and her jaw was clenched on her retort. Bateman stepped forward and leaned to whisper close to her ear.

"Don't say I never gave you anything."

It took all her self control from slapping him but she managed to maintain her dignity as she spat back.

"It is a gift from Silver actually."

Heston and Kate both looked at each other, their eyes accustomed to the dim light. Bateman continued to stare hard at Elizabeth, his eyes narrowed. She felt a pulse in her temple throb as she waited to see what effect this news had on him. Though she herself had never heard him doubt Silver's identity there had been plenty of reason to suspect that he knew more than he let on. She held her breath. Eventually, he spoke. His tone was thick with disdain and he curled his upper lip as though Elizabeth had something rotting about her.

"Miss Greenwood, I am surprised you can narrow it down to just the one man."

The insult washed over her. She simply felt a sense of great relief. Relieved that, with such an admission, Bateman both accepted Avery's identity but also rejected any connection with the child.

"You can keep your bastard child and Silver can keep his whore here but Heston here will be arrested. I shall see you jailed for assault, hear?" He jabbed a finger in the air as he touched the back of his hand to his bloodied nose. Heston held his head high but looked nervous.

"You will do no such thing," Elizabeth stated calmly.

"I beg your pardon?" retorted Bateman. Heston and Kate also looked startled. Her tone as authoritative and her voice was steady. With Avery out of danger, she felt suddenly back in control.

"I don't like to repeat myself, Mr. Bateman but in your case I see I shall need to make a concerted effort both to speak up and slow down. I said, you will do. No. Such. Thing," she enunciated loudly.

Bateman bristled and he drew himself up, stepping forwards to within a few inches of Elizabeth's face.

"And why is that?" he asked menacingly.

She did not blink as she replied amiably.

"Because you have made an enemy of me already, Mr. Bateman, you do not now wish to antagonize me. Do you?"

Bateman snorted loudly and began to turn away.

425

"I think I shall take my chances, Miss Greenwood." He shook his head. "Antagonise you? Ha!"

"I should explain, Mr. Bateman. I am merely a woman of no great importance and of course, whilst I am prone to spend evenings in the company of men with whom I should not be seen, yourself included, I am also prone to spend afternoons in places where I should also not be. Reading things I should not be reading."

Bateman halted in his steps and turned to consider Elizabeth, his face clouded with confusion.

"You probably do not know this about me Mr. Bateman but I have a penchant for reading just the most awful of fiction. I don't speak of those penny dreadfuls you can find in any old bookshop but the fascinating real life stories like the real life tragedies of the circus freak shows you can see on the common. I like stories about men who are tried for their crimes and, when found guilty, are punished. Then there are those crimes so heinous, against the laws of decency of God and of nature that I could not even conceive of a punishment. I have always found the light in my father's study all the better for reading. But then you should know that. Both yourself and your father have spent a good deal of time in there yourself."

Bateman's jaw clenched and a vein near his eye began to bulge with the tension of his anger.

"Its amazing what lengths a father might go to keep his family name clear whilst his son will go out of his way to sully it. Don't you think, Bateman?"

426

He snapped and leapt forward a foot, raising his hand towards her face. She did not flinch but Heston was quick to lunge forwards regardless.

~o~

The day they left London, Elizabeth kept expecting her father, Georgina or someone to rush alongside the coach and forbid her from leaving. Through Kent and overnight in Dover, she thought she saw familiar faces at every turn come to fetch her home. Across the Channel, sick with the rise and fall of the waves, she still thought that she saw the face of Cribbs among the lower deck. In fact, she did not quite shake the feeling until they arrived at Ostend and the foreign ground beneath her feet assured her she was free, if not of her predicament but certainly the immediate concern of her father.

The air of liberation and anticipation was not solely Elizabeth's to cherish and she witnessed the same elation in her travel companions the moment they stepped from the boat. Avery had arranged passage from Ostend to Ghent where they would stay for a few nights and as they continued their journey by coach, Elizabeth took the opportunity to consider the changes leaving England had wrought upon Silver, Heston and Kate. She knew very little about Heston. She knew that he had pretended to be a tutor, the son of a family friend, to convince her own father as to his suitability. However, she knew nothing about where he had come from nor what he did. That Bateman recognized him that night troubled her but his actions in saving her from him assured her he was firmly on their side. Later on in their travels, he was to be butler and foil to Avery's male counterpart but for the time being he was to be Avery's tutor. Kate was like an infant at Christmas time, she sat beside the window remarking on every small thing which they passed. Though not accustomed to foreign travel herself, Elizabeth could not bring herself to find pleasure in the sight of every plain looking street.

For the first weeks, the four travelled further into Europe avoiding the busy cities and the tourist routes they had promised Frederick Greenwood they would follow. Avery was yet to find a place he was comfortable to start his transition in and so they seemed to be permanently on the move. After another fortnight, they arrived in the town of Basel in Switzerland and Avery, pleased with what he saw, indicated to Heston that he should check the four of them in to a hotel as Mr. Silver and Miss Greenwood.

Basel was a bustling town with an exciting community of its own and with many visitors from all across Europe. Since Queen Victoria had holidayed in Switzerland the previous year, the area was thriving with the added tourism. As Elizabeth waited for Heston to check the four of them into a hotel, she walked with Avery down to the banks of the Rhine. As they stood on the meander of the river taking in the panorama, she watched him breathe in the chill November air and sensed a promise that had been absent from all of the other locations so far. Though she would have preferred somewhere warmer or more sophisticated like Paris or Florence she had to agree that the place was lively and beautiful. Though she did not know it then, as she watched Avery's shoulders relax as he exhaled, she felt some of her own anxieties dissipate along with the mist of his breath on the cold air.

"I need to find somewhere to change before we head back to the hotel," he said.

Elizabeth said nothing and Avery turned to explain. "The porter shall be expecting to escort you and Kate to your room and a *Mr.* Silver and Mr. Heston to their rooms."

Elizabeth nodded but shrugged. It was a gesture which said many things; that she did not know how to help, that she did not know what to say and that she did not care. Ignoring her, Avery's eyes lit upon the bridge that spanned the river to their right. Dark grey, it was made of several arches which reflected dully in the water. Where the bridge met the land, a deep pocket of trees and bushes proved to be too tempting an opportunity for Avery. Looking around quickly he grabbed Elizabeth by the arm and strode down towards the bushes.

"Oh, surely not!" Elizabeth exclaimed when she realized his intentions and she looked around furtively, craning to see if anyone would see them. By the time she had reached the dark bushes, Avery had slipped between them and the grey stone wall and called out to her.

"Keep a watch. This won't take more than a moment."

True to his word, only five minutes later, Avery emerged clutching the carpet bag in which his dress and boots were now stowed. He looked a lot more disheveled and Elizabeth stepped forward to correct the sweep of his hair and to pull his shirt collars more tightly around his neck. Above them, where the bridge

429

rose across the water, a pedestrian noticed them and wolf whistled, calling out in German. From the man's perspective, the pair looked as though they had just been caught out in a romantic clinch and Avery stepped back from Elizabeth abruptly.

Elizabeth looked up at the man and impulsively gave him a wave and a ready smile. Avery laughed and, caught up with the moment, he pulled Elizabeth too him and kissed her. As he did so, she closed her eyes and felt herself drawn upwards to him. By contrast, Avery drew away and looked sheepish. Rather than spoil the moment, he strode back to the main thoroughfare, calling over his shoulder.

"Come, Miss Greenwood. The day is young and there is much to do."

It was over in a second but the feel of his lips on hers stayed with her all that day. As they arrived back at the hotel Elizabeth could still feel it; over dinner that evening and when she woke the following morning, to the sound of Kate drawing water Elizabeth pressed her hands to her lips to assure herself that he had left nothing of himself upon them.

~o~

By the end of the month, Avery had explored much of the city and was beginning to grow restless. Now that he had begun to shed his female persona, he was keen to keep on with his first plan which was to see as much of Europe as possible. As amiable as ever, he had begun to build a network in the city and the familiarity with which he was met was beginning to make him feel uncomfortable. Though they had checked in as travelling companions with Kate posing as Elizabeth's maid and Heston as his valet, Avery had quickly been upset with Kate having to wait upon Elizabeth and he had employed the services of a young girl who could attend to her instead. This left Miss Ward with more free time at her disposal than she was comfortable with. Their days fell into a routine quickly enough with Kate and Avery taking morning walks around the city, they would all lunch together and then he would often spend his evenings alone or as a foursome with Heston, Kate and Elizabeth taking in some evening entertainment. With two women in his entourage he was beginning to get a reputation around the town which amused and annoyed Elizabeth.

"What on earth do you both find to talk about for so long on your walks?" Elizabeth asked one morning when Kate had returned from a walk with Avery.

It had been growing much colder and Elizabeth, though annoyed that Avery had not once asked her to join him on his morning stroll, was rather pleased to be inside on days such as those. Kate seemed to give her question much thought and then shrugging her shoulders she replied.

"We talk about lots of things. I seem to do much of the talking but he always listens. He asks me about the town I grew up in, about service, about how it is to sleep in a truckle bed in an attic room, about how it feels to wear his pretty dresses after the plain sacks I am used to." She blushed as she noticed Elizabeth watching her and she quickly tried to change the subject.

"We have not yet talked about you, if that is what you wish to know. Though quite what I am to tell him when he asks why you are beginning to look so thick around your stomach is beyond me."

Elizabeth shot her a glare. This was what came from Kate having too much time on her hands. If she was not kept busy, she had time enough only to press Elizabeth about what she planned to do. Thus far, Elizabeth had managed to avoid discussing it entirely but she was growing concerned too and, though she was cross with not having brought it up herself, she welcomed the opportunity to have someone else to talk about the matter with.

"I rather hoped he would never know," said Elizabeth finally. She had turned her face away from Kate's and she felt tears welling. It was unlike her to allow her emotions to run so close to the surface but in the last months she had found herself welling at the most ridiculous and sentimental things.

"But of course he must!" Kate spouted. "Sometime in the spring, you are going to be heavily pregnant and you won't be want to be gallivanting around Europe on your travels. We won't leave you on your own, so we need to think about a place to settle for a bit. A month after that you are due to be home and I'll bet you've given no thought to what your father is going to say when he sees you looking as large as a house. How is that going to look? That Avery concealed that from him will not go down well either. When you said you didn't want to tell anyone. I let you alone. You said you needed to get out of London and we got out of London. You said you wanted to get away from that Bateman. Well I reckon you won't see him again. Not in a long time. So now you are clear of him, and England, you must tell Avery." Kate fell silent and

Elizabeth continued to keep her face turned away. Of course she had heard everything that Kate had said and contrary to what the girl thought of her, Elizabeth had given all of those things a lot of thought. She knew exactly how her father's face would look if she arrived home either pregnant or carrying a baby. She also knew only too well that her fiancé would rather terminate their engagement than be shamed in such a way. She knew she was beginning to show and she suspected it would not be much longer before she would not be able to deny the changes in her body to the rest of the world. She knew all that but did not know what to do. Though she felt like a woman, the enormity of the problem made her feel like a child. She had hoped that something would happen, that somebody would make a decision for her or that Avery would just find out and plans would be made without her knowing.

"Elizabeth?" Kate prompted.

Elizabeth opened her eyes and turned to face Kate. She would have to deal with this herself.

"I will speak to Avery this evening."

Chapter Twenty Eight - Imogen, 1911

As I replaced the mouthpiece on the telephone stand, I felt at last as though I were back in control of my own self. John's mother had been kind but obstructive. She made no effort to conceal her distaste of the news of my father but her dislike of matters both personal and delicate ensured that neither of us spoke of the situation directly. Her concern, as was mine, was for her son.

"How is John bearing up?"

"John is being very practical Margaret. You know John."

"Of course, I can only imagine there is much to organize. Well, the boys must stay as long as possible to keep out of your way."

"Well actually, that is why I am calling Margaret. I'd like the boys to come home."

"Of course, you must want them with you. Well as soon as the funeral is all out of the way then we shall send them home."

"Actually, I'd like them home tomorrow," I paused and girded myself for the imminent disapproval, "in time for the funeral."

There was a heavy silence and I almost spoke again, believing the connection to have been lost, when Margaret Bancroft's reproachful voice came down the line.

"Does John think that is a good idea Imogen?"

I had weighed up what to say to such a question and it was tempting, simply to avoid any conflict, to simply say yes but in the end I had decided that honesty was the best policy.

"I have not spoken with John yet but you can be rest assured that he will support me in this Margaret."

"Imogen, I must insist…"

"Margaret. I don't wish to fall out with you on this matter and I am grateful to you for stepping in to look after them at such short notice."

"Naturally…"

"…but the boys are old enough to pay their last respects to their grandfather. They were very fond of my father and in the circumstances I would like them to be at home."

I heard her draw breath for a further objection but I simply continued. "I will have Stokes wait for the 2 o'clock train, if you will be so kind."

~o~

When John returned home that evening, rather than avoid him or be afraid of his silent disapproval, I was waiting for him in his study. I had only been in the room without him once before. It was before we had had the children and late one evening we had been sat together in the parlour. There had come the sound of breaking glass from upstairs. John had sprung into action and, taking me by the hand, he had pulled me behind him into the hall. A young Stokes was already mounting the stairs, a fire poker in hand and John whispered to him to wait. He had ushered me to the study and had kissed me and told me to stay. He had closed the door and turned the key in the lock. He had kept me safe, his most precious thing. The recollection was a fond one and when he opened the door, he looked many years older than the twelve that separated the memory from the present day. He looked surprised to see me but he regarded me kindly.

"Imogen?" he said. "It's late. What are you doing here?"

"I wanted to talk."

I saw his shoulders droop as if he could think of nothing worse than to talk to me. The gesture made me feel very sad and alone.

"Mother called the office this evening," he said. "Would this have anything to do with what you want to talk about?"

Though I knew that she would, I felt my temper rise nonetheless.

"What did you say to her?" I asked.

His shoulders dropped yet further and he sank into the chair in which I had myself sat only a few short nights ago and he had raged at me.

"I told her that you were under a lot of strain and that perhaps it would be best if the boys were to stay where they were for the time being. At least until after the funeral." he added quickly.

I did not feel angry, I had been expecting as much. I sat back on the desk and held the warm wood tightly beneath my fingers as I stared at him.

"Do you remember Wales?" I asked.

John's face remained drawn and he tipped his head back as he braced himself for a conversation he hadn't seen coming.

"Of course," he said. His tone was flat.

"Do you remember the river?"

"And the boat that capsized? Of course I remember."

"Capsized? You stood up so fast, the boat rocked for a full minute before I was pitched into the cold water."

"It can't have been that cold, it was summer!" he retorted. His face was softer but he remained guarded.

"I took a lungful of water. I thought I would drown but you saved me."

John looked at his me and shrugged his shoulders.

"The water was shallow. It was only waist deep."

I took his hand and shook my head at him.

"But you carried me anyway."

The silence in the room was full of our voices from every conversation we had ever had in this room and after a minute or so, the memory of them was deafening and I was grateful when John stood from his chair and, stepping forwards, took me in his arms and held me.

~o~

When I reached my father's house, there was already an air of dereliction. What furniture remained had been draped in white sheets and those fires which had once been lit with regularity were clean and cold. The only person who was left was Heston and he had not been expecting me. Having let myself in, I had found him sat in my father's study, his head upon his hands. He had not heard my approach and I had the luxury of watching him for a few moments, unobserved. His was as familiar a face as my own father's. I could not remember a day when I had not passed through Heston to see my father. Of a morning, he was upon the stair carrying some errand or other. Some paperwork, a newspaper, anything at all but all delivered with the same care and diligence as he treated his position. In some ways I suppose, I had seen more of this man before me than of my father and if I had not known my own father then how could I trust this man before me? So he had been my father's man since he had transitioned from Alice to Avery? He must know something and I had come to find the last of the truths. I drew back silently from the frame and into the hall where I coughed and allowed Heston to rouse before I re-entered the room.

"Mrs. Bancroft!"

He was unshaven and his suit was crumpled and he was apologetic from the off.

"Please. Forgive me. I was…I mean." He looked at me apologetically, picking at his shirt front and glancing around to where his jacket hung on another chair back.

I smiled at him and shook my head.

"Please. There is no need to apologise. I didn't mean to startle you."

"You didn't. I mean…, I didn't know you would be coming back again today. I would have…" He looked about himself at the empty shelves of my father's study and his eyes took in the whole of the house from top to bottom as if he could see each of the floors now stripped of any memory of my father, my mother or me. The house would be sold to fetch the highest price. The money would be placed in trust for Sebastian and Thomas and the rest conferred amongst myself,

Heston and Mrs. Rooksmith and the handful of charities to which my father was a benefactor. The house would no doubt be of some interest to those peculiar people who made other people's lives more interesting than their own but in a few short days there would be nothing left of my fathers'.

"Can I offer you something?" he looked around him. "Some refreshment? I will see if there is something I can ..."

"Can we sit for a while?" I indicated the leather chair he had just vacated and I drew up a chair before it and placed my bag on the desk. The small and only fire that was lit was dying and I drew my coat around me. Old habits died hard and noticing that small gesture, he quickly assembled some more wood upon the embers and, within a few moments, the fire had recovered its appetite. Heston, pleased to have satisfied at least some small service, sat more comfortably alongside me. The room began to settle around us as some warmth began to infuse the bare boards and furniture with life. A few faint creaks gave an impression that we were not alone and that there was no silence to break. After a time, the familiar smell of the room gave me some comfort and, though my feet were still like ice, I could feel myself begin to thaw. I glanced at Heston beside me and he was transfixed with the orange tongue of the fire licking around the fresh logs and he seemed to be somewhere else entirely. He, no doubt more uncomfortable than I with the situation, was the first to interject his thoughts into the emptiness of the room.

"The first time I saw your father was when he came out of a shabby thoroughfare round by the Seven

Dials accompanied by my employer at the time, John Goodwin, and a mutual friend of theirs. It was in the early hours of the morning and I had been waiting at the agreed spot for almost an hour. It was an unseemly place to be and I was glad of the driver for company. He was a large man and always carried a pistol after some trouble working for another employer in the North West. I had known my master would be three sheets to the wind by the time had found his way to us. He was out with this particular school chum of his whose influence the whole household had come to despise,'" he looked across at me and nodded. "A life of service is a great pleasure but there are a few individuals whose actions are as reprehensible as an animals. I have had occasion to only happen upon one such character in all my days and, that first evening I met your father, he was also in the same man's company. When I saw my drink weary charge staggering out of the alleyway with that man in tow, I was not surprised, but when I saw a third man following closely, I was taken immediately by him. He was brighter eyed than the others as if he had not been drinking. He held himself tightly and was cautious to every noise and shadow as if each was reaching for the edge of his coat. He did not seem scared, only cautious. I watched how he looked at my employer and I was taken by his concern. He was careful to make sure we were known to one another and that he would be taken care of. I was touched more greatly I think that, by contrast, this old school friend was oblivious to any such notion and was merely looking around for the next diversion."

I waited whilst Heston paused for breath and collected his thoughts.

'As the carriage drove off into the night, I turned to look at the stranger one more time and from under the gas light, he looked ghostly. His dark hair and dark coat seemed to fade into the shadow around him, leaving only a slight form of grey. He was looking directly at me and those deep eyes seemed shot like silver and my heart rose into my throat. He looked ethereal and in the days that followed I found myself thinking of him frequently. It may sound odd to you but there was something about him which was magnetic."

The silence was replaced with a rushing noise as I became all to aware of the way the cold air was being sucked into the room towards the fire. What did Heston mean, was he in love with my father? The old man continued as if his thoughts were nothing more than a matter of a misplaced table ring.

"Mr. Goodwin spoke of Avery all the time and I found myself more interested than usual with his exploits. I think he was suspicious of Avery but he could not place his finger on why. He talked about him as though he were a riddle which he must solve and far from forgetting the enigmatic young man, I found myself becoming infatuated with him. I know that this may sound strange but Goodwin admitted to finding Silver attractive and repulsive at the same time; he was charmed and bothered by him; confused but drawn to him. In turn, I decided that I must find out more about this young man and, of my own volition, I decided to follow him home one day. I waited outside Cleveland Street one evening and followed Silver home in a cab. Oddly, he alighted several streets away from his home and I was forced to follow him from the shadows, skulking like a predator. I watched from a distance as he entered the house through the servant's entrance and I made a note of the address. When I returned to the house a few days later, I waited in the gardens opposite but never saw any sign of him.

"The first time we met properly was some two months later, after his father's funeral. I caught sight of an announcement in the local society news of the death of a man leaving a grieving daughter, Alice Silver and my interest was roused. The address of the man was the same as the house I had seen Avery return to. I wondered whether Avery had been his son and decided to go to the funeral. When I arrived, I stood a decent distance back from the congregation and at first I was disappointed that there was no sign of him and then I caught sight of a young woman, dressed in a long black skirt, coat and large brimmed hat. Her face was familiar and I assumed she was the daughter. As for Avery, I could see no sign. After about a quarter of an hour, as soon as the earth had struck the coffin, the young woman walked away from the rest of the mourners and found her own way from the graveyard and I was tempted to take my leave empty handed. But then I caught another glance of her as she passed me by and her face was more than familiar. I was convinced that the woman was Avery. Having thought of him over several weeks, I decided I must know and I decided to find out for sure. I followed at a distance at first but by the time we reached the main road I seized my chance. On an instinct, I called out to him.

"'Mr. Silver?'"

"Of course he turned around and I don't believe he recognized me but as soon as I saw those grey eyes, I knew it was him. I was so shocked that I think I made some noise and Avery turned around to see who else had noticed our exchange. He shushed me and, grabbing me by the arm, pushed me across the road.

'"Who are you?"

'"My name is Heston. You know my employer. Goodwin. I am Goodwin's valet. We met in St Giles, sir."

"He was panicked. There were no two ways about it. Even after I had reassured him that I had come of my own accord and that neither Goodwin or Bateman had sent me, he was no more at ease.

'"What do you want? Why have you come here?"

"I could not answer him and was almost glad when we were interrupted by an elderly woman who recognized Avery and called to him, eyeing me suspiciously.

'"Miss Silver? Why are you here? You ran off in such a hurry."

"She bustled towards us but Avery was not content with the interruption and, lowering his voice, gave me his first order.

'"Don't go anywhere, say nothing and play along."

"The woman soon came alongside us and Avery was quick to introduce us.

'"Mrs. Fearncott, this is Heston. Heston is a tutor at the University of Bristol. He was a friend of my father's and sadly just missed the funeral. Heston this is Mrs. Fearncott, a friend of my father's."

"At the time, I had no idea she was affianced to his father and I simply gave her a courteous bow and offered some glib condolences. I was impressed with the speed at which he had concocted a story for me

443

and I went along with the conversation as best I could. The woman asked me a few questions, confessed she had never heard of me and asked how I knew Toby. Avery stepped in quickly and told her we had to go. He hailed a cab, ushered me inside and then we were alone again.

"I was still very much in shock over exactly who Avery was but the whole liaison was thrilling. At this point, I did not know whether Avery was a man disguised as a woman or a woman dressed as a man. I could not have guessed when I had left my employer this morning that I would find someone as fascinating. My interest in him had been roused tenfold and, compared to my dull life, those ten minutes with Avery were exhilarating. As we bumped along without a destination, Avery began to fill the silence. He had a bitter edge to him.

'*"I expect you have come to laugh at me? To report back to Bateman about how you find me?"*

"I shook my head and waited for him to finish.

'*"It is something of a cruel joke is it not Heston that God has either placed the right mind in the wrong body or the right body with the wrong mind? I don't expect you to understand nor do I expect Bateman or Goodwin or Elizabeth or anyone else to for that matter. I do not think I care what is to become of me. I cannot live like this any longer," he paused, "and I do not intend to."*

'*"Mr. Silver, you don't surely intend to take your own life?"*

"He looked at me cautiously. I had used his correct address and this had been taken well.

'"Of course not Mr. Heston. I intend to make a new one for myself. Today I buried my father and though his memory will be gone soon enough, his money will survive a lot longer. I expect it will afford me a change of scenery anyway."

"He looked at me again, his tone self-assured but without arrogance and I was charmed by him. He had untied his hat and the curls of his untidy hair fell about his face, he had tugged at the lace around the neck of his blouse as if the fabric irritated him. He smiled at me.

'"And what about you Mr. Heston? Why are you here? What are you come to do to me?"

"I don't believe I had any ready reply but rather stammered for an answer.

'"I wanted to see you again," I managed to say.

"He narrowed his eyes at me and gave me a questioning look. It was a few moments before he spoke again.

'"When we met before at St Giles," he said and I nodded, "I was not dressed like this. As a woman. I was dressed as a man. And you wanted to see me again?"

'"Yes, sir." I felt my face warm.

"He searched my face and then laughed, a great bellow of mirth and he leant across and placed a brotherly hand upon my knee. "Mr. Heston. I am sorry for your troubles. You came this morning looking for a wolf and found only a sheep. It must be funnier still to find that under the sheep's clothing there is a wolf after all!"

"I could not help but smile with him as he had indeed put my day thus far into perspective. What he did not know then was that rather than be disappointed,

I was only more intrigued by Avery Silver and, when I left him a few hours later, I would go so far as to say that I was infatuated with him.

"The next day, I took my leave of Goodwin again and went to find Avery. The cabbie had eventually deposited us in the city and we had walked for an hour or so before getting an Ombudsman our separate ways. He had talked about two women that he had fallen in love with and how he needed to leave the city and to find a place for himself. The grief, shock or toll that his father's death had had upon him made him reckless and he told me far more than he should or indeed would have done under normal circumstances. I found him, dressed once more as a man, in Green Park. I saw him before he saw me and I had the luxury of being able to watch his easy gait and how other people did not even look twice at him. I found it utterly mesmerizing, and always did. When I bumped into him, he was not surprised to see me. We talked for hours and hours and at the end of the day, he had offered me a job as his personal valet. I accepted on the spot with no hesitations. Goodwin had been a reasonable employer but he was a troubled and difficult young man. Being taken on without the need of any references and for someone who would travel to Europe was an exciting prospect. I had only dreamed about such a prospect. Within the week, I was installed at his father's house and he had begun to make plans for his escape to Europe.

"By the end of a fortnight we had grown more accustomed to one another and I felt more comfortable that I could serve him. In many ways, he remained very private and there would be things that for the rest of his life only he would attend to. In other ways, I was able to improve upon how he managed to pull together his already successful ensemble. After those first few weeks, he returned to his father's fiancé's house to collect your mother. He was expecting to stay for a single night and return with the rest of his belongings and bring Kate back to London. When he returned from Amersham it was not only with your mother but with Miss Elizabeth Greenwood in tow. He told me that his plans had changed and that he planned to take both women abroad with him. He asked me to make the necessary arrangements and so I did."

Heston fell silent and, for a moment, I wondered if he had suddenly lost his courage. I was about to prompt him to continue when he started speaking once more.

"We left London under a bit of a cloud. Miss Greenwood was in some sort of trouble and on our last night in the city we ran into the same thing that she was trying to escape. It looked pretty nasty for a while and I was afraid that our best laid plans would go to waste. Fortunately, Elizabeth was, and I suppose she still is, a strong minded character and she managed to get herself out of a hole. That her father was a well to do lawyer must have leant considerable credence to her bluffs. Anyway, we left the next day and though your father and mother never looked back, I believe that Elizabeth kept one eye on the road behind for some time."

Heston swallowed and continued to gaze into the fire. When he spoke again, he had an airier tone to his voice and he smiled.

"And so for almost half a year Miss Greenwood, your mother, Mr. Silver and I travelled around Europe. I saw things I never believed I would see. Paris, Madrid, Seville, the Alps, Turin, Milan and, of course, Florence. Eventually, the constant upheaval became too much for both Miss Greenwood and Mrs. Silver, or Miss Ward as she was then, and your father tasked me with finding a house in Southern Italy we might rent for the spring. I found a delightful little place about an hour from Verona which we could rent for a year. I remember the house came with a housekeeper and a young serving maid who looked for all the world like a fat poodle."

He laughed at the memory of her and I found myself smiling along with him. It seemed such a rare treat to see him so animated, I felt ashamed of myself for not knowing the man better over the last thirty years.

"She had the most unruly hair. Your mother could not abide her waiting on her whilst she was around and much of the work your mother did, believing she could do it better. The poor girl knew only a few words of English and she would repeat them until she was almost in tears trying to get Mrs. Silver to leave things be.

"Those were good days. The food was most excellent, the cook was a typical Italian woman of a certain age and she was pleased to prepare hearty meals as long as they were received with effusion. We learned very quickly to make a lot of appreciative noises and this was enough to satisfy her at her work. She spoke a little more English and, after three months, our own Italian was becoming rather less rudimentary. Of course, it could not remain thus."

He paused again and he looked at me as if willing me to say something but I did not know what to say. There was a pause as he considered where he was heading with his story and he continued though his pace had picked up as if he were late for something.

"After a few months, Elizabeth went home to England and as far as I know, married her politician and we only saw her once again. The three of us stayed in Italy for the next year and then we returned to England. As you know, we lived in Bristol for a few years before moving to Hamble Gardens when you were younger." He paused and licked his lips. "I can't tell you how much pleasure it has given me to be in your father's service. A life of service requires great strength but whenever I was placed in a room with Avery I felt weak. He had the most amazing courage and it was my life to be a part of his."

The room around us had grown quite dark and the fireplace was home only to glowing red embers. Heston had had his eyes closed to this room and his time. He had been drawn in to his memories and I was loathed to speak and wrench him from his recollection but time had left us standing and I needed to ask.

"You said that Miss Greenwood was in trouble," I said, slowly. "What kind of trouble?"

Heston twitched and looked away from me. The hairs on the back of my neck began to prickle as I considered the way Mrs. Evesham had looked at me that first time we had met.

"Was she pregnant?" I asked. My voice was small but filled the empty study like a cloud across the face of the sun and Heston opened his eyes to look at me and nodded. "No, don't tell me," I said. I didn't think that I could stand to lose my mother again.

Heston frowned and opened his mouth to speak but I rose quickly and stepped away from the heat of the fire. "I think I should go," I said.

He rose and nodded.

"I should have given this to you when I found it," he said quietly, crossing to his jacket and pulling out a thick envelope marked in my father's hand with my name written across it. Though I had been expecting some such letter, it caught me by surprise and my ears filled with the sound of rushing blood. I knew instantly what may be contained within and I was unsure but eager to find out the contents. I took it from him and pressed it to my chest. I wanted to know what was said within but without having to read any details.

"Thank you," I said simply.

"What for?" he had stammered.

"For loving us all so well," I said.

He had blushed and looked away, a tear rolling down his cheek.

Chapter Twenty Nine – Avery, 1869

In the end, they slowed down at the beginning of Spring. The house that Heston had found was enough to cheer everyone's spirits after a few months of hard travelling. The New Year had brought with it a spell of extreme cold across Europe and Spring looked unlikely until they had descended into Italy. The further South they had travelled, the warmer it had become and it was the lure of the sunnier climes that kept the four of them moving onwards. It was around the turn of March that it was obvious that Elizabeth was struggling with the constant upheaval of their travelling.

Despite her protestations that they continue as planned to Rome, Avery insisted that they take a house somewhere. Verona was a destination on their planned itinerary and he thought it would be easier for them to stay in touch with Elizabeth's father from a planned stop. If they deviated too far from the plan then he may notice the postmarks becoming more obscure and begin to worry. It had become obvious that Elizabeth would not be home when she had intended and it would be necessary to make some excuses.

Heston had come up with the idea that Elizabeth could write to her father that she had taken ill with Poliomyelitis. Evidently, his father's master had taken ill with the same illness some twenty years ago and the doctor had prescribed bed rest for several months. It was entirely feasible that Elizabeth could have the baby, recover and be home only a few months after she had intended but not too late to mean her wedding must be postponed. The only difficulty would come if her father or her fiancé were worried after her and came to find her. After deliberating, it was decided that this was a risk worth taking and Avery wrote the letter the same night they had arrived. Heston would post it the following day when he visited Verona to stock for provisions.

They had been travelling for six months and, though loathed to admit it, Avery was pleased to have the opportunity to settle somewhere. Since Basel he had not dressed as a woman at all but instead had presented himself at various banks to withdraw his funds as a man. There had been only a small amount of difficulty in Basel at first but he was able to persuade the bank manager that there must have been some misunderstanding. He was a short, pale and thin man with equally thin, ashen hair. It was no surprise when Avery found out that his name was Blass.

"Sir! I think that I should know if I were my father's daughter or my father's son!"

"Of course, sir. It's just that the paperwork here states that you are female," Blass had offered a conspiratorial laugh but Avery just stared at him coolly.

"Do you wish me to drop my trousers and prove it to you?"

Blass's pale face had coloured very quickly and through his embarrassment it had been easy enough to have his documents changed. He had apologised profusely and assured Avery that he should have no further problems with his paperwork. With such documents in his possession it was easier still to drop his female identity entirely. When they arrived at the house in Verona, the housekeeper who spoke very little English had begun to flap as soon as they arrived. As Avery had turned to help Elizabeth down from the carriage, they all heard the cry from the woman who turned on her heel and disappeared into the house, making tut tutting noises. Avery's first thought was that perhaps the woman had seen something in him that thus far nobody had, that this woman had seen through his disguise. Heston and Avery threw each other looks of confusion and Kate, rolling her eyes, was the first to enter the house to investigate.

"What's the matter?" Elizabeth asked as Kate returned a few minutes later. She looked downcast.

"I think that there has been some misunderstanding," she said, looking at Heston. "I don't speak Italian but I don't think she was expecting Miss Greenwood to be *con Bambino*. Does she think you and Miss Greenwood a couple?" she asked Avery.

Avery shook his head and indicated to Heston to stay silent.

"Heston has arranged accommodation for the four of us. We are to have the service of a maid to keep the place clean and someone to cook the meals."

"There are only three bedrooms," Kate stated baldly. "One of us must share."

It was Avery's turn to feel confused and he shot a look at Heston who shrugged his shoulders apologetically. Elizabeth had not yet heard and Avery felt his ears begin to burn with annoyance. If the woman assumed that he and Elizabeth were a couple then surely he must share a bedroom with her. He found himself uncomfortable at the very thought of sharing such an intimate space and cast around for a solution before the woman returned and began shepherding them to their rooms. Before he could think,

453

the dark shape of the housekeeper had descended the front porch and approached Elizabeth with open arms.

"Buon giorno, buona giornata. Devi essere signora Silver?"

Elizabeth turned to look at Avery who did not fully follow the woman's fast gabble. She smiled at him, a mischievous twinkle in her eye that he did not trust. The woman turned and gestured at Avery.

"E 'questo tuo marito?"

"My husband?" Elizabeth repeated. "Yes, this is my husband."

Avery bit his lip on a choice outburst and saw Kate cast him a look of annoyance.

"Signor Silver. Benvenuto!" The woman beckoned them all to enter and before he knew it, he was being shown the room he must share with Elizabeth Greenwood for the next few months. As the door closed behind them, he glared at her.

"Why did you say we were married?"

"I didn't want her thinking I was a woman of loose morals, Avery."

"But..."

"I am not sharing a bedroom with Heston," she added

He could think of nothing to say so had left to find Heston and see what alternative accommodation might be arranged. He was unable to find him and instead he found Kate unpacking in her room. The door was open and for a few moments he watched from the threshold as she moved from bed to chest of drawers, laying out the clothes she kept so tidy and clean. Much of her wardrobe had been adapted from his own but he barely recognized the same dresses as ones he used to wear. Where clothes had hung from his tall frame like willow leaves, the same fabric, clung around her chest and hips causing the eyes of whoever was looking to be drawn to them. It was as though in adapting the clothes she had stitched in magnets to draw the eye.

"Is yours and Miss Greenwoods room to your liking?" she asked, without looking at him.

Startled to be caught gazing at her so, he could only apologise as his face glowed pink. "Sorry. I, er.."

She turned to look at him and taking pity, she stepped to the door frame and pulled him in to the room, closing the door behind him.

"Are you okay?" she asked. "You seem a little distracted by something."

He was distracted. He was always distracted around her. Since leaving London, he had been excited and tired by the new sights and sounds. Most nights he had slept dreamlessly; however when he did have dreams, they were almost always about Kate. No longer where they restricted to an English Lake but they reflected his waking day until some mornings he could no longer discern if he had spent the day sightseeing with Elizabeth, Heston and Kate or whether he had slipped an arm around Kate's waist and led her to a quiet corner and pressed his cool lips against the warm skin of her neck and felt her shudder.

"It's Just..." he looked around at the bedroom she had been allocated and he took in the size of her bed and imagined himself asking to share it with her. Though she would likely say yes out of a sense of duty, he could not imagine how he could keep his dreams from her. Though less preferable, perhaps it was better that he share the bed with Elizabeth after all.

"It's nothing," he said. "I just wanted to make sure you were comfortable."

"Yes, of course. It's perfectly comfortable. And you?"

He looked again at the bed.

"If you would rather, you could stay here?" she offered. His heart lurched and he smiled without noticing. "And I can stay with Miss Greenwood?" she continued.

He stared at her not knowing what to say and instead he just shook his head slowly.

"It's okay. I think I shall be fine as we are."

"I see," she added smartly and turned to continue her unfolding. He wanted to say something else but had no idea what. In the end, he just turned and left the room without a word.

The house was in a small village to the west of Verona, a few minutes from Lake Garda. Within a few weeks things settled into a routine. At night the four of them had the house to themselves but by 6am the cook and the maid came from a few streets away to start breakfast. The days were getting much longer and the heat was beginning to make longer excursions more uncomfortable, not just for Elizabeth but for them all. Elizabeth was getting larger and as she did so, the more fractious she became.

One day in early April, Heston had taken himself off to Verona for the day to deliver the latest letter bound for England. Elizabeth was of course overdue to be home and they needed to advise that she would be staying in Italy for further rest. The letter had been written with a balance of assurances that she was well but that she could not travel. The house had been getting warmer all day and the only cool room was a small, North facing, parlour in which all three had been sat since lunch. Too uncomfortable to share the bed with Elizabeth, Avery had taken to sleeping in a variety of chairs refusing to admit to Kate or Heston that was what he was doing. As a result his own temper had grown quite short.

"Must you keep sniffing like that?" he said.

Elizabeth stopped fanning herself and looked across at where Avery was sat.

"I don't know why you didn't go with Heston to Verona. You are ill suited to being indoors. I am sure Miss Ward and I have done little to deserve the pleasure of your company."

He glared at her and wondered himself why he had not. He looked across at Kate, sat beside the open window, her skin glistening with the heat. He felt his eyelids grow heavy in the warmth of the room and he began to doze. As he did so, he dreamt that he stood from where he was sat to where Elizabeth and Kate had also fallen asleep. He had walked to where Kate was seated and, lowering his head until his lips were beside her ears, he had whispered 'I love you.'

"Avery!"

Avery jerked awake to the sound of Elizabeth laughing uproariously and he looked around to find the source of the amusement. Kate was staring at him.

"What is it?" he demanded after a few moments. "What's so funny?"

"Whom is it that you love, Avery?" Elizabeth asked, a teasing smile pulling her face wide.

He looked at her with bewilderment.

"What on earth do you mean?"

"Oh come now Avery, there is very little else to amuse me at the moment. Your waking moments are as dull as mine so please do entertain us all with your sleeping ones."

He was confused for a few moments before it dawned on him that he must have uttered something in his sleep. A hot panic swept over him as he wondered what he had said and his mind swam with the various enactments he had imagined and what he had managed to give away.

"Leave him alone." Kate said.

"Oh, come now, Kate. Aren't you just a teeny bit curious about who or what it is that Mr. Silver loves enough to keep only in his dreams."

"I am not," she returned and, avoiding Avery's gaze, she added. "I am quite sure it is something the two of you should keep private."

Avery was about to retort but Elizabeth, looking even more pleased with herself, cut across him.

"Well I shan't be fobbed off quite so easily. Tell me Avery. What, or who, is it that you love you so much that it interrupts even your sleeping moments?"

"It was nothing," he snapped. He was in two minds to leave the room but he was annoyed that Kate seemed to think that there was something between he and Elizabeth. "It was nothing to do with you," he added.

"Nothing to do with me! But of course, Silver! It was nothing to do with me, but of someone else in this room I am sure you spend your time thinking."

Avery was stunned. He had not expected Elizabeth to guess the truth of his heart so easily. Had he spoken in his sleep before? He shot a look over at Kate who was staring at Elizabeth in distrust. Elizabeth had returned her attention to her lap where she had been pretending to read. Her face was alight with mischief and she began to hum as she turned over the pages of the book in her hand. Kate turned to face Avery and when she found he was staring at her, she blushed and looked away.

"I don't... I don't know what you mean.." Avery stammered at the same time that Kate spoke up. "Avery?"

"What are you playing at?" he asked Elizabeth. "Kate, I'm so sorry. Miss Greenwood is bedeviled. She finds amusement in such lies."

Kate looked at Elizabeth who had cast her book down on the side table.

"Oh for God's sake. I cannot bear this anymore! Avery, look at her. The girl is madly in love with you and you cannot spend a night without uttering her name whilst you sleep." She stood and, in doing so too quickly, she swayed on the spot as the heat hit her. She threatened to collapse back in to the chair and, worried for the baby, Kate and Avery leapt forwards at the same time to assist.

"Leave me alone. If anyone needs help in this room, it is the two of you." Elizabeth mopped her brow with the back of her hand and left.

Both Avery and Kate watched her retreating back in silence until they were stood alone, side by side in awkward silence. After a few moments, Kate shrugged her shoulders.

"I expect you will want me to return to England," she offered into the silence between them.

He almost laughed but instead he turned to face her and no longer fought the urge to take her in his arms.

~o~

Heston barely raised an eyebrow when he saw Avery leaving Kate's room early next morning and over the next few days it became obvious even to the young Italian serving maid that Avery and Kate were doing more than just talking when they were alone together. Avery noticed that the housekeeper spent more time fussing over Elizabeth in a pitying way and cast furious looks at Kate and himself. Though he felt he should probably put the woman straight, at least to keep Kate's character free from blemish, he rather enjoyed the idea that she thought him such a scoundrel. For Kate's part she didn't seem to care any less about what the domestic staff thought of her. She acted no differently around anyone, she chided Avery in the same way and kept picking up after Elizabeth or offering her assistance to the cook. The only difference was the way she looked at Avery when he watched her, she turned a smile on him full of such open delight that he was sure he was still dreaming.

They spent most mornings together, either walking to the lake or in to the groves and chatting. They held hands and found secret spots to steal a kiss or for him to press her to him. Avery was the happiest he could imagine himself but still he found something which worried him. One afternoon, they had meandered

460

locally to a place they had found where there was a shady sweep of Swiss pines beneath which a selection of broad flat rocks afforded a comfortable place to sit. The view out towards Lake Garda was arresting and Kate's face was in profile as he listened to her talk. He loved the sound of her voice, the way some words sounded foreign in her thick accent and the way her sentences seemed to roll on and on without her even taking breath. She had been talking about all of the places she had seen so far on their trip. Though he had been alongside her all the time, the way she spoke of it made it sound like more of an adventure.

"You never speak about your family," he asked suddenly.

She fell silent and turned an apologetic smile on him.

"I have no family, Avery. Don't look at me like that and don't ask me again." She closed her eyes and he knew from the way she screwed her eyes up that she would not relent. "They weren't there when I needed them, that's all I will say. When I have my baby I won't let her down," she added sadly.

He watched her sitting there and he felt her words like a cold slap. It was something he had never thought about in his own future and yet she obviously had. It was a future he could not give her. By the time she had opened her eyes, Avery had stood up and was pulling his lip.

"Come on," he said without looking at her. "Let's go."

His tone was short and there was a tangible atmosphere that she did not fail to pick up upon.

"What's the matter? What did I say?"

461

"It's nothing. It's grown late, that's all.' He stepped down off the rock and brushed his seat of his trousers glancing towards the dusty path they must take to rejoin the main road.

"Avery?" she continued to press. "What have I said?"

"Just leave it."

Kate stared at him, open mouthed and frowning.

"I can't just leave it. Is it because I won't talk about them? That I was disowned? Are you ashamed of me? Are you angry?"

"Damn it, no! I am not angry or ashamed of you. I am angry and ashamed at myself."

She looked at him blankly.

"Kate. I am utterly in love with you. I want to spend the rest of my life with you."

"And I want to spend the rest of my life with you," she interrupted.

Avery shook his head and turned away.

"I cannot condemn you to a life with me. This…" he indicated himself, "..is my choosing but it is not yours."

She stepped off the rock and walked to his side. "Avery, you are my choice. I know what you are and I choose every part of it."

"But you will never be a mother," he said finally. "We would never have a family."

She looked at him sadly, realizing at last what he meant. Her shoulders dropped with the realization and he felt an ache at losing her. After a few moments, she reached out for his fingertips.

"Avery, I have something to tell you,' she said, staring hard as if to reassure him. "Promise me, you won't be angry with me."

Avery felt his stomach lurch as his mind wrestled with all the possibilities Kate might declare but at that moment, they heard a shout from the road. It was Heston.

"Mr. Silver, Miss Ward. It's Miss Greenwood." he shouted. "Her labour has started."

Heston looked panicked, he was pleased to have found Kate and when she began to run towards the road, a great look of relief washed over the man.

Chapter Thirty - Imogen, 1911

When I finally arrived home that evening, I felt almost hollow with all of the emotion that had drained away from me over the last several days. From shock to anger, disappointment to grief I felt that the evening with Heston had left me empty. In the space of a week, I had lost my father, not once but twice. His death had pitched me into grief but finding out he was not my father to begin with, took him even further away than death could. And now, I was losing my mother all over again. So, she had not been my mother. I had been Mrs. Evesham's reject. The house seemed darker than ever as I crossed over the threshold and I thanked Maud as she relieved me of my coat and hat.

"Is Mr. Bancroft at home?" I asked.

"No, Ma'am."

"He has gone to collect Master Thomas and Sebastian from the train, Ma'am."

"Very good, Maud. I think I shall change before dinner. I will call for you if I need any help." I wanted to have a moment to collect myself before the boys arrived home and with that I ascended to my room and sat before my dressing table, looking at myself in the mirror. As I regarded my familiar reflection, I looked hard like I had never done before. I am not a vain woman but I find nothing much that displeases me when I regard myself. This however not an appraisal of my beauty but a study of my features. As I sat before the glass I could see my father's eyes dancing in mine as I smiled, the way my eyes crinkled as I did so were the spitting image of my mother's. How could it be that they were a part of me? I looked again

464

and tried to discern the fine features of Mrs. Evesham. As I studied myself I saw, from the corner of my eye, the envelope that Heston had given to me. The sight of it made my heart miss a beat. I didn't know what it contained within it but I was in two minds about destroying it. The ink of my name was dark and I imagined that it had only been written in the last few years. After a few moments staring hard at the familiar hand of my father's writing, I decided that whatever was written within could not change what I had come to find out. There could surely be nothing left to know.

Inside, there was a short letter in my father's hand and a sheath of papers written in my mother's untidy hand. They were dated 1870.

Dearest Midge,
There is much truth in the world that is denied and there are lies which are accepted by all as indisputable. That I should have told you face to face is undeniable and for that I apologise with all my heart. I suppose that I had always hoped you and your mother would have had the conversation and that it would be something you just came to understand the way you just learned to talk, the way your sense of humour grew more enchanting each day or the way you inherited your mothers understanding of how to make people feel comfortable. If you are reading this letter then it means that I ran out of time or courage. My lovely Imogen, this does not change a thing. There is nothing that can take away from the past. You must only look forward and take care of your own family now. The boys are your future just as you are mine.
Always your father, Avery

Chapter Thirty One – Kate, 1870

Avery was shocked when I told him about Imogen. I could tell. He is like an open book though he tries to pretend otherwise. I think we had been interrupted at the right moment because I am not sure I was ready. Poor old Heston was all of a muddle and it was just as well he had found me because the women of the village were not doing a good job at keeping Elizabeth calm. When we arrived back at the house, her room was full of people we didn't know, all calmly drawing water and preparing clean rags. I could hear Elizabeth before I reached her room, she was on all fours, in the middle of her bed, racked with the familiar throws of labour. As soon as she saw me, she screamed with relief and reached out to me.

"Oh, Kate. Help me. Please, make it stop," she sobbed through gritted teeth.

"I'm here now, Elizabeth. It's okay. How close are your pains?" I asked, remembering the questions my own midwife had asked me.

"They haven't stopped," she cried. "Oh, please."

She arched her back as a fresh wave overtook her and she began to wail. As she did so, I stepped over to the bed and took her hand just as Avery came in. One of the women chased after him, ushering him away.

"No, señor. Usted no puede estar aquí."

"What's happening? What can I do?" he said, ignoring the women.

"Avery, help me," Elizabeth screamed. "Do something," she said.

He looked helplessly at me.

"Come, sit here and keep hold of her hand," I said, standing up and rolling up my sleeves. Elizabeth had begun to pant hard, her face glowing red and I recognized the signs of an imminent delivery. Two of the women had thrown up their hands and begun muttering to themselves, no doubt about Avery's continued presence but I think they put this down to English eccentricity. Although I spoke no Italian and the women attending Elizabeth spoke no Englis,h they accepted my help and I was quickly absorbed into the smooth and ordered chaos of the delivery. Unlike my own labour, it wasn't long before I could see the glistening crown of hair and a rush of emotions flooded through me; regret, pain and joy.

"I can see the baby's head," I said.

"Get it out," she cried, panting hard.

One of the women gathered up some cloth and between us we took delivery of Elizabeth's baby as she struggled to draw breath in between the pain.

"Es un niño," the woman beside me cried as she lifted the baby clear of the bed. "Es un niño!"

"What did she say?" Elizabeth croaked as she collapsed onto the bed.

"It's a boy," I said, my voice breaking like the flood of memories that washed inside me.

~o~

"How did you know what to do?" Avery asked that evening.

He had watched the whole thing from beside Elizabeth without a single word, pale-faced and lost, like a small boy.

467

"It was…," he searched for a word, "terrifying."

I smiled grimly, remembering my own fear as I had lain upon a strange bed not two years ago, giving birth to a baby I could not keep and knowing I had been cast out by my family in disgrace and after what had happened, there was no way I could keep my job. Yes, terrifying was an apt word and I felt the same pang of regret as I had when the midwife had asked me what to call my daughter. I have a daughter, I thought and her name is Imogen.

"Kate? Are you okay," he asked.

I kept my eyes down and took a deep breath before I told him everything.

"I have a daughter," I said, "and her name is Imogen."

I watched carefully and, though he said nothing, his eyes grew panicked and his body rose with a tension he need not have felt.

"You asked me why I don't talk about my family. Well, they disowned me," I whispered. Though I had long accepted that that was the truth, admitting it was like going through the pain all over again.

"I officially went into service when I was nine years old though in truth, it had been so all my life. I followed my mamma into the kitchens of the Darfould Estate. We all did. It was a big estate and most of our village depended on it for their livelihood. My brother was a groom and my two older sisters were employed in the house. My father was, probably still is, head gardener. He spent so much time outside in the grounds that his face was like the saddle of the master's horse. He was a tall man but his back was always bent like he was crouched over a herb bed.

"The Estate was vast and employed so many people yet the Broadwater family were only five in number. I remember how odd I found this thought when I had first found out. The master and mistress were always to remain a distant presence to me and my mother had coached me well; to stay out of their way and to fear them before I could respect them for their power over us all was second only to Gods. They had three boys, two of whom were away for lengths of a time at school but the youngest, Charles, was almost exactly my age and it was inevitable that we found each others company.

"I spent much of my girlhood running errands around the kitchens and for my father and I became as much a part of the place as the skirting boards or fountains in the garden. When he wasn't being tutored or occupied by his nanny, Charles would seek me out and we would play together. No-one seemed to mind. He was well-liked by all the staff and his mischievous nature was tolerated by his family. Mine were less pleased when our forays ended in tears. I remember one summer when we had got lost. I had followed Charles around the estate to an area of woodland, we must have been no more than eight and it had begun to grow dark. He had grown frightened and begun to cry. When we were found by one of the garden hands, he was miserable and cold. I had taken the full brunt of the misadventure. I didn't see Charles for several weeks as he had been kept to his bed; his parents fearing he had caught some dreadful chill. The cook kept needling me about it for weeks; Charles was her own favoured child and I fancy she reduced my portions as a way to punish me for my actions. It felt very unfair of course but that became the way of it. As Charles was the golden boy of his family, I became the black sheep of my own.

"Over many summers, we found each other out and talked about what we would become. You'll laugh but my ambition then was to own my own shop where I would sell wraps of sweets and sticks of licorice. He said he wanted to be a gardener like my father so he could always play in the garden. It was a foolish notion but his life was already as set for him as mine was for me though we would not see this for many years

"The only recognition of my official cross-over into service was my uniform, which I hated, and a wage which my mother took for my keep. At first, Charles found the uniform hysterical and would search me out more frequently just to mock me. It was after several afternoons of him sitting around the back of the kitchen where I was cleaning out one of the kitchen grates, black smut clogging up my fingernails, that he annoyed me too much. He had been circling me for at least half an hour, repeating over and over:

"'Cinderella, you can smell her. Cinderella, you can smell her.'

"It was childish but I was cross at him and I was cross at my life. It wasn't fair that I had to be cleaning that rotten grate and endure his taunts. I snapped and, dropping the grate, I chased him. It wasn't hard to catch him and when I did, I let fly with a shower of blows across his shoulders and head until I was pulled off by the furious face of my father. Charles's face was black where my smutty hands had made contact and he looked shocked.

"Needless to say, I wasn't popular with anyone in the house for a long time after that and, looking back, I was lucky to keep my job. Charles's visits below stairs stopped altogether and I only saw him from a distance for the rest of the year. When he was ten, he was sent to boarding school and he only came home at the end of term. The first time he came back, he came to find me, to apologise for teasing me. I was taken aback. I had not been expecting it. He confided in me that he had found school hard and I suspect that he had been the subject of some bullying. He seemed more timorous but I was grateful for the apology. Though no-one else knew, I felt some of the guilt leave me.

Avery watched me whilst I spoke and I knew from his face that he was jealous. No doubt, he already guessed the ending to my story but I felt I had to finish. It was important to me to explain.

"Each time he returned, he found some time to come and find me but we were careful not to let anyone find us together. I would sneak away on an errand to the orchard or the kitchen garden and Charles would meet me in one of the outbuildings; the summer hours, the orangery, the lake house. I knew mamma would be furious.

"Charles spoke about his future, about his father's plans for him, about school, about his plans to travel and I felt that these were the only times he talked about the things that troubled him. My life became a routine and each year I looked forward to seeing Charles, to hear about his term and to see how much he had changed. Don't get me wrong, I didn't spend the whole year pining after him but you have to understand that he was a friend and my life was extraordinarily dull.

By the time he came home at the age of seventeen, we were very different people and our summer chats grew shorter and less frequent. I had noticed how each year he had come home taller, broader and his voice deeper. By comparison, I don't think I changed a bit; perhaps only grew more tired and less interesting!

"But that summer, he came to find me on his first day back. He was pink faced with excitement and he asked me to meet him in the summerhouse. He was so excited; he didn't even bother to make sure we were alone. My older sister, Eve and one of the scullery maids, Greta were in the yard when he came to see us. You should have seen the look on Greta's face when the tall young master strode round the side of the kitchen and asked to meet me. She looked as though one of the garden ornaments had broken free of its stony pose and begun talking to her. That alone was enough to make me bold enough to walk straight after him without a further thought. It was reckless but I was carried away with his excitement and wasn't he a friend?

"He wanted to tell me that his father had agreed for him to study botany at university alongside his classical studies. I was pleased for him but when he presented me with a basket of twisted licorice sticks I was so thrilled. I forgot myself and I ran to hug him. Please don't look like that, Avery. It was a hundred moons ago and I didn't feel anything but gratitude to him, honestly. It must have taken him by surprise too because the next thing I knew he had pulled me to him and begun to kiss me.

I stopped as Avery interrupted me.

472

"'Please, you don't need to tell me anymore. So you had a baby with your childhood sweetheart? Do you love him still?"

"Avery. Please. Let me finish," I paused and the next time I spoke I kept my eyes closed so Avery couldn't interrupt me. "I was shocked. No-one had ever kissed me before and, if I'm honest, I had never thought about anyone in that way before. I was dazed and I responded. I was flattered and confused but I don't regret what I did."

"The kiss lasted a few minutes and when we pulled away I still felt just as confused. He asked me to meet him again that same evening and I agreed. The attention was nice and I half thought we would fall back into our usual talks like we always did but we didn't. I don't need to tell you details about that evening but I need you to understand that he didn't force me.

"Within a week, he was off on a tour of the country to join his school friends and within a few months I knew I was pregnant. I was terrified and so I wrote to him. He had returned to school and the weeks I waited for a reply were the longest ever. I never got the reply, my mother and I were summoned to the mistresses presence and I was dismissed and effectively disowned in the same moment.

I didn't know what else to say nor whether Avery would still feel the same about me. A few moments passed in silence and I felt relieved to have finally told him my own secret but afraid he would no longer need me or want me.

"'What happened to Imogen?" he asked eventually.

"I couldn't keep her," I said. "I couldn't keep her."

I began to cry and in one swift movement he had sat beside me and taken me in his arms, smoothing my hair and quieting me with his calming breath.

"'We will find her," he said, and I believed him.

Epilogue

You are becoming accustomed to the way Avery's face looks in his stiff repose but for the first time he seems truly dead. He is lain out again but this time within his casket. The outside of the coffin is well polished and finely crafted, the oak is crisp and the grain is finely buffed. The brass handles are well shined. The inside is as perfectly arranged as the out with silk lining and a crisp pillow upon which Avery's head now rests. People often say that the skin of a corpse looks as if it has drained of all colour but you can at once see that this is not true. The face before you has many hues about it from blue to grey and at his neck a yellowing where blood has pooled beneath the surface and is now congealed.

As you stand beside the body of this man you hear the gentle click of the latch behind you, a sallow faced gentleman ambles to the other side of the coffin in which Avery is laid. It is apparent as this man busies himself with the tools of his trade that he is an undertaker and he is now taking a few moments to ensure that he is satisfied with his work. You are at once disconcerted at the resemblance between this man and Silver. They both share the grey silhouette of age and the man's skin is almost as blue grey as Silvers is at this moment. The man glances up as you think this and for a moment you are staring straight into his dull grey eyes. It is as if a connection has been made and you can see this man's own life flashing before you. It is a looping series of the same still images just like a zoetrope but ultimately more

475

revealing than any confessional. He is standing before the body of a woman. He is a boy, no older than Sebastian Bancroft. The woman is slumped in an upright winged back chair, the anti-maccassar has been pulled down as she has slumped and it now sits atop her head like a mantilla. Her face is pulled down on one side and drool is slipping from her mouth in a long and silver line which glints in the light from the window. It is as if she has swallowed a necklace which now dangles from her jaws. Her eyes are open and the boy is frozen in fear; his mother. The next image spins around and a younger version of the man is stood at an altar, his upper lip is beaded with sweat and he looks paler than he does today if that can be possible. Over his shoulder there is a figure dressed in white being processed up the aisle. Spin. The man is pacing outside his bedroom; he is anxious and afraid. A door opens and another man with an apron steps out, his hands and shirt are bloodied. Spin. He is working over the body of a woman and his face is wet with tears. Spin. He is standing before a single grave into which two coffins are being lowered. One is smaller than the other. It is raining and he is shaking from the cold. Spin. He is standing before a bed in his nightgown, a nightcap perched snugly on his head. He looks serene. The bed is empty but he has arranged a bolster cushion which he now regards with a look of disappointment.

It is quite a surprise when he looks away from you and you consider if there is the possibility that he can see you. After all, he is a man who works with the dead and whilst he has holds no stock in the silly parlour games that were once rather popular; the psychics and the mediums that purport to make contact with the dead. He knows them only for rogues for he knows that the dead do not need smoke and mirrors to disturb the living. A well placed ice bucket can give any mortal a clammy and deathly cold grip but the fingers of the dead can reach inside you to deliver just such a chill.

He continues busying himself with his work, tidying away some small remnants of the wax and polish he has used to bring up the wood and the brass on the casket. Satisfied with the way the outside of the coffin looks he turns his attention to Avery. For a few moments, he merely toys with the dressing along the interior of the casket, he runs a finger along the creases, sharpening up the corners inside. It strikes you at once how strange this is when the only one who could appreciate such detail is the one man who will never see it. After primping the fabric interior he collects a clothes brush from the bench beside him and proceeds to dust the fabric of Avery's suit from his shoulders down his arms and then across his chest. Replacing the brush he collects a rag and with a small pot of polish he applies a final sheen to Avery's shoes. Content at his task, he manages to get the old leather to gleam and this makes him smile a little in satisfaction. After several minutes, he leans back to gain a different viewpoint, a second opinion when working alone and turns his head to one side to consider Avery. You notice immediately that this man is not regarding Avery with any degree of curiosity. He is a man merely intent on doing his job and you watch with fascination as he gently reaches out to brush the hair at Avery's fringe with a delicate touch of one finger. It is a most intimate of gestures; one so tender after the brutality of the intrusion to his privacy and dignity that you feel your presence here intrusive. The man steps back again and nods once in approval. His work will be appreciated only if no-one notices his hand across Avery's face and as the few friends and relatives arrive to pay their last respects a few hours later, the undertaker watches from a distance behind a drawn curtain to the rear of the church where the body has now been transferred. And where we now find ourselves.

Look around yourself. There are faces you will recognise and others you won't. There are many strangers here. Despite the best efforts of the Bancroft's to keep the funeral a secret, word, as it is want to do, has got out somehow. The cortege is processing from the church to the graveyard to join the huddle of people beside an open grave. You see Imogen immediately, her face is glistening with tear marks but she is not weeping. Instead, she is surveying the faces around her. Some are bold enough to stand beside the grave, they have their hats removed and are showing their respect. Others stand a way off, faces she doesn't recognize, their necks craned discretely to catch a glance of this side show. You notice that John stands at some distance to his wife. He is uncomfortable, that much is obvious even from your distance.

The readings in the church have been simple as John has requested they ought to be. He was anxious to get Avery buried quickly, out of sight and out of mind. His moustache bristles as he straightens his lip. He is already imagining how tomorrow will play out, business returned to usual. With the boy's home, his wife will perk up and things may get back to some semblance of normality. Yes, he can see that this miserable mess will be over very soon. His lips twitch upwards into a smile and he only catches himself after a moment. Not the time, dear boy. Not the place. He glances sidelong at Imogen to see if she has seen but Imogen is not watching her husband; indeed I wonder if she will ever look at him the same way again. She scans the assembled congregation, her face hopeful. It is almost as if she is looking for someone. After several scans of the same group, she turns to look beyond the crowd to the graveyard onlookers. She squints a little, studying each person from a distance.

Her two sons stand at her side, the youngest has his hand in hers. He stands still and silent like he has fallen asleep on his feet. His brother is watching his mother and tries to follow her gaze. He asks her something but she either doesn't hear or she ignores him. Her view is obscured for a moment as the coffin is brought from the church to the graveside, causing her to arch her neck to see around it. The heads of the pall bearers bob alongside the casket as buoys on a barge. The coffin rides unevenly along their shoulders. It is plain but expensively crafted. Everything about a death is about a statement and anyone freshly chancing upon this scene would determine only this. A man of wealth is lost to us. Of course the casket is closed now, as you well imagine it would be and you watch as the four men lower Avery to the waiting planks across the grave, their work is steady but inevitably not smooth and it is not hard to imagine Avery's head rocking gently from side to side on his last cradle.

Your attention wanders around the assembled crowd and you pick out Heston. He is directly behind Imogen and John, his head is bowed and he holds a hat in his hands. He does not pick at the rim of it like some men nor does he look at the coffin at all. He does not imagine Avery inside the coffin. He has no need to.

You recognise Mrs. Phelps standing some distance from the group. She lingers as if in two minds. She is here for crumbs. She still does not understand how it can be so. Her enquiries have been met with a mixture of lies or contemptuous silence. They think she is seeking a cheap thrill with this information but how can she admit to having had a genuine affection for Avery. She does not believe any of the lies and only half believes he is dead. The tears she is crying are real.

There is a silence settling over the grave and attention is drawn to the vicar who has now assumed a position at the foot of the burial plot. All eyes except for Imogen's. She is continuing to search the distance for someone until at last her eyes alight on you. She looks relieved. No, don't panic. She is not looking at you, but rather she is looking through you. You turn around and see another face you recognise. Elizabeth Evesham.

She hesitates at the sight of the grave. She has attended a few burials recently. They are a symptom of age. You grow old, you lose some of your old friends. The old die. It is the death of the young which affects us so. Avery is not young but of course when Elizabeth last saw him, he was in the prime of his youth, a tall muscled and handsome man. It is this Avery she is laying to rest and not the silver-haired man lain inside the coffin. Elizabeth plucks her way carefully closer to the graveside, hanging back a little. John notices his wife's gaze and he watches Elizabeth curiously. He has made a note but not wishing to make a scene he will ask Imogen later of this woman's significance. After a few more moments the vicar continues his speech. Imogen has paid handsomely for today's ceremony. The vicar could not be persuaded to commend Avery to the Kingdom of Heaven explicitly as a man but in the end he would not be so callous as to deny him a resting place alongside his wife, even if God had not allowed it. Whilst he was sure he knew the church's feelings on the matter, he had allowed for some minor, discretionary amendments to the prayers he sent and he hoped his Father would forgive him. So far, he has managed to avoid making any such prayers gender specific. The cold is intense and people are shuffling to stop their feet from growing numb. The movement seems coordinated and gives the impression of one animal moving, the steam rising from their uniform of black like a steaming hound fresh from the chase.

As the last of the vicar's words form into visible clouds of steam, everyone watches as they ascend in the cold January air as if they will eventually meet with heaven itself. The pallbearers step forward once more and take the slack of the weight of the casket on two silk ropes and the gravediggers remove the planks. There is a little indignity as the men puff out their cheeks and brace themselves, lowering the rope, little by little, fist over fist until finally the wood has reached the frozen earth below and they collectively breath out a sigh on the thin winters air.

"Forasmuch as it hath pleased Almighty God of his great mercy to take unto himself the soul of our dear brother here departed, we therefore commit his body to the ground; earth to earth, ashes to ashes, dust to dust."

The vicar is surprised by his slip of the tongue but allows the prayer to rest with Avery. He reaches down, as he has done on many occasions before and no doubt will do again, and collects a handful of the ice-cold earth and scatters this on the top of the coffin. It is a symbol of the dust from which we came and to which we must all return.

The sky is weak with a sunlight diluted with thin yellow smog. Fires are lit all across London and it shows. The ground is full of the earth and the sky is full of dust and Avery is at rest with his wife; her headstone already placed at the head of his grave is fresh with the new inscription of Avery's internment:

In Veritas Pax – Peace In Truth

Printed in Great Britain
by Amazon.co.uk, Ltd.,
Marston Gate.